T0144276

Martín Rivas

Martín Rivas
Alberto Blest Gana

MINT EDITIONS

Martín Rivas was first published in 1862.

This edition published by Mint Editions 2021.

ISBN 9781513282558 | E-ISBN 9781513287577

Published by Mint Editions®

 MINT
EDITIONS

minteditionbooks.com

Publishing Director: Jennifer Newens
Design & Production: Rachel Lopez Metzger
Translated By: Mrs. Charles Whitham
Project Manager: Micaela Clark
Typesetting: Westchester Publishing Services

To His Excellency
Señor Don Alberto Blest-Gana,
Ex-Chilian Minister and Envoy-Extraordinary
to London, Paris, Rome, Etc.

To you, my dear Cousin Alberto, I affectionately dedicate this translation of your celebrated novel "Martin Rivas."

It has been difficult to convey, in a translation, the charm of a book, that has been and still is, the delight of many thousands of readers. "Martin Rivas" is known and beloved not only over all South America, but wherever the Spanish language is spoken.

It may be said that as a rule, a heavy curtain hangs between the English reader and the beauties of a foreign literature; this translation of "Martin Rivas" has lifted a corner of the curtain, let us hope that the glimpse it affords may awaken a desire to know more of the treasures of poetry and prose that lie on the other side.

November, 1916

Contents

I

A t the beginning of the month of July, 1850, a young man of twenty-two or twenty-three crossed the courtyard of a beautiful house in Santiago.

His clothes and his appearance were far from resembling the appearance and the dress of the smart young men of the city, everything about him showed that he came from the country, and that it was the first time he had been in Santiago. His black trousers fastened round the knees with leather straps, in the style of 1842 and '43, his coat with short and narrow sleeves, his black satin waistcoat with large pointed revers forming a sharp angle, and making a straight line with the knee of the trousers, his hat of a peculiar shape, and his boots tied to his ankles by means of black bootstrings, made up the old-fashioned costume, in which country-people from time to time appear in the streets of the capital.

The manner in which the young man approached a lackey who, regarding him superciliously, lounged on the threshold of a door at the entrance of the first patio, showed the timidity that some people experience when entering an unknown place, uncertain of what reception to expect.

When the young countryman found himself near the servant, who continued observing him, he saluted him, which the other acknowledged with a patronizing air, probably suggested by the humble appearance of the stranger.

"Is this the house of Don Damaso Encina?" he asked, in a voice which tried to hide the annoyance caused by the insolence of the other's salute.

"It is," answered the servant.

"Will you tell him that a gentleman wishes to speak to him?"

At the word "gentleman," the servant made an attempt to conceal the mocking smile which was visible on his lips.

"And what is your name?" he asked in a surly tone.

"Martin Rivas," replied the countryman, trying to repress his irritation, although he was unable to control its expression in his eyes.

"Wait, then," said the servant, and slowly turned to enter the house. At this moment the clock struck twelve.

We will take the opportunity of the servant's departure to make you better acquainted with the young man who has just called himself Martin

Rivas. He was well-made and of medium height. His black eyes, without being very large, drew attention on account of the look of sadness they gave to his expression; their regard was thoughtful and pensive, and this was enhanced by the dark shadows which encircled them and which harmonized with the paleness of his face. A slight black moustachio on his upper lip which also shaded the rather prominent line of his under lip, gave him an air of resolution, an air which helped to increase the appearance of hauteur with which he carried his head, which was covered thickly with chestnut hair, judging from what could be seen of it from under the brim of his hat. Altogether he had an appearance of distinction that contrasted strangely with the poverty of his clothes, and it was easy to see that, properly dressed, he would be a handsome man in the eyes of those who consider that fine clothes are as necessary to a good appearance as a good complexion and regular features.

Martin did not move from the spot where he had first spoken to the servant, and remained quietly contemplating the walls of the patio, beautifully decorated with frescoes, and the windows, embellished with gilt mouldings around the glass panes. After a time he became impatient at the delay, and his eyes wandered inattentively from one object to another.

At last the door opened and the same servant appeared.

"You are to come in," he said.

Martin followed the servant to a door at which he stopped.

"You go in here," said the servant, pointing to the door.

Martin Rivas crossed the threshold and faced a man who, by his aspect, appeared to be, according to the significant French phrase, "between the two ages," that is to say he was on the eve of old age without having yet arrived at it. His black suit, his well-starched collar, the shininess of his boots, showed the methodical man, who regulates his person as well as his life by invariable rule. His look revealed nothing, he had none of the characteristic traces so prominent in some faces, by which an observer can divine in a great measure the character of an individual.

Perfectly shaven and groomed, the face and the style of this man manifested that extreme particularity about cleanliness was one of his rules of conduct. At the sight of Martin he raised his skull-cap, and came forward with one of those looks which are equivalent to a question. The young man thus interpreted it, and made a slight bow saying—

"Señor Don Encina?"

"Yes, Señor, at your service," he replied.

Martin took from his pocket a letter, which he placed in the hand of Don Damase, with these words, "Have the kindness to read this letter."

"Ah! are you Martin?" said Don Encina, reading the signature, having leisurely broken the seal. "And how is your father?"

"He is dead," replied Martin, sadly.

"Dead!" repeated Don Encina, with surprise. Then as if struck by a sudden idea he added—

"Sit down, Martin, excuse my not having already offered you a chair. And this letter—?"

"Have the kindness to read it," answered Martin.

Don Encina approached a writing-table, laid the letter on it, took up a pair of spectacles which he carefully polished with his handkerchief, and placed them on his nose. Whilst seating himself he glanced over them at Martin.

"I cannot read without glasses," he said, as an apology for the time he had taken with his preparations. Then he began to read the letter which was as follows:—

My Dear and Honoured Sir,

"I feel myself seriously ill, and desire before God calls me to His divine tribunal, to recommend to you my son, who soon will be the only support of my unfortunate family. I have very small means, and have made my last arrangements, so that after my death my wife and my children may be able to do the utmost possible with the little that I have been able to leave them. With the interest of my small capital my family would have to exist in poverty, to be able to give Martin what is necessary for him to finish his studies as a lawyer in Santiago. According to my calculations, he will be only able to receive 20 pesos a month, and as it would be impossible for him to satisfy his absolute necessities with such a small sum, I have thought of you, and take the liberty of asking you if you will receive him in your house until he is able to support himself. This boy is my sole hope, and if you will do him the kindness that I humbly beg for him, you will have the blessing of his mother on earth and mine in heaven, if God will grant me His eternal glory after death.

"Dispose of your humble servant who kisses your feet.

JOSE RIVAS

He took off his spectacles with the same care as he had put them on, and replaced them in the same drawer they had previously occupied.

"You know what your father has asked me in this letter?" he asked, rising from his seat.

"Yes, sir," replied Martin.

"And how did you come from Copiapo?"

"On the deck of a ship," replied Martin, with a certain pride.

"Friend," said Don Encina, "your father was a good man and I am indebted to him for some services, and it will please me to repay them to his son. I have two rooms at the top of this house and they are at your disposal. Have you any luggage?"

"Yes, Señor."

"Where is it?"

"In the Inn of Santa Domingo."

"The servant will fetch them, you will give him the address."

Martin rose from his seat, and Don Damaso called the man-servant.

"Follow this gentleman, and carry back whatever he gives you."

"Señor," said Martin, "I do not know how to thank you for your goodness."

"Well, well, Martin," replied Don Damaso, "here you must make yourself at home. Bring your luggage and instal yourself upstairs. I dine at five; come a little before that hour, that I may introduce you to my wife."

Martin said a few grateful words and went away.

"Juana, Juana!" cried Don Damaso, raising his voice so as to be heard in the next room, "let them bring me the newspapers."

II

The house at which we have seen Martin Rivas present himself was inhabited by a family composed of Don Damaso Encina, his wife, a daughter of nineteen years, and a son of twenty-three, and three younger children, who at present were receiving their education at the college of the Franciscan Fathers.

Don Damaso had married in his twenty-fourth year Doña Engracia-Nunez, more for advantage than for love. Doña Engracia at this time was no beauty, but she possessed a fortune of thirty thousand pesos, which influenced the passion of the young Encina till it rose to the point of proposing for her hand. Don Damaso was a clerk in a commercial house in Valparaiso, and had no other means than his modest salary. The day following his marriage he could dispose of thirty thousand pesos. His ambition from this moment knew no limit.

Sent by the house which he worked for, Don Damaso went to Copiapo a month after his marriage. His good luck was such that when suing for payment of a small bill which his Chief had endorsed, Encina met an honest man who said to him—

"Even if you killed me I have no means of paying. But if in place of suing me you would not mind taking a slight risk, I will give you a document twice the value of this, that will entitle you to half of a mine which I possess, and which is certain to be of great value after it has been worked for a month."

Don Damaso was a cautious man and returned to his house without uttering one word, either for or against this proposition. He consulted several people, and was told by all that Don Jose Rivas, the debtor, was a madman who had lost all his money in pursuit of an idea.

Encina weighed this information and what Rivas had said, for his frank manner had made a favourable impression on his mind.

"Let us look at the mine," he said to him next day. They started, and reached the spot talking all the time about mines and mining. Don Damaso Encina saw floating before his eyes during this conversation veins, pockets, whole strata and other deposits of imaginative richness without understanding anything about it.

Don Jose Rivas had all the eloquence of a miner who has still faith left, although he has lost all his capital, and his eloquence caused Encina to see silver shining even in the stones of the road. But in spite of this illusion Don Damaso had sense enough to deliberate in his mind what offer he would make to Rivas, should he be satisfied about the value of the mine, after having examined it. Following his plan, Encina commenced his attack.

"I don't understand anything about it," he said, "but I don't object to mines in general. Let me have twelve bars of the silver, and I will obtain time from my Chief before you pay the debt, and take off some of the interest. We will work the mine between us, and make a contract by which you will pay me one and a half per cent. on the capital that I will expend in exploring, and give me the preference whenever you wish to sell your share, or part of it."

Don Jose was on the eve of a debtor's prison, and of leaving his wife and his son Martin, then one year old, in the greatest poverty. Nevertheless before accepting Encina's proposal he made a few faint objections, but Encina was firm and compelled him to sign the agreement upon the basis that he had at first proposed.

Shortly afterwards Don Damaso established himself in Copiapo as agent of the commercial house in Valparaiso for which he had worked, and looked after some other businesses on his own account, which increased his capital. During a year, the mine repaid its expenses, and Don Damaso bought up Rivas' share little by little, until he only remained as superintendent. Six months after having bought the last share, the mine became a great success, and a few years later Don Damaso bought a very fine country seat near Santiago, and also the mansion in which we have seen him receive the son of the man to whom he owed his riches.

Thanks to this, the family of Don Damaso was considered as one of the most aristocratic in Santiago. Among Chilians, money has caused many more prejudices with regard to birth to disappear than obtained in society in Europe in former days. In Europe there exists, it is true, what is called the aristocracy of money, which, notwithstanding its great power, never quite succeeds in making society forget the obscurity of its birth, whilst in Chili money is everything, and the haughty disdain with which in former years social adventurers were treated, now pales in the brilliancy of their gold.

The family of Don Damaso Encina was noble in Santiago on account of its wealth, and as such enjoyed social distinction. It was noted for its love of luxury, which was now beginning to seize upon society, and the prestige of the family was augmented by the solidity of the credit of

Don Damaso, whose occupation was money-lending on a large scale, like so many of our Chilian capitalists.

A magnificent frame was formed by this luxury for the beauty of Leonor, the only daughter of Don Damaso and Doña Engracia. Whoever had seen this girl of nineteen years in a poor dwelling, would have railed at the caprice of a fate which could not give to so much beauty corresponding surroundings.

Leonor was resplendent, surrounded by this luxury as a jewel surrounded by gold, and precious stones in a rich setting. The olive colour of her skin, and the brilliance of the expression of her large green eyes furnished with long lashes, her rosy lips, her small forehead bounded by abundant and well-arranged black hair, her arched eyebrows, and her white teeth, to which the only comparison which can be given is that used for pearls; all her features, and finally the dark oval of her face, formed in their conjunction that exquisite beauty which turns the heads of young men, and revives pictures of the past in the minds of the old.

Don Damaso and Doña Engracia had for Leonor the predilection which all parents have for the most beautiful of their children, and she, spoiled from infancy, had accustomed herself to look upon her charms as weapons of absolute dominion over those who surrounded her, whilst often her vanity went so far as to oppose her wishes to the will and authority of her mother.

Doña Engracia, in effect, naturally strong-willed and overbearing, her haughtiness increased by the 30,000 pesos she had brought to the marriage—which were the origin of the riches which now aggrandized the family—saw herself little by little lowered by the ascendency of her daughter, even to the point of being regarded with indifference by the rest of her family, and did not know how to console herself for this long isolation and prolonged domestic struggle, except by her love for her little lap-dog and the aversion from all differences and worries, natural to her sanguine temperament.

At the time of this history, the Encina family had just celebrated by a magnificent ball the return from Europe of the young Augustin, who had come back from the Old World with a great store of ornaments and clothes, as a proof of the amount of knowledge and wisdom he had acquired on his journey. His well-cut hair, the grace of his form and his perfect elegance caused the vacancy of his brain to be forgotten, and the 30,000 pesos had helped the young Augustin to walk upon the pavements of the principal European cities.

The arrival of Augustin and some good mercantile transactions, had predisposed the soul of Don Damaso towards the kindness with which we have seen him offer Martin Rivas the hospitality of his house. This circumstance had also made him forget the constant pre-occupation about hygiene with which he sought to preserve his health, and he gave himself up with complete freedom of mind to the political ideas which inflamed the patriotism of this millionaire, which patriotism took the form of a vehement desire to occupy a place in the Senate. For this reason he asked for the newspapers, after the kind reception he had just given to the young countryman.

III

Martin Rivas had left the house of his fathers at a moment of sorrow and misery for him and his family. After the death of his father, the earth held no more cherished people for him than Doña Catalina Salazar and Matilde his only sister; he and those two women had watched during fifteen days by the bed of the dying Don Jose. At these supreme moments, in which sorrow appears to tighten the bonds which unite persons of the same family, the three had had equal courage in mutually sustaining one another by a feigned calmness, with which each sought to hide his anguish from the other two.

One day Don Jose, knowing that his end was approaching, called his wife and his two children.

"This is my will," he said to them, showing them what he had written the previous day, "and here is a letter that Martin will take in person to Don Damaso Encina, who lives in Santiago." Then, giving a hand to his son, "On these depends in the future," he said to him, "the fate of thy mother and thy sister. Go to Santiago and study there. God will reward your constancy and your work."

Eight days after the death of Don Jose, the separation from Martin revived the sorrow of the family, in which resignation was slowly succeeding the first despair of their grief.

Martin took a passage in the steamer and went to Valparaiso full of the desire to study. Nothing that he had seen in any port or in the capital attracted him. His sole thought was of Iris mother and his sister, and he almost seemed to hear in the air the last words of his father.

Of high character and lively imagination, Martin had lived from that time, isolated by poverty and separated from his family, in the house of an old aunt who resided at Coquimbo, where the young man had studied by means of the help of this relation. The only happy days were those which the holidays permitted him to pass with his family, and after this separation all his desires were centred in the idea of going to Santiago, and then of returning to Copiapo to strive to improve the lot of those in whom all his thoughts were centred.

"God will reward your constancy and your work," he said to himself, repeating the words of trust in God with which his father had said farewell. With such ideas Martin arranged his modest belongings in the uppermost rooms of the beautiful house of Don Damaso Encina.

At four o'clock in the afternoon of the same day, the eldest son of Don Damaso knocked at one of the doors of Leonor's apartments. The young man was dressed in a blue embroidered coat buttoned over light trousers, which extended to a pair of varnished boots, on the heels of which were seen golden spurs. In his left hand he had a whip with an ivory handle, and in his right an enormous Havana cigar, half-smoked. He knocked at the door, and heard the voice of his sister, who asked, "Who is there?"

"Can I come in?" asked Augustin, half-crossing the threshold. He did not wait for an answer, but entered the room with an air of consummate elegance.

Leonor was combing her hair before the looking-glass, and turned her face with a smile towards her brother.

"So here you come with your cigar."

"Do not ask me to put it out, little sister," said the fop, "it is an Imperial cigar at 200 pesos the thousand."

"But you could have finished it before coming to see me."

"That is what I wished to do, and I went to converse with mother, but she sent me away protesting that the smoke suffocated her."

"Have you been on horseback?" asked Leonor.

"Yes, and to repay your kindness in letting me finish my cigar, I will tell you something which will please you."

"What?" she said.

"I was with Clementi Valencia—"

"And what more?"

"He spoke to me of you with enthusiasm."

Leonor made with her lips a slight pout of contempt.

"What nonsense" exclaimed Augustin, "do not be a hypocrite, Clementi is not disagreeable to you."

"Like many others."

"That may be, but there are very few like him."

"Why?"

"Because he has 300,000 pesos."

"Yes, but he is not a nice man."

"Nothing is ugly that is rich, my little sister."

Leonor smiled, but it would have been impossible to decide if it was at her brother's maxim, or with satisfaction at the skilfulness with which she had just arranged part of her hair.

"Nowadays, little girl," continued this elegant person reclining in an armchair, "money is the best recommendation."

"Oh! or beauty." replied Leonor.

"That is to say that Emilio Mendoza pleases you more because he is a handsome man. Fi! ma belle!"

"I do not say any such thing."

"Nonsense! search your heart, you know that you adore him."

"I will search it for you in vain, I love nobody."

"That is impossible; let us talk of something else."

"Do you know that we have a guest here?"

"So I have heard, a young man from Copiapo."

"What sort is he?"

"Poverty stricken," replied Augustin with a face of contempt.

"What is he like to look at?"

"I have not seen him, he will be a rubicund countryman, burnt by the sun."

At this moment Leonor finished dressing her hair and turned to her brother.

"You are *charmante*," said Augustin to her; he had not learnt French very well in his journey to Europe, but liked to air a great profusion of Gallicisms and foreign words in that language, to make it appear that he understood it perfectly.

"Now I must dress myself," said Leonor.

"That is to say that you send me away. Very well, I am going; *un baiser, ma cherie*," lounging towards the girl and kissing her on the forehead, then just as he was at the door he turned round again towards Leonor.

"So you despise this poor Clementi?"

"Yes."

"What is he going to do?" the gallant replied with feigned sadness. "Look here! 300,000 pesos, do not forget it; you could go to Paris and return here to be the queen of the fashion. I give you *ma parole d'honneur* that you would have from Clementi *cire et pabile*," said he, striving to Frenchify a vulgar expression which indicates a patient individual, above all, humble in love.

Leonor, who knew French better than her brother, rocked with laughter at the fatuity with which Augustin fired this shot as he closed the door, and returned to her toilet.

The two young men whom Augustin had mentioned were distinguished amongst the most pressing suitors for the hand of the daughter of Don Damaso Encina. The voice of social gossip had not said up to now which of the two would win the heart of Leonor. As we have seen, the arguments in favour of the qualifications of these two suitors who presented themselves, were very different.

Clementi Valencia was a young man of twenty-eight years of age, of ordinary appearance, notwithstanding the luxury with which he was dressed, thanks to the 300,000 pesos which Augustin so strongly recommended to his sister.

In those days, that is to say in 1850, fashionable young men had not yet adopted the mode of showing themselves in the Alameda in coupés or dog-carts, as they do today. Those who aspired to the title of "bloods" contented themselves with a more or less elegant cabriolet, which was driven by a postilion, à la Daumont, on the days of the Dieziocho and great festivals. Clementi Valencia had brought one from Europe, and found it useful to him in displaying his great wealth. It drew the attention of the young women, and aroused the criticism of the old, who look with contempt upon any superfluous extravagance, whilst they take their daily exercise in the walks of Las Delicias. However, Clementi was not much concerned with any criticism, and confined himself to drawing the attention of the ladies, who, in contradiction to these respectable old people very seldom looked upon ostentatious expenditure as useless. Thus it was that this young capitalist was received everywhere with the welcome which is given to money, the idol of the day. The mothers offered him the softest armchair in their salons, the girls showed themselves enraptured with the beautiful enamel of his teeth, and kept for him a hundred languishing looks—the heritage of the elect; whilst the fathers consulted him deferentially about his business, and took his opinion into consideration as that of a man who, in case of necessity, could lend his interest in an important speculation.

Emilio Mendoza, the second gallant named by Augustin Encina in the preceding conversation, was remarkable for the good looks which were wanting in Clementi, and which served him as a passport into the most aristocratic salons of the capital. He was a poor and handsome man, but this poverty did not prevent him from presenting a good appearance amongst the "bloods," although his resources did not permit him to keep the cab in which his rival displayed himself in the daily drive in the Alameda.

Emilio belonged to one of those families who having found a lucrative speculation in politics have always enjoyed good salaries in various public employments. At this time he occupied a post with 3,000 pesos salary, by means of which he was able to display on his shirt jewelled studs and handsome embroidery, which his powerful adversary was hardly able to eclipse. Both of them, in love with the daughter of Don Damaso, were moved by the same ambition. Clementi Valencia wished to augment his capital with Leonor's probable fortune, and Emilio Mendoza knew that once married to her, besides the fortune which would come later, Don Damaso's patronage would be an immense asset to him in his political career.

Between these two young men there existed consequently two important points of rivalry; to conquer the heart of the girl, and gain the sympathy of the father. The attainment of either of these objects presented considerable difficulties which were, however, lessened by the indolence of Leonor and the character of Don Damaso.

The latter was wavering between the Ministry and the Opposition, according to the advice of his friends, and the editorials in the press on both sides; and Leonor, according to general opinion, had such an exalted opinion of her beauty, that she would never meet a man she would think worthy of her heart or her hand. Whilst Don Damaso, preoccupied with the desire of being a Senator, inclined to whichever side in which he thought he would find success, his daughter gave and took from each of her suitors the hopes with which, on the previous night, he had lulled himself to sleep. Thus it was that Clementi Valencia (in the opposition, more for family reasons than from political conviction) would one day find Don Damaso agreeing with him about the faults of the Government and the necessity of attacking it, and the next discarding the conservative principles to which the previous day he had been temporarily converted. Likewise he found a smile on Leonor's lips at times, when he approached her almost believing that Emilio Mendoza had gained her heart.

The same thing happened to his rival, who worked hard to endeavour to procure a seat in the Senate for Don Damaso, and at the same time to arrange for his blind adherence to the Government; also this unfortunate suitor had to suffer the disdain of the daughter, directly after he thought himself certain of her love.

Such were the opposing interests which were fighting for the victory in the house of Don Damaso Encina.

IV

After having arranged his small baggage in the attics which he owed to the hospitality of Don Damaso, Martin Rivas was plunged in profound meditation. Finding himself in the capital, about which he had heard so much in Copiapo, seeing himself separated from his relatives with whom he had shared sorrow and poverty, he thought of the opulent family into which he found himself so suddenly admitted; all these ideas were mingled in his imagination, and by degrees oppressed him with misery at the remembrance of the tears of those whom he had left; and then he trembled at the idea of presenting himself before rich people, accustomed to all the surroundings of luxury, in his modest dress, and with manners embarrassed by timidity and poverty. At this moment, all the hopes which busy the young in their continual thoughts of the future left him.

He learnt from the servant that this house was the most luxurious in Santiago; that in the family there were a young girl and a young man, types of grace and elegance. The thought that he, a poor provincial, would have to sit down beside these persons accustomed to all the refinements of wealth, wounded his native pride, and made him lose sight of the beliefs with which he had come to Santiago, and the ambitions which he had resolved to realise by force of will.

At half-past four in the afternoon, a servant presented himself before the young man and announced that his patron hoped to see him at dinner.

Martin looked at himself mechanically in a mirror which was over a mahogany wash-hand stand, and thought himself pale and ugly, but before his childish discouragement could damp his spirit, his energy made him shake off this despair, and his strength of will enabled him to see his situation in a more rational light.

On entering the room in which the family was assembled, the pallor which had dismayed him a moment before quickly turned to the most vivid red. Don Damaso presented him to his wife and to Leonor, who gave him a slight salute. At this moment Augustin entered, to whom his father also presented the young Rivas, who received from this elegant person a very slight inclination of the head. This frozen reception ended by disconcerting the provincial, who remained standing without knowing what to do with his arms, nor how to take up an attitude like that of Augustin, who carelessly ran his fingers through his perfumed hair.

The voice of Don Damaso offering him a seat, delivered him from the torture in which he found himself, and with downcast looks he took a chair somewhat distant from the group which was formed by Doña Engracia, Leonor, and Augustin, who began to talk of his horsemanship and the excellent qualities of the animal on which he had been showing himself off.

Martin envied with all his heart this insipid loquacity mixed with French words and empty observations, uttered with ridiculous affectation, but he found himself at the same time admiring the richness of the furniture. The profusion of gilding, the magnificence of the curtains which hung before the windows, and the variety of objects, which covered the adjoining tables, were of a luxurious quality hitherto unknown to him. His boyish inexperience made him consider all he saw to be the attributes of riches and true superiority, and aroused in his enthusiastic mind that desire for luxury which appears, above all, to be the patrimony of youth.

At first Martin made these observations raising his eyes by stealth; until, overcome by a timidity which he could not combat, he ended by not even glancing at his surroundings.

When Don Damaso, who was a great talker, spoke to him and asked questions about the mines in Copiapo, Martin, as he replied, saw the eyes of the Señora and her children directed towards him. Under these circumstances, far from augmenting his perturbation, it appeared to give him more security and an unexpected coolness, which showed itself in his quiet steady voice, as he turned his face tranquilly towards the persons who were observing him as if he were a curious object. Whilst he spoke the serenity of his mind returned, thanks to the strength of his will, naturally inclined to contend with difficulties, and he was now able to observe those who were listening to him in the semi-obscurity of the room. He made out Doña Engracia, who always settled herself in the shadiest place to avoid the heat. This lady held upon her lap a little white dog with long thick hair, which, it was obvious from the fluffiness of its curls, she had just finished combing. The little dog raised its head from time to time and looked with its luminous eyes at Martin slightly growling, to which Doña Engracia replied every time by saying to it in a low voice, "Diamela," accompanying this remonstrance by slight, affectionate taps, such as one gives to a pampered child, when it has been a little naughty. But Martin took little notice of the Señora, nor of the signals of discontent of Diamela, and also omitted to admire the pretentious manners of the fop. He kept his gaze steadily fixed upon Leonor. The beauty of this girl produced in him an indelible admiration. Those who have seen a traveller contemplating the cataract of Niagara, or an artist standing before the great picture by Raphael—"The Transfiguration," could perhaps give an idea of the sensations, sudden and strange, which surged within the soul of Martin in the presence of the sublime beauty of Leonor.

She was dressed in a white morning gown, the girdle of which hung loosely round her, over an embroidered skirt of which the lower part, bordered with the most beautiful openwork, showed the flounce of valenciennes of a rich petticoat. The under-vest, which was slightly *décolleté*, showed the pure contour of her throat, and gave a suspicion of the exquisite perfection of her bosom. This dress, simple in appearance but really most costly, appeared to realize an impossible thing, that of augmenting the beauty of Leonor, upon whom Martin stared with so much unconscious persistence that the girl turned her eyes another way with a slight sign of impatience.

A servant just then presented himself and announced that the meal was on the table, whilst Augustin was giving a description of the Boulevards of Paris to his mother, at the same time that Don Damaso, who this day was inclined to the Opposition, put in practice his republican principles by treating Martin with familiarity and attention.

Augustin offered his left arm to his mother, managing to seize upon Diamela with his right hand.

"Take care, take care, my boy," exclaimed the Señora, seeing the small reverence with which her eldest treated her favourite dog, "be more gentle."

"Do not be afraid, Mamma," replied the elegant one; "how could I do *mal* when I find this little dog *charmante?*"

Don Damaso offered his arm to Leonor, and turned towards Martin.

"Come and eat, friend," he said, following his wife and his son.

That word "friend" uttered by Don Damaso showed to Martin the immense distance which lay between him and the family of his host; he felt renewed loneliness as he humbly followed them to the dining-room, noticing the easy grace of the elegant Augustin and the haughty mien of Leonor, who bore herself with all the pride of beauty and wealth.

Whilst they were taking their soup, the voice of Augustin alone was heard.

ALBERTO BLEST GANA

"In the Frères Provencaux they take every day delicious turtle soup," he said, twirling the down which shaded his upper lip. "Oh, the bread of Paris," he added, breaking a French roll—"*C'est un pain* divine!"

"And how long did it take you to learn French?" inquired Doña Engracia, giving a spoonful of soup to Diamela, and looking proudly at Martin as if to show him the superiority of her son. But whether it was that this movement did not perfectly convey the spoon to the beloved mouth of Diamela, or whether it was that the high temperature of the soup offended its delicate lips, the dog uttered a howl which made Doña Engracia jump in her seat, and her movement was so rapid that she dragged off the cloth the plate which she was holding before her and the liquid which it contained.

"Now you see! What did I tell you! It is horrid to bring dogs to the table," exclaimed Don Damaso.

"Dearest little one of my soul," said Doña Engracia, paying no attention to him and pressing to her bosom Diamela, who was howling desperately.

"*Taisez-vous, polisson,*" said Augustin to the dog, who at that moment, being liberated from the arms of the Señora, suddenly stopped barking.

Doña Engracia raised her eyes to heaven as if to admire the power of the Creator, and lowering them upon her husband she said in feeling accents—

"Just look at that; it certainly understands French. What a wonder!"

"Oh, the dog is an animal full of intelligence," exclaimed Augustin; "in Paris I used to call them in Spanish, and they followed me when I showed them a piece of bread."

A new plate of soup came to appease the discontent of Diamela, and order was re-established in the room.

"And what do they say in the North about politics?" the master of the house asked Martin.

"I lived such an isolated life, sir, on account of the illness of my father," replied the young man, "that I do not know the opinions that prevail."

"In Paris there are many different political opinions," said Augustin, "the Orleanists, those of the Brancha or Bourbons, and the Republicans."

"The Brancha?" asked Don Damaso.

"That is to say, the side of the Bourbons," replied Augustin.

"But in the North, all are in opposition," said Don Damaso, turning towards Martin again.

"I believe that that is usual," he replied.

"Politics 'gâté' one's spirituality," observed sententiously the eldest son of the family.

"What is this 'gâteau'?" asked his father with admiration.

"I prefer to say that it vitiates the spirit," replied the young man.

"Nevertheless," replied Don Damaso, "every citizen ought to occupy himself in public affairs, and the will of the people is sacred."

Don Damaso who, as we have already said, held a different opinion each day, uttered this phrase with great emphasis, having just finished reading it in a daily Liberal paper.

"Mamma, what confiture is this?" asked Augustin, pointing to the sweets, to cut off the conversation about politics, which annoyed him.

"And the will of the people," continued Don Damaso, without remarking the discontent of his son, "is consecrated by the Gospels."

"They are apricots, my son," said Doña Engracia, at the same time replying to Augustin's question.

"What apricots?" replied Don Damaso, referring to the Gospels, thinking that his wife qualified with this word the will of the people.

"No, dear, I said that these sweets were apricots," replied Doña Engracia.

"*Confiture d'abricots*," said Augustin, with the emphasis of a preacher who recites a Latin text.

During the dialogue, Martin directed his glances at Leonor, who wore an air of indifference, and took no part in the conversation of her family.

The meal over, they all left the dining-room in the order in which they had entered it, and in the drawing-room each continued to talk on his favourite theme. Augustin talked to his mother about the coffee which he took at Tortoni's after dinner; Don Damaso recited to Martin, as his own views, the Liberal opinions which he learnt in the morning from the newspaper; Leonor idly turned over the leaves of a book of English engravings which lay on the table. At six o'clock Martin was able to free himself from the republican discourses of his host, and to retire from the salon.

V

M artin sat down at a table with the air of a man tired from a long walk. The emotions of his arrival in Santiago, the presentation to a rich family, the impression given by the elegance of Augustin Encina and the surprising beauty of Leonor, all passing confusedly before his mind like visions in a dream, had overcome him with fatigue. That disdainful beauty, who did not deign to take part in the conversation of her own family, humiliated him with her elegance and her luxury. Could it be that his intelligence was so mean beside that of her relations and her brother that it had caused her to be silent? Martin asked himself this mechanically, and tried to combat the anguish which oppressed him when he thought of the impossibility of attracting the attention of a girl like Leonor. Thinking of her, finding himself for the first time in love, what could he descry at his age? A Paradise of indefinite felicity, ardent as the hopes of youth, gilded as the dreams of poesy; this is the inseparable companion of the heart that loves and desires love.

The regretful remembrance of his family dissipated for a moment these sad ideas, and rescued his heart from the circle of fire which at first had surrounded it.

He took up his hat and went down into the street; the desire to know the people and to see the movement of them, had restored him to tranquillity. Moreover, he desired to buy some books, and he inquired for a library from the first person he met in the street. Following the instructions which he had received, Martin went to the Plaza de Armas.

In 1850 the fountain in the Plaza was not surrounded by a beautiful garden as it is today, nor presented to the passer-by who stopped to look at it, any better seat than its marble border, always occupied at night by men of the poorer class. Amongst them he saw groups of employees from shoemakers' shops, who were offering boots or shoes to any one who passed by at this hour.

Martin, animated by curiosity to look at the fountain, went round by the corner of the street of the Monjitas, in the middle of which he remained contemplating the Plaza. On arriving at the fountain, when he had looked for some time at the two marble figures which crowned it, a man approached him, saying, "Buy a pair of varnished boots, sir." These words brought back to his memory the remembrance of the brilliant boots of Augustin, and his recent ideas which had made him go out into the street. He thought that with a pair of varnished boots he would cut a better figure in the elegant family which had admitted him to their midst. Being young, he did not draw back from this consideration on account of the meagreness of his purse, but gave a glance at the man who had spoken to him, who was already retiring, but he came back immediately.

"Let us see those boots," said Martin.

"Here they are, my little master," replied the man, showing the boots, the mirror of whose light reflections succeeded in overcoming the scruples of the boy.

"Look here," added the vendor, placing a handkerchief on the border of the fountain; "sit down here and try them on."

Rivas sat down full of confidence, and took off his coarse boots, taking one of those which the man presented to him; but his astonishment was not little, when, having used force to put his foot in, he saw round him six individuals each of whom offered him a pair of boots, all talking at the same time.

Martin more confused than the Captain of the Guard when he found himself surrounded by those whom he met in the house of Bartelo, in the "Barber of Seville"—was bewildered by the different voices and forced his foot in vain into the boot.

"See, master, these are much better," said one of them.

"Try these, sir, I made them myself."

"There are none finer," added another, dangling a pair of boots before his nose.

"Here is a pair which will last you all your life," murmured a third in his ear; and they all burst into praise of their merchandise with similar arguments, confusing the poor boy by this strange manner of selling.

The first pair was rejected for tightness, the second because they were too large, and the third were too dear. Amongst them all, the number of bootsellers had increased considerably round the young man who, tired of the obstinate persistence of so many united sellers, put on his old boot and got up saying that he would buy on another occasion. At that moment he found himself abused in violent language by those who had a moment before accosted him, and he heard the first of the vendors say, "If he does not wish to buy, we must hustle him," and another added as an appendix to this, "Perhaps he has no money;" and immediately a third chimed in, "He is a poor-looking creature!"

Martin, just arrived, and ignorant of the insolence of the working men of the city, felt himself at the end of his patience.

"I have said nothing insulting," he said, turning towards the group, "and I will not permit any one to insult me either."

"And how did we insult you when we called you poor?"

"We are also poor," replied a voice.

"Henceforth we will say that he is rich," said another.

"And if he is so rich, why doesn't he buy something?" added the first who had spoken, getting still nearer to him than the other.

Rivas' patience was exhausted at this, and he pushed the man with such force that he fell at the feet of his companions.

"I will pay you for this," said one.

"Get up, man, don't be a coward!" said another.

In fact the bootseller got up and set upon the young man with fury. A wrestling match went on between them to the great joy of the others, who applauded with great animation, praising with impartiality the happiest blows which each of them gave to his adversary.

"Hit him hard on the nose," said one.

"That's a good one!" said another.

Suddenly they heard a voice which dispersed the crowd as if by enchantment, and the combatants alone remained.

"Here come the police!" it cried, and sure enough they came running in twos and threes; they were followed by others. A policeman took Martin by one arm and the bootmaker by the other, saying—

"Both of you come with me to the judge."

Rivas turned round with astonishment at the grip that had seized him, as he heard the voice, and saw the uniform of the man who was holding him.

"I am not the guilty one in this affair," he said, "let me go."

"Gently, gently, keep quiet!" replied the policeman, and continued to sound his whistle. In vain Martin sought to explain the origin of their quarrel; the policeman listened to nothing and continued sounding his whistle, until an officer presented himself, followed by other soldiers. Before these, his eloquence broke down in the middle.

The officer listened impassively to the tale which was told him, and his sole reply was the sacramental answer of the guardians of the security of the city—

"*Paselos pa entro.*"

In face of such a one-sided method of discussion, Martin knew that it would be better to resign himself, and let himself be led with his adversary to the guardroom of the police.

On arriving, Martin hoped that the Chief of the Police, before whom he was presented, would do more justice to his cause. But he only listened to the tale, and gave the order to bring him in to await the arrival of the mayor.

VI

At the same hour that Martin Rivas was taken to prison, the salon of Don Damaso Encina was resplendent with the light with which it was illuminated upon the evenings on which they received their friends.

Doña Engracia, seated on a sofa, was conversing with a lady, the sister of Don Damaso and the mother of a girl who occupied another sofa with Leonor and the elegant Augustin. In the corner of a neighbouring room, Don Damaso and three gentlemen of important appearance and hair turning grey were seated round a quadrille table. Near the table young Mendoza, one of the adorers of Leonor, was looking on. Dona Engracia was talking with her sister-in-law, Doña Francisca Encina, about the cleverness of Diamela and its progress in the language of Vaugelas and Voltaire, whilst the son of Doña Francisca, who belonged to the category of spoiled children, amused himself by pulling the hair and ears of his aunt's favourite.

The girl who was conversing with Leonor was a great contrast to her in appearance. On looking at her red hair, her white skin, and her azure eyes, a stranger would not have believed it possible that she could belong to the same race as the young brunette with black hair who sat beside her, and much less would believe that between Leonor and her cousin Matilde Elias could exist such near relationship. The face of this girl, moreover, revealed a certain languid melancholy which contrasted with the haughty pride of Leonor, and though the elegance of her dress was not less than that of the other, the beauty of Matilde was shadowed at first sight beside that of her cousin.

The two girls had their hands affectionately clasped, when Clementi Valencia entered the salon.

"Here comes this man with his watchchain and his brilliants; how vulgar to show off his riches," said Leonor.

The young man did not dare to sit down beside the two cousins, on account of the frigid inclination of the head with which Don Damaso had received him, so went and seated himself beside the elder ladies.

"Do you know that they say you are engaged to him?" said Matilde to her cousin.

"Jesus!" replied she. "Because he is rich!"

"And they think you are in love with him."

"Neither with him nor any one else," replied Leonor, in disdainful accents.

"With no one else? Not with Mendoza?" asked Matilde.

"Now, in truth, Matilde, you have been in love once," said Leonor, looking fixedly at her cousin, who blushed deeply and did not answer. "When you were going to be married, did you feel for Adriano that love of which they speak in the novels?" continued her cousin.

"No," she replied.

"And for Rafael San Luis?"

Matilde blushed again without replying.

"Observe, nothing would have made me dare to ask these questions, but you told me some time ago that you loved Rafael; then you denied me all confidence, and afterwards I saw you preparing your trousseau to be married to Adriano; which of the two do you love? Is it not so, tell me, which of them has succeeded? It is more than a year since your bridegroom died, and it appears to me that it is quite time for you to abandon your *rôle* of widow (without being a widow), and your unkind reserve towards your best friend. Tell me that you did not love Adriano."

"No."

"Then you have not forgotten Rafael?"

"How can I forget him? I would marry him today," replied Matilde, tears which she tried to restrain coming to her eyes.

"And why did you abandon him?"

"You know my father's severity."

"Nothing would force me to change," replied Leonor, with pride, "and make me love another."

"If you have never loved any one how can you understand it? Do not say that," replied Matilde.

"That is true, I have never loved any one, at least according to the real idea of love; sometimes I have liked a man, but no one for long. The idea that you must return a man's love annoys me. I do not find in them any of the superiority which they pretend to have over us, and this thought hardens me; also I have never met a man who had sufficient high-mindedness to disdain the prestige that money gives, nor sufficient pride not to be obsequious to beauty."

"I have never thought about it," said Matilde, "I loved Rafael from the moment I saw him, and he also loved me."

"And have you spoken with him since Adriano's death left you free?"

"No, I did not dare to speak to him; I had not strength to disobey my father. He is quite right, I have given him the right to despise me. Sometimes I have seen him in the street; he was pale, but always handsome. I assure you that I have felt myself ready to faint at the sight of him, but he has passed without looking at me, raising that haughty head which he carries with such grace."

Leonor listened with pleasure to the excitement with which her cousin spoke of her love and thought that it must be very sweet to feel this enthusiasm and poetic rapture.

"And do you think that he does not love you?" she said.

"Yes, I think so," said Matilde, giving a sigh.

"Poor Matilde! I would like to love as you do, even if it were to suffer as much."

"Ah, you never have suffered! do not desire it."

"I would a thousand times rather have this torment than the insipid life I lead. Sometimes I have wept, believing myself different to all other women. All my friends have been in love, and I have never been able to think of the same man for two consecutive days."

"That is to be happy."

"Who knows?" murmured Leonor, pensively.

The servant announced that the tea was ready, and every one went into the room which was next to that which was occupied by the quadrille players.

We have already said that there were three players with the master of the house; the two others were a friend of Don Damaso called Don Simon Arenal, and the father of Matilde—Don Fidel Elias. These last were the type of men who, as political parasites, live to support authority and do not profess any stronger political creed than their own convenience, and a strict adherence to the grand word "orders," realized in its most restrictive sense. The political arena of Chili is paved with this class of person, as some say Hell is with good intentions, without having any intention of establishing a simile between the country's politics and Hell, although there may be many points of similarity between them.

Don Simon Arenal and Don Fidel Elias approved without question of every form of authority, and qualified with the disdainful names of revolutionaries and demagogues, those who without being placed in authority, occupied themselves with public matters. Serious men above all do not approve that the authorities should permit the existence of an

Opposition press, and call public opinion the chatter of fools; embracing in this sentence all those who dared to raise their voices, without having position, a house or a country place, capital, or interest. These authoritative opinions which the two friends professed, had brought some domestic trouble to Don Fidel Elias. Doña Francisca Encina, his wife, had some books and ventured to think for herself, thus violating the social principles of her husband, who looked upon every book as useless when it was not pernicious. As a blue-stocking, Doña Francisca Encina was liberal in politics and fomented this tendency in her brother, whom Don Fidel and Don Simon had not been able to bring over entirely to the party of "order," which some had called with a certain felicity in former times, the party of the "energeticists."

All these persons were seated at the tea-table, and the conversation took a different tone in each of the groups which surrounded it, according to their ideas and age.

Doña Engracia told her relation the scene at dinner, to prove that Diamela knew French, in reply to which Doña Francisca related certain other authors who spoke of the cleverness of the canine race. Leonor and her cousin formed another group with the young people, and Don Damaso occupied the head of the table with his friend and his brother-in-law.

"Be convinced, Damaso," said Don Fidel to him; "this 'society of equality' is a conspiracy of rabble who wish to seize upon our fortunes."

"And above all," said Don Simon (who was always nominated by the Government for different trusts), "plenty of people are in the Opposition because they have nothing to do."

"But, man," replied Don Damaso, "what about the schools, which this society founded for educating the people?"

"What people? There is no people!" replied Don Fidel. "It is the greatest evil to be teaching these rotten conspirators to be gentlemen."

"And if I were the Governor," said Don Simon, "I would never allow them to meet. What is going to become of us when they are all mixed up in politics?"

"But if they are all citizens like ourselves," replied Don Damaso.

"Yes, but they are citizens without a cent, starving citizens," replied Don Fidel.

"But now we are a Republic," said Doña Francisca, joining in the conversation.

"Would to God we were not," replied her husband.

"Jesus!" exclaimed the scandalized lady.

"Look here, my dear, women should not mix up in politics," said Don Fidel, sententiously.

This maxim was approved by the grave Don Simon, who nodded his head as a sign of affirmation.

"For women—flowers and the toilette—dear aunt," said Don Augustin, who had heard the maxim of Don Fidel.

"This child has returned from Europe more foolish than ever," the literary lady murmured stingingly.

"In past days," said Don Simon to Don Damaso, "a minister spoke to me about you, and prophesied that you would be in Opposition."

"I in Opposition!" exclaimed Don Damaso, "I have never been so, I am Independent."

"And it appears they gave you, contrary to expectation, a commission."

Don Damaso remained thinking, repenting of his reply. "And what commission was it?" he asked.

"I do not remember it now," replied Don Simon. "You know that the Governor was looking for people of good means to hold positions, and—"

"And they were right," said Don Damaso, "it is the way to establish authority."

"Look here, Leonor, they have made a conquest of your father," said Doña Francisca.

"They have not made a conquest of me, sister," retorted Don Damaso. "But I have said that the Government should employ well-known people."

"I have not lost the hope of seeing you a Senator," said Don Fidel.

"I do not aspire to this," replied Don Damaso, "but if the public elect me."

"Those who can elect are the Governors," said Doña Francisca.

"And so it ought to be," replied Don Fidel, "they would not be able to govern otherwise."

"But governed thus, it would be better if they would leave us in peace," said Doña Francisca.

"But, wife," replied her husband, "I have already told you that you should not meddle in politics." Don Simon approved a second time, and Doña Francisca turned round in desperation to her sister-in-law.

After tea the ladies returned to the salon, whilst the elders continued their political conversation, and the young people surrounded Leonor who was seated at a table. Upon this lay a beautiful book, with the covers encrusted in mother-of-pearl.

"Look, Leonor," said her brother to her, "I have *apporté* you an album which I have borrowed."

"Does it belong to you?" Leonor asked Emilio Mendoza carelessly.

"I brought it this evening, Señorita, as I promised it to you."

"Did you take it away to write verses in it?" Clementi Valencia asked his rival. "I have never been able to bear verses," added the young millionaire, twirling the chain of his watch.

"Nor I either," said the elegant Augustin.

"Let me see the album," said Doña Francisca, taking the book.

"Aunt, they are literary *morceaux*," exclaimed Augustin.

"I would rather there was a little music."

"Read, Mamma," said Matilde; "there are many of what my cousin calls literary '*morceaux*.'"

Doña Francisca opened it.

"Here are some verses," she said, "and they are written by Señor Mendoza."

"You have written verses?" said young Augustin. "With whom are you in love?"

Emilio coloured and glanced at Leonor, who appeared not to see it.

"It is a short composition," said Doña Francisca, who was dying with desire that they should hear her read them.

"Read it then, aunt," said Augustin.

Doña Francisca, in an affected voice and a sentimental accent, read—

"To The Eyes Of. . .

"A Los Ojos De. . .

"Mas dulces habeisde ser
Si me volvéis a mirar,
Porque es malicia a mi ver
Siendo fuente de placer
Causarme tanto pesar.

"De seso me tiene ageno
El que en suerte tan cruel
Sea ese mirar sereno
Solo para mi veneno
Siendo para todos miel.

"Si es la venganza medida
Por mi amor, a tal rigor
El alma siento rendida;
Porque es mui poco una vida
Para vengar tanto amor.

—"Emilio Mendoza"

At the conclusion of the reading, Emilio Mendoza threw a languishing glance at Leonor as much as to say: "You are the goddess of my inspiration."

"And how long did it take you to write these verses?" Doña Francisca said to him.

"I finished them this morning," replied Mendoza, with affected modesty, carefully refraining from saying that he had only copied the words of a composition of the Spanish poet, Campo Amor, then little known in Chili.

"Here there is something in prose," said Doña Francisca. "'Humanity travels after progress, travelling in a circle which is called Love, and having for its centre the angel which is called Woman.'"

"What a sweet thought," said Doña Francisca, with a languid air.

"Always provided one understands it," replied Clementi Valencia.

Doña Francisca continued for some time turning over the leaves of the book filled with vacant phrases or stanzas, which ended by praying for a little love from the lady of the album, which she read with enthusiasm.

"If my aunt was left with this book she would sit up all night," said Augustin to his friend Valencia.

Don Fidel gave the signal for leaving by taking up his hat.

"Do you know that Don Damaso has given me to understand that he would like his son to marry Matilde?" he said to Doña Francisca when they were in the street; "Augustin is a magnificent *parti*."

"He is a very insignificant young man," replied Doña Francisca, remembering the little liking her nephew had for poetry.

"What! Insignificant! and his father has a million pesos," replied her husband, with choler.

Doña Francisca did not answer this positive opinion of her husband.

"A marriage between Matilde and Augustin would be a great happiness for us," continued Don Fidel; "remember, my dear, that next year the lease will terminate which I hold of Roble, and that the owner does not wish to prolong the lease."

"Up to the present that country place of Roble has not done much for you," said Doña Francisca.

"That is not the question," said Don Fidel, "I am considering in case he finishes the lease. Matilde once married to Augustin assures to us the well-being of our daughter. And also Damaso would not deny me his security, as heretofore he has done in some money matters."

"Finally, you seem to have made up your mind," replied the lady, with warmth, indignant at the prosaic calculations of her husband. The rest of the walk was taken in silence until they arrived at their own house.

Let us now go back to Don Damaso and his family whom we left in the salon.

"And our visitor, what has become of him?" asked the gentleman. The servant whom they had summoned to answer this question replied that he had not returned.

"I should not be surprised if he were lost," said Don Damaso.

"In Santiago?" exclaimed Augustin, with surprise; "in Paris certainly it is easy to lose one's self."

"I have thought," said Don Damaso to his wife, "that Martin would be of much use to me in keeping my accounts."

"He appears a good young fellow, and he pleases me because he does not smoke," answered Doña Engracia. In fact, Martin had said that he did not smoke when, after eating, Don Damaso had offered him a cigar in a rapture of republicanism. Yet when they had said good night his friends had left him half converted from any impulses towards equality by the news they had given him that one of the Ministers had thought of recommending him to a post.

"After all," thought Don Damaso when he found himself alone, "those Liberals are so extreme!"

VII

In vain Martin Rivas protested against the arbitrariness with which he had been seized, asking for his liberty and promising to appear the following day before the judge. The officer of the Court was firm about the first order he had given with the inflexibility of the Grenadiers of Napoleon the Great, who would die before yielding.

Martin, tired of protesting and imploring, finally resigned himself, waiting with patience for the arrival of the Mayor, overcome by the sad reflections to which his situation subjected him. Above all, he thought of the explanations which it would be necessary to give the following day to the family of Don Damaso, in case he could not obtain his liberty at once. He saw beforehand, with misery, the proud glance of Leonor, the insulting smile of Augustin, and the humiliating confession to their parents. In his mind Leonor was the cause of his disagreeable adventure. His memory recalled the beautiful image of this girl, whom it was impossible to look at without emotion, and a profound sadness grew in his mind when reflecting on the disdain with which she would listen to the story of his disgrace. After a few moments, the poor boy was cursing his destiny, and his desperate heart asked Heaven to account for the poverty of some, and the riches of others. It was then that he thought of the unjust inequalities of fate, and in his heart was born a vague rancour against the favourites of fortune.

"If Leonor would spare me from ridiculing the emergency in which I find myself," thought Martin, "the others will annoy me much less, and I will know how to punish the insults of those who dare to laugh."

This singular reflection shows that Rivas, however much he might wish to escape from the deep impression that the sight of Leonor had made on him, was unable to think of anything but her. "Will she despise me?" he thought with bitter sadness. Sometimes the idea came to him to return to Copiapo the shortest way he could, and devote himself there to working for his family, but soon his strong will made him ashamed of seeking to turn from his fixed purpose by the silly fear of being despised by a girl whom he had seen only once.

The Mayor arrived at two o'clock at night, and gave an audience to Martin. After hearing his story, the judge saw that the young man's words spoke more in his favour than the poverty of his clothes, and gave the order to set him at liberty.

Martin returned at half-past two to the house of his protector, and found the door bolted; he gave some light knocks which nobody in the house appeared to hear, and went away without daring to make any other attempt to enter. Arming himself with patience, he resolved to pass the night in walking the streets without going too far from the house of Don Damaso. Santiago was then a city that went to bed early; thus it was that Rivas found no other sight to look at during his wanderings than the outsides of the houses, and the night watchmen who snored in every corner, watching over the security of the population.

The following day, Martin was able to enter the house when the door was opened by the servant who was going to the Plaza. The servant looked at him with a jesting smile, which served as a forewarning to the young man of the humiliation which he might expect to meet with from the family of Don Damaso.

A little before the breakfast hour he went cautiously into the Court, resolved to face the shame of his situation, rather than leave the field clear for the conjectures of his host and his son. Don Damaso saw Martin as he was going to his desk, and opened the door to him.

"How have you passed the night, Martin?" he asked, replying to the salute of the young man.

"Very badly, sir," he replied.

"How, have you not slept well?"

"I have passed the night, or part of the night in the street."

Don Damaso opened astonished eyes. "In the street? And where were you at twelve o'clock when they bolted the door?"

"I was a prisoner in the police court." Martin at once circumstantially recounted his adventure. On finishing he saw that his protector made visible efforts not to laugh.

"I feel in my soul all that has happened to you," said Don Damaso summoning all his seriousness; "and to forget this disagreeable event, I will speak to you of a project which concerns you."

"I am at your orders," replied the young man, without endeavouring to extract a promise of secrecy from Don Damaso about his adventure.

"You will have many unoccupied hours in the day after attending to your studies," said the gentleman, "and I would like to know if you would find it inconvenient to occupy yourself with my correspondence and my account books for the arrangement of my business; I will give you for this service 30 pesos a month, and it would much please me if you would accept my proposal; you would be my secretary."

"Sir," replied Martin, "I accept the occasion which you offer me of repaying in any way the kindness with which you have treated me, and with pleasure I will attend to your books and correspondence. But you will permit me to refuse the salary with which you wish to repay such a slight service."

"But you are poor, Martin, and you can easily find a use for 50 pesos."

"I would much rather have your approbation," replied Martin, in a tone of dignity which caused Don Damaso to feel a certain respect for this poor provincial, who refused a salary which would have been much to him in his situation.

Martin made himself acquainted with what he had to do at the desk of Don Damaso, and the latter, whilst running over some papers, thought in spite of himself of the conduct of his *protégé*. Among certain men, an action which shows a contempt for money is the summit of magnanimity. In this way, Don Damaso admired, as an act of the greatest heroism, the words of Martin. The love of gold has held so many proselytes that an exception appeared incredible, especially at the epoch in which we now are. At the same time along with his surprise and perhaps as the only way of explanation the idea occurred to Don Damaso that Rivas had the punctiliousness of what some men called Quixotism, and preoccupied as Don Damaso was by political thoughts, he thought that with this young man it would be very easy to convert him from that which, since his conversation of the preceding night, he judged the empty phrases of liberalism and fraternity.

"Look here, Martin," he said after some moments of reflection, "Santiago is at the present day full of people whose sole occupation is politics. If you will permit me to advise you, I would tell you that there is much danger from this pretended liberalism; they are always down, none of them are contented, and there is nothing good in them. So between ourselves I believe that a man, in order to lose himself completely, has only to become a Liberal. In Chili, at least, I think it is very difficult for them to get the upper hand."

The frankness of these words made Martin understand the political principles which constituted the profession of faith with which Don Damaso aspired to occupy a seat in the Senate of the Republic. Separated from social intercourse, and only occupied with his studies, Martin was ignorant that this was the profession which the greater number of politicians ordinarily studied. His straightforward mind and his youthful pride made him conceive a very sad idea of his protector as a politician.

In this judgment his instinct took more part than his reason, because Martin had never considered the questions which agitate humanity like a fever, and which can only be calmed when human nature breathes the normal atmosphere of its existence; which is liberty.

A little before breakfast, Don Damaso related to his wife and his son the mishaps which had occurred to Rivas.

"So that this poor boy has not slept all night," said Doña Engracia fondling Diamela.

"That is to say, Mamma" said Augustin, "that he has passed the night '*a la belle étoile*'; it is a delicious adventure."

"But you must know," continued Don Damaso, "this boy who goes to buy shoes in the Plaza, and who only has 20 pesos a month for all his expenses, this morning refused a salary of 30 pesos which I offered him for his services as my secretary."

"Ha, ha," exclaimed astutely the silly Augustin, "that is to say he is taking on airs."

"He does not wish to serve as a secretary?" asked Doña Engracia.

"Oh yes, yes, he accepted at once, but would not take any salary."

Leonor looked at her father as if she now heard the conversation for the first time, and Augustin lolled upon a sofa.

"It appears that he lost one of his boots," said he, looking with satisfaction upon his elegant morocco slippers and his morning trousers.

At that moment Martin entered, having been called to breakfast.

"Friend Martin, it appears that you sleep badly in Santiago," Augustin said to him, saluting him.

Martin blushed, whilst Don Damaso made signals to his son to hold his tongue.

"It is true," replied Rivas, trying to accept the joke as well as he could.

"Poor man," replied the fop, "fancy going to buy boots in the Plaza! why did you not tell me about it, and I would have told you of a French bootmaker."

"What would you wish me to do," replied Martin with pride, "I am a provincial and poor; the first explains my adventure, and the second that a French boot-shop would be much too expensive for me."

"You never told us of the silly acts that you did when you arrived in Paris," said Leonor to her brother, "and yet you criticize this one with so much ease."

Leonor said these words with a smiling air, trying to soften the situation, and without looking at Martin.

Rivas knew that he owed thanks to the girl who had taken up his cause, but his perturbation did not allow him to say a single word. In the meantime, Augustin, who knew the cleverness of his sister, had no desire to reply, and hid his chagrin by petting Diamela, whom his mother was holding in her arms.

"I have related the adventure to my family," said Don Damaso, "to explain your absence last night."

"And you have done well, sir," replied Martin, who had recovered his serenity at the words of Leonor. "I hope that these ladies will now pardon me my involuntary fault."

"Why not, sir?" said Doña Engracia to him, "it is an incident that might have happened to anybody."

"Without doubt, to anybody," repeated Augustin, seeing that everybody was taking the part of Rivas. "What I said to you was only an unmeaning pleasantry."

Leonor had approved by a nod the words of her mother, and Martin received this small signal as an absolution from the ridicule which the story of his adventure might bring upon him.

After breakfast he informed himself as to where the National Institute was situated, and the steps which it was necessary to take to belong to the class of forensic practice in the University. He used all diligence to return to the house of Don Damaso, and began to work in his study, repeating to himself: "She did not despise me." This idea raised the enormous weight which was pressing on his heart, and once more he saw happiness in the distant horizon.

VIII

O n the following day, Martin took up his duties with the diligence of a youth who is convinced that study is the only foundation for future happiness, when fate has denied him riches.

His poor and antiquated provincial clothes from the first day drew the attention of his fellow-students, the greater part of them elegant young men, who arrived at the class with the remembrance of a ball of the evening before, or the emotions of some amusement much fresher in their memory than the precepts of the 7th Partidas or the Memorandum of the Courts of Judicature. Martin found himself isolated from all. Amongst our young men, the man who does not begin by showing his superiority by the elegance of his clothes, has to contend against much indifference, and sometimes a little contempt before conquering the sympathies of the others. They all looked upon Rivas as a poor devil who merited no more attention than his worn clothes and took good care not to give him a friendly hand. Martin knew that this arose from what might properly be called the snobbery of dress, and held his head high in his isolation without more satisfaction than that of being able to show his natural aptitude for study, each time that opportunity presented itself. One circumstance drew his attention. It was the absence of an individual about whom the others frequently spoke.

"Rafael San Luis has not come?" he heard asked almost every day; and after the reply in the negative he heard many various comments about the absence of the owner of this name, who, to judge by the frequency with which they mentioned it, must occupy a certain superiority amongst them since they interested themselves so much about him.

Two months after he had become a member of the class, Martin noticed the presence of a student whom all the others saluted cordially by the name which he had already heard. He was a young man between twenty-three and twenty-four years old, pale, and with features so chiselled as to be almost feminine, which were set off by a black moustache. An abundant head of hair parted in the centre of his forehead, showed its nobility, and his black shiny ringlets curled round his ears. His eyes, without being large, appeared to shine with great intelligence, and the fire of courage and vigour. His energetic expression agreed well with the elegant proportions of a figure of average height with symmetrical and well-proportioned limbs.

At the beginning of the class, Rivas fixed his gaze with interest on this young man whilst the latter spoke to a comrade, after glancing at him. At this moment the professor asked Martin's opinion on a judicial question which was being debated, and received an answer differing from the reply of the student whom he had just corrected. Martin had replied with energy and authority, giving his own reasons, which made his adversary red hot with indignation. Whilst between the young man who had drawn Martin's attention and the student who sat beside him, the following conversation took place:—

"Who is he?" asked Rafael, seeing the attention with which every one observed Rivas.

"He is a new-comer," replied his companion. "By his dress he seems a poor country-man; he knows nobody, and only speaks in the class when they ask him something; he does not appear to be anybody."

Rafael observed Rivas during some moments, and appeared to take an interest in the question which he was debating with his adversary. On coming out of the class the student who had showed his indignation at seeing himself conquered by Martin, approached him in an arrogant manner.

"I have got to correct you," he said, looking at him contemptuously; "I am not going to suffer the tone which you have used today."

"I do not suffer the arrogance of any one, and I will also speak in the tone which I prefer to use," said Martin. "And I certainly warn you who have addressed me," he added, "that the only lectures that I admit are from my professor in what concerns my studies."

"The gentleman is right," exclaimed Rafael San Luis, advancing. "You, Miguel, have replied to him with rudeness, when he only was doing his duty in correcting you; moreover, the Señor has only recently come, and we owe him at least the appearance of hospitality."

The discussion ended with these words, which the young San Luis uttered without either affectation or dogmatism. Martin approached him with a timid air.

"I believe I ought to thank you for what you have said in my favour," he said, "and trust that you will accept my thanks with the sincerity with which I offer them."

"So let it be," replied Rafael, extending his hand with frank cordiality.

"And, now that you have deigned to speak in my favour," continued Rivas, "I beg that when you can you will guide me with your advice; I have been a very short time in Santiago, and I do not know the customs here."

"By what I have seen," replied Rafael, "you do require advice, and what predominates in Santiago is pride. You appear to have sufficient energy to keep it within its just limits. Since we are speaking of this, I will confess to you that my interference can do very little in your favour, since you tell me that you are poor, and do not know any of our fellow-students. Here the young men pay great attention to external appearance, which to me is quite indifferent. Your poverty and isolation have inspired me with sympathy, for certain reasons which have nothing to do with this affair."

"Such sympathy makes me happy," said Martin, "and I shall be greatly delighted if you will permit me to cultivate your friendship."

"You will have a sad friend," replied San Luis, with a melancholy smile, "but I am not wanting in a certain amount of experience which can sometimes be found useful. *Hasta Mañana*." With these words he went away, leaving a strange impression on the mind of Martin Rivas, who looked thoughtfully after him as he went.

There was, in truth, surrounding this young man, whose poetical beauty drew the attention at first sight, a certain air of mystery. Martin watched him with curiosity and found in him a dignity mingled with simplicity, whilst the vague melancholy of his voice inspired him at times with sympathy. Rafael's dress also drew Rivas' attention. Caprice and an absolute contempt of the modes which were uniform amongst all the other students in the class seemed to dominate it. His turn-over collar contrasted with the stiffness of those worn by the others, and his black cravat, carelessly knotted, allowed a throat to be seen whose suave outline recalled to memory the lines which sculptors have given to the bust of Byron. Moreover, Martin found in the young man's last words some analogy to his own situation, and he took pleasure in imagining that he might be, like himself, neglected by fortune. This thought made him approach Rafael on the following day, and endeavour to continue the conversation interrupted on the previous one.

"When you wish it," said San Luis to him, "come and dine with me at a modest hotel which I often go to and there we will converse more at our ease. Where do you live?"

"In the house of Don Damaso Encina."

"In the house of Don Damaso," he exclaimed with surprise. "Are you a relation?"

"No. I brought a letter from my father to him and he has given me hospitality. Do you know him?"

"A little," replied San Luis, endeavouring to hide a certain amount of agitation.

After this the two young men remained silent for some moments until Rafael broke the silence, speaking of ordinary matters very different from those which had just occupied them. On going out of the class San Luis invited Martin to breakfast, and they directed their steps to a hotel of humble appearance. A bottle of wine gave more freedom to the conversation of the two young men.

"Here you won't eat like the son of Don Damaso," said Rafael, "but certainly more at your ease."

"Have you visited his house?" asked Rivas, whose curiosity was piqued by the agitation of his new friend when they spoke of his protector.

"Yes, in better times," he replied. "And his daughter, what do you think of her?"

"She is a most beautiful girl," said Martin, with enthusiasm.

"Take care! Your answer shows an admiration for her that may be fatal," said San Luis, becoming serious.

"Why?" asked Rivas.

"Because the worst which could happen to a poor young man like you is to be in love with a rich girl. Goodbye 'to studies, prospects, hopes,'" exclaimed San Luis, swallowing with feverish haste a glass of wine. "You asked my advice yesterday; then here you have the best I can give: Love, for the young student, should be like the apple of Paradise—forbidden fruit. If you wish to succeed, Martin (I tell you this because you appear gifted with the noble ambition which forms distinguished men), cover your heart with a cloak of indifference, as impenetrable as a rock."

"I am not thinking of being in love," replied Martin, "and I have many powerful reasons against it, besides those which you have pointed out."

San Luis then turned the conversation, and spoke about many different things with much verbosity; he appeared wishful to make Martin forget the first words of counsel which he had given him.

In, Don Damaso's house Martin spoke of his new friend.

"This young man is very crafty," said Don Damaso, "he is looking for a girl with a good dot."

"But, Papa," replied Leonor, "it is not necessary to be unjust; I have a better idea of San Luis."

"He is a parvenu," said Augustin; "Papa is right, in the times in which we live every one wants money."

"And they are right, since the poor require it more than the rich," exclaimed Leonor.

The energy with which Leonor had defended Rafael from the attacks of her father and her brother, and the words of his friend on the subject of love, suddenly brought a light to Martin's mind and a strange pain to his heart. He could not but think that San Luis had been in love with Leonor, and that his addresses had been rejected by Don Damaso. Such a discovery upset him almost as if he had received bad news, and he returned to his work unable to explain to himself why he regarded the future as if through clouded glass.

When he had finished Don Damaso's correspondence, his thoughts, after returning a thousand times to the same idea, got no further than a conclusion which filled him with discouragement. "There is no doubt that he loves her, and as Leonor still defends him she must love him in return."

IX

The idea that Leonor was in love with his new friend caused Rivas to treat him with a certain reserve in spite of the lively sympathy which he felt towards him. During several days, he vainly tried to solve his doubts in his conversation with Rafael San Luis. Their confidential chats did nothing towards satisfying his mind.

One evening, after dinner, Martin retired as usual before the hour when the visitors arrived.

"Are you fond of music?" Leonor said to him whilst he was taking up his hat.

Martin felt agitated as he replied. It appeared to him so extraordinary that this haughty girl should address him, that he almost thought he was dreaming. With this impression he turned towards Leonor without answering, and as if he had heard her indistinctly. Leonor repeated her question with a slight smile.

"Señorita," replied Rivas, nervously, "I have heard so little that I do not know whether I am fond of it or not."

"It doesn't matter," replied the girl, in a commanding tone, "you will listen to what I am going to play to you and sit down by the piano, because I want to talk to you." Martin followed Leonor almost overwhelmed with emotion. Don Damaso, his wife, and Augustin were playing a French "Patience" which the young man was teaching them. Leonor began by playing the introduction to a waltz, after indicating to Rivas a seat quite close to her. The young man looked at her in delight at her beauty, doubting the reality of his situation, which a moment before he would not even have dared to imagine.

Leonor played the introduction and the first bars of the waltz without addressing him. And just as Martin was beginning to imagine that he was the sport of a caprice of the girl, she gave him a haughty look.

"You know Rafael San Luis?" she asked him.

"Yes, Señorita," replied Martin, seeing in this question the confirmation of the suspicions which were tormenting him.

"Has he spoken to you of any of my relations?" Leonor turned and asked him.

"Very little, I think he is very reserved," he replied.

"You are a friend of his?"

"Very recently; I met him in the College a few days ago."

"But at least you have spoken to him?"

"Almost every day since we became acquainted."

"And he never said anything to you particularly about any member of my family?"

"Nothing. Oh yes! he asked me once about you." Martin added the second part of that reply in the hope of reading in the face of the girl the confirmation of the suspicions which were increasing in his mind.

"Ah!" said Leonor, "nothing more?"

"Nothing more, Señorita," he replied in despair at the proud impassibility of that beautiful face. Leonor went on playing some moments without saying a word. Martin felt himself suffocating, inquiet, discontented, before the arrogance of this girl who only addressed him in order to speak of a man whom perhaps she loved. His *amour-propre* made him long to be also a handsome man; he longed to have an immense fortune or to be a great celebrity; something at least that would raise him to the level of Leonor, that would arrest her attention and occupy her mind, which perhaps at this moment was thinking as little of him as of the surrounding furniture. Humiliated more than ever by his obscurity and his poverty, he felt himself capable of committing a crime in order to occupy the thoughts of the girl, even if they were thoughts of terror. At the end of a few moments she looked at him again.

"But at least," she said, returning to the subject, "you ought to know what this young man does and where he visits."

"I regret deeply, Señorita, not to be able to gratify the curiosity that you show," replied Martin with a certain acerbity of tone. "I have never possessed the confidence of San Luis, nor do I know at all the houses where he visits; we only see each other at the College." Leonor stopped playing, looked over some music, and got up.

"Certainly you are getting on well with your game," she said, approaching the table at which her parents and her brother were playing.

"They play as well as I do," said Augustin.

Rivas blushed with shame and contempt. Leonor neither looked at nor spoke at him. She left him as if she had no remembrance of having asked him to stay.

"You don't understand this game?" Leonor asked him at last, as if she had just remembered that she had left him standing by the piano.

"No, Señorita," he replied.

He left, at the end of a few moments' reflection as to how to do so without attracting attention. He entered his room with despair in his heart. His anguish kept him from understanding the conflicting and violent feelings which overcame him. Mute curses against his fate and the pride of the rich rose to his lips; mad projects of vengeance rushed through his brain, as he gazed into the future with a hopelessness which had no limits. Resolutions to make himself a name that would attract the admiration of all, a thousand confused ideas, flashed through his brain, dilating his heart, agitating the current of his blood, oppressing his breath, drawing from him tears of fire, whilst he cast himself in convulsions on a seat, or gazed at himself in the mirror with frightened eyes; and like a burst of lightning in the middle of a raging tempest cutting through the clouds in his brain, came to his mind at every moment the thought which his lips did not dare to utter, but which was rending his heart: "Ah! and to be so beautiful! so beautiful!" Calmness supervened little by little, restoring him to the enchanted realms of first love. He had forgiven. Leonor was suddenly to discover the treasures of his pure and loving heart; she would accept a love full of submission and tenderness, she would allow herself to be adored. Martin thus created for himself an imaginary world; listening to the heavenly music of a waltz to whose strains he and Leonor repeated vows for life, vows which ignored old age, and prayed for a sepulchre together from which to emerge to the mansions of eternal life. He saw that suddenly a passion could be born which would trample on pride, which would find on earth the elements of a happiness supposed to be imaginary, and he retired with a mind unsettled—forgetful of the truth.

Whilst Rivas was passing through this crisis, from which his love emerged radiantly, as silver appears in the depths of a crucible when fire has purged it of dross, Leonor had gone with Matilde to a sofa at some distance from the grand salon, in which some visitors were conversing.

"As I told you the other day," Leonor began by saying, extending her hand to her cousin, "Martin spoke at table about San Luis, whom I defended from my father's attacks." Matilde pressed Leonor's hand with gratitude, and Leonor continued—

"This afternoon I made Martin come and sit by the piano, and asked him many questions about San Luis. He is a friend of his, but a very recent one. He was not able to tell me anything about him, because Rafael does not appear to have made any confidences to him as regards his love-affairs, but I promise that I will find it out. Rivas is intelligent, and I hope that soon he will give him his entire confidence. Thus we will learn if he still continues to love you."

The two girls continued their conversation until Emilio Mendoza came and sat down by Leonor and began to pay his addresses to her, whilst she manifested not the least displeasure, although she gave no encouragement.

On the following day, Martin returned with coolness his friend's salute. San Luis having taken a great fancy to him, immediately remarked his manner.

"What is the matter?" he said, using for the first time a tone of familiarity; "you seem sad!"

Martin felt himself disarmed in the presence of the cordiality of his friend, whom he had seen treat his other fellow-students with indifference, and at the same time remembering that Rafael was not to blame for his unhappiness, had sufficient sense to feel the absurdity of his jealousy.

"It is true," he said, shaking his hand, "last night I was miserable."

"May I know the cause?" asked Rafael.

"Why should I tell you?" replied Rivas; "you could not give me back happiness."

"Take care, Martin! Don't forget my advice. Love for a poor student is the apple of Paradise—if you taste it you are lost!"

"And what can I do, when—?" San Luis did not let him finish.

"I wish to know nothing," he said. "There are some feelings which become exaggerated in the mind once they are confided to another. And Love is one of them. Don't tell me anything. I have a true interest in you; I would like to cure you before the disease is too strongly rooted. Solitude is a fatal counsellor, and you live too much alone. You must have something to divert your mind," he added, seeing Martin looking down-hearted; "and I will do all I can to help you."

"It will be difficult," said Martin, who was still depressed by the previous day's events.

"It doesn't matter, we will try. Nothing is lost. Come to my house tomorrow evening at eight o'clock and I will take you to see some amusing people." Then the two friends separated, Martin turning his steps to the house of Don Damaso.

X

At the dinner hour he entered the drawing-room, and found Leonor seated at the piano. The timidity with which she had inspired him from their first meeting, showed itself in his manner more markedly than before. It appeared to him that if he allowed his timidity to be seen when she was alone, Leonor would discover the love he felt in his heart for her. Love without hope infuses this feeling in every class, and in the strongest men.

She will pity me, he immediately thought, drawing back and feeling that the humiliation which this thought alone gave him was burning in his cheeks. Leonor had already seen him. Far from showing her previous indifference towards the young man, she quickly rose and went to the door to call him. Martin returned, divided between surprise and perturbation at being called so unexpectedly.

"Why did you go away?" Leonor asked him, noting the confusion which was depicted on his countenance.

"I thought you were busy, and I did not wish to disturb you," he replied.

"To disturb me! Oh no! You see I had to call you."

"A thousand thanks."

"Come and sit down, we must talk."

Martin felt with anger that the pleasant tone in which Leonor spoke was a new method of questioning him on the same subject as the day before. He entered the room behind the girl, and remained standing some distance from the armchair in which she had seated herself. Leonor pointed to a chair with a smile.

"Yesterday you went away without my seeing you," she said, looking at him fixedly.

"Señorita," replied Martin, feeling slightly relieved, "I thought that you had nothing more to ask me."

"That was not the only object which made me invite you; certainly I left you without thinking, and that is why I wanted to see you to tell you how grieved I am to think that I may have quite unintentionally offended you; I was preoccupied, and not thinking of what I was doing."

These soothing words were lacking in the tone which generally accompanies them. It seemed that the girl struggled with her pride when uttering them, and wished to show to Rivas the distance which separated them, speaking in the rather imperious tone which at times is used towards an inferior. Her soothing words had, in fact, been dictated from a certain straightforwardness, which, in spite of the pride which her family had inculcated in her, prevailed in her nature, and spoke strongly to her conscience. Leonor had remarked Martin's departure the day before, and knew on the moment that, humble as he might be, he was right in being offended. If, instead of Rivas, poor and insignificant, she had met one of her elegant and rich admirers, she might perhaps not have remarked this circumstance, nor thought for a moment of examining her conduct. But on seeing Rivas depart, she felt a certain amount of guilt, and recognized that she had behaved discourteously towards him. Hence she decided on making amends directly she found the opportunity, that is to say at this moment. However, when she found herself in the young man's presence and under the necessity of making apologies, Leonor felt that the affair was not going to be so easy as at first she had imagined. It was such an unusual situation for her to be placed in that it was only the strength of her will which decided her to persevere with a task which, without knowing its difficulties, she had resolved upon. Thus it was that when speaking, she feared that her words might find a different interpretation in Martin's mind, and used a tone of voice which indicated her station as far above that of the man to whom they were addressed. When she had spoken she looked at Martin to read in his expression what impression he had received. The first words awakened his suspicions, and his disapprobation shone in his eyes. Then, using the same tone as Leonor—

"For my part, Señorita," he said, "yesterday I regretted deeply that I could not give you more certain information about the person in whom you appear to be interested."

"It is not on my own account," replied Leonor, with surprise, forgetting all her promises of secrecy, and the affected tone of superiority which she had assumed.

"Ah!" said Martin, unable to hide his satisfaction; "it is not for yourself?"

Leonor, with the penetration usual to her sex in affairs of the heart, knew how to interpret the joy that was depicted on the young man's face.

"What! does he love me?" she asked herself, feeling a vague timidity before the ardent look which accompanied Rivas' last words. Afterwards, as if annoyed at the surprise which he had shown on telling him that she did not inquire about San Luis on her own account, she returned to her former attitude, as if she wished to punish Rivas for his temerity in daring to love her.

"I see, sir, that you have a very lively imagination, you found suspicions upon nothing."

"It is true, Señorita, I confess that I was too impulsive," he replied, bewildered in his efforts to understand this girl who had summoned him to make her apologies, and shortly after reproached him in a tone even more bitter than her words.

"What motive could you find to think that I had any interest in San Luis when I questioned you about him?"

"None, and I protest to you with the greatest sincerity, that if such a suspicion was born involuntarily in my imagination, I have not, and never would have mentioned it to any one."

"I hope so!" said Leonor, with a haughty stare, which painfully oppressed him. At this moment entered Doña Engracia, followed by her husband. When crossing the ante-room adjoining the salon, Don Damaso saw that Rivas and Leonor were alone.

"Why is the girl alone with this young man?" he asked Doña Engracia. Entering, he began a business conversation with Martin, whilst the lady repeated to her daughter Don Damaso's observation.

"But my father doesn't know what he is talking about," Leonor exclaimed with indignation, "and gives too much importance to his *protégé*. It is all very well that he considers him clever, if, as he says, he helps him so much in his business, but I do not allow that my father should suppose that he is good enough for me to take notice of."

The mother looked down without daring to reply, and consoled herself for her want of authority over her daughter by taking Diamela, who was jumping about to attract her attention, on her lap. Don Damaso, in the meantime, had already forgotten the impression which he had just received on seeing Martin alone with his daughter, and was listening to the opinion he was giving him concerning an important speculation which Don Damaso was wishing to undertake.

Leonor's answer to her mother showed that Don Damaso had frequently praised the secretary who, initiated in his commercial secrets, and being the writer of the correspondence which he maintained with his agents in the provinces, had more than once helped him with good advice. Thus Martin had been able to be of use to him by means of the clear intelligence which heaven had given him, as he was almost completely ignorant of commercial matters. Moved by the desire to repay in some fashion the hospitality which he was receiving, he took the greatest pains in order that Don Damaso would find him useful and be pleased to retain him. So that in the short time in which he had lent his services, Martin had reached a high standard in the mind of his employer, and he consulted him in many of the business matters relating to his enormous fortune. At this moment, as we have already said, the conversation between them was on a business matter, and Martin had just given an opinion which opened a new field for Don Damaso's speculations. The latter—full of satisfaction, sought for the means of showing his gratitude to the young man.

"I notice," he said, "that you do not come in the evenings to the drawing-room."

"My studies, sir, leave me little time," Rivas answered, feeling much gratified by this remark, because he saw the possibility of being more in the company of Leonor, and of becoming acquainted with her admirers.

"All the same, when you have time," said Don Damaso, "you are most welcome. I wish you to become acquainted with our visitors, and thus you would know the people in our society. For a young man entering the law, friends are always an advantage."

That night Martin took advantage of this invitation to present himself in the salons of Doña Engracia, where at nine o'clock were to be found the guests already known to our reader.

It is also necessary to mention that in the short time that Rivas had spent in Santiago he had made a notable change in the appearance of his dress, thanks to an arrangement which San Luis had told him of. This consisted in buying articles from a tailor and paying for them at the rate of 12 pesos a month, which Martin commenced to pay on receiving a complete suit. In this way he was able to present a decent appearance, and retain eight pesos a month for his other necessities.

To understand the agitation which reigned that night in Don Damaso's house, we will give an idea of the situation of the capital, and explain the conversation of Doña Engracia's guests, and depict the state of the public mind at this period of ardent political preoccupation. The Society of Equality, of which we have twice made mention in this history, composed at the beginning of 1850 of a few members only, had seen its ranks increase with great rapidity and became at last the object of general attention at the time of the events to which we are about to refer. Its numbers alone would have been sufficient to arouse the suspicion of the authorities, if it had not been that the programme of the principles which it sought to spread, and the ardour with which it was received, were owing to the inspiration of the upper classes in the social life of the capital. At the end of a short time the Society contained more than eight hundred members, and influenced by its discussions many grave social and political questions. By this means, a new life was awakened in the inert population of Santiago, and politics became the topic of every conversation, the preoccupation of every mind, the hope of some and the nightmare of others. Now was to be seen the peaceful citizen turning his drawing-room into a court of justice for inflamed debates; brothers, agitated by the most violent passions, enlisted themselves on opposite sides, rebellious sons defied the will of their fathers, and political frenzy disturbed the peace of an enormous number of families. In 1850, and afterwards in 1851, at times there was not a single house in Chili where there did not resound the disconcerting voice of political argument, nor a single person who was not enthusiastic for one of the parties which divided us. Lycurgus would not have been able at that time to enforce his law about those indifferent to the public welfare, because he would not have been able to find a delinquent.

The Society of Equality had already celebrated four sessions before the 19th August, in which took place the famous session commonly called "The Session of Cudgels." It was the same night that Martin Rivas was to attend for the first time the evening reception at his patron's house.

XI

As we have already said, much excitement reigned in the company which ordinarily composed the circle of guests of Don Damaso Encina. It was the night of the 19th August, and the news was already spreading that the Society of Equality was going to be dissolved by order of the Governor. As a proof, was cited the affair of the attack made by four armed men a few nights previously, at the time when group No. 7 of those who composed this Society were being installed in la Chimba.

Martin seated himself after having been presented by Don Damaso to his guests, and the conversation, for a moment interrupted, began again.

"The authorities," said Don Fidel Elias, replying to an objection which had just been made, "are within their rights in dissolving this reunion of demagogues; for what is authority? the right to command; therefore in commanding to dissolve, I tell you they are within their rights."

Doña Francisca, a woman of intelligence, covered her face, horrified at such logic.

"Besides," continued Don Simon Arenal, an old bachelor who posed as a man of political importance, "a well-conducted nation should be content with the right to amuse itself at public festivals and not mix up in matters that it does not understand."

Don Damaso, who regarded as lost the hope of being made deputy by the Government, which he had heretofore expected, found himself on this evening under the influence of the Liberal papers, whose views he remembered perfectly.

"The right of assembling is sacred," he said. "It is one of the conquests of civilization over barbarism. To prohibit it is to render of no avail the blood of the martyrs for liberty, and besides. . ."

"I will hear you speak about the martyrs for liberty when you have given up your fortune," interrupted Don Fidel.

"This has nothing to do with attacking property," replied Don Damaso.

"You are equivocating," said Don Simon Arenal. "Do you think that this step is taken without premeditation? Society of Equality; which means a Society which will work to establish equality, and as that which is most opposed to it is the inequality of fortune, it is clear that the rich will be the scapegoats."

"That is so, *Les Canards des noces*," said the elegant Augustin.

"About that there is no doubt, sir," said Emilio Mendoza, who had been giving approving nods with his head.

Don Damaso remained thoughtful. Such arguments against the security of large fortunes which were now beginning to intimidate all the rich who showed tendencies towards Liberalism, left him perplexed and taciturn.

"Brave men like you," said Emilio to him, "should take advantage of this opportunity to offer their support to the Government."

"Clearly," continued Don Fidel, with his affection for syllogisms; "it is the duty of every good patriot, because the country is represented by the Government, to support it is to manifest patriotism."

"But, man," replied Doña Francisca, "your proposition is false because. . ."

"Ta, ta, ta!" interrupted Don Fidel, "women don't understand politics; isn't that so, sir?" he added, turning towards Martin, who was nearest to him.

"That is not my opinion, sir," replied Rivas, modestly.

Don Fidel looked at him with surprise. "What!" he exclaimed; then, as if a sudden idea enlightened him, "Are you a bachelor?" he asked.

"Yes, Señor."

"Ah! that's the reason! We won't say anything more about it."

At this moment, Clementi Valencia, who was always later than the others, arrived.

"I have come from the street of las Monjitas," said he, "where the crowd of people detained me."

"What! is it a revolution?" Don Fidel and Don Simon asked at the same moment, turning pale.

"No, it is not a revolution, although if it were the Government is to blame," replied Valencia, by this sentence creating the greatest admiration in those who heard him, every one being accustomed to the difficulty of the capitalist to speak thus.

"I think that politics can make even fools eloquent!" said Doña Francisca to Leonor who sat beside her.

"Come on, man, what's the matter, you are out of breath," said Augustin to Valencia, who was mute whilst every one was waiting in silence the explanation of his words.

"Yes, what is the matter?" said the rest of the company.

"There was a general assemblage of the Society of Equality," replied Clementi.

"We know that."

"The session ended about ten o'clock."

"Great news!" said Doña Francisca in a low voice.

"That's what they told me in the street," continued the young man.

"And what more?" asked Augustin. "What happened afterwards?"

"Some men entered the room where the members of the Society were and attacked them with sticks."

"With sticks!" exclaimed his hearers.

"With blows of a cane," exclaimed Augustin, in a French accent.

"It is an atrocity," said Doña Francisca, indignantly. "It appears as if we did not live in a civilized country."

"Wife, wife!" replied Don Fidel; "the Governor knows what he is doing, don't mix yourself up in politics."

"Yes, but this is a little too strong," said Augustin; "this passes the limits."

"The duty of the authorities," said Don Simon, "is to watch over tranquillity and to suppress this association, if those in revolt threaten to disturb that tranquillity."

"But this is exasperating," cried Doña Francisca.

"What does it matter? The Governor has the power! He does well, he does well to be harsh, they have no right to mix themselves up in what is not their business."

"But it may bring on a revolution," said Don Damaso.

"You may smile at that," replied Don Simon; "it is the way to make one's self respected; every Governor should manifest his strength to the people, it is the way to govern."

"But this is cudgelling, not governing," replied Martin, whose fair and generous instincts revolted against the arguments of these authorities.

"Señor Don Simon speaks with judgment," replied Emilio Mendoza, "always be as harsh as possible to the enemy."

"Extraordinary theory, sir"—Martin was stung—"until now I always believed that nobility showed itself in generosity to the enemy!"

"Against other kinds of enemies, but not against Liberals," replied Mendoza with disdain.

Rivas rose, repressing his derision.

"Don't discuss anything, for he will not listen to reason," Doña Francisca said to him.

The political conversation continued between the two men, and the ladies approached a table on which the butler had just placed a tray with cups of chocolate. Martin was observing Leonor all the evening, and found it impossible to read the mind of the girl with regard to the different opinions given. The same thing happened when he wished to discover if Leonor gave the preference to either of her admirers, with each of whom he remarked she conversed alternately without her face expressing anything more than the polite interest demanded by good breeding. Very different from the expression seen on a woman's face when she listens to words to which her heart responds. This discovery far from cheering Martin made him deeply disconsolate. He thought that if Leonor regarded with indifference both the elegant politician and the fastidious capitalist, her attention could never possibly be gained by him, he had nothing to attract her to him capable of competing with the advantages possessed by his rivals, and at the same time he felt his heart still more troubled by the proud beauty whom his love surrounded with a divine aureole. Each of his thoughts at this moment was a sentimental idyll born of hopeless love, and he imagined at moments that Leonor was too beautiful to condescend to the love of mortal man.

In the meantime he struggled not to look to Leonor, fearing lest the others would guess what was passing in his thoughts. Matilde and her cousin had left the table.

"That young man is Rafael's friend," said Leonor.

"Do you know that I find him interesting," replied Matilde.

"Your opinion is not an impartial one," answered Leonor, smilingly.

"Have you asked him anything more about Rafael?"

"No, because my former questions made him think that *I* was the one in love with Rafael, and besides he was offended because I only called him to question him."

"Ah, he is proud!"

"Very, and it surprises me that he should have come here tonight, for never has he done it before. At table he seldom speaks unless he is addressed, and when he does it is to show his disdain for idle chatter."

"I see that you have studied him with attention," said Matilde, in a playfully malicious tone to her cousin, "and I think that you are more interested in him than in all the young men who come here."

"What an idea!" replied Leonor, tossing her head disdainfully.

This observation of Matilde had nevertheless made Leonor reflect that Martin, without her knowing it herself, was occupying her thoughts more than the other young men who surrounded her everywhere she went. This idea caused a strange perturbation in her mind, and she blushed to the ears when she remembered that this coincided with the thought which occurred to her when she saw the joy that the young man showed upon her confession of the motive for her questions concerning his friend San Luis.

This perturbation and these blushes in one who disdained the homage of the most distinguished young men of the city are perfectly explicable in the character of a girl spoiled by her parents and by the gifts of nature. Although Leonor had shown to her cousin her desire to be able to love, it could be seen that a great deal of her pride was centered in the indifference with which she treated the young men most admired by her friends. So that the very idea of having fixed her attentions on one whom she looked upon as so insignificant, disgusted her with herself, and made her form the resolution to put her will to the proof and triumph over what she considered as an involuntary weakness. Leonor looked upon Rivas as an adversary from this moment, without discovering that her proposition obliged her to fall into the error which she had just reproached herself with as a weakness: that is to say of occupying her mind with him.

Whilst she was forming this resolution, Martin had gone away in despair. Like every one who is in love for the first time, he did not attempt to overcome his passion, but seemed to revel in the sufferings that it awakened in his heart. He was under the dominion of the melancholy dreams which envelope the first pangs of the heart and took a new pleasure in augmenting their magnitude. Love in these cases produces a vertigo similar to that experienced by one who looks down from a great height into vacant depths beneath his feet. Rivas divined in his soul that this depth was vacant of all hope, and felt shattered against the certainty of the impossibility of being loved. These thoughts made him forget the appointment that Rafael had given him for the following day, and he only remembered it when his friend said to him coming from the class—

"Don't forget that you are coming tonight to my house!"

"Where are you taking me to?" he asked.

"Be sure to come, and you will see; I want to try a remedy!"

"For whom?"

"For you, I see that you have some very alarming symptoms."

"I'm afraid it is useless," said Martin, sadly, shaking hands with San Luis as they parted. He answered nothing, and at two paces from Rivas gave a sigh which contradicted the certainty with which he had spoken of being able to brighten the hopes of his friend.

XII

At eight o'clock at night Martin entered an old house, occupied by San Luis in the Street of Ceniza.

San Luis came to meet him and led him into an apartment which drew Rivas' attention by the elegance with which it was furnished.

"This is my nest," said Rafael, as he motioned Martin to a seat covered with green silk.

"To pass down this street," said Rivas, "one would never suspect the existence of a room so luxuriously furnished as this."

"What you see around you are the relics of better days," replied Rafael. "Amongst many things that I have lost," he added in a sad voice, "there still remains to me the liking for pleasant surroundings, and I have kept this furniture. But let us talk of other things because I want you to be bright and wish to be so also. Do you know where I am going to take you?"

"No indeed," answered Rivas.

"Then I am going to tell you while I am shaving." Rafael took a razor, prepared some soap lather and sat down opposite an oval mirror which could be raised or lowered. Then he began to shave, speaking whenever the operation allowed it.

"Now I will tell you. I am going to take you to a house where there are some daughters and where I am going to assist at what is called in technical terms a 'picholeo.' If you know the signification of this word, you will understand that it is not on an aristocratic scene that you are entering. The people who receive you belong to the middle class."

"And the girls, what are they like?" asked Rivas, to fill up a pause made by Rafael.

"I am going to tell you, but let us go by degrees. The family consists of a widow, a young man, and two girls. The widow's name is Doña Bernarda Coldero de Molina. She is about fifty years of age, and is different from most women in that she is inordinately fond of gaming. The girls are called Adelaida and Edelmira. The first owes her name to her godfather, and the second to her mother, who shortly before her birth went to see 'Othello,' and wished to give her a name which would recall her impressions of an evening at the theatre. You should hear her talk of these artistic recollections. Adelaida nurses in her mind an ambition worthy of an adventuress in a drama. She wishes to marry a Caballero.

Amongst middle-class people, who are not acquainted with our salons, a Caballero, or, as they call it, a man of good family, is a type of perfections. They judge the monk by the dress. The second sister Edelmira, is a gentle and romantic girl like the heroines of some serial novels, and has a leaning towards literature. The two sisters rather resemble each other, both have chestnut hair, white skin, grey eyes and pretty teeth; but the expression of each of them reveals the stores of ambition imprisoned in the heart of Adelaida, and the treasure of love and unselfishness in that of Edelmira. Her heart, as Balzac said of one of his heroines, is like a sponge and dilates to the smallest drop of sentiment.

"Lastly we come to the young man, who is twenty-six, and hasn't half an ounce of sense in his brain. He is the type of what every one knows by the name of 'sintico,' and in addition he is endowed with the Christian name of Amador. He is a curious object to study. You will see Now to tell you how this family lives without any more support than a young fool, can only be done by conjecturing. Don Damian Molina, the husband of Doña Bernarda, pretended to be of good family. He lived in poverty all his life, and left, as I am told, a small sum of 8000 pesos which lifted the family above misery. The eldest, when he had wasted his share, lives at the mother's cost, and defrays his small expenses by card-playing. At election times he is an active patriot, if opposition pays him better than the Government, and a pure Conservative if the Government is willing to give a better price. At times his philosophy rises to the height of his serving the two parties at the same time—like the rest of his compatriots—as he says."

"With two pretty girls it would be impossible that love should not find a hospitable shelter near, and such has been the case. But you will hardly believe me when I tell you the name of the lover of Adelaida."

"Who is it?" asked Martin.

"The elegant son of your patron."

"Augustin!"

"The same," answered Rafael. "A short time after his return from Europe, one of his friends brought him to call on them. At first he thought to make the conquest of Adelaida with his Gallicisms and his travels, but his love for the girl took serious proportions, when he found he met with a stronger resistance than he had expected. If the girl had loved him I think he would have had no scruples in deceiving and then abandoning her, but when resisted, his caprice became a genuine and overwhelming passion."

"And the other, who does she favour?"

"No one until now, notwithstanding the heartfelt sighing of a police official, who seriously wishes to marry her. Edelmira has wept so many times over more poetical and romantic heroes on the weekly novelettes she disdains the homage of this minor son of Mars—who sulks inside his uniform and takes to heart her indifference as if it were a blot on his career."

Whilst speaking Rafael had finished dressing and passed a final comb through his hair. At that moment Rivas' eye fell on a daguerreotype which was placed upon a writing-table.

"Oh," said he, "I have seen this face somewhere."

"Yes, very likely," said San Luis, extinguishing the light. "Are you ready to come?" he added, putting out one of the candles and taking up the other.

"Yes, let us be off," answered Martin, and went out arm in arm with his friend.

From the house of San Luis they directed their steps to a house in College Street. The outer door was bolted, as was then the custom followed by many people in Santiago when they were entertaining their friends. Rafael gave several knocks at the door, when a servant came and opened it.

To give an idea of this servant, the type of a servant of the poorer classes with his soiled worn-out jacket smelling of the kitchen, would be to weary the reader. What the pen refuses to describe, can better be seen in a picture, and a proof of it may be found in Murillo's "Beggar Boy," who has nothing in his appearance either agreeable or picturesque.

"We are in full swing," said Rafael, pausing before a window which looked on to the narrow courtyard by which they had entered.

"But," replied Martin, "there are a great many more people than you had described."

"They are their friends asked to the party. Look! There is the ambitious Adelaida. What do you think of her?"

"Very pretty, but there is something hard in her expression, which shows a calculating mind and repels confidence. But this opinion may possibly be the result of the description you have given me of her."

"No, no! All this is really shown in her face, you are right, but in the eyes of most people this hardness is considered an expression of dignity. Augustin Encina says she looks like a queen in disguise. Look!—notwithstanding that the other is her sister—what an immense difference there is between her and Edelmira, who is close by. Get rid of some of that languor that romanticism lends to her eyes and she would be an adorable creature!"

"You are right," replied Rivas. "I find her more beautiful than her sister."

"Look, look!" said San Luis, seizing Martin's arm, "here comes Amador, the brother; he is carrying a glass of punch, that they call 'Chicolito' at these re-unions. Don't you find Amador superb of his kind? His white waist coat embroidered in colours by some lady-love, speaks eloquently for him. On his cravat two large spots of sealing wax give a special glow to his person, and his hair which is curled like an angel's in a procession, speaks with the mute eloquence of the cleverest painting to characterize the perfection with which he is endowed. Just look at him! quite in his element, offering a glass of wine to a girl."

At this moment a young man approached the object of their attention and said something in his ear. Amador came out of the room and passing through another which adjoined the Court, crossed to the other place where San Luis and Rivas were waiting.

"Gentlemen," said he, bowing, "will you favour me by entering 'la cuadra.'"

"We were taking off our gloves before coming in," answered Rafael. Then, indicating his friend, "Don Amador," said he, "I have the pleasure of presenting to you Señor Don Martin Rivas—Señor Don Amador Molina," he said to Martin.

"Your servant. Command me in all things," said Amador, returning young Rivas' salute.

The three then entered the room next to that which Amador had called "la cuadra."

XIII

The glances of the guests were all directed to the new arrivals who were preceded by Amador. The young men saluted them in a friendly but distant manner, the girls whispering together as soon as they were introduced to them.

The clamour which prevailed when San Luis and Rivas were in the courtyard ceased suddenly as soon as they entered. In the midst of a dead silence a woman's voice was heard saying—

"Why, they are all as silent as the grave! One would think they never saw gentry before!"

It was the voice of Doña Bernarda who spoke with her arms akimbo in the middle of the room, animated with the desire to please the assembly. The girls smiled, casting down their eyes, and the young men appeared to squirm under such an eloquent remark.

"You are quite right, Bernardita," exclaimed one of them. "Let us dance quadrilles then."

"Quadrilles, quadrilles!" repeated the others, following his lead.

A friend of the family sat down at the piano, which he had himself brought to the house in the morning, and commenced to play a set of quadrilles, whilst the couples took their places. There was no distinction of age or condition amongst them. A matron of fifty faced her daughter of fourteen, who every now and then pulled down her skirt from the belt at the risk of tearing it, to make it longer, so that she should appear grown up.

"Leave off jerking at your skirt," said her mother, to the desperation of her partner, who was affecting a superior air in the presence of Rivas and his friend.

Near them a young man was making tender professions of love at the top of his voice to his partner, to show every one that he was not shy in the presence of the new arrivals.

"Señorita," said he, "I tell you, you are a thief, for you go about stealing every heart."

To which she answered blushing, and in a low voice—

"You are flattering me, sir."

Doña Bernarda went about the room amongst the different couples, in her *rôle* of hostess, paying compliments to every one. On arriving opposite the mother whose *vis-à-vis* was her own daughter, she looked at her, shaking her head archly.

"Look at the old party who is so gay," she exclaimed, "and has such a fine young man for a partner! That's right, my daughter, do your best to keep young!"

Amador was rushing in every direction looking for a necessary partner.

"And you, Señorita," he said to a girl, after having received excuses from many others, "will you not have the kindness to dance with me?"

"I have never danced quadrilles," she replied in an affected voice. "If you wish I will dance a polka."

"No nonsense, Mariquita," said Doña Bernarda, "you can learn here. Whoever brought you up? I find you very ill-mannered!"

At the end of a few moments Mariquita decided to dance, and the quadrille time gave way to discordant thumps on the piano. With a foot on the loud pedal, the excited player made tremendous efforts, swaying upon the piano seat as if each movement upon it had to produce a sound as loud as the instrument. The yells of the dancers and spectators contributed not a little to drowning the sound of the music, and Mariquita and the girl of fourteen made mistakes in the figures every moment and were prompted by three or four onlookers at the same time.

"This way, Mariquita," said one.

"This way. Now curtsey," said another.

"Here, here," shrieked a voice.

"Look at me and do what I do," said Amador, contorting himself in the forward and backward movements with his *vis-à-vis*.

"Don't yell so loud," shouted the piano-player, "no one can hear the music."

"Take a drop of wine on account of the heat," said Doña Bernarda to him, passing a glass, whilst Amador clapped his hands to indicate to the player to change the figure.

At the second figure the girl of fourteen began to dance the first over again, making the greatest disorder amongst those dancing opposite her and causing general confusion because every one wanted to set her right at the same time, striving to re-establish order by means of explanations.

This disorder, which caused despair to the young men and girls who desired to give an appearance of refinement to the reunion, gave great pleasure to Doña Bernarda, who, with a glass of wine in her hand, applauded the mistakes of the dancers and shouted every now and then, carried away by the animation of her entertainment. "Go it, my children! Keep it up!"

Rafael San Luis was, to Rivas' great surprise, one of the gayest present, doing all he could to still further entangle the quadrille and mix the dancers in inextricable confusion; his voice could be heard above all the rest, and every now and again he took occasion suddenly to abandon his partner for another and begin to dance with her a different figure, which upset the scarcely established tranquillity afresh. Martin saw his friend from a new point of view, which contrasted strangely with the serious melancholy which was previously so marked, and he guessed something rather forced in the pains that San Luis took to appear so happy and light-hearted.

"Your friend is the life of the house," said Doña Bernarda, approaching Rivas.

"I never would have thought he could be so gay," replied Martin.

"He is always the same—loud and noisy, but he has the heart of a seraph. Did they ever tell you what he did for me?"

"No, no one has told me anything."

"That is another thing about him, he never tells a soul the works of charity he does, but I will tell it you because I know it well. Last year I was at death's door, and when I recovered and wished to pay the doctor and the apothecary, they told me that I owed them nothing as he had paid them; Ah, he is a good fellow!"

The profound gratitude with which Doña Bernarda pronounced these words, made a strong impression on Martin's mind, and drew his attention anew to the mad gaiety of San Luis, who at this moment had led the confusion and the yelling of the dancers to its culuminating height. Seeing his friend looking at him, Rafael hastened towards him. In the short interval necessary to reach Martin his face had already exchanged its happy expression for the aspect of quiet sadness which it generally wore.

"This is a good beginning," he said, "as we become less shy we amuse ourselves more!"

"And are you really amusing yourself?" Martin asked him.

"Real or pretended matters little," replied San Luis, with a certain exaltation. "The principle thing is not to let one's self think." And with these words he moved away, leaving Rivas standing in the same place. Then Rivas went into a neighbouring room where he found himself face to face with Augustin Encina, who was dazzling in his elegance. The two young men looked at each other indecisively for a moment, and a slight flush appeared on both their faces.

"You here, friend Rivas!" exclaimed the elegant one.

"And I see you here," replied Martin, "and can't guess why you should be surprised, since *you* frequent the house."

"Surprised: why not? I said it because you are so reserved a man; I come because it reminds me of the grisette dances in Paris. Here in Santiago there are few amusements for young men."

Augustin took himself off after this to pay his respects to the lady of the house, who, to show her pleasure, exhibited the best which remained to her of her former charms.

At this moment Rafael, who had just caught sight of young Encina, took Rivas' arm and approached him.

"Have you saluted this elegant person?" he said, stretching out his hand to Augustin. "Here all the girls are dying about him."

"You are jesting, my dear boy," answered Encina, blushing slightly; "you flatter me too much," and he went into the salon, fingering ostentatiously an enormous watchchain with which he hoped to subjugate the proud Adelaida.

The quadrille finished, Doña Bernarda called to some of her friends—

"Let us go and play 'Montecito,'" she said; "that is the way to amuse ourselves."

Several people surrounded a table on which Doña Bernarda placed a cloth, and the others, including Rivas and San Luis, entered the salon, where could be heard the sound of a guitar. Amador was playing it, seated on a low chair and glancing at the spectators, whilst the servant who had opened the door to Rafael, carried about a tray with wine glasses.

Men and girls drank the liquor gratefully and Amador leaving the guitar presented a glass to Rivas and another to Rafael, insisting on their tossing off all the contents. To this libation succeeded several others which augmented the hilarity of the assembly, and they acclaimed with enthusiasm the voice of one of them who shouted—

"Cueca! Cueca! Let us have the Cueca!"

Various handkerchiefs were waved in the air, and Rivas saw with some astonishment a girl step out into the middle of the room and give her hand to the same official who had received him in the police station on the night of his arrest.

"It is the police officer who was in charge when they took me to the prison," he said to Rafael.

"And he is Edelmira's lover," answered the latter. "He must have just arrived, for I did not see him earlier."

The gay music of the Zamacueca sounded from under Amador's fingers and the couple launched themselves into the evolutions and movements of this dance and the voice of Doña Bernarda's son arose. He sang with his eyes gazing at the ceiling the following verse, which was as old as the dance itself—

> *"Antenoche soñé un sueño*
> *Que dos negros me mataban*
> *Ieran tus hermosos ojos*
> *Que enojados me miraban."*

Many of the spectators clapped their hands in time to the music and others encouraged the dancers with loud voices.

"Ai! Morena!" shouted a voice (the first word was loudly yelled).

"Ha, ha, hurrah!" shouted another at the same time.

"Go it, my girl!"

"Don't let her stop!"

"Twist the handkerchief!"

Voices followed in repetition whilst Amador sang—

> *"A dos niñas bonitas*
> *Queriendo me hallo;*
> *Si feliz es el hombre*
> *Mas lo es el gallo."*

At the end of these last words a general "Bravo!" greeted the old-world gallantry of the police officer who knelt before his partner at the end of the last turn. The drinking continued, augmenting the enthusiasm of the guests, who flung tender expressions to the girls, and jokes of doubtful morality to each other. To the difficulty which they had found in the beginning in copying the manners and habits of good society, succeeded the mixture of confidence and exaggerated politeness which gives a peculiar tone to this class of reunions. The people whom we call the middle class were placed between the democracy who despise the aristocracy, and those who envy and imitate it. Their manners present a curious mixture, in which one sees them as it were vitiated with vulgarity, and present also, up to a point, a caricature of those of the higher social class, hiding its absurdity under the repose of pretended riches and good breeding. Rafael made these observations to Rivas whilst they were escaping from a pursuer who wished to make them drink a glass of punch.

"As to that," said San Luis, "love-matters advance with more celerity amongst this class of people, for they dispense with the preliminaries which lovers in the higher ranks of society employ to lead up to a warmer declaration. The use of glances, the resource of all timid lovers and those not timid, is quite superfluous in this case. Does a girl please you? You tell her so without hesitation; do not believe that she will resent your frank declarations as you might imagine. Here, in matters that touch the heart, woman is the same as elsewhere; if she likes the compliment she will meet you halfway."

"I confess, Rafael," said Rivas, "I could not possibly find amusement here."

"I don't want to force you to amuse yourself," replied San Luis, "but I declare you are hopeless if the scenes we have just witnessed do not at least distract your thoughts. You have just seen something you have never beheld."

"What is it?"

"The sight of a rich man, thanks to a devouring passion, as unhappy as the most wretched of men. Look at him!"

Rafael indicated young Encina who, seated beside Adelaida, was pouring out protestations of love. The young man's face was burning from the fumes of the wine he had drunk, and from the desperation he felt at the coldness with which the girl received his advances.

"How is the love-affair progressing?" San Luis asked him.

"Not very quickly," answered Augustin, wriggling.

"Would you like me to give you a word of advice?"

"What is it?"

"At the rate you are going, you will never be loved in return."

"Why?"

"Because you pay court to Adelaida as if she were a great lady. It is necessary, in order to please these people, to act as if you were on an equality with them, and not to take the tone you are giving yourself."

"But how?"

"Have you danced?"

"No."

"Then ask Adelaida to dance the Zamacueca, and she will see at once that you do not disdain to dance with her.

"Do you think that will have a good effect?"

"Certainly."

Augustin, whose ideas after his libations were not very lucid, found the argument very logical, but he made one objection.

"The pity of it is that I don't know how to dance the Zamacueca."

"That doesn't matter; didn't you say that you had danced the 'Can-can' when in France?"

"Oh yes."

"Very well then, it's the same, with very little difference." This decided Augustin, and he asked Adelaida for a Zamacueca. A "Bravo!" greeted the appearance of the new couple. Rafael put the guitar into Amador's hands, who sang—improvising—in a voice which mistela had rendered still more sonorous—

"Sufriendo estoi vida mida
De mi suerte los rigores
Mientras que, nigrata tyrana
Tu ries de mis dolores."

Augustin, urged on by San Luis, at the first words of the song, flung himself with such ardour into the dance that he stumbled and staggered about for some seconds, finally falling at the feet of Adelaida. Then all the "hand-clappers" shouted, each of them directing some pleasantry to the unfortunate fop.

"There goes the dandy."

"Come along, my boy, let me help you up."

"Don't be alarmed, you have fallen in a delightful place."

"Pasenle la balanza que esta en la cuerda."

Augustin was up now, and dancing with such liveliness and so many contortions that the shouting and clapping increased, and Amador, in a feigned treble voice, sang, to the great joy of his hearers—

"To jump over the stream
Send the lame girl.
You must hold my legs
So that they don't get wet."

They were all echoing these last words whilst the fop, believing that the voices he heard were overwhelming him with their enthusiasm, fell on his knees at the feet of his partner, in imitation of the preceding dancers. Adelaida received this demonstration of gallantry with a laugh, running to her seat, and the others heartily echoed her laughter at the sight of the young man going down on his knees in the middle of the dance. Rafael followed Rivas into the next room, for Rivas looked distressed at the spectacle presented by the son of his protector.

"He is a silly ass," said San Luis, in reply to something that Martin said to this effect, "and imagines that his money is enough to save him from ridicule."

Rivas left his friend standing near the table where Doña Bernarda was playing at Monte. There was a chair beside Edelmira in which Martin seated himself.

"I have not seen you take much part in the fun," said the girl.

"I am not very fond of noise, Señorita," he replied.

"So you must not have enjoyed yourself."

"No; but I see that I am not made for these amusements."

"You are right; I have seen much of them, but I have never been able to get accustomed to them."

"Why?" asked Martin, his curiosity piqued by these words.

"Because I think we lose our dignity by them. And the young men who come here—like you and your friend San Luis—only come for the amusement of the thing, but do not consider us good enough to be their friends."

"In this I think that you are mistaken, at least as far as my respect is concerned. And since you have spoken with so much frankness I may tell you that, looking at you, I could guess your feeling about what you have just told me."

"Ah, did you remark it?"

"Yes, and I confess that I am pleased at your dislike of all this, and I think with sympathy of how many times you must have suffered under these circumstances."

"Never, as I have already said, have I been able to get used to these reunions which delight my mother and brother. Between young men like you, and ourselves, there is too great a distance for disinterested and friendly relations to exist."

"Poor girl," thought Rivas, meeting now another heart wounded like his by the curse of poverty. And Martin added another thought to this—

that of love—by imagining that perhaps like himself Edelmira loved another, and without hope.

"I don't understand," he said to her, "the sorrow with which you express yourself, when I know that you are young and beautiful. Don't you think that it may be all an illusion?" he added, observing that Edelmira lowered her face sadly. "My observation arose from the probability that surely you must have been loved, and it was in your power to be happy."

"In our class," replied Edelmira, sadly, "they do not love as the rich do. Sometimes those with whom we are mad enough to fall in love most offend us with their love, and oblige us to feel the misfortune of not being able to be content with those around us in our own station."

"So that you do not think you can find a heart which will understand yours?"

"It may be so, but never shall I meet one which will love me sufficiently to forget the position which I occupy in society."

"I feel I am not enough in your confidence to combat that idea," said Rivas.

"And I have spoken so frankly to you," she answered, "because your friend has told me about you, and because you have justified in part what he said."

"How?"

"Because you have talked to me without making love to me—unlike nearly all the other men when they wish to pass the time with us."

Many of the guests now came begging Rivas to dance the Zamacueca with Edelmira, but both firmly refused. But they would not have been able to free themselves from the exigencies of the situation, if Rafael had not come to the aid of his friend, assuring them that he never had danced in his life.

XIV

A nd now the fun was waxing fast and furious, and the fumes of the mistela were rising to an alarming height in the brains of the thirsty. Each of them, as generally happens in these cases, raised his voice to make himself heard above the others, and those who at the beginning showed themselves quiet and circumspect, displayed by degrees a loquacity which, however, was confined to a limited number of words, on account of the impediment placed on speech by the wine they had drunk. A harp was added to the guitar, and the piano abandoned as superfluous. The two instruments were played together, and to the voice of a lady, who raised it in a duet with Amador, was added an animated chorus of other voices joining in with a roar like thunder. Doña Bernarda looked up from her cards and shouted loudly, trying to re-establish order.

"Adios! You are behaving like hump-backed niggers! That's enough; this house is like a mad-house!"

The police official, whom they named Ricardo Castaños, taking advantage of the moment when Rivas got up to escape from the Zamacueca, sat down next Edelmira and began to annoy her about her conversation with Rivas, whilst Augustin, forgetting his aristocratic dignity, tossed off the contents of a glass which Adelaida had touched with her lips.

"And if you don't care for him," said the official to Edelmira, "why did you whisper to him?"

"My heart is entirely yours," said Augustin. "I give it alone to thee!"

From the harp Amador was singing—

"Me voi, pero voi contigo
Te llevo en mi corazon
Si quieres otro lugar
No permite otro el amor."

And all the others, wandering through the rooms glass in hand, repeated in voices more or less sober—

"No permite otro el amor."

And Rivas amongst the others heard the last word, and it awakened in him the bitter melancholy of his isolation, and the thought that never would it realize for him the joy that it promises to young and pure hearts. The noise worried him, and he felt oppressed by the facility with which the others seemed to yield their whole hearts to an imaginary love, created by the fumes of wine. Whilst he made these reflections, Rafael called the guests into the courtyard and lit some fireworks, which on exploding in the air, drew frantic applause and prolonged cheers for Doña Bernarda, the lady of the *fête*.

The voice of Amador called to the guests from the interior—

"Now, boys," he said, "let us go to supper!"

"To supper," exclaimed some of them, "what luxury!"

"And what did you expect, then?" replied the son of Doña Bernarda. "Here things are done properly."

The noisy crowd invaded a tiny whitewashed room, in which a supper-table had been prepared. Each sought a place at the side of the lady he liked best, and others who could find no seat at the table, stood about.

"My sons," exclaimed Doña Bernarda, "those who can't find seats must stand up and scratch themselves."

This preliminary announcement was celebrated with fresh applause, and gave the signal for the attack on the viands, which all undertook with valour. Opposite to Doña Bernarda, who occupied the head of the table, its skin a golden brown from the oven, was the turkey, which figures as a classical morsel at suppers in Chili whatever may be the rank of those who offer it. Fried fish and salad gave the table a characteristic look, and made a good effect with the rolled-up sucking pig and a centre-piece of olives, which Doña Bernarda told her guests she had received that morning from a cousin—an Augustinian nun. To facilitate the digestion of so many different dishes, there were some decanters of the famous vintage from Garcia Pica, and a tureen of punch, into which each guest had the right to dip his glass on condition he did not dip his fingers into the liquid, according to the warning given by Amador when filling a glass, which he swallowed at a gulp so as to give his opinion on its quality. The young men besieged the girls by a series of delicate attentions and finesses, which are not written in books on etiquette. One young man offered to the object of his attentions the portion of the turkey whence spring the tail feathers, and in presenting this choice morsel on his fork, he remarked that it was typical of his heart transfixed by a dart of Cupid. The officer of police would drink from no other cup than that from which Edelmira had drunk; Amador was on the road to ruin his health for ever by swallowing great glasses of chicha, whilst drinking the health of the young girl beside him. Augustin at the same time, having finished his amatory eloquence with Adelaida, recounted his souvenirs of Parisian restaurants, and spoke of the "*suprême de volaille*," whilst swallowing a supreme morsel of rolled sucking pig. The frequent libations commenced at last to develop their evil influence on the official's brain, who, wishing to prove his love, gave Edelmira a kiss, at which she screamed. At this sound, the maternal dignity of Doña Bernarda made her rise from her chair and give the aggressor a reprimand in which figured the official's grandmother, who for this occasion squinted—as one may well imagine. This incident suspended for a moment the general gaiety and had even an effect upon the mixture of liqueurs in the stomach of Augustin, who was carried out by the others as the wounded are in battle, whilst the official began shouting words of command as if he were at the head of his squadron. Others, at the same time, became extremely sorrowful, and related their griefs to the walls, their faces bathed in tears; whilst in another corner a group of young men embracing each other swore eternal friendship, whilst others kept telling Doña Bernarda over and over again that she must not be annoyed because Edelmira had been kissed. These different tableaux, in which every one acted under the influence of drink, had all the grotesque aspect of those pictures of the Flemish school, in which the artist depicts the consequences of (what is called in the language of the people we are speaking of) "borrachera." The few who were able to stand, nevertheless, did not wish to end the evening, and hid the key of the street door to prevent Rivas and San Luis, who wished to leave, from getting out. Then took place, as a final scene, a discussion which lasted a quarter of an hour, in which every one who wished to leave and every one who wished to prolong the evening took part. At last the prayers of Doña Bernarda prevailed on those who were keeping the door, which allowed those to leave who were still able to walk away on their feet. Doña Bernarda and her daughters then returned to the scene where the official and other visitors were lying on the ground and placed blankets over them. The young heir of Don Damaso Encina slept soundly in Amador's bed, where they had carried him a short time previously without his knowing anything about it. Doña Bernarda and her daughters retired to a room which served the three for a bedroom. Scarcely had they entered it when Amador appeared. Better armed than most for this kind of campaign, he had recovered his senses a little.

"Look here, my dear," he said to Adelaida, "I think that youth is in love to the points of his toes."

"And that other little fool," said Doña Bernarda, pointing to Edelmira, "who pretends such timidity and shrinks from the advances of her officialito, she ought to learn from her sister."

"But, mama! I don't want to marry," replied the young girl.

"And what! You think I am going to keep you all your life? Girls ought to marry. Look here, the officialito has plenty of money, and the sergeant, who is a cousin of our servant's, tells me that he will be promoted."

"We can't all find Marquises," replied Amador, directing his glance towards Adelaida.

"But pay attention then!" exclaimed the mother; "advance with caution, these sons of millionaires only want to amuse themselves. Adelaida, the one who doesn't take care—loses."

"If he doesn't talk of marriage, Amador is here to throw him out," replied Adelaida.

"Leave him to me," said Amador "Before a year is out, mother, we shall be related to these millionaires."

With this he said good night, begging the lady of the house to wake up the invalids of the *fête* early next morning so as to get rid of them before the family went to Mass.

In the meantime, Augustin was snoring loudly in a drunken sleep, ignorant of the kind projects of his hosts for receiving him into the bosom of the family.

XV

Rafael accompanied by Martin arrived at his house shortly after leaving Doña Bernarda's. It was about three o'clock in the morning when the young men came to the dwelling in the street called la Ceniza, occupied by San Luis.

"It is certainly too late for you to go on," he said to Rivas, "and it would be much better for you to remain with me. Augustin is not in a state to be moved, so no one will notice your absence."

Whilst speaking, Rafael lit two candles and pushed forward an armchair.

"Have you been amused?" he asked.

"A little," answered Martin, wearily leaning back in the chair.

"I noticed you were talking to Edelmira; she is a poor, unhappy girl, for she is discontented with her surroundings, and aspires to be with those who would understand her and her feelings."

"What I learned of her sentiments during the short conversation I had with her, filled me with melancholy," said Martin. "Poor girl!"

"You pity her?"

"Yes, she has refined sensibilities and seems to be suffering."

"That is quite true! But what can be done? Hers is a heart that would burn if it came too near the fire of happiness," said Rafael, sighing. Then he continued, passing his hand through his hair—

"It is the history of the butterflies Martin, those which are not burned carry for ever the scorch of the fire which has burned their wings. Vaza! I appear to be getting quite poetical, but it's the wine that is speaking."

"Go on!" said Rivas, the state of whose mind was in sympathy with the sadness with which San Luis had uttered these words.

"This cursed mixture has set my head on fire. Let us have some tea and we will talk. The fumes of liquor loosen the tongue and expand the heart." He lit a spirit-lamp, and then a cigar with the same paper with which he had lighted the spirit. "I see that you have not been amused," he said, throwing himself on the sofa.

"That is true."

"You have a grave fault, Martin."

"What?"

"You take life too seriously at your age."

"How?"

"Because you have fallen deeply and truly in love."

"You are right."

"Let us see—we must consider the subject, because one must always calculate. What do you think your hopes are worth?"

"Hopes of what?"

"Of being loved by Leonor, since you love her."

"I have no hope."

"Nonsense! don't be so miserable," exclaimed Rafael, getting up.

Rivas looked at him in astonishment, he could not conceive a greater misfortune than to love without any hope of success.

"That is to say," continued San Luis, "not a glance? not one of those almost imperceptible signs by which one may have a glimpse at the heart of a girl?"

"Not one."

"So much the better."

"Do you know Leonor?" Martin asked him, still more astonished.

"Yes, she is most beautiful."

"Then I don't understand you!"

"I will explain. I suppose she loves you."

"Oh never! She never will!"

"It is a supposition, but I have the opinion that a love that is returned has a thousand times more strength than the love that lives hopelessly on signs. You have conquered the whole world, and to confirm the conquest you wish to marry her. Such is life, and you will bless the saints when the moment arrives for you to ask her hand from her parents. Your love is that of an angel which raises you in your own eyes to the height of a demigod, has made you forget your poverty, and the reality arrives under the form of the father who will put his finger in the wound. You are a leper, and will be driven from the house like a dog. This history, my friend, loses nothing of the truth because every day it is repeated in what is called civilized society. Do you wish to be the hero of it?"

Martin saw that San Luis was excited to such an extent that he finished with a harsh and suffocated laugh.

"Poor Martin," continued San Luis, preparing the tea, "I have the experience even in my short life, and I will tell you my own story. I have never spoken of it to any one. But now, at this moment, its remembrance chokes me, and I will tell you about it as it will be a lesson to you. I have studied you ever since I first knew you, and I sought your friendship because you are good and noble; I would not like to see you unhappy."

"I thank you," said Martin, "I owe to your friendship the little happiness I have found in Santiago."

San Luis served the two cups of tea, placing a little table beside Rivas and seating himself at it.

"Listen to me, then," he said to him. "It is not an extraordinary romance I am going to tell you; it is the history of my heart. If you were not a lover I would take good care not to tell it to you because you would not understand it, although it is simplicity itself. I am obliged to begin at the beginning, as they say, because you know nothing of my life.

"My mother died when I was only six years old—I see her face sometimes in my dreams, I know it by the instinct of an orphan, but when I wake I can hardly remember what she is like. I was brought up in a college where my father came frequently to see me. Childhood passed; after its innocent gaiety came adolescence. I had been an innocent child, and continued to be so when my mind began to influence my actions. At eighteen poetry delighted me, and I wrote poems with the burning thoughts of which Descartes spoke when he described love. At this age I knew the original of this portrait."

Martin looked at the daguerreotype which Rafael gave him. It was the same that had excited his attention some hours before.

"It is Matilde—Leonor's cousin?" he said, looking well at the portrait.

"Herself," answered San Luis, not looking at it.

"I saw her yesterday evening at Don Damaso's house."

"This love," continued Rafael, "drew my very heartstrings, and was a safeguard to me from those pitfalls into which the nascent passions of youth so often fall. I loved Matilde for two years without ever speaking to her of my love. Our hearts spoke for a long time before our tongues. At twenty, I knew that she had loved me for two years. I found myself then in the same situation which I alluded to just now in telling you that you had conquered the world. This world, to a young man of twenty, gives him in all the glory of its freshness the heart of the well-beloved woman." Rafael paused to light his cigar, which had gone out.

"So far you must be very happy," said Rivas, who considered that the fact of being once beloved was sufficient repayment for the sufferings any other sorrows might bring.

"I had lived for twenty years in a world of roseate light," continued San Luis. "Matilde's parents welcomed me because my people were rich and their business was on a large scale. She had made me bless life. I was, as I have just told you, very happy. The most beautiful days of Spring are sometimes swiftly overclouded, and Matilde and I were in the flower stage of existence. I had a rival, young, rich, and handsome. The rose-coloured world sometimes had a tinge of grey which made my nerves tremble, and then at night on my pillow visions came to oppress my heart. After wrestling with jealousy for some time, my pride opposed my love. I was jealous! I had no dignity before such a tremendous passion, and mine was such that it will live as long as I am alive. Matilde chased some of the clouds from my heaven by swearing to me that never had she ceased to love me, and I saw, linked in my being, a love and a passion which were absolutely without limits when I believed I had reconquered her heart. The clouds dispersed and gathered again; often I saw the sun shine and again hidden behind fresh doubts. In this struggle a year passed by. My father called me one day into his study, and when I entered threw himself into my arms. My own preoccupations had hindered me from seeing that his face had been haggard and anxious for some time past. His first words were these: 'Rafael, I have lost everything!' I gazed at him with astonishment because the world considered him a rich man. 'I pay my debts,' he said, 'and enough alone is left to support us in poverty.'"

"'And we can live thus,' said I kindly. 'Why do you let it grieve you so? I shall work.'

"To explain my father's ruin would be to recount a history that repeats itself every day in business. Ships lost with valuable cargoes; wheat blighted in California—that mine of wealth for a few, and ruin for many. To sum up, all the mishaps of mercantile speculation. This news grieved me on my father's account; as for myself, it was as if one spoke to the Emperor of China of the death of one of his subjects. I owned seventy thousand millions in happiness, because Matilde loved me. What mattered the loss of fifty or sixty thousand pesos?"

"She loved you in spite of your poverty," said Rivas, still with his idea fixed.

"Still I continued my visits to Matilde, talking of love to her and literature to her mother. You know love has a bandage on his eyes. This bandage prevented me from seeing the coldness with which Don Fidel replaced the attentions which he formerly lavished on me. One night I arrived at Matilde's, and found, alone in the salon, Don Damaso, your patron. I don't know why I felt my blood run cold when he bowed to me.

"'They have charged me with a disagreeable message,' he said to me, 'and I hope you will receive it without annoyance and with the calmness of a gentleman.'

"'Sir,' I replied, 'you can speak. I hope I am sufficiently a gentleman not to require to be reminded to act as one.'

"'You are aware,' said Don Damaso, 'that the situation of a young unmarried girl is always a delicate one, and that her relatives' duty is to avoid anything that might compromise her. My brother-in-law Elias has learnt that society talks a great deal of your repeated visits to his house, and fears that Matilde's reputation may suffer by it.' The poniard's point entered in the middle of my breast, and I felt an agony which almost deprived me of consciousness.

"'That is to say that Don Fidel shuts his doors on me?'

"'He begs you to cease your visits,' Don Damaso replied.

"My boast about my good breeding had an unlooked-for result, for in a rage I threw myself on Don Damaso, and took him by the throat. (Here I ought to tell you that a friend had informed me that this gentleman, urged by Adriano, the other suitor of Matilde, for the payment of a large sum which was very inconvenient to give at the moment, had obtained more time for payment by promising to obtain Matilde's hand from his brother-in-law for his creditor. I refused to believe it, but my doubts in this respect were dispersed when I saw him empowered to dismiss me from Don Fidel's house, and my rage was uncontrollable.) Seeing Don Damaso's face turning purple from the furious pressure of my fingers on his throat, and alarmed by the suffocation in his voice, I let go, threw him on a sofa, and rushed in despair from the house. In my own house I found my father in bed and ill. My aunt Clare, who lives here with me, I found by his bedside, and she only left when she saw him fall asleep. I sat down by the bed and watched him all the night. At one time I tried to read, but it was impossible. Sorrow was choking me, and my eyes made vain efforts to understand the words of the book, for in my imagination a volcano was burning. For two hours I suffered a martyrdom impossible to describe. The painful breathing of my father—in place of inspiring anxiety—was that of Don Damaso, whom I was castigating for the terrible news which was slaying my happiness for ever. At last my father began coughing with such violence that the sorrow in my breast gave place to fears on his account. The following day the doctor declared that my father had a violent attack of pneumonia. The seriousness of the attack was so great that in three days he was dead. I did not leave his room for a moment, watching with my aunt who came to stay in the house. In the daytime we were aided by a brother of my father who was then poor, but since then has become rich. My poor father died in my arms, blessing me. You can imagine that I had need of almost superhuman force to resist such great sorrow. When, after a month I went out to pay some morning visits, I learned that Matilde and Adriano were soon to be married. The rosy world was changed to darkness for me henceforth. To suffer as I suffered, without counting my father's death, does it not seem almost too much?"

"It is true," said Martin.

"That is why I told you that your misfortune is not irreparable, since your love is not returned. You have still a chance of forgetting."

"Forget, when love is beginning! It is not easy," exclaimed Rivas; "I would rather suffer."

"Try and love some one else then."

"I could not. Besides, my poverty closes the doors of society to me, or at least gains me little consideration."

"That is just what I found," said Rafael. "After a year of grief I renounced all self-respect and became a libertine. Desperation dragged me down to abysses of licentiousness where I thought I would find forgetfulness. I learned the real meaning of this new phase with pain, which was not wanting in attraction, and found that to revenge a disgrace upon one's self, is to be doubly disgraced. It appeared to me that the sacrifice of any poor girl was nothing when weighed against the tortures which my abandonment had imposed on me. From that time I neglected my studies, which I had heretofore followed with exemplary application in order to marry Matilde and pass my examination for the law. Instead of attending the classes I frequented the *cafés*, and spent entire days learning to play billiards. There I made friends with some young men of the class who shout at the waiters, and try to make their voices listened to no matter what they have to say. My reputation as an idler began to be known, without my being able to lose in this dissipation the agonizing remembrance of my lost love, when one evening I was passing a parade of the Señor del Mazo at the Plaza de Armas with one of my new friends, and he called my attention to a group of three women of that special type which appears to like showing itself in processions. One of them was elderly, but the two others were young and pretty. There was something about them that distinguishes a true Santiagan from ordinary people.

"'Pretty girls!' I said to my companion.

"'Don't you know them?' he inquired, 'they are the Molinas, daughters of the old lady who is with them.'

"'Do you visit them?' I asked.

"'Why not? they give very pleasant parties,' he answered.

"Adelaida most drew my attention by the peculiar charm of her beauty. Her fresh and rosy lips promised me in advance forgetfulness of my misery. Her eyes, with their warm and ardent glances, her black and thick eyelashes and black hair, which escaped from her shawl, her noble stature, offered me a conquest worthy of my new career. Confident in my good appearance and in the audacity which had before served me in my *rôle* of cavalier, I obtained an introduction to the family, and spoke of love to Adelaida on the first visit. 'I looked neither at the procession nor the pretty girls, once I saw you,' I said, when I sat by her. This compliment of doubtful taste did not seem to offend her. The man who introduced me to the house had told them I was rich, and this surrounded me with an aureole which fascinated them all. At night, when as usual, I gazed on Matilde's photograph, the pure brow and candid look made me ashamed of the kind of life I was leading. But jealousy was stronger than any twinges of conscience. I continued visiting Adelaida, and took a mad part in every diversion to escape memory. There are people who refuse to believe that in the nineteenth century an unfortunate love can drive a young man desperate, without remembering that the heart of humanity cannot grow old. I was laden with the recollection of my misfortunes in the midst of tumultuous orgies, and I heard the voice of Matilde in the vows of Adelaida, for at the end of a month she loved me. Many times I tried to withdraw from the villainy of my purpose, but I yielded to the fatal aberration which sought, by the sacrifice of one girl, to avenge itself for the deceit of another. Besides, Martin, bitterness destroys the purest thoughts of the soul, and of all the unfortunate wretches who seek forgetfulness in a life of dissipation, the victims of love are the first. Ah! in that solemn compact of two hearts who exchange their being to live in the existence of each other, that which turns traitor does not know that, in breaking the compact, it deprives the other of its vital atmosphere. I ought to have thought of this reflection before betraying Adelaida, but desperation had blinded me. The few persons who knew me, related to me with barbarous prolixity the details of the approaching marriage of Matilde and Adriano. A lady, an old friend of my family, praised Matilde's happiness, telling me that her lover had given her three thousand pesos' worth of jewels. After that I was far from approving the virtue of Joseph, and deemed that I, whose heart had been trampled on so cruelly by destiny, had the right to trample morality underfoot. A very short time sufficed to convince me that the only true way to endure misfortune is resignation, since I found myself more unhappy than before. The impure life of a seducer without a conscience, made me feel ashamed of myself before my people, and the illicit pleasures to which I had abandoned myself—far from curing me—made me conscious of my baseness and my unworthiness of Matilde's love, to be worthy of which had always been my aim before I lost hope. After a few months, my obligation to the family of Adelaida was overpowering because she had a son. From that time I employed all my pecuniary resources to ameliorate the material condition of the family of Doña Bernarda, and formed the resolution of breaking off my relations with Adelaida. She received this announcement with admirable coolness. Her heart, in which I had often remarked a certain hardness, appeared to listen unmoved to what I said, and when I had finished speaking she did not utter a single complaint. Since that day she has treated me as if never a word of love had been spoken between us. Does she love me now, or does she hate me? I don't know. Now you will ask me why I took you to this house if I did not think you would succeed no better in forgetting than I did."

"Yes," was all that Martin said.

"I have the experience, bought at the cost of much remorse," said San Luis, "and I only wished to give you a little distraction. I saw you entering on a life of melancholy, and I wished to save you. For this purpose I offered you a little change, and related to you at the same time what I have done. If I could have seen in you the lightness of character common to most young men, I would have carefully guarded myself from taking you to this house."

"You are right, and have judged me wisely," replied Martin; "for me, Leonor, or no other woman! I have no right to complain, because she has done nothing to make me love her. But let us talk of you. What would you say if Matilde's love returned to you?"

Rafael jumped from his seat. "You! What do you say? And how?"

"I don't know, but it might happen."

San Luis let his forehead sink on his arms outstretched on the table.

"It is impossible," he murmured. "Her affianced husband is dead, it is true, but I remain always poor." Raising himself when he said these words, he busied himself for some time preparing a bed on a sofa.

"You can sleep here, Martin," he said. "Good night;" and without undressing he threw himself upon his bed.

authority arms are necessary, and in this case those who resist by force of arms are thus converted into soldiers."

"Don't you see?" said Don Fidel, carried away by the loquacity of his countryman.

Doña Francisca turned to Doña Engracia, who was caressing Diamela.

"To discuss with these politicians is only to get heated," she said.

"That is true, my dear, I already begin to feel the heat," replied Doña Engracia, who, as we have already said, suffered from difficulty in breathing.

"I said that these disputes heat one," replied Doña Francisca, cursing in her inmost mind the stupidity of her friend.

"And I, my dear, add this, that after any discussion the day passes for me with my head burning and my feet like ice." Whereupon Doña Francisca sought to calm herself by turning over the leaves of Leonor's album.

Leonor had retired with Matilde to a corner of the room when Martin put his hat down in the antechamber (familiarly called dormitoria in our language). Augustin went to Rivas immediately he saw him appear.

"Do not say anything about last night," he said to him before Martin could enter the salon; "in this house they do not know that we were together."

At the same time Leonor said to Matilde, "This night I am going to see if I can conquer his discretion, and make him give me news of Rafael." A very natural circumstance quickly arrived to further Leonor's project, for a servant entered bringing in several yards of stuff, that Doña Eugracia had sent him to look for in a shop. At the sight of the cloth Doña Francisca forgot her bad temper, and left off thinking about politics in order to enter upon a long discussion about the fashions with her lifelong friend, whilst Don Damaso and his friends disputed with warmth upon the destinies of the country, using the sort of argument beloved by a great number of those politicians who take notes upon everything. In the meanwhile Augustin, tired of politics, sat down by Matilde to speak to her of Paris, and the other young men followed the political discussion because they did not dare to cross the room and mix with the group of girls.

When Leonor announced to her cousin that she was going to speak with Rivas, she not only did so to explain what she was going to do, but she also sought to excuse herself in her own eyes from what her conscience told her was weakness. Martin's absence, and her vow to try her will-power against a man who had claimed her attention for a moment, were the ideas which really predominated, but which she refused to confess to herself, and thus she sought a pretext that would exonerate her for the desire which drew her to speak with him. Leonor, in this fashion, made the first step in this preliminary skirmish in the war of Love, which has been so poetically described in the well-known expression "to play with fire." Her presumptuous heart sought to triumph over that to which she had seen so many of her friends succumb, and she entered the lists with the pride of her beauty for her principal weapon.

Martin sought her eyes and found them fixed on him. When he went to the salon of Don Damaso, he went seeking (as Leonor did, although for another reason) an excuse for the weakness which drew him to the feet of a girl whom his love clothed in divinity.

"This excuse," he said to himself, "is founded on the desire to serve my friend by giving Leonor more ample information than in our last conversation." He saw in the eyes of the girl an order to approach her, and he proceeded to occupy a seat at her side with the reverence of a subject who is presenting himself before a sovereign. The emotion with which Martin approached her caused a flutter in the breast of Leonor, and she felt a singular impatience against her heart whose beating had quickened against her will. The slight movement of rebellion which accompanied this feeling persuaded Martin that he had made a mistake in interpreting the glance of the girl. Under this persuasion he wished himself a thousand leagues from the spot, and cursed his stupidity, his face showing the desperation that agitated him. Finally, when Leonor felt secure of herself she turned towards Rivas, putting an end to the awful moment during which the young man was swearing to fly from the house.

XVII

O ur conversation of the day before yesterday," she said to him, "was interrupted by my mother, and I regret it very much." Rivas found nothing to answer, neither could he explain to himself the last part of Leonor's sentence; she, without waiting for a reply, continued, "I regret it because I labour under the fear of not having plainly expressed myself in the questions that I asked you about your friend San Luis."

Disillusioned from his idea of having deceived himself and committed an absurdity by seating himself at the side of the girl, Martin began to feel calmer.

"You explained yourself perfectly, Señorita," he replied.

"Did you understand that I was not asking for myself?"

"I understood then and I now know the object with which you did it."

"Ah!" exclaimed Leonor, "you have discovered something new."

"As you say, I have discovered the object of the questions you have asked me."

"And that object is—?"

"Is, according to my belief, to serve a friend."

"That is true; tell me how you knew it."

"This friend is interested in Rafael."

"Yes; and what more?"

"Certain circumstances have separated them."

"Oh, I see you have been receiving confidences."

"That is true."

"And now you have decided to become communicative," said Leonor with an accent of reproach.

"Only yesterday did I receive this confidence," replied Martin, who was quivering with happiness at seeing himself in such familiar conversation with her whose coldness a day previously had driven him to despair.

"Consequently," replied Leonor, "you can tell me all."

"I believe so."

"Since you appear to know all, you will understand that the principal object of my questions is to make one point clear. Does your friend still love Matilde?"

"With all his soul!"

"Truly?"

"I firmly believe it. The enthusiasm with which he has spoken to me of his love, the sadness which disillusion has left in his soul, and the misery with which he looks at the future, appear to me to confirm my opinion."

Martin said these words with as much warmth as if he were advocating his own cause. His tone drew from Leonor this remark—

"You speak as if you alluded to your own heart."

"I believe in love, Señorita," said Martin, with a certain melancholy.

The girl saw a danger in this answer, and instinctively felt a desire to change the conversation. But her pride made her feel ashamed of this fear, and suggested to her a question which, under ordinary circumstances, she would not have asked any man.

"Are you in love?"

Martin could not hide the surprise which such a question caused him, nor the irresistible desire to show to Leonor that in the breast of a poor and obscure young countryman a heart could beat as worthy as any of those of the fashionable people who now surrounded him.

"A person in my position," he said, "is not allowed to be in love, but I can believe in love as a well of hope which gives strength in the struggle for which fortune has destined me."

"I can see that the disillusion from which your friend suffers has also contaminated you."

"No, Señorita, but the kind of wonder with which you ask me your question has made me examine myself. Principally I believe from the little that I know of Santiago, that here love is considered as a pastime for the rich, and can hardly be considered by those for whom time is immensely valuable."

"But you said," replied Leonor, "that nothing could impose laws on the heart."

"On this point I have very little experience," replied Martin.

"From what then comes the feeling which you have just made manifest? You say that you believe in love."

"My feeling is born in my own heart. There is something which tells me frequently that my heart was not made solely to beat in order to make my blood flow regularly; that life holds a less material side than the speculations with which one seeks for fortune, that in the streets, in the theatre, in the dances, the soul of a young man is seeking for some other pleasure than that of seeing, that of hearing, and that of conversation more or less insipid."

"And this pleasure, this unknown thing which he seeks, do you call it love?"

"Is it not so? I believe that those who are not aware of its existence," replied Martin, with a certain pride, "either have been born with an incomplete organization, or are happier than others."

"Happier! Why?"

"Because they have less to suffer, Señorita."

"That is to say that love is a sorrow."

"Every man can consider it according to his position in life. As for me, for example, I believe that I may consider it as a sorrow."

"Then you are in love, since you have such fixed ideas on this matter." These words sounded in a mocking tone, which made the cheeks of Rivas burn. His impetuous character made him forget the nervousness which he had at first suffered from at the side of the girl.

"I suppose," he said, "that this matter does not interest you to such a point that you desire a sincere reply on my part, but I have no difficulty in giving it to you, and since I ought to consider love as a misfortune I have resolved to keep myself aloof from such an infliction."

"That is to say you consider yourself superior to others."

"I may be an egotist and nothing more. I do not think it is a very great merit for me to take the path that I find the easiest."

Leonor, who had hoped to bend him to her will, saw herself thwarted by the apparent humility with which Rivas manifested a strength which she must try to conquer. She summoned up a haughty look and the imperious tone which she generally employed with men.

"We have wandered much from the object of this conversation," she said, accentuating these harsh words in order to show her displeasure.

"If you have anything else to ask me," replied Martin, pretending to take no notice of her meaning, "I am ready, Señorita, to satisfy your curiosity, or to withdraw as soon as you order me."

"Let us speak of your friend," said Leonor in a dry tone.

"Rafael loves, and is unhappy, Señorita."

"Can you not teach him the philosophy of resignation?"

"It is he who has taught me that when disillusion arrives, it is more prudent not to seek for a response."

"You count yourself amongst the disillusioned?"

"That is a proof that I do not think myself as superior as you suppose, and shows that I have suffered modesty to qualify my daring."

"Your modesty sounds much like pride still," said Leonor, "and in that case proves that you are quite contrary to what you say. It does not appear that it is necessary for me to tell you what pride is, and pride always seeks a point of superiority in order to manifest itself."

She did not wait for the reply of the young man, and left her seat without looking at him. For the first time in her life Leonor felt worsted in a contest which she herself had provoked. In place of those obsequious and banal compliments which she had hitherto received in this game of vanity, she found the proud submission of a poor and obscure man who would not bend the knee before her imperious self-love, and made no protestations about aspiring to have the happiness of pleasing her. This conversation made her think that she had been mistaken in supposing that Rivas was in love with her on account of the happiness which she thought she saw in his face, when she told him that she had no personal interest in Rafael San Luis; and this disillusion, which crushed her belief in the supreme power of her beauty, irritated her vanity, that vanity which was counting on a new slave to be attached to the chariot of her numerous triumphs. When she abandoned her seat she thought no more of amusing herself with Martin by trying the power of her will in an amorous flirtation, but she promised herself vengeance for his reproof by inspiring him with the passionate love from which he had boasted that he had sufficient strength to fly.

Martin, at the same time, was sunk in the sadness which each of his conversations with Leonor left him in; he persuaded himself more and more each time that he was a plaything of this girl who, during the past few moments, had amused herself by mocking at the love which his eyes must have confessed from the first. Scarcely had he seen her leave, when the memory of what he had said returned to him, and he cursed his stupidity for having let slip so many opportunities for letting her see that he had a heart capable of understanding her, and an intelligence that she could not despise. Leonor's last words left him hopeless, and brought clearly to his mind that neither heart nor intelligence were of any value whatever if not accompanied by riches and distinguished birth. This reflection rendered him disconsolate, and he withdrew desperate, praying to Heaven—as all unhappy lovers pray—for supernatural power, if not to forget, then to infuse into the breast of the beloved girl one of those passions which would draw her to submit to his will.

In this fashion Leonor and Martin, both devoted themselves to the same object, she confiding in her beauty, he hopelessly praying Heaven for what seemed to him impossible. At the moment when Leonor left her seat Doña Francisca was going away with her husband and Matilde.

Whilst Leonor was arranging a scarf on the head of her cousin, she found the opportunity to whisper: "He loves you! Tomorrow I am going to see you and we will talk." Matilde clasped her hands with indescribable gratitude. Never had she returned to her house happier or more light-hearted.

Don Damaso, finding himself alone with his wife, gave her some of the Conservative ideas to which his friends had converted him at the end of their political discussion.

"Above all," he said to her, "those Ministerialists are not wanting in reason; what has the Liberal party ever done that is right? and I am not deceived in the part that I am taking because in all parts of the world rich men are on the side of the Government, as in England, for example, all the Lords are rich."

After making this observation he went to bed reflecting that with these ideas he would very shortly occupy a seat in the Senate of the Republican Government.

XVIII

We have said that Rafael San Luis occupied with his aunt a house in the street of Ceniza. This aunt, whose want of money and beauty had made her an old maid, had concentrated little by little all her affections on Rafael, when she saw him fatherless and abandoned by fortune. Joining the little sum that she possessed to the 8000 pesos her nephew had received at the time of his father's death under his will, after the creditors had been paid, Doña Clara San Luis consecrated her life to Rafael and went to live with him. Having no other occupation than going to the Mass and the Novenas of her religion, the lady studied Rafael's thoughts as written in his face with the devotion of one quite free from all thought of self. Without ever inviting his confidence, she was able to follow him step by step in his sorrow, sometimes venturing to give a little religious advice about the necessity of resignation and virtue. During those days in which the scenes to which we have just referred were taking place, Doña Clara was very busy seeking for Rafael some occupation which would take him away from Santiago where she saw that he was neglecting his studies, and was losing himself in dissipation and amusements in which he hoped to find forgetfulness from his thoughts.

On the morning of the 21st, when Rafael was asleep after having told his story to Martin, Doña Clara went out of the house wrapped in her mantilla, and directed her steps to the house of her brother, Don Pedro San Luis, who lived in one of the principal streets of Santiago. Don Pedro, as San Luis had told Martin, was rich. He possessed, not very far from Santiago, two large farms, which the delicacy of his health had obliged him to let on lease, being unable to work them himself. His family was composed of a wife and a son called Demetrio, who was fifteen years old.

Doña Clara was going to the house of her brother because an idea had occurred to her by means of which she hoped to help her nephew. Don Pedro had a true affection for his own relations and was always disposed to help them. He received his sister with affection, and when Doña Clara told him that she had just come to talk of some important things he led her into his library.

"How is Rafael?" he asked, when he saw his sister seated in an armchair.

"He is well. I came to talk to you about him. You know how spoiled he is by me."

"I have been sorry for it many a time," replied Don Pedro, "and it is a pity, because he is a capable boy."

"Is he not? poor boy! But, brother, his sadness increases, and little by little it is going to upset all his studies."

"That is bad, but you ought to advise him."

"I have another project which depends upon you."

"Upon me! Let us see what it is."

"By dint of thinking," said Doña Clara, "I see that the best thing for this boy would be for him to leave Santiago and go into the country, where the hope of increasing his means and an active life of work, will help him to forget the melancholy which is consuming him."

"You are right; would you like me to find him a farm?"

"Better than that; many a time you have told me you wish that your son would live in the country and work there, is not that so?"

"Precisely; for, sister, this boy is too delicate to study, and it is necessary that he should know the land which will be his after me."

"Very well then, why don't you send him to work on one of your farms in company with Rafael?"

"Well thought of," exclaimed Don Pedro, who had for a long time been disquieted at the idea of sending his son alone into the country. "Do you know if Rafael would like to leave Santiago?"

"I have never asked him, but we will see now. When will Roblè's lease be out?"

"In May next year. And yesterday Don Simon came here on account of his friend Don Fidel and wished me to promise him the lease for another nine years."

"And——?"

"I did not promise anything because I want to think over the matter, and consider whether I would like to send my Demetrio there."

"Now," said the lady, brightly, "you are going to rep that you cannot."

"That will be best, if Rafael would like to abandon his career as a lawyer."

"I will advise him to do it; I do hope he will accept, because I have no hope of his studies."

Doña Clara returned to her house full of happiness, and imparted her new projects to her nephew. Rafael asked for some days to think it over. The following day, after the class, he went out of the college with Martin. Martin inwardly thought of the impression left by his interview with Leonor. He thought of telling San Luis of his conversation with the girl, but an instinct of delicacy made him reject this idea because he had received no permission from Leonor to reveal it.

Whilst Rivas was making these reflections, San Luis said to him, breaking the silence—

"I have a project, Martin, about which I want you to give me your opinion."

"What project?"

"To go and live in the country."

"And does it promise any gain?"

"Probably."

"Are you fond of your studies?"

"Not very nowadays."

"Well then, accept."

"I am going now to explain to you the reasons that make me hesitate. Do you know who is the actual tenant of the Hacienda, who wishes to renew the lease? Don Fidel, Matilde's father!"

"Ah! that quite alters the case; but tell me more about it."

"Don Fidel has not always been the intolerant ministerialist whom you know. Before turning his coat in politics, like so many of the old 'pepiolis' to whose party he belonged, Don Fidel joined in the war against all those conservative principles which unfortunately lasted so many years in Chili. His principles bound him strongly to those of the same political opinion generally but particularly to my father, and my uncle in the country; my uncle had invested his money in good securities, not losing it in business, as my father did his hard-earned savings, in two or three unfortunate speculations. When my Uncle Pedro took up house in Santiago, he added to his income by letting his Hacienda in Del Roblè, and naturally the preference was given to his friend and political colleague Don Fidel, who asked for the lease. For Don Fidel the bargain was also more profitable than for the others; because he possessed near Roblè a little farm of 100 acres well watered and planted with good alfalfa, which pasture was wanting in my uncle's Hacienda. At the time that the bargain was being drawn up a difficulty presented itself: it was the need of some one to go security. Don Damaso was not then established in Santiago and the other friends of Don Fidel were not in a position to do him this service. My uncle exacted a surety; because Del Roblè was part of his wife's fortune and he did not wish, even for the sake of a friend, to divest the lease of the necessary guarantees. Under these circumstances Don Fidel received the offer of

Don Simon Arenal as that of a Guardian Angel. Don Simon knew him very little; but he had an object in offering to become security with so much generosity; and this object was the satisfaction of a political ambition. Don Fidel, in effect, exercised then and continued to exercise a great influence over the elections in the department in which his farm was situated, and Don Simon wanted to get this influence to ensure his own election as deputy. And now you will ask me what interest could a rich man like Don Simon have in becoming a deputy. This interest will be explained when you learn that Don Simon came of a family of low origin recently become rich, which made it necessary to occupy some post of honour in order to mix with the Society which is coveted by all caballeros and improvisados, who are common enough types amongst us, and to which he belonged.

"From that time Don Fidel and Don Simon became intimate friends. They were comrades—Don Simon was related to the best families in Santiago and Don Fidel turned (owing to these and other influences) from Liberal to Conservative; for Don Simon talked him over from the very first to the Conservative party, because he had been taught by long experience that in politics there is nothing to be gained amongst those who are not on the side of the party in power.

"My uncle saw by degrees that he was losing a friend in his tenant; but the contract was signed and there was no retreat and he was absolutely bound by it. Now that the termination of the lease was approaching, Don Fidel wished to continue it at all costs; for very prosperous days had arrived for agriculture in trading with the new market of California, and he wrote to his great friend Don Simon to obtain a new lease from my uncle. The latter proposes to me to go to Del Roblè with his own son, whose fortune he naturally wishes to increase by the project. Now you know the whole story."

"Do you think that you ought to accept the offer?" questioned Martin.

"I have asked for some days before giving a reply," answered San Luis, "and now I am going to show you my weak spot. This delay I have asked for, because I cannot completely abandon the hope that Matilde may love me."

"And what is the good of that when you will always be poor?" asked Rivas, conquering with difficulty the temptation which urged him to inform his friend of his strong suspicions on this point.

"It is true, I may remain poor," answered San Luis; "but if she loves me, perhaps I might be able to gain her hand by giving up the lease to her father, which is to him a matter of such importance. If I am able to recommend myself to him in this way, it is possible that the past may be forgotten. Matilde would be the link of union between the two families, and I, with the help of my uncle, would undertake some other business in company with his son."

Martin kept thinking that his last conversation with Leonor might decide the fate of his friend; but he still doubted whether the repeated questions which the girl had asked about him might not have been from pure curiosity.

"You are right," he said to San Luis. "But instead of asking for a few days to make up your mind, I think it would be better to explain your plan to your uncle and speak to him with complete frankness. In this way the matter would be much better arranged than going on hoping indefinitely!"

Whilst giving this council, Martin privately proposed to himself to tell the daughter of Don Damaso all that had occurred if she sent for him again to talk about Rafael.

XIX

Leonor, in fulfilment of the promise she had made to her cousin, presented herself at her house at two o'clock on the following day.

Matilde received her with a kiss. A night of hope had given her cheek the flush of happiness, and her eyes the vivacity transmitted to them by a heart palpitating in the expectation of love.

"We are alone," she said, "my mother is out. I began to think you might not be able to come."

"As I told you last night I sent for Martin to ask him fresh news about Rafael."

"And he must have given you a lot because the conversation was long," observed Matilde, laughing.

"All the news I have," said Leonor, "is contained in what I told you last night. Rafael loves you!"

"How does Martin know?"

"Because he told him so himself, it appears."

"Yes; but it is not enough that he says it," exclaimed Matilde, sadly. "What can I do?"

"You love him also?"

"It is true; but we shall still be separate."

"Then that will be your own fault."

"Mine! and what do you want me to do?"

"The case seems to me very clear. Was it Rafael who left you?"

"No, but—"

"You left him. That is the truth."

"But you know very well that I cannot disobey my father."

"That excuse is of no value to him," answered Leonor. "San Luis, forbidden your house without a word from you, had abundant reason to think himself forgotten."

"I swear to you a thousand times that I have never forgotten him."

"But you were going to be married to some one else, was not that sufficient to give the lie to all your promises?"

"He ought to know that I did it against my will."

"Look here, Matilde!" said Leonor, in a serious tone. "I believe that vows of love should be sacred above everything else; above all if they are made to a man whom your relations received and made much of.

If he becomes poor afterwards your vows should not disappear on that account. They should be fulfilled."

"You know," replied Matilde, with her eyes full of tears, "that I am not able to oppose my father's will."

"I know it," rejoined Leonor, "and I only said this to you to show you that, if you really love San Luis, you can make amends; since I know certainly that he has not forgotten you."

"Yes, but how am I to do it?"

"Write to him," said Leonor, in a determined voice.

"Ah! I have not the courage," cried Matilde.

"In that case give up all hope of his love, since you do not care to make the first step towards reconciliation."

Matilde covered her face with her hands and burst into a flood of tears.

"Poor girl," said Leonor to her in a softer voice than she had used hitherto, and fondly caressing her. "There is nothing to cry about; it simply means this, that for once in your life you must have courage."

"Ah! you speak like that because you are not in my place."

"That is not the reason," answered Leonor, quickly. "I would have the strength to keep my vows when I had once made them!"

"It is certainly true that I am wanting in courage; but you can help me."

"How?"

"Make Martin tell you."

"It is true," said Leonor, reflecting, "from the questions that I have been asking about Rafael, and from the confidences that he must have had from him, Martin must know all; but still, supposing that by this means San Luis knows that you still love him, is that sufficient? Is it not necessary that you should give him some explanation to account for your treatment of him in the past?"

"You are right," said Matilde, despairingly.

"It is necessary," added Leonor, "that, before taking a decisive step, you should carefully measure the distance that separates you from Rafael. You must remember that as soon as he gets the news through Rivas, San Luis will want to see you and to hear the justification of your conduct from your own lips, and you must not refuse to meet him; because that would mean breaking with him a second time and finally, and he would be quite right in thinking you were making him the victim of a jest."

"I love him, and I will be courageous enough to do anything if you will only help me," exclaimed Matilde, drying the tears which wetted her cheeks and stretching out her hands caressingly to Leonor.

"At last you are decided," said the latter. "With all this vacillation I had begun to doubt the sincerity of your love."

"Ah! believe me, Leonor, I love him above everything. I have cried so much all this time that, to return to him and hear from his lips the vows of love he used to make long ago, I sometimes believe would give me strength enough to conquer all my fears."

"Let us see now what we can do," said Leonor.

"I leave everything to you; do not abandon me," said Matilde, kissing her tenderly.

"I believe you ought to see him, and certainly you run no risk in writing to him by this Martin who I tell you can help us. I will let him know that I can see him with you in the grove of poplar trees."

"When?" asked Matilde, without being able to hide the eagerness with which even the idea was received.

"Tomorrow you will come with me, and Augustin will accompany us."

"My God!" murmured Matilde, who trembled with as much emotion as if she was in the presence of Rafael. "If my father ever came to know it!"

"I make myself responsible for everything," answered Leonor, who appeared to get more courageous in proportion as her cousin grew more timid.

Matilde embraced her, murmuring thanks mingled with the sobs that she could not suppress.

"You owe me nothing," replied Leonor, returning her caresses; "because, besides my love for you, I have another object to consider."

"Another object!" exclaimed Matilde, raising her head, which had been lying on her cousin's bosom.

"Yes, another object," she replied, "I want to atone for a fault of my father's, which was in a great measure the cause of Rafael being forbidden your house as you have told me many times."

In this explanation of her interest in Matilde Leonor was hiding a still weightier object than that she had mentioned. It is quite true that a desire to repair the evil caused by her father was not a little influenced by her desire to distract herself and help her to combat the trouble that her last conversation with Martin had left in her mind. She felt this necessity the more, because it was she herself who had provoked this conversation, which had given her bitter disappointment on seeing the triumph escape from her grasp on which her pride had been feeding in anticipation. This was the first blow which her self-love had ever received, and she was naturally preoccupied—dejected by it. Without relinquishing the idea of revenge for this humiliation to her vanity, she experienced an ardent desire to occupy herself with something else, a desire natural to vehement natures like hers, for whom reflection and calm are a martyrdom. This same vehemence prevented her from thinking of the consequences that the plan they had made might entail on her cousin's reputation, and on her own.

"Don't you think that some one who knows us might see us in the Poplar Grove, and tell my father?" asked Matilde, after a short pause.

"It seems to me, Matilde," exclaimed Leonor, whom every sign of weakness irritated, "that you have formed a resolution to adopt none of the plans I make for you and which are perfectly simple to me. They are either to give up Rafael's love, or to face with courage the idea that your father can oblige you to accept any husband whom he may wish to force on you in his place—the advice I have been giving you was based on the idea that you were absolutely decided to marry no one but Rafael—if this is not the case, take no further steps, but forget him."

"I have so often hoped that an occasion would present itself to—"

"Tell me, have not you been hoping it for more than a year?"

"Yes."

"And in all this time have you given San Luis the least opportunity to have an explanation with you?"

"No, none," replied Matilde, with a deep sigh; "because I thought he must hate me."

"And, nevertheless, he loves you; but it appears that his resentment, or perhaps fear, has made him hide it from you. One thing certain is, he was given no food for hope—the consequence is that he believes that he is despised, and appearances justify him in that opinion."

"I know it well, but I feared so much that my father might come to suspect."

"I, in your case, would prefer his suspicions. If your love is sincere and you will never, as you say, love any other but Rafael, sooner or later what you fear so much is bound to happen."

"I had made up my mind to suffer in silence."

"But you wanted to know if San Luis had forgotten you?"

"Yes."

"And you told me you would give your life to get back his love?"

"That is true. Ah! how I would like to have your courage!"

"If you have not got it, give up your love: there is still time. You have asked me for counsel and help. I have told you what I would do in your place; but if you do not possess sufficient strength to conquer your fears for the sake of the man you love, then you are right. You must not take any compromising step because society will look down upon you and disgrace will ensue."

"Ah, but I will never renounce the love of Rafael," exclaimed Matilde, "you are right. I have suffered much, I have suffered too much by it, and I have a right to look for my own happiness."

"In that case, if you have courage, go forward. Between suffering in silence and being despised; and suffering after having justified one's self—I prefer the latter."

"And I also," said Matilde, with resolution.

"That is to say that I am to speak to Martin?"

"What will you tell him?"

"That you love Rafael, which Rivas must have already suspected."

"And what more?"

"That tomorrow you will come with me to the Grove of Poplars, near the fountain between one and two o'clock in the afternoon. He can go there and meet us as if by accident, and join us if you bow to him."

"Very well," replied Matilde, trying to check the trembling which seized her.

"Now I must go quickly," said Leonor; "because I have to speak to Martin before he goes out of my father's library, for in the evening there is no chance of speaking to him."

When the two girls took leave of each other, Don Damaso's coachman was waiting at the door for Leonor's orders. Embracing each other for the third time and saying good-bye till they met in the evening, Leonor sprang into the carriage which quickly drove away.

XX

Whilst Leonor and thoughts of Rafael were overcoming the fears in Matilde's heart, Don Fidel Elias returned to his house dispirited at the news he had just received from Don Simon Arenal concerning the lease of the Hacienda del Roblè.

Thoughtfully he entered the room in which his wife passed the greater part of the day reading novels and her favourite poets. At the present moment she was reading the "Dream of Adan and the Devilish World of Espronceda"; and she heard the voice of her husband at the moment that the hero was begging Saladin for a horse, just as Richard III begged for one at the price of his kingdom. The presence of Don Fidel tore her from her poetic ecstasy to plunge her into the prose of everyday life.

"My friend Arenal tells me," Don Fidel began by saying, "that we cannot be sure of the lease of Del Roblè."

Doña Francisca looked at him without understanding what she heard; besides she had been accustomed for a long time now to listen and never to give her opinion about anything that her husband said, except that sometimes she gave it in the presence of others, to show her intellectual superiority.

"Don Simon has just told me," he went on, thinking that Doña Francisca had not heard him, "that Don Pedro San Luis says that he must take time to consider before committing himself to the renewal of the lease of the Hacienda."

"Well, let us hope for the best," she said, anxious to go on with her reading.

"It is easy to say that," replied Don Fidel; "but to me it is a vital matter to have a definite reply; because if I lose the Hacienda, I may be ruined."

"Well, then, let us look for something else through Don Pedro."

"I had thought of that; but the worst of these cursed politics is, that they have deprived me of his friendship when I wanted it most."

"Ah! now are you convinced that I am right?" said Doña Francisca, excitedly, seeing an opportunity to pay off some of the humiliation that her husband condemned her to in society.

"I know very well what I have got to do, and I'm not a child asking for advice," replied Don Fidel, in an acid tone. "But let us leave the

Hacienda to speak of something else. Do you think that Augustin will propose for Matilde?"

"I don't know. Who knows?"

"It does not require much penetration to reply like that," said Don Fidel, impatiently. "I am asking you; because a man occupied as I am has no time to go mixing in these things which are more fitted for women."

"I have not seen anything to make me think otherwise," replied Doña Francisca, impatiently taking up the book which she had just laid down on the table.

"Why are you always thinking about books and nonsense, leaving it to me unaided to look after the wellbeing of the family?"

"What! how can you wish me to occupy myself in such matters when you think that no one can do things as well as you can!"

"And that is true; man is born for business matters. However, as I have not time for everything, it is necessary that you do your share. Augustin is a good *parti* whom we must not allow to escape, and I will speak with Damaso about this matter, as I have to do everything in this case."

Doña Francisca caught up the book and appeared to be reading. Don Fidel took up his hat and went out, persuaded that he alone was capable, with his powerful mind, of directing various businesses at once; for like the generality of fathers he counted as a business the establishment of a daughter.

Doña Francisca watched his departure with a yawn, which was her customary method of ending her conversations with her husband.

She then returned to the visions of Adan, deploring the want of poetic feeling in the man to whom she was united by indissoluble ties; and this idea made her suspend her reading and her mind turned upon George Sand, to whom she compared herself in her aversion to the conjugal yoke.

In the meantime Don Damaso's carriage bore Leonor quickly to her house in spite of the abominable paving of the Santiago streets, the condition of which was long in securing the attention of the local authorities.

Leonor crossed the courtyard of her house with light steps and came to the door of a room. It was her father's study.

Whilst driving from Don Fidel's house to her own she had thought of a way of accomplishing her design about Martin, and her natural disposition counselled her to be entirely frank in the matter. So it happened that, after having assured herself that Rivas was alone, she entered the room and went up to the desk at which he was working.

On seeing her, Martin sprang to his feet; his heart was beating with violence and the colour at once left his cheeks.

"Sit down," said Leonor to him in a slightly haughty manner.

"Permit me, Señorita, to remain standing," replied the young man, seeing that Leonor leant her hand upon the table and showed no inclination to sit down.

"I have come about the same thing I have already spoken to you about," said Leonor, accentuating these words as if she was anxious to deprive Rivas of forming any other idea about this step that she had taken.

"I am at your service, Señorita," answered Martin, with the accent of proud humility which formerly had drawn the attention of the girl.

"It is about your friend San Luis, of whose affairs you spoke to me yesterday evening. Will you give me the name of the person that he loves?"

"It is the Señorita Matilde Elias, your cousin."

"According to what you have told me, Rafael still loves her?"

"It is true."

"Do you think that he would be glad to know that Matilde still returns his affection?"

"I think that such news would give him happiness, Señorita."

"Very well then, you can tell him so; such news as that, received through a friend, would give him double happiness—at least I think so."

"I shall only be too delighted to tell him," answered Martin.

The sincerity with which the young man uttered these words showed Leonor that Rivas possessed a heart capable of the warmest and truest friendship. These observations in a manner softened the ill-will with which she had sought to regard him since the previous night.

Finding that, on her return to her house, she had accomplished her object in accordance with the plan arranged with her cousin, she made a motion to leave the room.

"One word, Señorita," said Martin. "Rafael has believed himself deceived. Will he now believe what I am going to tell him?"

"I don't know. It seems to me that, if he is interested, he can find means to verify the truth."

With these words Leonor went away, and Rivas hid his face in his hands which were on the table before him.

"It is plain," he said to himself, with sorrowful bitterness, "she looks upon me as a little better than a servant, and much beneath the young men who visit her."

The imperious accent with which Leonor had spoken to him and the profound tranquillity which she showed in the presence of his agitation gave rise to his reflections.

Rivas remained preoccupied with these ideas until he had finished his work for the day and retired to his room.

After a few minutes he went out in the direction of San Luis' house.

"You never will be able in all your life," he said to Rafael, who received him with warmth, "to give me such news as I bring to you."

"News!" exclaimed Rafael, with a vague presentiment of the truth, "speak, what is it?"

"Matilde loves you!"

Rafael looked sadly at his friend.

"Look here, Martin," he said to him, "do not jest with what is to me the most serious thing in life—you are putting me at this moment to the most horrible torture, because not believing what you have told me with so little ceremony, I could never believe anything which you would ever tell me again."

"It is quite true," replied Martin, "I respect your sorrow too much to deceive you. Listen to me."

He then related to San Luis his former conversations with Leonor, ending with that which had just taken place.

Rafael wrung Martin's hands with joy impossible to describe.

"You give me more than happiness," he said, "you give me life."

He began to walk up and down the room, speaking of his recollections and of his hopes with incredible fluency. At the end of a quarter of an hour, Martin knew in detail all the scenes of this pure and ardent love which had formed the very life of his friend, and he envied his happiness.

"I was forgetting you, Martin," said Rafael, suddenly. "Are you also in love?"

"I have no love-story to tell," replied Martin. "Its past, its present, and its future hold nothing but sorrow. It is a madness that I must cure myself of, as I am always trying to do. She looks upon me as good enough to employ to let you know your happiness; that is all!"

"Nonsense, keep up your courage. Who knows that Leonor will love you some day—the very interest that she shows in her cousin indicates that she has got a noble heart and is able to understand you: that reconciles me to her and, after her, to her father; and I forgive him the wrong he has done me."

Martin took up his hat and was leaving.

"Do not go away," said San Luis to him, "come with me to lunch; we shall lunch with my aunt. She will be almost as happy as I am at what has happened, besides I must speak further with you. The last words Leonor said now make me think, since I must see Matilde, what I shall say to her. You tell me that Leonor said—"

"That it was necessary to tell you the whole truth."

"Oh yes; but I must find some means of seeing Matilde. Tell me, you are clever, what would you do in my place?"

"I would write to her, that seems to me very simple."

"I do not care about letters—I want to hear her voice; I want to tell her that I love her more than ever. Let us think of some better means than that; love-letters are either cold, or else ridiculous and affected: besides, a letter from her would not satisfy me long, I must see her."

"In a letter you could ask for an interview."

"Yes, and then—"

"She would herself solve this problem."

"Very well—I'll write to her."

Lunch was announced, and Rafael told his aunt, before going into the dining-room, the story that Martin had told him, and his joy was shared by the lady.

When at table, San Luis sent away the servant and said to his aunt—

"I want you to speak with my Uncle Pedro and tell him what has happened. Ah! That was a happy inspiration, when I asked for some days for reflection about the business he proposed to make."

"And what shall I tell him about it?" asked Doña Clara.

"Tell him that this is an excellent means to obtain the consent of Don Fidel. I will give him up the lease of Del Roblè, if my uncle will allow me to do him this service, and in this way he will be reconciled to me. If he exacts from Don Fidel the promise of Matilde's hand, I will study until I am received as a lawyer, or if he prefers it, I will work in the country with the help of my uncle. Supposing that you are able to persuade him, my uncle is generous and he loves us. I have no doubt but that he will help me."

After lunch Martin said good-bye to the Señorita and to Rafael and returned to Don Damaso's house just as the family were going out of the dining-room. As he went up the stairs which led to his room, he heard the sound of the piano which Leonor usually played to her father at this hour.

Leonor had hoped to see Martin at lunch, she was anxious to go on with the pose of indifferent disdain by means of which she hoped to have revenge for the words with which she thought Rivas had humiliated her self-love. Perceiving the absence of the young man, she guessed that he had gone to San Luis' house, and it seemed certain to her that he would come in the evening to the assembly.

This idea pleased her, because she hoped to make Rivas repent his words.

XXI

At this very moment Augustin Encina walked into Rivas' room. The elegant fop had become very intimate with Martin from the night when he had seen him at Doña Bernarda's. The egotistical principle which directs the major part of human actions impelled Augustin to seek Rivas' friendship, although he looked upon him with the contempt that the elegant Santiaguino has for those he sees badly dressed.

"Martin could accompany me to the house of the Molinas and would be very useful to me," said Augustin to himself.

This idea helped him to conquer his mighty pride so far as to treat Rivas with a certain familiarity.

The expression, "would be very useful to me," which Augustin had used when calling upon Martin, necessitates explanation as to the social point of view in which Encina used it in making this reflection.

A young man visits a house. Love, that star which guides the steps of youth, has directed him there.

The want of animation, which is to be noted in our assemblies; chokes the voice in the throat of those who are obliged to confine to glances the amorous phrases, which the fear of being overheard by the profane, prevents them from uttering.

But love takes the seal off the lips. He felt that he must explain himself in order to progress. The glances, which had hitherto sufficed for attesting admiration, are not sufficient to satisfy the demands of the heart which soon arrives at what may be distinguished by the name of "tender admiration." It was now necessary that he should hear the voice of the loved one and also confide to her the sweet affection of an enamoured heart; but the conversation at the assemblies is general and formal, it is not easy to say a word in private to any of the girls.

Therefore, he sought for a friend. The friend can entertain the Mama with more or less insipid chatter, or the sisters who are always more ready to listen than the mother.

Then the lover can display at his leisure the eloquence of short and thrilling sentences.

In this matter Augustin thought that Rivas would be very useful to him in Doña Bernarda's house, in which the vigilance of the mother was all the greater on account of her love of gambling, which aggravated the danger of the situation, as she knew that the lover of her daughter was a young man of rich family.

Augustin entered Rivas' room humming the air of a French song.

"Do you not wish to *rendre visite* to the Molinas'?" he said to Martin, offering him a fine cigar.

"No, I do not care about it," answered Martin.

"Have you never thought of repeating your visit?"

"No, I never thought about it."

"They are such nice girls."

"Yes, they appeared so."

"I thought of going over to see them this evening—would you like to come with me?"

"With much pleasure."

"What did you think of Adelaida?"

"Oh! I think she is well enough; but I don't admire her as much as you do," said Martin, smiling.

"Have they told you that I am in love with her?" asked Augustin.

"I knew at the first glance."

"Yes, my boy, it is true, there is no girl in our drawing-room who pleases me as much as Adelaida."

"That is unfortunate," said Rivas.

"Why?"

"Because this love can be converted into such a passion that it may make you commit some madness."

"What do you call madness? In Paris everybody has this kind of love-affair."

"I call it a madness; because it is possible that it might lead you to marry her."

"Nonsense, my dear fellow, you don't know the world. All these girls know very well that a young man like me does not marry one of them."

Then Martin made use of all the moral reflections that occurred to him to combat the Parisian ideas of this elegant young man, who contented himself with replying that Martin did not know the world.

"All that I know for certain is that I love her," said Augustin to terminate the remonstrances of Rivas, "and that, either alone or accompanied by you, I shall go to visit her; please yourself whether you will come with me or not."

"If you wish it, I will accompany you," answered Martin. Rivas made this reply recollecting the picture that San Luis had drawn of Adelaida's character and her desire to marry a rich man.

"That is all right," said Augustin, contented with his answer, "one must be obliging amongst friends, besides, one must find amusement in something, for life at Santiago is so insipid. Now I am going to dress myself and I will be ready to meet you in half an hour."

"Very well, I will be punctual," answered Martin—thinking how necessary it was for him to try in any manner to forget his sadness.

After Don Damaso's son had left, Martin made the reflection:—"I feel all the time my passion increase in proportion as the hope of being loved becomes less. Would it not be better, like Rafael and Augustin, to indulge in a passing love-affair and so endeavour to restore the tranquillity of my mind?"

This idea remained in his mind whilst he prepared for the visit which he was going to make with Augustin. The tendency of love to cure its sorrows in the homeopathic remedy, like cures like, quickened his pride which had been humiliated by the haughty majesty of Leonor.

He was aroused from his meditation by the return of Augustin who was dressed with irreproachable elegance.

He immediately monopolized the conversation talking about his love-affairs until he arrived at Doña Bernarda's house.

At this moment Leonor was seated at the piano playing with enthusiasm. She was delighted to be able to show Rivas that she could meet him without the least emotion and she was longing for his arrival to paralyse him with her disdain. She could not forget the words of the young man when he told her of his intention never to fall in love. Was not this an insolent threat flung at her beauty, which no one up to now had ever dared to make? Finally, tired of playing, she left the piano and seated herself pensively on a sofa.

The sound of every step that she heard in the courtyard made her heart beat with violence; and so it happened that she received the people who arrived with a frigid salute. The absence of her cousin augmented the duration of this long evening, in which she had hoped to explain to her her reasons for not having told Rivas the whole of the plan arranged during the day.

When she had quite lost the hope of seeing Martin arrive, her irritation increased with every slight incident which deprived her of the pleasure of a victory. It appeared to her that Rivas was committing an unpardonable fault by not presenting himself to receive the insulting indifference with which she was prepared to show him the contempt with which his presumptuous intention of never falling in love had inspired her.

Leonor believed in all good faith that this intention would be overthrown by the force of her beauty which every one must admire.

Don Damaso, on his part, without noticing the impatience of his daughter or the sleep into which Doña Engracia had fallen with Diamela on her lap, kept up during the whole of the evening a manifest opposition to the ministry against Don Fidel and Don Simon, who attacked him vigorously.

When Don Fidel arrived at his house, where Matilde, professing to have a very bad headache, had stayed quietly with Doña Francisca, he found his wife alone and buried in the reading of George Sand.

Don Fidel, after having argued against the opposition in the presence of his friend and protector, asked himself, as he returned to his house, whether he could not perhaps obtain the prolongation of the lease of Del Roblè if he went over to the opposition. Before Doña Francisca he continued this reflection aloud—the turning of the wheel of probabilities which the case presented taking the form indicated by the following words:—

"The thing is to hit the right mark; because if I go over to the opposition now, I shall lose the confidence of my protector, who, as he mixes with fashionable people, will get me out of society. Cursed politics!"

Doña Francisca, who, much impressed by what she was reading, felt disposed to reduce everything to theory, exclaimed—

"Look here! Politics, as some author, whom I don't know, has said, are a flaming circle—"

"No matter what circle, wife, nor what author," replied Don Fidel, impatiently: "if Don Pedro will promise me a new lease of Del Roblè, I will laugh at all the world."

Doña Francisca contented herself with raising her eyes as if calling upon heaven to look down upon the prosaic heart to which she had united her own.

XXII

Rivas and Augustin entered the house of Doña Bernarda just as the Señora was preparing the gaming-table, and she called to Amador's two friends, who, with him and the official of the police, were chatting with the girls.

"Go along, my sons," said Doña Bernarda, "you are not here to talk nonsense, go and take a hand."

The two friends of Amador came forward at the call of the lady of the house, who received the arrivals at this moment, with the cards in her hands.

Doña Bernarda wished to rise to receive them.

"Do not incommode yourself for us," said Augustin to her, "remain seated."

"No, my son, it is not polite," insisted Bernarda.

"I do wish you would not disturb yourself," replied the young Encina, with a gracious smile.

"Ah! what a sweet way you have of showing your French politeness," exclaimed Doña Bernarda, with a hoarse laugh. "Will you take a hand?"

"Later on, Señora," replied Augustin, "we are going to salute the young ladies."

The girls, who were in the next room, were called by their mother.

"Bring a candle here," she said, "and let us all be together."

Edelmira and Adelaida obeyed the order, and the official of police followed them carrying a flat candle-stick.

"Military men please me very much," were the words with which Doña Bernarda praised the gallantry of Ricardo Castanos, who placed the flat candle-stick upon a table and sat down beside Edelmira.

Augustin saw that in such a room it would be difficult to carry on an animated conversation with Adelaida without being overheard, and so hastened to praise loudly Amador's singing.

"Oh! I am mad about singing," he said to the young Molina, who immediately took up his guitar.

"What song would you like best?" he asked.

"Whatever you prefer, they all please me," replied Augustin.

Amador twanged the guitar, whilst Augustin stopped talking, and he sang some verses, accompanying himself with the monotonous music of our antiquated tunes.

"Yo no me pieaso matar
Por quieir por mi no se meure
Querer a quier un quisiere
Jal que no me quiera andar."

Augustin, taking advantage of the sound, said to Adelaida in impassioned accents—

"I must have a proof of your love."

"And you, what proof are you going to give me?" she asked.

"I? Whatever you ask."

"If you love me as you say," replied the girl, "you will be content with my word and not ask me for proofs."

"It is that I never can speak with you freely, and therefore I insist upon what I asked for the other night."

"The other night? What thing? I do not understand."

"A rendezvous."

"*Ai por Dios!* that is a good deal to ask for."

"Why not?" asked Augustin, in a most humble tone of voice.

"I give you a rendezvous ! ! ! Who would have ever thought of such a thing! Am I. . . no, it is not true."

"Do you not think I am gentleman enough?"

"On the contrary, too much so. Because, to speak the truth, you will never marry me."

With these words Adelaida cast a penetrating glance at the young man. It was the first time that she had had so frank an explanation with Augustin.

He, confused with such a question, hesitated for a moment; but, remembering the moral elasticity and its theories which he had unrolled to Rivas the previous evening, he answered—

"Yes, why should you doubt it?"

Adelaida read in his hesitation the duplicity of his answer; but she gave no sign of disgust. Pretending, on the contrary, that she believed him, she went on to question him.

"You are not deceiving me? You swear it?"

Augustin launched into a campaign of lies, and did not scruple to answer immediately—

"Yes, I swear it."

The lightness with which he said it, served to confirm Adelaida in the opinion which his first response had given her, of the untrustworthiness of the young man.

"Ah! if you were only speaking the truth!" she said in an impassioned accent, which Augustin thought was sincere.

"I swear to you that I am speaking the truth," replied the young man. "Give me a rendezvous and we will talk together."

At this moment Amador's song was finished, and Adelaida said shortly—

"Tomorrow at two o'clock in the morning, the street door will be open."

Augustin jumped clean over his chair, joy lighted his face and shone in his eyes.

"You make me the most happy of mortals," he said, lowering his voice, which mingled with the last vibrations of the song.

"Now, go away because my mother is looking at us," said Adelaida, between her teeth.

The dandy went towards the card-table, lavishing compliments on Amador for the song which he had just finished.

"Look here, little Frenchman," Doña Bernarda, who was playing Monté, said to him, "you may have a bet on the knave."

During all this time Martin had remained alone in his seat. With a sentiment common to young lovers, he found himself isolated in the midst of the people who surrounded him, and listening to the notes of Amador's song, he sang to himself his hopeless love in incoherent verses, which sounded only in his own imagination.

When the song was finished, his eyes and those of Edelmira's met. The idea of seeking her sympathy again returned to his mind. In Edelmira's look lay a sadness which seemed in sympathy with his own.

At this moment Amador called on the official to give him his opinion of some home-made mistela, and Ricardo Castanos could not refuse such a complimentary request.

Rivas took advantage of this circumstance to sit down beside Edelmira.

"I had not hoped to see you here so soon again," the girl said to him.

"Why?" asked Martin.

"Because the other evening I didn't think you found it very amusing."

"But I spoke a few words with you, and they were sufficient to make me wish to return."

Rivas said these words in order to see how they would be received, dominated by the idea of seeking consolation in a new love.

Edelmira looked at him with an air of surprise.

"And you, are you like all the rest?" she asked him.

"Why do you ask me this question?"

"Because I imagined that you were different from the others."

Rivas did not know the meaning that women generally give to phrases like Edelmira's.

He thought that the pleasure with which she received his attention, and what she had just said to him might be securely looked upon as a happy augury for the new love-affair to which he aspired.

"Then what have you considered me to be hitherto?" he asked her.

"Sincere in your words," replied Edelmira, "and incapable of jesting at serious things."

These words, appealing to his honour, had for the lofty and noble soul of Martin all the strength of a bitter reproach. He saw immediately that he was going to take a step unworthy of a man of honour, and the story of Rafael vividly pictured in his memory the remorse which his friend had described to him in conversations subsequent to his first confession.

"Do not believe," he said, "that I lied to you, when I told you that the recollection of the conversation that I had with you made me desire to return here; it was the truth. The manner in which you described to me the sorrow you felt at your position in the world, inspired me with a lively sympathy; because I found in it much that is similar to my own situation."

"I am much more pleased that you should talk to me like this," said Edelmira, "than in the way you began."

"What I have just said to you is sincere," replied Martin.

"If you think so, it will please me much if some day you will have sufficient confidence to treat me with the same frankness that I showed to you the other night."

"Certainly I will, since I have told you that I find your situation very similar to mine."

They continued this conversation for a long time. Edelmira found in Martin the type of hero, whom girls fond of reading novels worship in their youth, and she yielded to a very natural timidity, when she did not desire to hear from his lips the flatteries which she daily heard from Ricardo Castanos and the other young men who frequented the house. She found a real satisfaction in penetrating into the heart of Rivas in proportion as their friendship expanded, a resource instinctively used by sentimental minds which have a horror of the hackneyed forms of ordinary love-making.

Martin, whose conscience had already condemned the idea of inspiring a love which he could not return, felt on his side much sweetness in the romantic friendship which Edelmira offered him. In a short time his sympathy for this girl occupied a considerable place in his heart. He found in her an exquisite sensibility united to a profound contempt for the people who sought her love whilst they were incapable of understanding her. In her unhappiness there was a certain perfume of poetry, which at times seemed to find a friendly echo in the heart of the young man. Thus Martin, captured by the refinement which he found in Edelmira, arrived at a point in his conversation when he said—

"I will confess the truth to you, I am in love, and I have no hope."

The frank confession, which Rivas made when he found it impossible to seek for consolation in the love of Edelmira, weighed heavily on the girl's heart. It appeared to her that a veiled hope was being torn from her—at the same time these words awakened in her mind a feeling that is very natural to a woman, curiosity.

"It will be some rich and beautiful lady?" she asked.

"She is most beautiful," said Martin, with an enthusiasm which he was not able to hide. There was a pause after this reply, which was interrupted by Amador and the official, who entered declaring that the mistela was first rate.

Martin got up from his seat.

"I hope it will not be long before you come to see me again," said Edelmira.

"Having such a friend as you," Martin replied, "I do not want to seek any other company."

All were now standing round the gaming-table, and Amador took the cards given over to him by Doña Bernarda, who was very pleased at having won a hundred pesos. The player who lost the most was Augustin Encina, who, almost beside himself at the unexpected outcome of his love-affair, was defying all the chances of the game, even after he had already lost, to show Adelaida how little he thought of money.

Amador opened a bottle of the new mistela in order to foment Augustin's animation, and the stakes rose with the drinks. Without doubt the son of Doña Bernarda had learned some of the methods whereby a certain class of players know how to appropriate the money of the others with more courtesy but with no more honour than highway robbers; because he seemed to be adding to his fortune all the time during the quarter of an hour that Augustin was losing.

"I shall have to stake my word," exclaimed the latter, swallowing a glass of mistela, "as I no longer have any money."

"As you like," replied Amador, "but in your place I would stop playing."

"Why?" asked the young Encina.

"Because you are having bad luck."

"That doesn't matter to me," replied the dandy, with a pride which showed how much he despised such a poor argument.

Amador and the others who were round the table exchanged a significant glance.

"How much do you wager?" asked the son of Doña Bernarda, shuffling the cards.

"Sixteen onzas on the seven of diamonds," said Augustin.

At the end of an hour he had lost a thousand pesos, and double that amount in another half hour. Martin then intervened and tried to stop the play.

"Bring some paper and I will sign an I.O.U.," said Augustin to Amador.

The paper was drawn up for two thousand pesos but Augustin signed it for four thousand; because at that moment he had received from Adelaida a glance of amorous admiration.

On leaving Doña Bernarda's house, the young Encina, excited by his conquest and the fumes of the mistela, related to Martin in his peculiar jargon, the irresistible method which he had employed to soften Adelaida's heart.

After the visitors had left there remained in the room beside the gaming table—Doña Bernarda, Adelaida, and Amador; Edelmira had retired after her mother had admonished her on the necessity that every girl has to look for a good husband.

When Amador found himself alone with his mother and his elder sister, he shut the door of the room into which Edelmira had just passed.

"What is going to happen?" he asked, turning to Adelaida.

"It is to be tomorrow night," she answered.

"Ha, ha!" exclaimed Doña Bernarda, "the sweet little Frenchman has asked for an interview?"

"It isn't the first time," said Adelaida.

"He is rich," continued Amador, "many girls are running after him: he can afford to pay dearly."

"Then tomorrow you will trap your friend?" added Doña Bernarda.

"Certainly I will," replied Amador.

"And if he does not wish to?" asked the mother.

"I shall see to that, little mama," said Amador, taking up the candle to retire. Then he returned and approached her to add, "Don't you forget anything that he may say."

"I'm not so stupid as to go and forget," she replied; "you'll see how I can manage things."

At the moment that Amador was retiring he heard a light step on the other side of the door, which he had shut at the beginning of this conversation.

"It is that fool of an Edelmira who has been listening," exclaimed Doña Bernarda.

"What does it matter if she did hear us?" said Amador: "Tomorrow she will have to know everything that has passed."

The mother appeared satisfied with this answer and bade her children good night.

XXIII

Rafael San Luis had passed so quickly from profound despair to happiness that, when leaving Martin, the unhoped-for news that his friend had brought him seemed like a dream.

His first care was to send his aunt to explain to Don Pedro his new projects about the Hacienda del Roblè, with the lease of which he hoped to conquer the difficulties which separated him from Matilde, and to gain the consent of Don Fidel Elias.

When he found himself in his room surrounded by all his belongings, witnesses of his constant sorrow, he covered with kisses the portrait he had kept of his beloved one, and his memory returned to former times of happiness, not without a sad impression when he remembered the actions of his life after fate had separated him from Matilde. Remorse at having sacrificed the honour of Adelaida Molina in seeking consolation for his trouble, now cried more loudly in his conscience than in former days. Happiness made him return to virtue as desperation had caused him to break its laws. He felt with shame that he could no longer come, as formerly, without reproach to the feet of her whom he knew was the immaculate guardian of his heart, and his faith. This was the first idea which came to cloud the crystal wave of his happiness, and which also drew him from the contemplation in which he was merged, to make him feel the necessity of higher emotions which should employ his returned energy.

To see Matilde and to hear from her lips the eternal protestations of her love, so sacredly preserved for him alone, was the only thing that at this moment occupied his imagination. He remembered with this that Leonor's last words, transmitted to him by Rivas, opened the way for a means of meeting Matilde. Seating himself at his table he began to write with feverish ardour. At the end of an hour he had torn up two letters, and wrote the following which was the only one which satisfied his impatience:—

"A friend has told me that you still love me. I cannot tell you the happiness that this news has given me; it is absolutely necessary that you should hear me, because a letter cannot contain the story of the misery of my sufferings—now banished by renewed hope. If it is true that you have preserved for me this love which has been for me, until now, my only joy, and my only dearest thought, let me hear it from your lips. I beg you for this on my knees; if you would only see me. Sorrow has almost ruined me, and if I had again to return to my bitter desolation it would kill me."

San Luis had to be content with this letter because it was the only one which he found in harmony with the agitation of his mind. The words of love which he had written in the first two appeared to him very inadequate to depict the state of his mind under the violent emotion which was agitating him. After sealing the letter he went to call on Don Fidel Elias. On arriving at the threshold of the door, which he had passed through last time with a broken heart, he felt as if he were close to a terrible danger.

To deliver his letter he had not thought of any other means than the simplest invented ever since the origin of writing. The hour favoured his intention, because the night had arrived, and the inferior lighting of the streets allowed him to go to the house without fear of being recognized. In the courtyard of the entrance he asked for an old servant of Doña Francisca's whom he knew when he used to visit the house. Four reales sufficed to make the servant, who was in the courtyard, hurry to summon the person whom Rafael asked for; and ten minutes afterwards the letter was in the hands of Matilde.

The hour having arrived at which Don Fidel with Doña Francisca and his daughter were to be at the house of his brother-in-law, Matilde pretended to have a headache in order to excuse herself, fearing that at the assembly at Don Damaso's some one would be able to read in her face the perturbation which she felt after reading San Luis' letter.

At eight o'clock in the morning on the following day Leonor came out of church wrapped in her mantle and accompanied by a maid. From the church she turned to the house of her cousin, who received her in the same room in which she had been the day before.

"You are really ill as they told me yesterday?" she asked Matilde, in whose cheeks she saw the pallor which generally follows a sleepless night.

"Look at this," was Matilde's reply, placing in her cousin's hands Rafael's letter.

"And your mother?" asked Leonor, sitting down without looking at the letter.

"She is sleeping."

Leonor pushed back the veil which covered her face, and began to read. When she had finished, she raised her eyes and looked at her cousin. The latter remained standing opposite in the attitude of a culprit before a judge.

"I understand," said Leonor, "why San Luis asks you for an interview since our conversation of yesterday."

Matilde, in her perturbation, had not thought of this circumstance, and only now remembered that, in her arrangements with Leonor, they had resolved to have an interview with Rafael on that day.

"It is true," she answered.

"On leaving here," continued Leonor, "I altered the plan. It appeared to be more natural to try to arrange that San Luis should ask for this interview. This letter shows that I was not deceived. Have you replied to it?"

"No, I was waiting to see you before doing so."

"Have you altered your resolution since last night?"

"Not in the least," said Matilde, "it is true that I am nervous; but I shall conquer that. Now that Rafael has written to me it is impossible to alter my determination because, if I do, he will believe that I do not love him."

"You are right, it is just what I told you."

"What shall I say to him?"

"Plainly and clearly what we arranged yesterday. It is not too late and your reply will arrive in time. Don't forget it is for two o'clock, I shall be there with Augustin at one."

When her cousin had left, Matilde wrote as she had been advised, and sent her letter by the servant who had received Rafael's.

Leonor returned quickly to her house and went to her brother's rooms; at one of the doors she gave three light knocks, and the voice of Augustin asked from inside—

"Who is that?"

"Are you up?" asked Leonor.

"Come in, sister," he said to the girl. "How are you up so early; do you come from church?"

Leonor replied in the affirmative to the last question and sat down in an armchair covered with green silk which the dandy pushed forward.

"And you, how are you so early on foot?" asked the girl, taking off her veil.

Augustin's happiness had given him a bad night, happiness sometimes is as bad as sorrow for keeping one awake.

"I did not know it was so early," he replied.

"You returned late last night."

"Yes, I amused myself," replied Augustin. He was glad to find an opportunity to relate his visit of the night before.

"Where were you?" asked Leonor, with an air of abstraction.

"Visiting some girls."

"Were there any young people?"

"Some; I was there with Martin."

"With Martin," said Leonor, "visiting some girls?"

"Ah! sister, you are very inquisitive, I'm reading you a missal without naming the saint."

"I did not know that you would care to visit such people," said Leonor, playing with the music which she held in her hands.

"I'm like all other young men."

"Are the girls pretty?"

"Oh, enchanting!"

The enthusiasm of this reply gave Leonor a strange sensation.

"Do I know them?" she asked with curiosity.

"I don't know, perhaps you do."

Augustin made this reply because, much as he desired to relate that he was beloved, on the other hand he didn't wish to let his sister suspect in what an inferior circle he had found his lady-love.

"And of these girls which has pleased you the most?"

"The most beautiful," swaggered Augustin.

"And she loves you?"

"Proofs are not wanting to show it."

Leonor had begun with these questions in order not to let her brother remark the following words—

"Is Martin playing court to one of the girls?"

"I don't know exactly; but I have seen him talking a good deal to the sister of my girl."

Augustin gave to the possessive pronoun all the fatuity which inspired him at the recollection of the rendezvous which he had obtained with Adelaida.

"And is she also pretty?" asked Leonor.

"Pretty? Yes; but not so much so as the other; but she is interesting."

The girl remained thoughtful for a few moments. She felt herself humiliated by what she had just heard. It was plain that Rivas had lied, when, with pretended modesty, he had informed her of his intention of never falling in love; and that he had been making love to another girl when she was thinking of overwhelming him with her disdain. While she was making these reflections, it occurred to her that her silence would arouse her brother's suspicions as to her motives and she determined to call his attention to the object of her visit.

"Ah!" she instantly exclaimed, "I was forgetting the object of my visit. I want you to do me a service."

"A service, little girl?" said Augustin, "you have only to tell me and I am quite at your orders."

"I want you to come with me today to the Alameda between one and two in the afternoon."

"Why? this is not Sunday."

"I will tell you afterwards, promise me first that you will come with me."

"I promise you. I don't see any difficulty about it."

"Tell me, Augustin, are you truly in love with this girl you have just been talking about?"

"Oh! I love her with all my heart."

"So that if you could not see her, you would feel it deeply?"

"Frightfully; but I don't think that will happen."

"What does it matter, suppose that you were separated from her?"

"Caramba, that would not be very easy!"

"I know that; but suppose it."

"Ah! It is a supposition! Well?"

"That being so, and you unable to see her, would you not be grateful to the person who could contrive an interview for you?"

"Indeed, I would be grateful to that person from my very soul!"

"Then that is exactly what you are going to do when you come with me to the Alameda today."

"Ha! you rogue, you have got a love-affair? Eh?"

"No, my dear, it's not me," said Leonor, with a certain sadness in her tone.

"Then who is it?"

"Matilde."

"The little cousin! Is it? And who with? Because when I was in Europe and it was supposed that she was in love with Rafael San Luis, you wrote to me that she was going to be married to another; and now you want me to go to the Alameda to see her without doubt with a third. Oh, fie! Excuse my astonishment."

"It's not to meet a third, Matilde never has loved any one but Rafael San Luis."

"Then how was it she was going to marry Adriano?"

"In a great measure it was my father's fault."

"Our father, little sister, I don't understand."

"Because you never knew that it was our father who advised Uncle Fidel to turn San Luis out of his house."

"And why?"

"They say it was because Rafael was poor."

"That was no reason."

"No matter what it may have been, my father had no business to interfere and to bring such a misfortune upon such a good fellow."

"That is true."

"I think we are only doing our duty in making all the reparation we can to him."

"That seems to me only just."

"Matilde loves San Luis still and will never love another."

"She is quite right, I am all for constancy."

Leonor explained in detail the rest of her plan, leaving her brother quite convinced of the necessity of supporting Matilde in her love-affair.

They parted after this conversation, Augustin promising not to fail at the appointed hour.

The dandy gave himself a holiday on account of the happiness which the expectation of the rendezvous caused him, and so it happened that he could not find one moment to remember Matilde and her love-affair.

XXIV

A little before one o'clock in the day Leonor left her room and went into the ante-sala. The perfect elegance of her toilette showed off her dazzling beauty. A dress of light poplin clothed her delicate figure, worn with a little mantle of chantilly lace bordered with black velvet. The numerous folds of the pollero fell down to the ground, showing the dignity of her carriage, and the fichu of fine valencienne held in place by a clasp of opals, mingled its white border with the delicacy of her beautifully made throat.

Leonor sat down to wait for her brother, playing with a parasol which she held in her hand. After a few moments she left her seat and paused before the looking-glass over the mantel-piece, passing her hand over her lustrous bandeau of hair with a care which showed the attention she gave to her appearance.

Leonor was very far from knowing that at this moment she was being devoured by the ardent glances of a pair of eyes, which were looking through the window over the door which divided the ante-room from her father's study.

These eyes were those of Martin who, having heard the door close through which Leonor had just passed, put himself in a position of observation, as he had often done before, to see the girl, who at this time generally practised the piano.

Such beauty and elegance made the enamoured boy's heart beat with desperate violence. With the need of all lovers Martin wanted to draw nearer to his idol, and sought for the moment a pretext to approach her. He felt a strange fascination which drew him in his love to despise the haughtiness with which he was treated: it was the effect of the mysterious strength which forces all the unhappy to exaggerate their sorrows, all criminals to follow the obscure path into which their first fault has led them. Martin wanted to immerse himself in his own disgrace, to feel the oppression of his lot under the haughty glance of Leonor, to compare by her side the misery of his fate with the opulent riches and beauty of the girl. This sensation made him cross the threshold with a feverish ardour, having no understanding of what he was doing, driven there by the desperation of his lot, which the sight of Leonor had brought home to him.

The girl turned her head quickly towards the wall where the door was and saw Martin, pale and disordered, standing before her.

At this moment the story of the evening before recurred to Leonor, and she received the young man's salute with a frigid glance and a haughty manner.

Before she had saluted him Martin knew the folly of what he had done.

"Señorita," he said in a timid voice, "I have taken the liberty to present myself in order to tell you I have accomplished the task you gave me."

"I had hoped to receive that reply last night," said Leonor, sententiously.

Martin, with his hand on the handle of the door, was about to retire.

"My brother told me something in confidence this morning," said Leonor, without giving Martin time to carry out his intention, "which explained to me why the thing I had hoped for did not succeed."

Martin's pallor disappeared beneath a lively blush on hearing these words, because he imagined that Augustin must have told her about the house of Doña Bernarda.

"I didn't think, Señorita," he replied, "that you were waiting with so much impatience for the answer."

"So you brought happiness to your friend?" said Leonor, not taking the slightest notice of the young man's excuse.

"Thanks to you, Señorita," replied Martin, bowing.

"This is going to be a bad example for you," she replied, with a slightly malicious smile.

"I don't know how, Señorita."

"Because the happiness of your friend may overcome the heroic propositions that you made the other night."

"Rafael occupies a position very different from mine," said Rivas, in such a melancholy tone, that Leonor threw a penetrating glance at him.

"Is it because he is certain of being loved?" she asked.

"Precisely so."

"And you?"

"I! I don't expect to be," replied Martin, with genuine modesty.

"You are too easily discouraged," said Leonor, with the smile which a moment before had lingered upon her lips.

"I think that my want of confidence can serve me as a better shield than that of not being loved."

"Greater misfortune? Than what? For example."

"Than that of loving without hope."

Martin pronounced these words with a voice so profoundly moved, that Leonor, in spite of her power over herself, blushed, and dropped her eyes at meeting the ardent gaze of the young man. Her invincible pride made her for the moment ashamed of her involuntary emotion. At the moment when she lowered her eyes, she heard the voice of her self-love scoffing at her for her weakness, so that hardly had her eyelids covered the pupils, when she raised them anew, allowing her arrogant gaze of offended pride to be seen.

"Ought you not to remove yourself further from this misfortune?" she said. "There are few men who do not meet at some time some one who will love them. According to what Augustin tells me you are soon on the road to meet a shelter from that which you fear so much."

Rising from her seat with the majesty of a queen after having said this, she launched these words at the young man, gazing at him with a scoffing air, which in no way diminished her dignity—

"One of the girls whom you visited last night, Augustin says, shows a liking for you, therefore you see you may have some confidence in your star."

She went out of the room calling for a servant, leaving Rivas standing motionless on the spot where he had remained during the whole of the conversation. In the distance he heard Leonor's voice saying—

"Tell Augustin that I have been waiting for him over an hour."

These words awakened him from his stupefaction. He opened the door and entered Don Damaso's study with the tears brimming in his eyes. Leonor's last words and what she had afterwards said to the servant forced him to believe that she looked upon him as an object for pastime and jest. This belief awoke in his soul a sadness which clouded the brightness that all youth expects in the future. "Vamos," he said to himself with anger, striking his forehead distractedly—"I must work!" He took the pen with desperate ardour, evoking the recollection of his poor family to calm the desperation which oppressed his breast, and made him wish to sob like a boy.

Leonor returned and sat down pensively on the sofa which she had occupied when speaking to Martin. Mechanically she turned her eyes towards the door which the young man had just closed and she seemed to see him again before her, standing close to this door, pale and agitated, his ardent gaze fixed upon her, and to hear the moving sound of this phrase which in a few words depicted the disconsolate melancholy of his mind, "Love without Hope," and she again lowered her gaze by an involuntary movement to raise it again once more, her eyes not now scintillating with the rays of pride which they recently had shown, but with a wondering expression which depicts the dawn of a new emotion in the soul. Leonor then thought but without precisely formulating the idea in her mind, that these words of youthful sentiment, the eloquent glance of the dark eyes of Martin, the deep emotion which sounded in his voice, were a thousand times more attractive than the studied compliments of the elegant young men, who every night repeated their annoying flatteries, and this short interview aroused in her a deep and unknown emotion which dismissed from her memory the image of the poor provincial, nervous and badly dressed, to give place to the young man, intellectual and modest, who, in a few words, had given a glimpse of a great and noble heart.

The arrival of Augustin cut short these reflections, formless as they were, but into which Leonor's mind had wandered.

The dandy had studied the combination of his cravat, waistcoat, and trousers in the most perfect harmony of colours, the shininess of his cheek attested to the passing of the razor over a budding beard, and his hair was perfumed with the richest jasmin pomade from Paris.

"I have made you wait, my beauty," he said to Leonor, artfully showing off the elegance of his trousers, cut by Dussotoy in the capital of fashion.

"Let us go," replied Leonor, rising.

They went out of the house and soon arrived at that of Don Fidel where Matilde was expecting them. She also had given much thought to a toilette which rivalled in beauty that of her cousin. The strong resolution with which she had armed herself added a certain grace to a loveliness modest even to timidity, and her eyes were animated by a vivacity which augmented her brightness and her beauty.

When they were on the road they pretended an indifference which only Augustin thought was real, because Leonor, and still more Matilde, could not overcome the nervousness which they felt at getting nearer to the Alameda. On arriving at the place of which we are all so proud as good Santiagons, Leonor had recovered her serenity, and encouraged Matilde—whom fright had deprived of the vivacity and animation which distinguished her on first leaving the house. The Alameda was deserted as it always is on non-festival days. The light sun of springtime played on the red branches of the poplars and threw its golden rays over the walk.

The two girls advanced with Augustin to the open place where the fountain stands. The calm of the place gave Matilde confidence and the conversation which had languished on the way recovered its animation when they were seated not far from the Maiten trees—which some curator with a flair for National trees had planted in the circle round the fountain as a proof of his patriotic obsession.

Shortly after they found themselves in this place Augustin whispered in Leonor's ear—

"Here comes Rafael."

Matilde had already perceived him and had the greatest difficulty in suppressing the trembling of her whole body.

San Luis approached the seat and gracefully saluted Leonor and her cousin, giving his hand to Augustin who received him with a smile. Equal courtesy was shown in saluting each of the girls; no one would have been able to guess that one of them had occupied his whole heart for many years.

Rafael also was able to take the opportunity to join in the general conversation, in this way getting rid of the natural embarrassment which would have succeeded his arrival.

During this conversation Matilde became calm and was able to look at Rafael without trembling, with all the ardour of true love; and disdaining disguise, she showed in her face the strong emotion which overwhelmed her.

Leonor soon gave the signal to return, rising and taking her brother's arm.

Rafael offered his to Matilde and the two couples went slowly on.

San Luis told her all that he had endured during his days of sadness, he depicted warmly his terrible trouble, he made the heart of his beloved one overflow with joy, by the passionate expressions of a love which had formed his whole existence, and he received with a happiness which he found difficult to repress the few and trembling words with which Matilde related to him her sorrow at the sacrifice which she had so nearly made at her father's command.

In this mutual confidence of two hearts united by a sincere passion and separated by ambition, this boundless expansion which overflowed from thoughts inundated by complete felicity, words were uttered as if life had no limits, glances were given which shone with almost celestial light.

"Now," said Rafael, "all my sorrows are gone from this moment. I see that the maddest dreams of my imagination may be realized—you love me!" he uttered this phrase when Matilde related to him the fears she had had to conquer before granting him this interview.

"Now," added the girl, who in this moment of supreme happiness, felt in her soul a decided courage, "my resolution is irrevocable, I have suffered so much that I have for the future strength to resist."

Now Rafael related his new plan and the probabilities on which he counted to conquer the obstinacy of Don Fidel. Joyful hopes extended their golden wings over the lovers and the Heavens appeared to them bluer and the air in which their words were spoken purer than ever they had been before.

Three-quarters of an hour had elapsed during which Augustin related his love affairs to Leonor, transforming in his narrative Adelaida into the only daughter of one of the principal families in Santiago and then dragging into his story of the interview a thousand proofs of a violent passion invented by the imagination of the dandy. At the end of the fourth quarter Leonor turned and said they must go.

Matilde and Rafael thought they had scarcely spoken at all, but the young man having saluted them took his leave and left his friends and his beloved.

He took with him the hope of another interview if Leonor would consent to accompany Matilde again, and meanwhile he would put in execution the plan which was to result in gaining the consent of Don Fidel Elias.

XXV

O ur story must go back at this point to the day following the evening party at Doña Bernarda's house to explain the conversation which took place between her, Adelaida, and Amador after the visit at which Augustin Encina had obtained a rendezvous.

The secret that Rafael had revealed to Martin about his love-affair with Adelaida Molina was also well known to Edelmira and Amador, to whom this girl had confided it to conceal from her mother the result of her fault. Amador had aided his sister in this design and helped to get his mother to go away from the house for a whole month, at the end of which Adelaida returned from a journey to Renca, in which she gave her son to the sister of Doña Bernarda.

Edelmira, for her part, contented herself with weeping for her sister's fault.

It seems useless to give the circumstantial account of the means by which Amador avoided suspicions in this delicate matter. The result was that Adelaida returned to the family residence without the least suspicion on her reputation in the eyes of the world, for Amador was a man who liked to exact gain from the accidents of life to compensate him for the unhappy fate of always having a frugal purse. By this means he was able to take advantage of this secret to have an ascendency over his sister and to oblige her to be less disdainful towards the love-sick son of Don Damaso Encina.

Adelaida was only thinking of what vengeance she could take against the man who had abandoned her when Augustin began to visit the house, attracted by her lustrous eyes; the dandy arrived, so to speak, at a bad time, and naturally had to suffer for several days the disdain to which his unlucky star had destined him.

Nevertheless, Augustin was not discouraged at his first reverses and attributed the sweet smile which occasionally rested on the lips of Adelaida, to the constancy of his attention. The smile only came when Amador had ordered that some amiability should be shown, as he had an idea of gaining something good from this love for the son of the family.

Ambition had taken such a hold on Amador that he even thought of the possibilities of blending his poor and plebeian race with the gold of the new lover of Adelaida. She allowed herself to be ruled and consented to act the part in the comedy assigned to her by her ambitious brother, without hoping for any further advantage for her obedience than the possiblity of bettering her fortune, and also that more probably she would find a means of avenging herself on San Luis.

On the day following the party given by Doña Bernarda in honour of her birthday, Amador entered Adelaida's room whilst Doña Bernarda and Edelmira had gone out shopping.

"How was Augustin last night?" asked Amador, sitting down, "still in love?"

"Always," said Adelaida without raising her eyes from the dress with which she was occupied.

"And you? what did you say to him?"

The girl looked at her brother with the resolution which naturally showed upon her face.

"I have nothing to tell you, because up to the present moment you have not told me what you wanted me to do."

"What I want you to do? Have I not told you that you have got to do what I wish!"

"And why?"

"First because you are poor," said Amador, lighting his cigarette and throwing away the match.

"I know what it is to be poor when every night we have almost empty plates!"

"I have won lots of money from him, he has signed papers for it."

"And why don't you recover it?"

"Do you think I would succeed? Something always happens: one wins from the son of a rich man, and if he doesn't wish to pay it one goes to the father, who gets furious and threatens to send one to prison. And the money that Augustin owes me, that is very little, only one or two onzas, I could put it between my toes."

Adelaida remained silent.

Amador waited for a little and then said, "What I want you to do would be of great advantage to you, would you not like to marry Augustin?"

"You know I would, the first thing that I would like to do would be to pay out Rafael."

This vulgar reply sounded a little strange from the lips of Adelaida, whose eyes shone at the same time with the dark reflection of a concentrated and tenacious hatred.

"I will help you if you will help me," said Amador to her. "Listen to me, if you will do what I tell you, you'll marry Augustin, and he is rich. What more do you require?"

"You speak of getting married as if it was so easy," replied Adelaida, who didn't dare to contradict her brother, who was the guardian of her secret.

"It is true that it is difficult," he answered, "but I know how to manage it."

"How?"

"You must give Augustin hopes. Have you not told me that he is always asking you for a rendezvous!"

"Certainly."

"Very well, when I tell you to do so, give him a rendezvous, then I will arrive with a friend who'll be a witness and I'll oblige him to marry you."

"Yes, but who marries us?"

"My friend; don't worry yourself."

"Your friend is only a sacristan."

"What does that matter! First listen to me, as we have to tell it all to my mother, and she will never consent if she suspects that my friend is no more than a sacristan. We'll tell her that he is a curate and has a licence to perform marriages."

"And afterwards?"

"I'll tell my mother that as soon as she knows you are married you are not to live with him till he has told his family he has married you. This makes us secure against any opposition from my mother. Augustin knows that he must tell his father, and the latter seeing that there is no remedy will agree, and tell his friends. I'll advise Augustin to tell his family that he had got married in the country or some other place. Once this has been done I'll explain to Augustin that not to have the shame of relating it, and that all Santiago may not be able to laugh at him, he must always hold his tongue about the truth."

"But he will always hate me for what I've done to him."

"And what is to prevent you saying that you never knew anything about it? Look here—hardly has the interview commenced when my mother and I will burst in upon you, you must play the innocent and weep and sob as much as you like—in the midst of this I'll oblige Augustin to marry you. Augustin will believe you know nothing about the plot."

Adelaida opposed some feeble objections to this plan, but they were not strong enough to overcome her brother's will, who threatened to ruin her if she resisted. Besides this plan did not a little flatter her pride, seeing herself received as the wife of a rich young man in the highest class of society—with which she would be able to mingle henceforth as an equal, triumphing over the envy of her friends. Another cause acted besides on Adelaida and helped her to submit to her brother's will with very little resistance: this cause had its origin in the state of her mind. Stricken by the consciousness of her disgrace it was easy for her to follow this plan, which offered her a chance to change her destiny for the happiness of an existence full of the material enjoyment of the luxury which to many is so great a temptation. After this conversation Adelaida moderated her coolness to Augustin until she made him believe that she returned his love, and gave him the rendezvous for which the dandy was preparing after his walk to the Alameda with Leonor and his cousin.

Amador in the days which intervened between his conversation with Adelaida and that fixed for the rendezvous, found means to bring Doña Bernarda to his way of thinking, to whom the idea of seeing her family united to the rich Encina made her feel the greatest pride in having given to the light of day a man like Amador, capable of conceiving a plan like that which he had revealed to her. Under the influence of these sweet hopes she promised her co-operation, believing what Amador told her and that the complacent friend of her son was a sacristan licensed to bless the union of Adelaida and Augustin.

"If we didn't do this, mother," said Amador, to her in explaining his plan, "on some unexpected day one of those rich men might seduce the girl and get off scot-free."

"You are quite right," replied Doña Bernarda, her eyes wet with the lively emotion caused by the idea of the gifts which the rich family of her son-in-law by force, would necessarily have to give to her daughter, if not for love, at least from ostentation.

"I don't quite believe," added Amador, "that all this will marry them securely, because it is necessary also that Augustin's family should recognize the marriage."

"That is true," replied his mother.

"Then you must do what I tell you, you will say to the young man that after his family has been informed then he can have his wife."

"And if he won't?"

"I'll threaten him and tell him that he is a coward."

This explanation will now reveal the meaning of the conversation which took place between Doña Bernarda and her two eldest children after Augustin and Rivas had left on the night before that fixed for the rendezvous.

XXVI

Augustin returned with his sister from the walk on which they had accompanied Matilde, every moment consulting his watch, the hands of which he kept changing, imagining that it was going slower, so impatient was he for the night to arrive.

He had arranged with Adelaida that to avoid all suspicion he would not present himself at the ordinary entrance of Doña Bernarda's house, and that a postern door with a tiny window and a wicker grating which looked on the street would be the place where his beloved might expect him.

On this day Martin did not present himself at the dinner hour; he had received a few lines from San Luis summoning him to go and listen to his history of the past and to speak to him of the happiness of which his heart was full.

Augustin sustained the conversation at the table with great prodigality of Gallicisms and Frenchified phrases, every one of which, according to Doña Engracia, the pampered Diamela understood, as one could easily see by the movements of her ears.

Don Damaso preoccupied by his political doubts added a few words to the conversation of his son, which had so little analogy with the matter that one would have thought he was either asleep or deaf. And Leonor, evoking without either thinking or wishing to do so the image of Martin, looked at the door with the same glance which formerly had made his heart feel an indescribable sensation of heat and cold.

After dinner Augustin went away to his room and smoked several cigarettes to calm his impatience, following in the capricious forms depicted by the smoke as it mounted to the roof the capricious turn given to his hopes and his pursuit. At nine o'clock he entered the family drawing-room, exhaling an odour mingled of eau de Cologne and various scents favoured by many princesses and European duchesses, revealing the careful scrupulousness with which the dandy had perfumed himself for the better success of his amorous career.

To check his impatience he sat down beside Matilde who had arrived a few moments before with her parents.

The heart of the daughter of Don Fidel had lent to her appearance some of the happiness with which it was beating. In Matilde's face there appeared that transparent and brilliant colour with which the emotions of happy love tint women's faces, when they appear to acquire new life in its atmosphere.

She was like this when Augustin met her and it was easy to have an animated conversation with her, of which San Luis soon became the subject.

Don Fidel and Doña Francisca, who from some distance were looking at their daughter, noted the animation with which Matilde was chatting and suspected on the moment, believing themselves to be of great experience, that it must be the commencement of love between those two young people, who conversed with such vivacity. This idea suggested certain reflections to the observant parents of Matilde.

"Ha, Ha! I never make a mistake. I have often thought that they were in love," thought Don Fidel.

Doña Francisca said, looking at her daughter, "Above all there is no doubt a happiness there that soars above vulgar love, a stranger to the delicate ecstasies of privileged souls who traverse the aerial of existence without encountering another capable of comprehending the delicacy which they aspire to realize, etc., etc."

And both imagined that the vivacity which shone in Matilde's face could only arise from the attentions with which Augustin must be paying his court to her.

Martin entered the salon at this moment. His mind was depressed by the confidences of his friend which naturally left him in the position of envying a happiness which it appeared to him impossible that he should ever attain. The desire to be loved, the constant dream of youth, took up immense proportions in his mind and enslaved him with absurd tenacity.

Leonor, who was afraid she would not see him come that evening, far from confessing to herself the satisfaction which she felt at seeing him appear, found in her own pride reasons to look upon the visit of the young man as an audacity after the scene in the morning.

The proud heart of this girl, spoiled by nature and by her parents, could not perceive that the contest which she had undertaken for making sport of her natural sentiments, and scoffing at the overwhelming power of love, was by degrees losing its haughty security, and making room for certain strange emotions whose sweet power appear to her a humiliation to her dignity.

Martin, after saluting, sat down alone not far from the piano, and without appearing to do so, glanced frequently over to where Leonor was talking with Emilio Mendoza. From his seat he could not notice the change which had come to Leonor's expression, who agitated by the sentiments we have just described, apparently listened with great interest to Mendoza's words which a moment before she had hardly paid any attention to. At the end of some moments Leonor appeared to tire of the affected attention with which she was listening to the amorous phrases of the young man, and showed again her want of attention. Taking advantage of a moment when Emilio Mendoza was answering a question of Dona Francisca's, Leonor went to the piano and sat down on the music-stool and began to run her fingers over the keys.

Martin at this moment remembered the past happiness of the conversation, which some days before he had had with Leonor in this very place.

A heart which loves without hope finds itself forced to "poetize" the most insignificant scenes of the past, because it has no hope for the present, or the future. For this reason Rivas recalled this conversation, striving to forget the sorrow which it had since given him.

"Martin, in that book that is beside you is the piece I am looking for, have the kindness to pass it to me."

These words said by Leonor in a very natural manner, roused the young man from his meditation.

At the moment of handing the book his mind sought the reason for this order with the inclination that all lovers have to find a hidden meaning for every word they hear from the person they love.

The frigidity with which Leonor thanked him, turning over the leaves of the book, persuaded him that in asking him for it she had no other intention than looking for her piece of music.

Martin, a novice in love, always thought the contrary to what any of those young men who abound in our salons would have thought, imagining that to conquer a heart nothing more is necessary than to cast a glance at the victim whom they wish to enslave, as a Sultan throws his handkerchief.

Martin was going to retire when Leonor turned to him.

"The leaves of this book won't stay down," at the same moment she held the book with her free hand and struck some notes with the other.

"If you will permit me," he said, rising, "I will turn over for you."

Leonor without replying, let the hand of the young man take the place where her hand had been and began to play the introduction to a favourite waltz.

"Can you turn over the leaves alone?" she asked him at the end of a few moments.

"No, Señorita," answered Rivas, who trembled with emotion, "I hope you will tell me the right moment."

The conversation was principally about this and would be firmly adhered to, at least so thought Leonor; whilst Rivas, having forgotten all his trouble, gave himself up to looking at the girl who was turning her face alternately to the book and to the piano.

"Today I saw you and your friend," said Leonor, when she found an opportunity to glance at Rivas to indicate that he must turn over the leaf.

"Yes, Señorita," answered Martin, "I have met today the happiest man in the world."

"So that you must pity him very much," said Leonor, looking fixedly at the young man.

"I? And why, Señorita?" he exclaimed, surprised.

"On account of your theory of flying from love as from an affliction."

"My theory refers to love without hope."

"Ah! I had forgotten; and can this love exist?"

Momentarily Martin had an idea of giving himself as an example of what Leonor apparently doubted, with the eloquence of deep melancholy to portray to her the sorrows which destroy the spirit of him who loves without hope, to reveal to her the madness of his adoration, in words which would describe the treasures of love which he held in his bosom for her, who, without knowing it, held absolute dominion over him, but at this moment his voice stuck in his throat, and the remembrance of the glacial disdain with which Leonor received his words in the conversation of the morning froze the courage with which he had been animated; he saw beforehand his love scoffed at, he imagined with consternation the haughty and sarcastic look with which the girl would receive his words, and his palpitating heart returned to the reserve which his condition imposed upon him. These reflections passed through his mind with such rapidity that only a short instant intervened between Leonor's question and his reply.

"I imagine that it can, Señorita," he replied, striving to conquer his emotion.

"That is to say that you are not certain?"

"No, not certain, Señorita."

"Nevertheless in your friend you have an example that you cannot consider as an object of pity."

"Rafael had been loved before, so had some hope of regaining it."

"But if he had thought as you do he would have tried to forget it, but now he is worthy of his happiness because he has been so constant."

"What is the good of constancy to a man who never dares to confess his love?" said Rivas, emboldened by the arguments and conclusions of Leonor.

"I don't know," she answered, "for my part I don't understand this timidity in a man."

"Señorita, it has to do with his happiness and sometimes his life," replied Martin, with emotion.

"Don't men risk their lives often for much less worthy causes?"

"That is true, but now we combat against an enemy, and in the case of which we're speaking sometimes one counts one's love more precious than one's life. Rafael, for example, amongst the men of whom we are speaking, I don't believe would tremble in the presence of any adversary, nothing would be strong enough to take him from your cousin after the happy circumstances which have reunited them. True love, Señorita, can make a strong man as timid as a child, and if this love is without hope it will make him more timid still."

"They say that everything can be learned by practice," said Leonor, with a slight smile, "and I suppose that the means of conquering this timidity is subject to the same law."

Martin did not answer because he was trying to guess the object of this remark.

"Don't you think so?" Leonor asked him.

"It seems difficult to me," he replied.

"Nevertheless nothing is lost by trying, and I think that you are on the road to do it."

"I—I never thought of it."

Leonor didn't think this required an answer.

"You forget to turn over the leaves," she said to him. "I've had to play the whole of the valse from memory."

"I was waiting for the signal," replied Martin, disturbed at the cold way in which Leonor had said these words. The girl had now begun to play the waltz over again.

"And what is your friend's plan now?" she asked him.

"In the first place," Rivas replied, "I think his only idea is to see the Señorita Matilde again."

"On Monday we are thinking of riding to the Campo del Marte, where he could see her."

"This news will gratify me greatly if you will permit me to tell it to him," said Rivas.

Leonor ceased playing and left the piano.

Martin, who for want of hope looked upon everything in the most pessimistic manner, thought that this conversation had been sustained by Leonor in order to tell him this last sentence, as a postscript in a letter often contains the object for which it was written.

Augustin woke him up from his meditation and conversed with him until eleven o'clock, the hour when everybody went away.

Shortly after, Don Fidel Elias with his wife and Matilde left also.

"Did you see," he said softly to Doña Francisca, "how Augustin and Matilde were talking? What did I tell you, they love each other, I am certain of it, and tomorrow I'm going to talk to Damaso to arrange about the marriage."

"Would it not be better to wait until you are sure they are in love?" observed Doña Francisca.

"To wait—do you imagine that a *parti* like Augustin is easily met with? If we wait somebody else may catch him! Who knows what may happen! No, Señora, in these things it is necessary to look alive! Tomorrow I will speak with Damaso."

At the same time Augustin gave some finishing touches to his elegant costume, and scattered on his clothes a few drops of the most fashionable essence of perfume before going to the rendezvous.

XXVII

Shortly before the hour agreed upon Augustin was to be found in the neighbourhood of Doña Bernarda's house. All her visitors had left and the servant had bolted the door of the street, which grated as it turned on its hinges.

Not far from Augustin, who concealed his face in the collar of an old overcoat, passed two of the visitors of Doña Bernarda with Ricardo Castanos, the official of police.

The heart of the son of Don Damaso palpitated with eagerness as he found himself in the shelter of the postern door, waiting for the expected signal. He looked upon himself at this moment as the happy hero of a novel, and, above all, it flattered his pride to think that a beautiful girl loved him enough to sacrifice her honour. This reflection made it all the more real in his eyes—humid with love and gratitude to the divine creature who had given him her heart, fascinated by the irresistible attraction of his person. In the sweet expectation of his good fortune, he was surprised on hearing the bells of the church striking two. It was the hour agreed upon, and Augustin, rousing himself from his fond reflections, gently pushed the door, which opened with the same noise with which it had shut. On hearing this noise the dandy felt ready to drop, and drew back some steps, but seeing nothing was moving inside the house he advanced with more security and entered the courtyard. The courtyard was dark, which permitted him the better to distinguish a ray of shaded light which showed itself through the door of the ante-room which was not quite shut.

Adelaida had not told him that she expected him with a light, and this circumstance did not fail to quench his valour. After some moments of perplexity which he spent in trying to look through the crack in the door, the silence which reigned over all the house decided him to enter, which he did with the greatest caution in order to avoid the noise of this new door which he had to pass. The instinct of precaution counselled him to leave the door half open so as to leave the way clear for flight in case it was necessary. The room which Augustin entered was empty, and lighted by a candle which shone through the green shade in the flat candlestick of gilded copper.

Augustin tried to overcome the apprehension with which he entered. On finding himself alone the idea of being trapped crossed his mind. As courage had no place in his moral qualities, he was obliged to call upon all the strength of his passion and his very weak will to overcome the counsels of fear which impelled him to turn back by the way which he had just come. The entrance of Adelaida under circumstances which he could not but regard as a support, made him give up this idea, and he returned to tranquillity and the thought of his happiness.

"I was afraid you might not come," he said to the girl, trying to take her hand, which she drew back.

"I was waiting for you in my room," replied Adelaida, "until everything was quiet."

"What imprudence to have a light!" he exclaimed, in a soft and tender accent, going towards the table to put it out.

"Don't put it out," said Adelaida, pretending a delicious perturbation which filled the young man with pride, on seeing the timorous love which he was able to inspire.

"Have you no confidence in me?" he asked, again attempting to take one of Adelaida's hands.

"Yes, but we are better with the light," she replied, withdrawing her hand.

"Why will you not give me your hand?" asked the young man.

"For what?"

"In order that I may speak to you of my love and feel between my own this divine hand which—"

A loud noise cut short the declaration of the gallant, who saw with horror the door open and Doña Bernarda and Amador appear with candles in their hands.

Augustin's first impulse was to fly by the door which he had left half open, whilst Adelaida flung herself upon a chair, hiding her face between her hands.

Amador ran quicker than Augustin and got between him and the door threatening him with a stick.

The cheek of the dandy became as pale as that of a corpse, and the sight of the stick made him give a terrified jump backwards.

"Don't you see, mother?" exclaimed Amador. "What did I tell you? These are the gentlemen who come to the houses of poor but honourable people to make a jest of them, but I will not put up with it."

Whilst he was saying this Amador rushed to the door, locked it, and put the key in his pocket, and then planted himself in the middle of the room with a most menacing air.

"What are you doing here?" he exclaimed in a thundering voice to Augustin.

"I—I thought that the family hadn't gone to bed, and as I was passing—"

"Liar!" shouted Amador, interrupting him.

"Ha, ha, little Frenchman!" exclaimed Doña Bernarda, "that is the way you get into houses to seduce young girls."

"My lady, I didn't come here with bad intentions," replied Augustin.

"*This* culprit is the guilty one," said Amador—appearing to be in the last stage of exasperation—"because, if she hadn't consented he couldn't have got in. She has got to pay for it first." With these words he rushed at Adelaida in such a furious manner and aimed a blow at her with the stick with such violence that any one would have sworn that it was only the agility with which Adelaida left her seat that saved her from a bloody death.

Doña Bernarda threw herself into the arms of her son, uttering shouts of fear and calling upon him to be merciful in the name of a great number of saints. Amador appeared not to hear her and struggled in the maternal embrace, which to all appearances prevented him from being able to move.

"Since you don't wish that I should pay out this evildoer," he exclaimed, "then let me get at this young blackguard; he thinks he can dishonour us because he is rich."

His glance was now directed to Augustin, who trembled with fright as he got behind a chair to save himself. On hearing these words, and seeing how Amador struggled with his mother to escape from her arms, Augustin thought his last moment had come and fervently supplicated the Almighty that he would deliver him from this awful and unexpected death. With a supreme effort Amador succeeded in throwing his mother on the carpet and with a bound he arrived at the place in which Augustin was commending himself to the Almighty, sheltering himself as well as he could behind the chair. On seeing Amador raise the tremendous stick Augustin fell upon his knees imploring pardon.

"And what do you offer me for your pardon?" asked the son of Doña Bernarda, with a most threatening air and accent.

"Anything that you like," replied the prostrate lover, "my father is rich and would pay—"

"Money! that is not the question!" exclaimed Amador, his eyes flashing with pretended rage. "Do you imagine that I'm going to sell my honour for money; the rich are like that. If you have no better thing to offer me than that I'll dispatch you on the spot."

"I'll do whatever you like," said the terrified voice of Augustin, wrung with fright at the sight of the ferocity in Amador's face.

"What I want is that you shall marry her, or I'll kill you," replied Amador, in a tone of resolution.

"Very good, I'll get married tomorrow," said Augustin, who looked upon this condition as the only means of saving his life.

"Tomorrow! You are laughing at us, who would believe that you would keep your word. No, it is to be done at once."

"But I can't do it at once, what would my papa say?"

"Your father may say whatever he likes, because he has a son who wishes to deceive honourable people; now, will you get married or not?"

"But now. It's impossible!" exclaimed the dandy, in desperation.

"Impossible! don't be a fool!" said Amador, turning to his sister. "Don't you see what he wanted to make of you? He wants to laugh at you. I know the sort you are," he exclaimed, looking at Augustin, "for the last time, will you get married or not?"

"I swear to you that tomorrow—"

Amador did not give him time to finish his sentence, but tearing away the chairs which separated him from Augustin, he tried to throw himself upon the young man. But moving the chairs gave Doña Bernarda time to get to him and seize him in her arms, hanging on to him whilst he waved the stick in the air.

Augustin who did not see Doña Bernarda's movement, grovelled on the floor, promising to get married.

"Ha, ha! you consent now," said Amador. "You do well, since, only for my mother, I would have pierced you to the heart. Let us see, you will tell the priest whom I shall bring here that you wish to get married?"

"Yes, I'll tell him."

"I see that he is only doing it out of fright," exclaimed Adelaida, "and I don't want to get married like this."

"No, no, it's not from fright," replied the young man, abashed; "I offered to do it tomorrow, but your brother won't believe me."

"On the moment!" said Amador. "I demand it."

Going to all the doors in the room, locking them and taking the keys, he went out, putting into his pocket the key of the door which communicated with the courtyard.

"You are all to wait for me here," he said, "I am going to look for the curate who lives close by. If you escape," he added, turning to Augustin, "you will see me tomorrow at your house, where I'll tell your father everything, besides settling my account with you."

"Don't fear," replied Augustin, who was now feeling intense humiliation before Adelaida.

Amador went out, bolting the door leading into the courtyard.

They could hear the sound of his footsteps on the pavement leading to the door of the street, which he opened and bolted after him.

Immediately afterwards Augustin appeared to rouse himself from the fright which the well-feigned anger of Amador had given him, and he turned to Doña Bernarda.

"Señora, I promise that I'll get married tomorrow if you will let me out. Today it is impossible for me to do it because papa would never pardon me if I got married without letting him know."

"What rubbish the little Frenchman talks," exclaimed Doña Bernarda, shrugging her shoulders. "Don't you see that Amador is capable of killing me if I let you out? How stupid you are, have you not seen that just for nothing he would have stabbed the girl?"

"But, Señora, for God's sake, I swear to you that I'll come back tomorrow and get married."

"If I dared I would let him out," exclaimed Adelaida, looking at him with disdain; "and I wouldn't marry him only I am forced to do so, because I see that you are tired of me."

"I tired of you!" he exclaimed in a supplicating voice, "I should truly love you, but I believed that you did not think me worthy of you, you who oblige me to do it. I would marry you without it being necessary to force me to do so."

"Do what you can with Amador," said Doña Bernarda. "How can you expect us to do anything?"

The quarter of an hour passed in supplications and prayers. Augustin was in desperation and hid his face in his hands, his elbows on his knees. Sometimes it appeared to him like a horrible dream, when he thought of the daily shame he would have to suffer before his family and the aristocratic society in which he moved.

A sound of steps was heard on the courtyard, and Amador entered the room.

"Here is the priest," he said to Augustin, in a threatening tone. "Whoever says a single word against what I've arranged, no matter who is the first to say it, they will be stabbed." Saying these words he returned to the door which led to the courtyard.

"Enter, my father," he said; "we are all here."

The sacristan entered the room with an air of gravity. A cotton pocket-handkerchief knotted at each corner was on his head, which besides was covered by the hood of his cloak, and partly hid his face, but allowed to be seen a bulky swelling which rose in rebellion on his left cheek. A pair of old green spectacles hid his eyes and concealed the real aspect of his physiognomy with the aid of a pocket-handkerchief in which his face was half buried.

"Come on, begin the ceremony," said Amador.

Doña Bernarda, Adelaida, and Augustin stood up.

The priest made Adelaida and Augustin take hands—Doña Bernarda and Amador stood beside them.

Putting the candle which he held in one hand close to the book which he held in the other hand, he began in a monotonous voice the reading of the marriage service. When the benediction was given Augustin fell upon a seat paler than a corpse and the priest retired accompanied by Amador, after verifying the rite which he had performed.

Amador returned to the room where the newly married pair and the mother had remained in silence.

"Go, Don Augustin," he said with scorn, "you are free."

"Never shall I dare to confess to a marriage celebrated in this fashion," said the unfortunate fop in a sombre voice.

"This little Frenchman is annoying himself for nothing," said Doña Bernarda. "You don't want Adelaida, then?"

"For the same reason that I love her I would like to marry her with the consent of my family," replied Augustin, who seeing himself married wished at least to destroy the bad impression he had made in Adelaida's mind by his former resistance.

"Go; it's the same thing whether you do it before or after," said Amador. "In place of begging for your father's consent before marrying, you can do it after."

"It's not the same thing," answered the newly married one, "and it will be a long time before I can tell papa that I'm married."

These words choked the voice of Augustin, as the idea drove him to despair at finding himself bound to her whom a few hours before he considered only worthy to serve his caprice.

"Then, little boy," said Doña Bernarda to him, "I don't think they will take in your wife before you tell them you're married to her. Go to your papa's house, it is from there that you should receive her."

This new declaration had not so much effect on the mind of Augustin because he was searching in it an excuse for the real tragedy of his sad adventure.

"And if he doesn't tell it, mother, I can hold my tongue also, and who is there that would imagine it? I would bite out my tongue rather than tell any one that my sister is married to him."

Amador's contempt appeared to impress the stricken youth more strongly than Doña Bernarda's words.

"At least you must give me time to prepare my father's mind," he said, exasperated; "you don't want me to do it suddenly."

"I'll give you some days," replied Amador, "and in those days you promise to do it?"

"I promise."

"Go, then, it's very late," said Doña Bernarda, "it will be a good thing if you go off to your house."

Augustin turned to Adelaida, who feigned in a most perfect manner a terrible sorrow.

"I see," he said to her, "you suffer as much as I do from the violence committed by your relations."

All the reply that Adelaida gave was to lower her eyes and sigh.

"I would have preferred to have given you my hand in another fashion," continued the dandy.

"And I felt much that—" here sobs stifled the voice of Adelaida, conveying by this reticence a more agreeable impression to the young man than if she had spoken, because he thought that Adelaida, like himself, was the victim of the drama.

"Don't cry, my girl," said Doña Bernarda to her daughter.

"This grief proves to me that she had no part in what you have done," said Augustin.

To put the seal upon the tardy interest with which he pronounced these words, he rose to leave, clapping on his hat down to his eyebrows.

"Don't forget what we've arranged," said Amador to him, going to the door of the ante-chamber when Augustin had arrived at that of the hall. He gave a blow at this door as all weak persons do, discharging their anger on inanimate objects, and returned to his house with his mind overwhelmed with despair, shame, and fury.

Amador in the meantime had bolted the door, and burst out laughing.

"Ha, ha! what a fright I've given him," he exclaimed, "sufficient to make him forget all the French phrases that he ever knew."

After some commentaries on their future conduct, the two children and the mother separated, each of them going to their room. Adelaida met her sister standing outside.

"How could you have consented to take part in such a farce?" said Edelmira, who apparently had observed the whole scene of the supposed marriage without being seen herself.

"I like that question," replied Adelaida. "Don't you see that Augustin would have made a fool of me if he had been able to. All these rich young men imagine that our class is born simply for their pleasure. Ah! if I had only known this before, I wouldn't have given away my heart; but now I hate them all alike."

Edelmira renounced the idea of combating the sentiments that disgrace had given birth to in her sister's heart.

"This one would have played with my heart just the way the other one did if I had allowed it, it's not too much to give him a good lesson."

As Edelmira made no answer to these words Adelaida went away, following in her imagination these reflections, which manifested the constant pre-occupation of her mind.

Adelaida, like so many other victims of seduction (who, in their very first love have received a terrible awakening), had lost the delicate sentiments which germinate in the heart of a woman, between the grief of her disenchantment and the violent desire for vengeance which Rafael's abandonment of her had left in her breast. Her disposition, naturally refined and noble, shattered in its youth, and at the moment of its purest expansion by disgrace, now appeared only capable of hatred and the darkest passions. Ignorant of her history, every one attributed to pride the indifference with which Adelaida looked upon life. This story of a heart destroyed at the very spring and commencement of love, is common enough in every class, particularly in the sphere to which Adelaida belonged, because there are no safeguards for it in this social circle.

Adelaida had added to her rancour the thought of many similar instances so that in her mind there existed no difference between the young men of society and the professional libertine. For this reason she had not a single feeling of compassion for the sorrows of Augustin, who, from the moment that he entered his room, threw himself upon the bed, giving way to despair.

XXVIII

The days which intervened between the scenes we have referred to in the previous chapter and the Sunday on which Leonor had told Rivas that she would go out with her cousin to the Campo del Marte, were fruitful in torments and terrors for Augustin. He was always watching, he felt the misery that tortures the mind of the guilty, and he told himself that the trivial accidents of life are all prepared beforehand by destiny to reveal that guilt to the eyes of the world. A question from Leonor about the love-affair which he had confided to her, an observation from his father about his frequent absences from the house, gave him the most desperate fright, and made him imagine that he saw the fatal words which would reveal his secret upon the lips of every one. Offspring of a society which tolerates with a good grace the seduction of the lower classes (a practice common amongst his friends), but not an honourable act which marries in order to repair a fault, Augustin Encina feared not only the anger of his father, the complaints and bitter reproaches of his mother, and the proud disdain of his sister, which all threatened him after his secret was discovered, but also that besides this sword of Damocles suspended over his head, was the sarcastic and implacable mockery which dominates our refined society, this burning and terrible judge whom we call Mrs. Grundy. The unhappy dandy, whose unsuccessful attempt at libertinage had cost him so dear in the country of easy access formed by the lower classes, lost his colour, his sleep, and his appetite at the idea of seeing his fated adventure divulged in the gilded salons of the society families, and heard in imagination the spiteful comments which the dearest of his friends would make upon his situation. The burden of these thoughts deprived him of his genial vivacity and his decided tendency to Frenchify his own language.

The consciousness of his situation made him look with indifference on the most elegant articles in his wardrobe; the world had no further interest for him, a black cravat was enough for his neck for a whole day. He had seen the flowery crown of Don Juan or Lovelace with which he had hoped to deck his brow to the envy of everybody, change into the binding cord of a clandestine marriage contracted in a low circle! It was only his want of courage that prevented him from committing suicide; the only escape of which he thought in this awful and shameful moment. He no longer looked upon seduction as a triumph, but concluded that in truth it was a reproach which would overwhelm him for ever with shame. This was the situation which Augustin could not dissimulate from himself and which by dint of thinking over filled him at times with the most terrifying anticipations.

During these days of continued apprehension, Augustin went every evening to Doña Bernarda's house and by the advice of Amador played the part of lover, in which the other friends of the house knew him so well, in order to divert in this way any suspicions of his marriage. On all these visits he was accompanied by Martin, whom he deceived also, referring to imaginary conversations with Adelaida in order to make him believe that he was still in the preliminaries of a love-affair. Martin followed him willingly because he found in his conversations with Edelmira a consolation for the troubles with which he was oppressed. The confidence with which she had inspired him increased from day to day, and he never left her without having spoken of his love for the daughter of Don Damaso.

Rivas displayed to Edelmira the longing of his heart, and the youthful fire of his passion exalted by a hopeless love.

Edelmira heard with pleasure these comments upon love which for young people, who live principally for the moment, are so attractive. Each conversation revealed to her new treasures in the mind of Rivas, whom she saw crowned with the halo with which the imagination of sentimental girls encircles the brows of heroes of novels, and we have already said that Edelmira, notwithstanding her obscure condition, read with avidity the feuilletons and the romantic periodicals which a friend of the family lent her.

Ricardo Castanos saw with the greatest disgust the intimacy between Edelmira and Martin, whom he considered as his rival. In vain he tried to depreciate him, referring very unfavourably for Rivas to the adventure in the Square and the imprisonment of the young man; these petty attempts to make little of him produced exactly the contrary effect in Edelmira's mind to what he had expected. The attempts that an unwelcome lover makes to disparage his rival in the eyes of a woman often help to augment his value because of the tendency to take the part of the absent natural to the female mind.

For this reason the greater trouble the official took to lower Martin in the thoughts of Edelmira the more highly she thought of this young man, so melancholy, whose language was so refined, who gave to love the poetry which enchants the mind of a girl.

Between Edelmira and Martin, nevertheless, none of those phrases had ever been uttered with which lovers seek for the road to the heart of the beloved.

Martin had a true and affectionate friendship for Edelmira, which increased as he found how superior the girl was to the rest of her class, whilst Edelmira looked upon him with that sympathy which, in a woman, frequently becomes love, above all when love is not asked for.

The frequency of Rivas' visits to the house of Doña Bernarda was very agreeable to Augustin. Afraid of exasperating the family by his absence, he did not dare to miss a single night, and he thought that being accompanied by a friend made the absurdity of the position in which he found himself less remarkable in his own eyes and those of Adelaida.

In the meantime Amador had begun to reap some of the fruit of his intrigue, receiving from his supposed brother-in-law money which he paid him to ensure his silence, Augustin telling his father when borrowing the money from him that it was to pay some tailor's bills.

Amador chuckled with glee at seeing the facility with which Augustin had obeyed his orders, and hastened to take all the money he could get from him, with the ease of those who get it without having to work for it. Besides his present expenses it had also been necessary for Augustin to feign an enormous amount of other debts which were in arrear, to try to stop for any time the continued persecutions to which he was condemned.

With a decided love for pleasure, without having any income, or any other way of obtaining money than play, Amador found himself always under the weight of very considerable debts considering his path in life. Augustin's money gave him also a certain ease which was necessary for the undertaking of the plan which he had begun. With a watch which he had been clever enough to swindle him out of, and an enormous chain which he had just bought, Amador had acquired great importance in his own eyes, and affected all the air of a gentleman, in the *cafés*.

The Saturday which preceded the day fixed for the walk to Pampilla in the house of Don Damaso Encina, there took place a conversation between Doña Bernarda and Amador, which threatened once more to attack Augustin's tranquillity.

It was in the morning, and Amador was trying to get over the drowsiness caused in his brain by a night of orgie, his eyelids were weighed down, and the whole of his body was suffering under the agitation of fever.

Doña Bernarda entered her son's room calling to him to get up.

"Look here, lazy one," she said to him, "how long are you going to sleep?"

"Ah, is it you, mama!" replied Amador, turning over in his bed. He raised his arm and stretched himself, gave an enormous and loud yawn, and taking his cigar from the box he lit it with a match.

"I got up thinking about something," said Doña Bernarda, sitting down at the head of her son's bed.

"And what thing?" he asked.

"You see that several days have passed since Adelaida was married, and Augustin has not even asked for a kiss."

"It is true also that he has never given her anything."

"What use is it that she is now rich? a poor man would have given her something."

"I am managing this affair," said Amador, in a magisterial tone, "don't worry about it, mother. If the young man wishes to make us believe that he doesn't understand, he is mistaken, he doesn't get away from here without my telling him so."

"That isn't enough," observed the mother, "not only does he not avow his marriage to his family, but he also pretends to be ignorant of the custom of giving presents."

"Say no more, I'll settle him," said Amador.

Doña Bernarda now entered into a description of the clothes which would suit her daughter, not forgetting those which she would like to have herself, mentioning the shops in which they could be bought. The prolixity of these details showed that the good Señora had well thought over this business before she so minutely described it to Amador. On her list were mentioned besides coloured clothes, a lovely black petticoat and a mantle of chiffon, because she never could bear merino on account of the heat.

With the help of the little arithmetic that Amador had acquired in the school of Professor Vera (of which he had a lively remembrance on account of certain escapades for which he received the rod), Doña Bernarda arrived at the price of a great number of things, which included a dozen chemises for Adelaida and several embroidered petticoats with flounces, two dozen pairs of stockings, various pairs of French boots, and divers necessary articles, in order that she, according to Doña Bernarda, might figure in the best society in Santiago.

"But, mother," said Amador to her, "how can you imagine that Augustin or I can go and buy all this? Wouldn't it be better if he gave you the money to buy them with?"

"That might be," replied Doña Bernarda, "you could tell him that fifty pesos would buy the articles most needed at the moment, or sixty pesos, better more than less," said the mother.

In the evening Augustin presented himself, accompanied by Rivas. Amador called him away to a corner of the room which was distant to that occupied by the others.

"And when are you going to tell your family?" he said to the dandy, who turned pale under the glance of his master.

"It's just that I'm looking for a suitable time," he answered, "because if the opportunity is not well chosen papa could turn me out and disinherit me."

"That's all very well," replied Amador, "but you forget that you've got a wife, and up to now I haven't noticed that you've given her a single present."

"I did think about it, but you know I can't ask papa for money every day."

"What! a rich man like you could trouble himself about a trifle like a thousand pesos! On Monday I'll go and look for him in his house."

"Oh, Monday is too soon!" exclaimed the terrified Augustin; "the other day I asked him for a thousand pesos, now it's impossible! What will papa say?"

"Papa will say whatever he likes. The fact of the matter is that I'll go there on Monday and ask for a thousand pesos."

"Oh! I hope you'll give me at least fifteen days?"

"Fifteen days! What more! During that time you'll have me ashamed before my mother and the girls, because I gave them my word that they would all receive presents also."

"That is my intention, but I must have time before I can ask my father for the money, otherwise he'll get suspicious."

"And, if he does, what does it matter? Do you imagine that we're always going to remain silent? I don't tell you that you haven't got the courage to tell your father about the marriage, but the money is another matter! The old man is very rich and he doesn't care what he pays."

"But how can I tell him so soon?"

"I don't know how you are to do it, but you must, otherwise next Monday I go to him."

Amador went away, leaving the unhappy young man whom he had in his power perplexed and crushed.

The frenzy that the want of money roused in Augustin appeared nothing compared with the fear of revealing the secret of his marriage, which, he persuaded himself, could wait for a more opportune time, imagining, like all those of a weak character who find themselves in any difficulty, that time reserves for them some method of getting out of the difficulty in which they were placed at the critical moment. With this load on his mind Augustin went away at eleven o'clock in the evening. Neither the words of Adelaida nor the endearments showered upon him by Doña Bernarda having been able to calm his mind.

On the way home he kept silence, walking beside Martin, who took no notice of this dulness on the part of his new friend, because like all lovers, not in the company of their confidant, he preferred to walk in silence giving the rein to his thoughts about Leonor.

XXIX

The Sunday arrived on which Leonor had announced her intention of going out with her cousin to the Campo del Marte.

Some details that we shall give about these promenades will be dedicated to those who read this story and who have never had an opportunity of seeing this glorious capital of Chili, when it was preparing to celebrate the memory of the month of September, 1810.

These preparations were the cause of the walks in the Campo del Marte in which Society displays itself in all the allure of fashion, first going there, and then afterwards to the Alameda, to celebrate the *revue* which annually takes place in the Campo del Marte on the 19th September; the Civic battalions come to this Campo on the Sundays during the previous months, beginning in June, to practise the use of firearms and the military evolutions and sham-fights showing the overthrow of the dominating Spaniards.

On these Sundays, our Society, which is always looking for an excuse for amusement, comes to the Campo del Marte to see the troops start. Before the wealthy families of Santiago had found elegant coaches indispensable in which to display themselves, ladies went to this rendezvous in "calashes" (or Spanish chaises) and sometimes in long narrow carts, vehicles which are now only used by the inferior classes of Santiagan society. The elegant world instead of the English saddles and English horses in which they show themselves at present in the side walks of the paseo, liked then to show enormous mountains of pellones (old-fashioned country boots) and spurs of marvellous dimensions, which now only are used by genuine huasos. But then, as now, the departure of the troops for the Pampilla was the pretext for these promenades. The disposition of the Santiagan is always the same, and amongst the ladies especially, they do not care for a walk for its hygienic qualities, but as an opportunity to show each other the progress of fashion and the power of the purse of their father or husband to pay the cost of the magnificent clothes which adorn them on these occasions. In Santiago it would be a crime for any woman of fashion to show herself in the paseo two Sundays following in the same dress. This was the reason why in Santiago only the men went there every day, and why the ladies felt the necessity to take the air in the public walks on Sundays only.

Those who wish to go to the *revue* and have no carriages in which to drive, walk in the central street of the Alemada with the seriousness which distinguishes the national character, and wait for the arrival of the battalions, remarking each other's dresses if they are women, or looking for glances from the ladies if they are men.

Before the trumpet has announced the coming of the soldiers the coaches station themselves in rows on the border of the Alemada, and the fashionable world on horseback show off their equestrian powers, trotting their horses up and down, making them caracole to provoke admiration from those who are looking at them on foot.

The critic, that inseparable companion of all good society, takes notes of the beautiful clothes and the skill with which the dandies try to gain the admiration of the spectators. In our circle of men, there was not wanting a good jester, who made ridiculous remarks about the clothes of those who passed.

The ladies for their part applied their minds to analysing each other's dress, taking note of the make of each garment.

"Look at Frilana; that green pollera, that is the same dress that she had trimmed with flounces last year; she bought it eighteen years ago. Look at Mengana, wearing the mantle that she has had for the last three years; she thinks nobody will remember it because she has sewn on some lace that she took off her mother's dress. The dress that Perengana is wearing belonged to her sister before she got married and was her mother's before that; she bought it at the same time as my aunt bought hers."

With these observations, which prove the privileges of a feminine memory, were mingled expressions of admiration for the clothes of their friends.

Finally the troops defile in a column in the central road of the Alemada, amidst the people, who give a loud cheer, and the officers, who march before their companies, salute right and left with their swords, at times being so absorbed in this occupation that they allow their heels to be trodden on by the troop which marches behind them.

In 1850, the epoch of this history, the same enthusiasm obtained for this festival, precursor of the Dieziocho as nowadays, although then the north side of the Alemada was not completely covered as it is today with brilliant carriages, as since those times many families assist at the *revue* without moving off spring cushions.

Leonor had told her father that she wanted to go to the Pampilla on horseback with her cousin, and from this desire arose an order given by Don Damaso that at twelve o'clock on Sunday two horses should be ready. One was for Leonor and the other for Matilde; beautifully shaped and high-spirited horses. There was another riding horse for Don Damaso, who had promised his daughter to accompany her, and two more intended for Augustin and Rivas, whom his new friend had invited to join the company.

The day was one of the most beautiful of our springtime.

At three o'clock in the afternoon there were a great many people in the Campo del Marte looking on at the evolutions and listening to the firing and observing the soldiers.

Carriages laden with beautiful women drove over the green pasture of the Campo, flanked by elegant cavaliers, who trotted beside the doors seeking for smiles and glances.

Happy groups of girls and young men galloped in the distance, enjoying the air, the sun, and flirtations.

Amongst these groups could be seen Leonor, her cousin, and the riders who accompanied them.

The cavaliers trotted here and there, whilst the girls were sometimes alone and sometimes surrounded by men.

Emilio Mendoza and Clementi Valencia, who manœuvred their horses to get near Leonor, were added to this group.

Always far from her, and gazing at her with admiration, Martin followed without looking at the beauty of the scenery which was so remarkable in this place.

Leonor presented herself to him in these moments in a new aspect, which added hitherto unknown enchantments to her. The air gave her cheeks a diaphanous blush, the warlike sound of the bands made her eyes brilliant with animation, and her figure clothed in a black jacket, and a long riding skirt, showed all the beauty of her form. The most lively pleasure shone in her face. At this moment she was not the proud girl of the salons, the haughty beauty in whose presence Rivas lost all his strength of will. She was a girl, who was giving herself up without affectation to the pleasure of a ride, which delighted her by the novelty of the situation, by the beauty of the day and the landscape, by the breath of the air, full of sweet odours of the country, and fresh with the dew of the evening which caressed her cheek.

The retinue had waited a moment near a battalion which was firing. At the sound of the first discharge the horses began to move, some of them shying—which they repeated at the second discharge. Amongst the most uneasy was Don Damaso's horse, which, at the sound of the firing, lost its peaceable aspect and transformed itself into a most unruly rebel.

"And they told me that it was tame," said Don Damaso, turning pale when it reared furiously, when at the end of the second discharge the cannons began to fire.

At the continuous sound of this fire all the horses began to lose patience and to follow the example of Don Damaso's horse, who in its consternation had overthrown a hamper of oranges and lemons that the vendor was presenting to the young men.

This incident made a change in every one's position, so that with an intentional movement Leonor found herself suddenly beside Rivas: and Matilde, who was trying to restrain the movements of her horse, heard beside her the voice of San Luis, who saluted her.

"It's not very pleasant here," Leonor said to Martin. "Would you like to have a gallop?"

"Yes, Señorita," answered Rivas.

"Follow me, then," said Leonor, turning her horse to the south.

This took place at the same time that Matilde's horse began to gallop, whilst Don Damaso was bargaining with the orange-seller for the price of the oranges, which, on account of his horse, had fallen into the hands of the boys who always escort the battalions when they set out for the field.

"Go on, I'll overtake you," said Don Damaso to Augustin, when he saw the others galloping away.

Leonor lashed her horse which was on the verge of passing from a gallop to a race, excited by the movement of Martin's horse behind. This race beside Leonor made him feel for the first time the shadow of a hope in his heart. The invitation of the girl to follow her, the frankness of her words, the undissembled joy with which she gave herself up to the pleasure of the ride, appeared to him all to be auguries of the future.

Under the influence of such ideas, whilst he rode he contemplated with indescribable admiration Leonor, who, animated by the swiftness of the horse, her face lashed by the wind, her large eyes shining with almost infantile content, appeared to him a modest and sensitive girl who must have a tender heart, free from the pride, which until now it had shown.

The gallop ended very close to the penitentiary prison. Here Leonor pulled up and waited for some moments for the others of the party, who had only galloped a short distance from the point at which she had met Rivas.

"They have left us alone," said Leonor, looking at Martin, who at this moment felt happy for the first time since he had fallen in love.

During the gallop, and influenced by the ideas I have described, Martin resolved to abandon his timidity and to stake his happiness on one stroke of audacity. When Leonor spoke he felt his heart beat with violence because he found an occasion to realize his new idea. Arming himself then with resolution and in a trembling voice—

"Do you mind?" he asked her.

To follow step by step the haughty spirit of the girl we are obliged to interrupt with frequent remarks the conversations between her and Martin. Between two hearts which seek each other and, above all when they find themselves alone together at such a time as we have mentioned, each conversation marks the gradual steps which conduct them to the closest bonds or separates them for ever. A lack of words is a peculiarity of these situations. In the present circumstances very few words were sufficient to place these two hearts face to face. Leonor was very far from thinking that she was going to be asked this question, and this question alone was sufficient to awaken her pride. She had caused Martin to be invited to get away from the infallible attentions of her two elegant lovers, who were boring her more particularly the last few days. In Rivas, Leonor saw only an object whom she wished to conquer to gratify her vanity, and she counted upon the timidity of the young man as well as on his real or calculated dulness, but not on the courage which this question showed.

For reply Leonor turned with the glacial indifference with which she had castigated Martin on another occasion, pretending not to hear and only saying—

"What did you say?"

The blood of the young man appeared to rush to his cheeks and his youthful smile was changed to the sudden red of shame. For Rivas, like every naturally manly man, felt himself rebel against this contrariness, and in measure as his heart beat with violence and his tongue appeared unable to utter a single word, he found the strength to answer.

"I asked you, Señorita, if you minded being alone with me, to explain to you that I followed you by your orders in case any accident might happen."

"Ha, ha!" exclaimed Leonor, certainly not indifferent, yet with a biting tone, "you came to look after me in case of necessity."

"To serve you, Señorita," replied the young man, haughtily.

Leonor heard with pleasure the accent of these words, which showed a certain pride on the part of the speaker.

"You impose so many duties upon yourself to pay for our hospitality," she said to him, "isn't it enough that you help my father in all his business?"

"Señorita," replied Martin, "I placed myself in the position which you mention because I am far from having exalted ideas of my social importance."

"Are you comparing yourself with any of those who appear your superiors?"

"With those gentlemen who come to your house, for example."

"With Augustin?"

"No, Señorita, with the Señores Mendoza and Valencia."

"And why with those particularly?" asked Leonor, with a slight nervousness which she cleverly dissimulated.

"Because they, from their position, can hope for what I dare not aspire to."

When Rivas said these words, the cavalcade who were galloping towards the place in which he was with Leonor was very near.

"I don't see the difference that you indicate," replied Leonor, in a voice which appeared affectionate, and confidential, "a man has no value in my eyes on account of his social position and much less for his name. You see," she added, with a little smile, which bathed the soul of Rivas in the most supreme felicity, "that in this case we always think differently."

She gave a slight blow with her whip to her horse and rode off to join the new arrivals.

Martin said to himself as he watched her leaving, "Extraordinary creature, has she got a heart or only a head? Is she laughing at me, or does she really wish to elevate me in my own eyes?"

The group which formed the party had arrived at the spot where Martin was as he made these reflections, they, as has been seen, were very far from them when his conversation with Leonor had occurred. Hope gilded his reflections and the horizon of his ideas unveiled new vistas to the sensations of his breast and to the delirium of his mind. Hope alone was felicity for Martin.

Whilst Leonor and Martin held the preceding conversation the others of the party were coming towards them as we said, at a gallop, which, little by little, was changed into a trot.

Rafael was riding beside Matilde and holding a conversation with her very like the first, and very like that in which all lovers indulge. Happiness shone in his face and his eyes, and his lips swore the eternal love sworn by all lovers. But, finally, San Luis, who wished to take advantage of this moment to tell his sweetheart of the favourable progress of their prospects of marriage, left the amorous idyll to speak of realities.

"My uncle," he said, "is quite disposed to help me and advance me, and my hopes increase. If your father wishes to go on with the lease of the Hacienda it is more than probable that we shall be happy. May I count upon it that you will have the courage to confess to your father that you love me now?"

"Yes, I have the courage," answered Matilde; "if I don't belong to you I will never belong to any one."

"These words," replied Rafael, "I receive on my knees: my love for you has augmented with suffering, I can tell you, until it has struck root for ever in my breast."

Insensibly they returned to the eternal variations on the same theme, which forms the paradise of all true lovers.

Thus they arrived at the place where they found Martin. After this San Luis spoke a few words with Leonor and Rivas, and then, seeing Don Damaso approach, he galloped off.

Don Damaso had finished his affair with the orange-seller and set out to join the others. At his age, as he very rarely rode on horseback, he was very quickly tired of the exercise, particularly when he had a mettlesome steed like the one on which he was mounted now.

On arriving at the group amongst which were his children, Don Damaso hoped to have some rest from the fatigue which he had had, but Leonor rode away, and the others followed her, to the great discontent of Don Damaso, to whom the sun and fatigue had given a sorry aspect.

When they arrived at the rear of the carriages and the riders who surrounded the battalions and the party met the coach in which was seated Doña Engracia, accompanied by Doña Francisca with Diamela on her lap, Don Damaso assured his wife that he was not tired, and he and the others ate the limes, oranges, and sweets which on such occasions are handed from the carriages to the riders.

But, unfortunately for him, Leonor appeared indefatigable and he was obliged to follow her on new excursions until the hour of returning to the Alemada. Thence they returned, and remained near the coach of

Doña Engracia. After ten minutes of repose Don Damaso imagined that he had recovered from his weariness, but on again starting out his chilled body felt all the force of the fatigue, and the pace of the horse seemed to pull him up by the roots, and the jogging caused him such anguish that the good cavalier swore in the most solemn manner never to find himself again in such a situation. His oaths were repeated many times, for numerous were the promenades that his daughter gave him all along the Alemada, only stopping for a few moments, of which Don Damaso took advantage to put his cravat into its place (it appeared to wish to make the tour of his neck) and to put his hat back in its proper position.

On dismounting from the horse in the courtyard of the house Don Damaso made some gestures descriptive of his lamentable state and implored Leonor that at least for this year she would never invite him again to go for such a ride.

XXX

The most reiterated supplications and prayers and an immense stock of patience were necessary before Augustin Encina could obtain a few days of rest from Amador's incessant demands for money.

Without any other view than that of gaining time he had asked for a respite, because he knew that a new demand for money from his father would excite the suspicions of the latter and probably lead to the discovery of the marriage. The probable idea of Augustin was to conceal this marriage, animated by the vague hopes of those who finding themselves in a difficult position, trust to time more than to their own energy to escape from the difficulties which surround them.

His love for Adelaida, based upon the elastic ideas of morality professed by the generality of young men, had singularly modified since he believed himself united to her by indissoluble bonds, finding a wife where he had hoped for a mistress. The feelings of passion which he had thought sincere cooled before the imminence of the peril which threatened him at every moment. Always afraid of being scoffed at and despised according to the code of laws existing in the most aristocratic society, Augustin only thought that to pay his addresses to Adelaida was to avert this peril as long as possible. Thus passed the days until the 10th of September.

Doña Bernarda on this day pointed out to her son that the 18th was very near, and that they had bought nothing to solemnize this festival.

In all social classes in Chili, there is a law that nobody wishes to infringe, that of buying new clothes for the Dias de la Patria.

Doña Bernarda observed this law with all the strength of her will and thought that on such an occasion she and her daughters could be better dressed than ever with the help of the money Augustin was to give to Amador; this consideration led to an argument between the mother and son as to exacting the payment of the stipulated sum without waiting one day longer than that agreed upon.

On the evening of the day on which this agreement was made, Augustin came as usual, with Rivas, to Doña Bernarda's house.

Amador notified his supposed brother-in-law that the time was up, and announced to him that he would present himself without fail the following day to receive the sum. Augustin's entreaties were useless against Amador's will, and Amador fulminated the terrible threat of disclosing the secret of the marriage.

ALBERTO BLEST GANA

Edelmira in the meantime conversed with Martin on the occasions when she could escape the perfidious vigilance of Ricardo Castanos.

The girl found new enchantments every day in these conversations and abandoned her heart to the sentiments which Martin inspired in it, without running any risk of showing the young man that she had for him an affection which he had never shown the slightest wish to create. Edelmira, as we have said on other occasions, was naturally romantic and given to reading novels: this quality enabled her to cultivate in her breast a love which expected no return, and which little by little engrossed her mind without any other hope than to go on living with the melancholy voluptuousness which passions of this kind create in the heart of a woman who possesses an organization more passive than that of a man, in most cases because her sentiments are purer also.

On returning to the house Augustin did not wish to go into the salon and went to his room. On the road he had struggled vigorously against the weakness which was advising him to confide entirely in Martin and to be guided by his counsels, but his *amour propre* had triumphed, and Augustin kept his secret and his trouble to himself, looking forward with fear to the arrival of the next day.

Martin also went to his room without going to the salon as he had done on previous nights.

Since the ride the hope that Leonor's words had raised in his breast remained, but the girl had destroyed with studied indifference the desire which encouraged Rivas to declare his love; but neither was he in despair, because at times he remembered the question which he had asked her when in the Pampilla, and it returned now to calm the doubt of his mind.

During these days, Don Fidel for his part had made serious reflections about the determination which he had previously mentioned to his wife.

Notwithstanding that he apparently followed exclusively his own ideas, the observation made by Doña Francisca about the prematureness of his project found sufficient strength in his eyes to make him take note of it.

But Don Fidel was a man with very little patience, and it was thus that in the course of the days that intervened between the last conversation with his wife to which we have referred and the 10th of September at which date our story has arrived, that Don Fidel determined to give effect to his idea of speaking to Don Damaso about his desire to see

Matilde and Augustin married. This union he calculated would be a good business matter because his nephew would inherit at least a hundred thousand pesos: thus calculated Don Fidel with the precision of a man for whom the illusions of the world take on a metallic colour which fascinates the sight in proportion as life advances. Thinking thus Don Fidel did not overlook the affair of the lease of Del Roblè. His ambition counselled him to chew with both cheeks, to use the vulgar expression, and it appeared to him that it was an affair worthy of his genius to marry Matilde to Augustin, and at the same time to obtain a new lease for nine years of the Hacienda on which he placed his strongest expectations of future riches. With this view he again begged his friend Don Simon Arenal to make another attempt to obtain the desired lease from Rafael's uncle.

Don Fidel did not think it was necessary to wait for his friend's reply, and on the eleventh day he hastened to go to Don Damaso's house before two o'clock, the hour at which his brother-in-law went out to take a turn, and to talk for some time in the promenades with his friends; an occupation which few of the Santiagan millionaires forego.

Whilst Don Fidel was on the way, we shall return to Amador Molina who arrived at Don Damaso's house, as he had forewarned Augustin the night before.

The son of Doña Bernarda was punctual on this occasion, like all those who want money, and he wore the stamp of "devil-may-care" more marked on his person than on many of the other occasions in which he has figured in these scenes. A hat, very well brushed, but rather old, was dashingly placed over his right ear. A cravat of lively and varied colours embroidered with large butterflies' wings, a shirt, the frill of which was embroidered by his sisters, beneath which could be perceived a small cushion of red satin which all the dandies wore at that period to display a tall form and an elevated chest, a coloured waist-coat well open to match the cravat fastened by two buttons only, and allowing to be seen to the right and left silk lining with flame-coloured embroidery worked by some dear one as a present on his saint's day. A dress coat of doubtful colour from one of the pockets of which hung the point of a white handkerchief, trousers bought as a bargain, a little short, pearl colour, but somewhat deteriorated, and finally calf-skin boots with a slight patch over the little toe, of the right foot, and polished with the greatest care. Add to all these a thick stick which Amador twiddled between his fingers like a windmill, a paper cigarette, bent by the pressure of his thumb and forefinger, on the next finger a ring with this motto in black enamel. *Viva mi amor*, and you have a perfect picture of Amador, who, on entering the house of Don Damaso, twisted his moustache and imperial as if to give himself an air of ferocity suitable for striking terror into the heart of his victim.

Augustin, a prey to mortifying anxiety, was waiting for him. In his sunken eyes, and in the paleness of his face could be seen not only the fear of the moment but the anguish of a night of insomnia and restlessness.

The family of Don Damaso had only just finished breakfast when Amador arrived in the courtyard of the house. One could hear from the interior the sound of the piano where Leonor was practising her scales. Don Damaso and Martin were in the study despatching business letters, and Augustin, through the glass over the door, was observing with an unquiet eye the people who might arrive in the courtyard.

On seeing Amador he precipitately opened the door and made him come in. Amador sat down without waiting to be offered a chair, and put his hat on the carpet.

"Caramba!" he said, noting the furniture and the adornments of the room. "Here I am!"

Augustin shut the doors carefully whilst Amador struck a match and lit his cigar, which had gone out.

"And you are ready with the money?" he asked the young man standing opposite to him with his pallid face.

"Not yet," said Augustin, "I am sure that papa would be too annoyed with this continued asking for money."

"Well, then, what is going to be done? One of two things—to tell him all, or to hand over the money?"

"And if he won't give it we lose everything," replied Augustin, supplicatingly. "Why not wait a few days?"

"If I had a house like this with servants and furniture and good drink, I would certainly wait; but, my boy, our family is poor and your wife can't go out dressed like everybody else. If the old man is annoyed it's because he doesn't know that you're married. I'll go and give him the pill if you are so chary about it; so no more."

Augustin turned in desperation to the door which opened on the courtyard and saw Don Fidel Elias, who was going into his father's study. This visit appeared to him a favour from Heaven.

"Look," he said to Amador, "there is my uncle Fidel going into my father's room; how can you expect me to go and ask him for money now?"

"We'll wait until your uncle Fidel goes away," replied Amador. "Haven't you got anything to drink? Then we shall converse like good brothers."

Augustin gave him a Havannah cigar and got ready a tray and poured himself out a glass of cognac which Amador drank like a drop of water; he filled the cup up again and looked at his victim with satisfaction.

"It isn't bad," he said, "see what it is to be rich. I'm usually obliged to fill my stomach with ordinary anisodo."

We shall leave them to finish their conversation whilst we relate what took place between Don Fidel and Don Damaso.

Don Fidel led his brother-in-law to one end of the room, whilst Rivas wrote at the other end.

"I have come to speak to you about something that has been occupying my mind for some days, and which interests us both," he said in a low tone.

"What is it?" asked Don Damaso, replying in the same air of mystery in which Don Fidel had spoken to him.

"As you are not very observing you have not remarked something."

"What? No?"

"Your son and my little girl love each other," whispered Don Fidel into the ear of his brother-in-law.

"Really!" said Don Damaso, with surprise, "I haven't noticed it."

"But I notice everything, and I am never mistaken; I am sure that they are in love."

"It may be."

"Very well then, I have come to you to tell you about it and we ought to arrange something. Augustin appears to me a good boy, and he wouldn't be a bad husband."

"But, man, he's too young to marry yet!"

"And I! What age do you think I was when I married? I was no more than twenty. It's the best age; those who marry early avoid dissipation. If you wish your son to become a rake let him remain a bachelor and you'll see he'll spend the eyes out of your head. Ah! I have a knowledge of these things, don't you see that I am never mistaken."

"It may be, it may be," replied Don Damaso, following his weakness of agreeing with whoever he was speaking with, "but we must first see what Engracia says. Don't you see that I alone cannot dispose of the future of my son."

"Ah! that is to say that you're looking for excuses," said Don Fidel, forgetting in his impatience to speak in a low tone.

ALBERTO BLEST GANA

"No, man, I swear it," replied Don Damaso, "I'm not looking for excuses; but doesn't it seem very natural to you that I should first speak to his mother, because, after all, she is Augustin's mother."

"But what I want to know is your determination; do you approve or not of the proposition I have made to you?"

"For my part, why not? with much pleasure."

"And you will do your best with your wife to gain her consent?"

"Certainly."

"Listen to what I tell you, if your son is a bachelor the day you least expect it he will launch into utter recklessness and cost you the eyes in your head. I know what these sons are, nothing is ever hidden from me."

Assured by fresh promises from Don Damaso, Don Fidel went away, satisfied with the manner in which he had conducted this business and leaving his brother-in-law reflecting.

"There must be something in this," he murmured, remembering the frequent requests for money that Augustin had been making lately. He put his hands in his pockets and began to walk pensively up and down the room.

Amador in the meantime was getting impatient at waiting, and got up when he saw Don Fidel go out.

"Now your uncle has left; I've just seen him go out."

Augustin looked at Don Fidel who was crossing the courtyard. With him went all Augustin's hopes of being liberated for one day at least from asking his father for money. He tried once more to get a concession, but Amador showed himself immovable.

"It's all nonsense," he said; "I'm going to speak to your father myself, this is child's play for me."

"Well, then, look for me tonight at your house and I'll bring the money or papa's consent," exclaimed Augustin, pulling himself together with desperate resolution.

"No, no, I'm very well here," replied Amador, sitting down and lighting another cigar; "do nothing, and I'll speak to papa and get his answer myself."

Augustin raised his eyes to Heaven, imploring its help, and went to Don Damaso's room like a victim to the stake.

XXXI

D on Damaso continued his walk and his reflections. The visit of his brother-in-law appeared to him an opportunity to look more carefully into the conduct of his son.

Martin finished his writing and quitted the study, leaving his patron sunk in these reflections. When Augustin entered the room Don Damaso looked at him, his mind occupied with these ideas.

"Augustin, what are you here for now?" he asked him.

Augustin, who had carefully prepared the sentence in which he was going to ask for money, was disturbed on hearing his father's question. In the fear of finding his secret discovered, it appeared to him that such a question evidently indicated that Don Damaso had some suspicion of his marriage.

"I!" he answered stammering, "I come here as you know I—"

"It is time that you thought of beginning to work at something," said Don Damaso, interrupting him.

"Oh! I'm most willing to work, I'm only waiting for the opportunity to present itself."

"That is well, I'm pleased to hear it," said the father, again looking at him with a searching air; "young men shouldn't be idle, because they lose both time and money."

This reflection did not sound very well for Augustin's success, nevertheless the dread of seeing Amador appear and of being discovered gave him strength to persist in the task that he had undertaken.

"That is so, papa," he said; "you are right, and for those reasons I would like to work."

"That is well, my son, and I'll look for some occupation for you."

"Yes, and when I'm working I'll not be able to make debts, which now without my noticing have amounted to one thousand pesos."

Augustin pronounced these words as serenely as he possibly could and anxiously observed the effect they produced on his father. Don Damaso, who had resumed his walk, stopped and fixed his eyes on his son. The words that Don Fidel had just said took a prophetic tone in his imagination.

"One thousand pesos!" he exclaimed, "only a few days ago I gave you that amount."

"That's true, papa, but I don't know how, I've forgotten—and besides, with friends—and the tailor."

"Fidel was right," agitatedly said Don Damaso, "these boys think of nothing but spending money." Then, turning towards Augustin, "Nonsense, man! One thousand pesos! that is to say two thousand pesos in less than two months! Caramba amigo! you're more extravagant than one could possibly imagine."

"In the future it will be different—and you'll see it when I'm working," replied the dandy, in dulcet tones.

"Eh, and what work can you do? Nowadays boys think of nothing but spending the money that their fathers have made by dint of work. Yes, sir, Fidel is right, you are all spendthrifts."

"I promise you that I'll work, and when I pay the one thousand pesos that I owe, I'll never spend another centime."

"These promises are worth nothing, my little friend. Do you know what you must do? You must commence a regular life."

"Oh! I'm quite willing to."

"That's all very well; every one says that. Observe, my friend, what I call a regular life is matrimony. Do you understand me?"

Augustin dropped his eyes, terrified at the turn the interview had taken; it was impossible to retract, and the most important thing at this moment was to gain time. This was the only reflection that survived in the mind of the agonized youth.

"It is necessary, then, that you think about getting married," continued Don Damaso in a more tranquil tone, for on seeing that Augustin had lowered his eyes he believed that it was a signal of submission and obedience.

Don Damaso, who was only energetic at rare intervals, felt a true pleasure when he saw his authority respected. The attitude in which his son listened to him, and the terror which his words inspired disposed him more favourably towards him. As Augustin remained looking at the carpet Don Damaso continued more kindly—

"Look here, Augustin, let us talk together as friends. It pleases me that you respect me, that is certain; but I also desire that my children should have confidence in me. How do you like your little cousin Matilde, she's a pretty girl."

"Oh yes, a very pretty girl."

"And has a good disposition; isn't that so?"

"Excellent, papa, a very good disposition."

"How would you like her for a wife?"

"Very much, papa," replied Augustin, whose only desire being to get out of the room, was therefore showing himself submissive and complacent.

"Well, my son," exclaimed Don Damaso, cheerily, "your uncle has just been here to tell me that it would be happiness to see you married to his daughter."

"If it pleases you, I—"

"It pleases me well, my boy, very well; it's necessary to make a good decision early in life, to secure a happy old age."

"Yes, papa, without doubt, but I must tell you that Matilde doesn't love me."

"Bah! that's nonsense," replied Don Damaso, "I thought the same before marriage; there are timid girls who like a young man well enough, and yet don't dare to become better acquainted with him; your cousin is like that. But I'm going to tell you the truth. I'm certain that she is in love with you. Look here, I'm not certain, but I believe what your uncle told me today." Don Damaso aggregated this doubt which was not in his mind to show his son his docility.

"No, papa, it can't be. Matilde loves another."

"How many, my son? All girls have little flirtations until some one comes who speaks of marriage."

"Finally, papa," replied Augustin, who did not wish under these circumstances to contradict his father, "I don't think that the matter is so urgent that—"

"Urgent, and very urgent!" said the father, in a different tone from the affection with which he had spoken up to now.

"I want to know if she loves me, and if—"

"All that is very fine, but I also require that you don't come here asking me for money; it's absolutely necessary that you take this advice most seriously."

"Without doubt, and as soon as you have given me enough to pay what I owe—"

"How much is it?"

"One thousand pesos."

"Nothing more?"

"Nothing more."

"Don't come back and tell me that you've forgotten anything."

"It's all that's necessary."

"Very well, then, tomorrow you bring me the account of what you have got to pay and your reply about your cousin and all will be paid, that's all, it's understood."

Augustin looked stupidly at his father, who gave him no time to answer but immediately left the room.

"Accounts, and my reply about Matilde!" repeated the dandy, almost stunned. "Now I'm worse off than ever. How shall I get out of this awful situation?"

In a state of desperation he went to his room where Amador was waiting for him.

"I've done nothing," he said, in reply to the questioning glance with which Amador received him. In his despair he was desperate.

"What is this? What have you done?" asked Amador, looking anxiously at the distracted appearance of his victim.

"I've lost everything through you," replied Augustin, throwing himself upon a chair in the profoundest dejection.

"But say on. What has happened? What did you do?"

"Papa was angry."

"Was angry! What a pity! And then?"

"He said he would pay when he saw the bills."

"What bills?"

"The bills I told him I owed."

"Well, and why worry yourself about that, bring him the bills."

"But how can I do that when they don't exist?"

"Look here, my friend, for very little I would murder you; you can have all the bills that you want."

Augustin listened with amazement at the coolness with which he spoke to him of presenting documents that did not exist, whilst the appearance of Amador breathed perfect serenity, and in his eyes was a tranquil look which astounded Augustin. With a sudden presentiment Augustin saw himself linked with this man in the shameful life of falsification and trickery to which Amador so calmly invited him. This presentiment alone made him shudder and tremble. With this was awakened also in his mind the instincts of honesty which fear had until now suffocated, and they gave him the strength which he needed to make a frank confession of all that had happened before becoming an accomplice in fraud with one who offered him the means of deceiving his father.

"Tomorrow," he said, "without requiring any documents, I shall see that my father will give me the money."

"Very well, I'll not wait after tomorrow," replied Amador, taking up his hat. "If papa is annoyed and doesn't wish to give the money, I'll let the cat out of the bag, and tell him everything then. Until tomorrow." Saluting with a menacing air, he left the room.

Augustin clasped his head with his hands and remained motionless for some moments. Then, raising his eyes, in which burnt a ray of resolution, and leaving his seat, he went out of the room and mounted the stairs which led to Rivas' rooms. Martin, sitting at a table, was studying or rather reading a book without understanding it. Surprise was depicted on his face when he saw Augustin rush in, his drawn and pallid features showing the agitation which his mind was undergoing.

Rivas got up, saluting Augustin warmly; the latter began to walk about the room thoughtfully. After a few strides he stopped and looked in silence at Martin.

"Friend," he said, "I am very unhappy."

"You!" exclaimed Rivas, in amazement.

"Yes I. If I had followed your council I wouldn't be as I am, I am lost for ever."

Martin offered him a chair. "I see that you are very upset, Augustin," he said, "sit down here."

"If you have come to confide your troubles to me," he added, "you will find that, besides thanking you for your confidence, I'll do all I possibly can to help you."

"I thank you gratefully," said Augustin, sitting down. "It is true that I have come here to tell you everything. Ah! for many days, my friend, I have suffered, and, as I had no one to speak to about it I was overcome with trouble. Now I remember that you gave me good advice which unhappily I did not follow. Now I have come to unburden myself to you because I believe you are a good friend."

These words were so sorrowful that Martin felt moved. The dandy, who had borne his burden alone, was expressing himself with such abandonment that Rivas felt a sincere and affectionate interest in him.

"If you will allow me," he said, "I will be your friend. But what has happened? It may be something to which you give more importance than necessary."

"No, no, I give it the importance that it requires. Do you know what it is? I am married!"

"Married!" exclaimed Martin, in the same tone as Augustin's.

"Yes, married! And do you know to whom?"

"I cannot imagine."

"To Adelaida Molina."

"To Adelaida! But when? Certainly this is very strange!"

"Listen and hear what happened just because I did not take your advice."

Augustin related the matrimonial affair to the minutest circumstance, and told of the constant demands for money to that very day—and of the scenes with his father, and with Amador.

"I find something very suspicious in the audacity of Amador's threat to reveal all to your father," said Martin, reflectively. "Do you know if the man who performed the ceremony was a *curi?*"

"I don't know; he was a priest whom I have never seen before."

"Did he show any licence empowering him to perform the ceremony?"

"I don't know—I was so upset that I did not remark what was passing."

"There is one thing we must do first of all."

"What is it?"

"We must search every parish register and inform ourselves what marriages have been celebrated from the day you were married."

"And why?"

"To see if a marriage exists—because I have suspicions that you have been the victim of a fraud—from what you have told me."

"That may be true; perhaps you are right!" exclaimed Augustin—suddenly illuminated by a ray of hope.

"If we cannot find it registered in any parish—it is certainly null."

"If you are right in this," said Augustin, enthusiastically, "you will be my saviour; I shall owe you my life."

"Amador has said that he will return tomorrow?"

"Yes—at the same time as today."

Martin then made a list of the parishes which he was going to search—and gave another to Augustin with the same object.

"You must not spare expense," he said, "it is necessary to act quickly—we must be quite certain about the matter before Amador presents himself here, and we must warn your father."

"My father! Why?"

"To prevent Amador or some one else telling him."

"And if the marriage is legal?"

"You must be courageous and frank. Would not Don Damaso have a right to be angry if some one, in place of you, gave him the news?"

"That is true."

"Besides, if unfortunately the marriage is valid, by warning your father in time, it might be possible to arrange the affair in some way that we have not yet had time to think of."

"Certainly," replied Augustin, admiring the way in which Rivas reasoned.

"Come, then," said the latter, "we must set out."

"Go to my room and take the money there. It is two hundred pesos, and we will divide it between us."

"The quicker the better," said Rivas, taking his hat and going downstairs with Augustin. A few moments afterwards they set out, each in a different direction, to pursue his investigations.

XXXII

Don Fidel Elias returned home congratulating himself, as we have said, on his activity and his mastery in business matters.

This type of man, who directs every step in his life by business, is well known. For such men, everything that has not to do with business is superfluous. Art, history, literature, all these for them is the pastime of fools. Science may appear a good thing in their eyes if science brings money, that is, in a business point of view. Politics may merit attention for the same cause, and these men can be sociable because friendly relations are necessary in business. They have a superb disdain for all that is no use in material interests, and find the list of current prices the most interesting column in the newspaper. As the reader may have remarked, Don Fidel Elias was amongst the followers of the religion of business, and had been so for ten years, and in ten years his exhortations and example had made numerous converts.

Don Fidel looked on a marriage between Matilde and Augustin Encina as a good piece of business. But what interested him still more was the other piece of business he had on hand—the lease of Del Roblè.

They told him when he arrived at his house that Don Simon Arenal had been there looking for him, and without entering or telling Doña Francisca about his interview with Don Damaso, he went to Don Simon's house full of curiosity.

Doña Francisca saw him set out with the pleasure that many women feel when they find they can be free from their husbands for a few hours. There are a great number of marriages in which the husband is a cross which can be carried with patience, but is laid down with joy, and Don Fidel was a marital cross in the full extent of the word. Doña Francisca was now reading about Valentina, in George Sand, and Don Fidel, a man of business, cut a poor figure compared with the ardent and impassioned Benedicto.

For this reason Doña Francisca saw with pleasure her cross go out, and eagerly returned to her reading.

Don Fidel thought no more of George Sand than he did of the poor in the hospital, and so he went out without noticing the romantic excitement that shone in the eyes of his consort: the business of Del Roblè interested him much more than the study of the impressions of his wife.

He arrived at Don Simon's breathing quickly, his mind filled with doubts. Don Simon offered him a seat and a fine cigar, assuring him that it was one of the best from the cigar-factory of Reyes, situated in the Plaza of San Augustin.

A cigar, with Chilians, commences all conversations, and it may be said that a cigar is one of the principal agents in sociable intercourse. Don Fidel Elias lit his, and hoped, not without agitation, that his friend might tell him the object of the visit that he had just paid him. "Did they tell you I called at your house?" asked Don Simon.

"Yes, compadre," replied Don Fidel, "and as soon as I knew it I came on here to see you."

"It was to tell you that I have accomplished your business."

"Ah! then you were with Don Pedro San Luis?"

"Just now."

"And what did he say about the Hacienda?"

"He made fresh conditions about a new lease."

"What conditions?"

"One that is very difficult to describe."

"Is it harder?"

"That is how you may regard it."

"Let us see, tell me, compadre; let us talk about it as business men."

"Don Pedro told me that he wishes his son to begin to work."

"Yes; and what have I to do with that?"

"It appears that he wishes his nephew to join his son in the work."

"Rafael San Luis?"

"Yes."

"At present I cannot see what it has to do with me."

"He thinks of giving the lease of Roblè to his son and his nephew, unless you consent to something that Rafael has asked him."

"What has he asked?"

"He asks for Matilde's hand."

Don Fidel was not prepared for this. He did not find an answer quickly. His features contracted like those of a man in deep thought.

"Truly I never could have imagined this," he said.

"Those are his conditions," replied his friend.

"And if I accede to them?" asked Don Fidel, after a short pause.

"In that case Del Roblè will be yours, and his son and nephew can work in another Hacienda."

"What do you think of it, compadre?"

"I! I don't know; it is an affair for your family."

"That is true," said Don Fidel, returning to his calculations.

"Before everything," he said to himself, "the affair wants thinking over, because at first sight Don Pedro's proposition is not easy to answer." We have said that Don Fidel had put a large part of his fortune in the Hacienda del Roblè, and this was a powerful consideration in making up his mind about Matilde's marriage with Rafael or with Augustin.

According to every probability the latter would be very rich, but only after his father's death; and Don Fidel calculated that Don Damaso, with his perfect health, would go on living for many years longer. Besides, the help that his brother-in-law could give him was very problematical, and not so advantageous to his business as a lease of Del Roblè for nine years would be.

"You know that some time ago Rafael was to have married Matilde," he said after some moments of consideration.

"So I heard," answered Don Simon.

"The affair was upset by my brother-in-law," continued Don Fidel; "Rafael had nothing, but he is a good fellow."

Don Simon approved by a nod.

"If his uncle helps him, he would not be a bad match," continued Don Fidel.

"So it seems."

"The best thing, compadre, would be not to be too hurried in deciding. Let us take time and think it over."

The conversation then changed; he remained about half an hour longer with his friend and then returned home.

He arrived there at the moment that Doña Francisca was reading the passage in which Benedicto found himself in the alcove with Valentina. The arrival of Don Fidel interrupted her reading whilst her mind was bathed in romance. Don Fidel spoke of the two visits he had paid that day; his compromise with Don Damaso, and the unexpected condition imposed on the lease of Del Roblè.

Doña Francisca discarded the prosy business part of the story with which Don Fidel had seasoned it, and let her thoughts dwell on the poetic idea of the constancy shown by Rafael San Luis. In the state produced in her mind by the reading of Valentina, this circumstance was enough to decide her in favour of Don Pedro's proposal. "Ah!" she exclaimed, "that is indeed true love!"

"And by working in the country," said Don Fidel, "the young man might become a desirable *parti*."

"This is a proof of a faithful heart!" she continued with enthusiasm.

"Also the other Hacienda of Don Pedro is a good investment," observed Don Fidel, disposed for the first time to endure the romantic wanderings of his spouse, because he saw that she was of his opinion in the affair.

"Oh, I am certain it will make Matilde happy! With three thousand cows he could have a good profit every year. I don't think we should hesitate, my dear, it is an excellent thing for us all."

"So it appears to me, it is a Hacienda where at the very least five to six thousand bushels of wheat can be reaped annually."

"Rafael, besides, is a clever young man."

"Without counting the wool and the coal, which yield a good income."

"You reduce everything to money," exclaimed Doña Francisca, impatiently, horrified at the prolixity with which her husband counted over future profits, when the matter had to do with the happiness of Matilde.

"My dear, all the rest is only a trifle," replied Don Fidel, already impatient of the romantic enthusiasm of his consort; "when one has not much money, and has a family, one ought, before everything else, to make positive inquiries. I tell you that I know the world better than any one, no one knows it as well as I do. It would be useless for Rafael to be as much in love as Abelard, if he had not the means to support a family."

"Money does not make happiness," said Doña Francisca, raising her eyes to the ceiling with a dreamy expression.

"Let me have the money and I mock at the rest," said Don Fidel.

"Very well, then, let us talk of something else, we hold such different opinions on this subject."

"It is clear to me I should not discuss anything with you," replied Don Fidel, seeing that his wife, instead of being converted to his doctrine, avoided discussion.

Doña Francisca took up her book, seeking consolation in some poetic thought.

"That is to say that we accept what Don Pedro proposes," said Don Fidel, after a pause, which he employed in trying to get calmer.

"Do whatever you like," answered Doña Francisca.

"I intend to do so. I don't require any lessons, because I know well what should be done: the lease of Del Roblè for nine years is better for us than anything your brother can do for us."

"But you should speak to Damaso, telling him what you are going to do."

"I shall tell him that Matilde's constancy has conquered me, and—nothing else occurs to me just now."

He left the room, and Doña Francisca went to look for her daughter in order to tell her the happy news.

Whilst Don Fidel conducted his business in this manner, Don Damaso had told his wife and daughter of the object for which the brother-in-law had visited him. For Don Damaso his daughter's opinion was as important as his wife's, since Doña Engracia, as a mother, began by opposing any marriage for her son.

"And you, little girl, what do you say about it?" asked the caballero of Leonor.

"I, papa?" she answered. "I think you should not be in a hurry."

"Don't you see? I said the same," exclaimed Doña Engracia, squeezing Diamela, an action that she always employed when agitated by emotion.

"But if we allow this boy to remain a bachelor he is going to waste an insufferable amount of money! That's the only thing he learnt in Europe," said Don Damaso, who as a capitalist and a former man of commerce, looked at things from a material point of view.

"Let us try to improve him," said Doña Engracia, scratching Diamela's head.

"That doesn't matter," said Leonor, "we are rich enough," giving her father one of her haughty looks.

"Anyway, I have requested a reply tomorrow," replied Don Damaso; "we shall see then."

Don Damaso left to take his daily exercise, and the mother and daughter remained alone.

"You must speak to Augustin, little daughter," said Doña Engracia, who counted more on Leonor's influence in the family than on her own.

"Don't worry yourself, mama," replied the girl, "this marriage will not take place."

Doña Engracia embraced Diamela in her joy, and the little dog responded to her caresses, by wagging its tail in every direction.

At the dinner hour the family were all in the ante-salon. Martin, who arrived at this moment, was called when he was going up to his room.

Augustin arrived a few moments after, in a frame of mind that showed itself at table. His eyes sought for hope in those of Rivas, but the latter, finding himself in Leonor's presence, was not capable of thinking of anything but her.

Doña Engracia tried to break the monotony of the general silence and preoccupation by calling attention to the accomplishments of Diamela. But in vain did Diamela feign death, whilst her mistress made little punches on her body, representing the carriages and horses which were passing over her corpse. This accomplishment, which is taught to every pet-dog in Chili, drew Augustin's attention very slightly, for his heart was fluctuating between fear and hope, and much less the attention of Martin, who found himself, mentally, prostrate at the feet of his idol, with the reverence of a heart overflowing with its first love.

On leaving the dining-room Augustin approached Rivas, who always stood aside to allow the family to pass. "Come to my room," he said in the voice of an actor, who gives an assignation to his friend, in order to reveal to him the secret of his birth.

Augustin in his anxieties of the last few days had quite lost his natural affections and his silly phraseology. His mind was filled with drama of the most lurid description, and this is why he spoke in this tone to Martin.

The latter followed him to his room, and sat down in the chair Augustin offered him.

"How did you get on?" was his first question, after turning the key in the door.

"Very well indeed," replied Martin; "in the parish registers that I searched there was no mention of your marriage. Have you discovered anything?"

"Nothing either," answered Augustin, joyfully.

"Early tomorrow I shall have the certificates," said Martin.

"And I also."

"Don't you see. The marriage is null: what is important now is, that the story is not known outside the family."

Augustin could not restrain himself, and hugged Martin, saying—

"You are my saviour, Martin."

Hardly had he uttered these words when they heard some one knocking at the door.

"Who is there?" asked Augustin.

The voice of Leonor answered this question through the door.

"Shall we open it?" the dandy asked Martin.

Rivas made a sign in the affirmative, his heart beat with violence when he heard the girl's voice.

Augustin opened the door. The girl entered.

"It seems that you are talking secrets, and very important ones when you are shut up so closely," she said, looking at Martin, who got up and went to the door as if to withdraw.

"Why do you go away?" she asked him.

"Perhaps you have something to say to Augustin," replied the young man.

"That is true, I have something to say to him, but you are not in the way."

Leonor sat down on a sofa with Augustin beside her, and Martin on a chair at a little distance.

"Papa has told me everything before dinner."

"What, everything!" exclaimed Augustin.

"The visit of the uncle and his intentions."

"About what?" asked Augustin.

"Didn't papa speak to you about getting married?"

"Yes."

"To Matilde?"

"Yes."

"My uncle Fidel came here about that."

"Yes, I know it," said Augustin.

"What are you going to answer?"

"That I can't do it."

"Papa expects the contrary."

"I can believe that from the way I answered him today, but I didn't speak clearly," said Augustin, looking at Rivas.

"And now?"

"That is to say tomorrow will be different."

"Why?"

"Little sister, in all this there is a secret which I cannot confide to you."

"A secret?"

"The only thing that I can tell you is that I have been in the greatest peril, and would have been lost if Martin had not come to my aid."

Leonor looked at this young man whom her father was always praising and who appeared now as the saviour of her brother.

"I shall know this secret," she said to herself on seeing the ardent glance with which Martin returned hers. The conversation continued for some time, strengthening her brother in the refusal which he must give to his father. By degrees the subject was changed and she spoke of music, of her study of the piano, and the pieces most in fashion, consulting at times Augustin's and Rivas' opinion, and concluding with these words, "Tonight they are going to play the new valse which neither of you know perhaps."

Martin thus felt himself invited for the evening, for in saying these words Leonor had looked at him. Under this impression he went down in the evening and joined Don Damaso's circle, from which Don Fidel and his family were absent, having judged it prudent not to present themselves that night. A few moments after Martin's arrival Leonor went to the piano and called the young man with a glance. Martin approached her, trembling. The invitation which he had received and the glance with which the girl had called him to her side were sufficient to fill him with emotion.

"This is the valse," said Leonor to him, placing a piece of music on the piano. She began to play and Martin remained standing to turn over the leaves.

"Apparently," said Leonor to him, as she played the first bars, "you are playing Providence to the family."

"I, Señorita?" he asked. "How?"

"My father says that you are his right hand in business."

"That is because he exaggerates the few services that I am able to give him."

"Added to that, without you there was a time when Matilde would have been always unhappy."

"In that I have played a very insignificant part, and you attribute to me merits that do not exist."

"Certainly at first you were very reserved."

"It was not my secret, it belonged to my friend."

"Whom you supposed at the commencement I was in love with."

"An involuntary suspicion, Señorita, of which I was quickly undeceived."

"There is more to come now; Augustin says that you are his saviour."

"Another exaggeration, Señorita; I have done very little for him in comparison to what I owe his family."

"I don't think that that is very much, according to what Augustin says."

"I never can have sufficient consideration or gratitude towards your father."

"Augustin has made me uneasy telling me that the danger which threatens him had not altogether disappeared."

"I have more hope than he has, Señorita."

"Is it such a very grave thing that you cannot tell it?" asked Leonor, beginning to get impatient at Martin's evasive replies.

"Señorita, it is a secret that does not belong to me."

"I thought," she replied, her pride returning, "that I had given you sufficient proofs of confidence to enable you to trust me."

"I would do it with all my soul if I could."

"That is to say that nothing has any influence over you?" exclaimed Leonor, in a sarcastic tone.

"You exercise it most imperiously over me, Señorita," replied Martin, accompanying these daring words with an ardent gaze.

Leonor did not deign to look at him although she felt keenly the fire of this gaze. She went on for some moments playing the valse without speaking a single word, and left the piano when it was finished. For the rest of the evening she never looked once at Rivas and conversed for a long time with Emilio Mendoza, who, on retiring, thought himself the favourite.

Leonor on thinking it over confessed herself conquered by the obstinancy with which Rivas had hidden his secret, but this reflection, made to herself alone and without any self-deception, created a feeling of admiration for this loyal and knightly character which preferred to risk her disdain rather than betray a friend. She had sufficient elevation of mind to understand the delicacy of Martin's reserve; and the appreciation of this reserve prevailed in her spirit above the desire of enslaving the young man, a desire which formerly her will and her pride had so imperiously demanded.

XXXIII

At nine o'clock the following morning Augustin and Martin found themselves once more together, after having gone out an hour earlier looking for the certificates which the previous day they had searched for in all the parishes nearest to Doña Bernarda's house. With these certificates Augustin had returned to the vivacity natural to his character, and showered upon Rivas a thousand professions of friendship and eternal gratitude.

"I'm yours for the whole of my life," he said, reading the certificates. "With these papers we are going to stun Amador. Now we're going to see which of us two is the injured one!"

"I insist," said Martin, "that it is necessary to tell your father everything that has happened."

"You think so, I don't see the absolute necessity."

"From what you tell me," replied Martin, "Amador is capable of going to see Don Damaso and learning for himself whether he refused you the money."

"That's true."

"In that case it would be very difficult to explain the affair when Don Damaso is under the impression produced on him by news such as Amador has to give him."

"You're right. But the fact is that I don't dare to go and talk to my father."

"I will go and tell him all that has happened."

Augustin was most grateful to Rivas for this new service, thanking him in his peculiar language of Frenchified Spanish phrases.

Martin went to Don Damaso's study because he knew that at this hour he would be writing while waiting for breakfast. He began the conversation without any preface, relating Augustin's unfortunate adventure and excusing his conduct as much as he could. Don Damaso listened to him with the inquietude of a father who sees his son's and his own honour compromised. The honour of the Molinas was nothing to him and he wondered at the insolence of these people, who to preserve their reputation desired a marriage with the son of a caballero.

Finally Rivas related his interview with Augustin on the previous day, the steps that he had taken and the suspicions that he felt about the validity of the marriage. These suspicions permitted Don Damaso to breathe with freedom.

"With these certificates from the clergyman," he said, taking the papers which Rivas had handed to him, "I think that there will be no doubt about the affair."

"The brother of the girl," said Martin, "is coming here today to ask for money."

"How do you think we should receive him?"

"I think the best thing would be to take a decided step before he presents himself," replied Rivas.

"How?"

"Present yourself this very day at his house and tell the mother that the marriage is null. From the knowledge that I have of Amador I believe there is some mystery in all this; he is a man capable of anything."

Don Damaso accustomed to follow the instructions of Martin in his business received this counsel gratefully.

"What time do you think I ought to go there?"

"Before Amador comes here, shortly after breakfast. Amador ought to come about two o'clock."

They arranged the attitude Don Damaso should take during the interview.

"Will you not come with me?" said Don Damaso, to Martin.

"Sir," said the young man, "I owe some consideration to this poor family and beg you to excuse me from accompanying you. Apart from Amador the others of them are good people, Adelaida is an unhappy girl."

"If it is arranged as I hope," said Don Damaso, "it will be a new service that we owe to you."

"I beg that you will not be angry with Augustin about this affair; he has suffered enough the last few days and is very penitent."

"Very well, I will do it for you."

A servant announcing that breakfast was on the table, Don Damaso went towards the dining-room speaking about other business matters with Martin.

During breakfast Rivas sought in vain to meet Leonor's eyes. The girl became more reserved and cooler towards him as the interest she took in him increased. Her reflections of the preceding night had been fruitful in deductions in favour of Martin; but Leonor finally had asked herself for the first time a frank question.

"Are you in love with him?" This question came to her like a flash of lightning at the moment when across her deep reflection sleep was arriving to close her lovely eyes fringed with their beautiful lashes. Leonor closed her eyes but heard it with her heart. Sleep was driven away although she sought it, laying her perfumed hair on the pillow which supported her head. A thousand incoherent ideas were now mingled in her mind. Like the rise of the sun whose rays bathe some objects in vivid light, leaving others in shadow, this luminous radiant idea of love accompanied by its train of unexpected reflections, illuminated part of her spirit, if one may say so, with glorious beauty and left the other in obscurity and confusion. Love appeared to her an enchanted and bewildering dream, but her pride also spoke at this supreme moment. To love a poor and unknown man, one who had not until now drawn the attention of any girl, appeared a shame to her; but at the same time, although her cheeks burned at the thought of what society would say of the union, in her own heart she united the name of Martin Rivas with hers. The imagination of this girl during this insomnia was a mirror in which were reflected all the efforts of a heart struggling with a powerful sentiment. She dreaded the haughty disdain of so many fashionable people. She saw herself in love with a man who had lived on sufferance in her house, and who had for his sole fortune an income of twenty pesos, whilst her friends, whom she had always looked upon as a beautiful queen looks upon the ladies of her court, were married to rich young men of good families whose arms they were proud to take in the promenade. "I'll not think anything more of this madness," was what Leonor said to herself as she turned on her side in order not to hear upon her pillow the violent beatings of her heart. And she again sought for sleep, but sought it in vain. The following morning Leonor mistook the fatigue of insomnia for the victory of her will. The dawning of daylight which chases away the fantastic proportions which ideas generally take at night disposed her mind to a torpidity which she took for her usual cold indifference, but on seeing Martin enter with her father, her mind was again unsettled, and again returned the struggle between her proud will and her heart with the strong vigour of illusion and youth. But Martin knew nothing of all this, and perceived in Leonor's indifference nothing but the influence of his evil star and the constant sequence of endless disappointments.

Thus it was that the breakfast was a silent one. Doña Engracia alone spoke from time to time with her beloved Diamela, and Augustin looked at his father, trying to read in his face the impression which the revelation of his secret had produced.

Don Damaso was so preoccupied with the interview recommended by Rivas that he was impenetrable to the eyes of his son, and he went away at the end of breakfast without Augustin being able to guess whether he was pardoned or not.

Don Damaso called Martin, and they went out together in the direction of Doña Bernarda's dwelling.

"That is the house," said Rivas, as he pointed it out.

Don Damaso left Martin and entered the house that had been indicated to him. He met Doña Bernarda chatting with her daughters in the ante-room.

"La Señora Doña Bernarda Coldero?" asked Don Damaso.

"Yes, sir," replied Doña Bernarda.

Don Damaso entered the room.

From his appearance Doña Bernarda knew on the moment that he was a gentleman and got up and offered him a seat.

"Señora," said Dom Damaso, "which of these two young ladies is called Adelaida?"

"This one, sir," replied the mother, indicating the elder of her daughters.

Adelaida had a vague presentiment that this gentleman had come there about something concerning her marriage to Augustin; the question which she had just heard gave her strong foundations for this suspicion.

"I wish to speak a few words to you alone," said Don Damaso, "because I have to speak to you of a very disagreeable affair."

"Of what affair, señor?" asked Doña Bernarda.

"A dishonourable act has been committed here which may have grave consequences for you and your family," replied Don Damaso, in a solemn tone.

"And who are you?" she asked, surprised at what she heard.

"I am the father of Augustin Encina, Señora."

"Ah!" exclaimed Doña Bernarda, turning pale.

"I suppose that you thought you had done a good piece of business when you married Augustin to your daughter?"

"Who has told you about it? What do you want then, Señor? Your son came here and it was necessary that they should get married."

"But perhaps you don't know that this marriage is null?"

"How null?"

"That is to say that Augustin and your daughter are not married."

"What is all this talk? Married they are, and well married."

"But I hold proofs to the contrary."

"You have no proofs that are worth anything; you'd better take care of yourself." On saying these words Doña Bernarda turned to the door of the courtyard.

"Amador, Amador," she said, calling him.

Amador was at this moment dressing himself to go to Don Damaso's house. He came at his mother's call and turned pale when he saw Don Damaso, whom he knew by sight.

"Look here, my son," exclaimed the mother, "listen to what this caballero has come to tell me."

"What is it?" asked Amador, in a subdued voice.

"He says that it isn't true that his son is married to Adelaida!"

Amador tried to smile contemptuously, but the smile froze on his lips. He was so far from imagining that he was going to hear such an assertion that he felt disconcerted and vacillating in the face of it. But he imagined that there was no possible salvation except in the most obstinate negation, and he again tried to find strength to smile.

"This gentleman perhaps doesn't know what happened," he answered in a scoffing tone.

"I know very well that you have committed an offence against the law," exclaimed Don Damaso, "and I hold documents to prove that the marriage into which you dragged my son is absolutely null."

"Let us see them, then, where are the proofs?" asked Amador.

"Here they are," said Don Damaso, showing the papers which Martin had given him, "and I shall make use of them if necessary."

Amador saw that the affair was taking on a very serious aspect, but he did not dare to propose an arrangement in the presence of his mother.

"Well, if you have proofs so have we," he replied; "let us see who will win."

Don Damaso reflected that it would be better to conduct the business amicably, and continued—

"The proofs that I hold are incontestable, the marriage is null from every point of view, but as this is an affair which might be prejudicial to my honour and to that of my family, I've come to have a conversation with this lady in order that we should come to some agreement without creating gossip and scandal."

"What scandal can there be if they're married?" said Doña Bernarda, consulting her son's face.

Amador avoided the look because he felt himself standing on very shaky ground.

"I am convinced," said Don Damaso, "that my son did wrong to come here for a rendezvous, because that rendezvous was a trap held out for him."

"If then! I don't wish you to say anything more about it," exclaimed Doña Bernarda; "and why do the rich imagine that there's no honour among the poor? When you are about it why don't you say that he was the girl's lover! Ave Maria, Señor!"

"Calm yourself, Señora," said Don Damaso to her, "you must look at the thing as it is."

"How am I to look at it? Saints above! They're married and there's nothing more to say."

"I can take this affair into court and I can prove there the nullity of the marriage, but in that case I shall not be contented because I shall ask punishment for those who have laid a trap for an inexperienced young man."

"Yes, very inexperienced, he came and got into my house at two o'clock in the morning!" exclaimed Doña Bernarda.

"What are you doing over there?" she added, looking at her son, "have you lost your tongue?"

"Look here, Señor, my mother is right," said Amador, "you can't prove that the marriage is null, because we hold proofs to the contrary."

"Where are these proofs?"

"You'll know, and when the case comes on—"

"Does the registration of the marriage exist in any parish?

Amador remained silent and Doña Bernarda said to him—

"Didn't you tell me that you had left it to the curate?"

"Say no more, mother," he replied, not knowing how to get out of the difficulty, "when the case comes on there will be proofs."

"Don't you see, caballero, there are proofs, and they are married, and you've got to make up your mind to it," exclaimed Doña Bernarda.

"What my mother says is the truth," continued Amador. "If you don't like it as it is we can wait until you find it out."

"For my part I shall not wait, and this very day I shall take steps to bring a criminal action against you."

"Take what steps you like, we shall see," replied Doña Bernarda, once more consulting her son's face.

"Just so," said Amador, to content his mother.

Don Damaso rose impatiently. "You are doing very wrong," he said, "to be obstinate about it, because you'll lose everything. I find myself disposed to give you something in the way of indemnity within reason, for the foolish action of my son, if you consent to be silent about the affair, but if you oblige me to disclose it before the judge, I will be inflexible and punishment will fall upon the culprits."

"As you like," said Doña Bernarda; "nothing will ever prevent me from thinking that I saw them married. Isn't that so, Amador?"

"Certainly, mother, it was so."

"You must think over this," said Don Damaso, "and if tomorrow I do not receive a favourable reply, I shall present myself to the judge."

He left without saluting and crossed the courtyard, a prey to mortal anxiety.

The confidence with which Doña Bernarda declared the fact, and the testimony of Amador, whose weakness Don Damaso was not able to appreciate, gave him desperate perplexity. In spite of the certificate which he had, it appeared that Doña Bernarda and Amador also had some irrefutable proof in their possession, which might make him lose his cause. Under the weight of such fears he returned to his house, his face burning and his mind vacillating in the midst of such terrible doubt.

XXXIV

D on Damaso Encina was not capable of coming to any resolution in his own mind in any affair of importance, so that when he arrived at his house he called his wife and Leonor to consult them about the steps he ought to take in this delicate and difficult crisis.

On hearing the story Doña Engracia nearly had a fit, and in her aristocratic pride she uttered an exclamation which depicted the horror and surprise which in waves of fire sent the blood to her cheeks.

"Married! to a 'china,'" she exclaimed in a choking voice, clasping Diamela convulsively in her arms; and the little dog uttered a howl of pain at this unexpected squeeze, which, joining in a chorus with the voice of its mistress, gave her words noble importance.

Don Damaso took his head between his hands, exclaiming, "But the matrimony is null, we have proofs of it."

"What are you saying? before God, what are you saying?" kept on exclaiming Doña Engracia, again seizing Diamela, who immediately gave a growl of impatience which augmented the desperation of Don Damaso.

This time he turned to Leonor, who remained impassible in the midst of the excitement of her parents.

"Tell her, girl, the marriage is null, and that we have proofs of it."

"That is not enough, that is not enough," replied Doña Engracia, "all society is going to know what has happened, and they will never speak of anything else."

"Papa," said Leonor, "didn't you say that Martin was the one who thought of looking for the proofs that you have?"

"Yes, my little girl, Martin."

"I think that the best thing for us would be to call him, and perhaps he would tell us what is best to be done."

"You are right," replied Don Damaso, as if he had been given an infallible medium to get out of the dilemma.

They sent for Martin, who came after a few moments.

Don Damaso told him about his visit to Doña Bernarda and the difficulty he had found with her and her son.

"And now what are we to do?" were the words with which he finished his story.

"I am persuaded that the whole thing is a farce," replied Martin, "because, according to what you tell me, if they have the proofs they talk about, they would have shown them, and Amador above all, whom I know, would not have been so humble."

"What is necessary is to be quite certain of all this, to have an irrefutable proof of the nullity of the marriage, and to buy these people's silence," said Leonor to Martin, in a determined tone, as if she and the young man alone had to arrange this family affair.

"You solve the difficulty, Señorita," said Martin, "it's a matter of buying them off. I also have a suspicion that Amador is at the bottom of this plot, and I think that money will settle the matter, as you suggest."

"My father," replied Leonor, "is ready as I understand, to spend the necessary amount."

"How much do you think it will be?" exclaimed Don Damaso.

"One thousand pesos will be enough," said Martin.

"Will you take charge of the affair?" asked Don Damaso.

"I will promise to do all that I can to settle it at least," replied Rivas, in a determined tone.

"Excellent!" exclaimed Don Damaso. "I wish you to carry a cheque on sight against my account."

"That is not a bad idea, because it would be valued more than any promise I could give," said Martin.

Don Damaso went to his study to write the cheque.

During this time Doña Engracia was fighting against the suffocation brought on by this news, and Diamela, who tired of her lap, was making terrible efforts to jump on the carpet.

Leonor approached Martin, who remained standing some distance from the sofa on which Doña Engracia and her daughter were seated.

"In a fashion which you are not aware of," she said, I have learnt the secret that you were hiding from me."

"I hope you will do me justice," replied Rivas. "Could divulge another's secret?"

"I understand it," replied the girl, haughtily, "since were more interested in finding it out than in divulging you say."

"Interested! in what way?"

"It has to do with people whom you visited with Augustin."

"It is true that I accompanied him there several times."

"According to what my father says there are two daughters, both beautiful," said Leonor, maliciously, "and I believe Augustin was only courting one of them."

Martin did not know how to justify himself before this direct imputation. We have already said that in Leonor's presence the young man lost his natural serenity. Disturbed by the accusation which was hidden in the words he had just heard, he found no better reply than that which he now dared to give with entire coolness.

"From today I shall never enter the house," he replied. "I don't see how I can offer a better justification."

"You impose an enormous sacrifice upon yourself," said Leonor, with a mocking smile. At that moment Don Damaso returned with the cheque which he had offered to pay, and Leonor went back to her mother's side. Martin listened to the injunctions of Augustin's father without giving them much attention, and went out, more occupied by Leonor's words than by the task which he had just undertaken. Those words and the smile which accompanied them renewed his belief that he was the plaything of Leonor's caprices. He was persuaded that she owned a cruel and empty heart. "She is too proud to allow a man like me without social position to love her," he said to himself with profound bitterness; and on the wings of this sad reflection Martin flew to the immense country in which unhappy lovers breathe the acrid perfume of the pale flowers of melancholy. All suffering has a poetic side for young people's minds. Martin was drowned in the poetry of his unhappiness. Promising to himself to serve Leonor's family in spite of the disdain with which she treated him, he hugged to his hopeless heart those ideas of sacrifice with which unhappy lovers sustain their pain as if to extract advantage from its misfortunes. "To suffer for her," he said, "is it not preferable to a tired-out indifference?" Thus little by little recurred to his mind the distinct duties of true love, and he now found himself inclined to persist in his grief as in a relative good, in place of desiring the calm of indifference, that Lethe, whose magic waters are only begged for by broken hearts. Thinking of Leonor, he left to accomplish his promise made to Augustin's family. "If it turns out well," he thought, "she will be obliged to be grateful to me since she cannot be quite indifferent to the peace of mind of her family."

In Doña Bernarda's house agreement was established after Don Damaso had left. Doña Bernarda, Adelaida and Amador were talking in his room about the visit which they had just received.

"I always feel pleased when those millionaires are made fools of," said the mother, without noticing the preoccupation depicted on the faces of her children.

After gossiping about the affair and building castles in the air—taking the validity of the marriage for certain—Doña Bernarda went away with these words directed to her daughter, who lowered her face to hide the fears which seized her—

"Don't worry, Adelaida, this rich man will have to swallow the pill, even if he makes as many faces as a man being hanged; you are his daughter all the same, and he'll have to take you to his house."

When Adelaida and Amador found themselves alone, they looked fixedly at one another.

"Some one has lent a hand to this," said Amador "because Augustin left to himself is not capable of doubting that he is married; I shouldn't wonder if it is that fool of an Edelmira."

"Amongst other things," said Adelaida, "if they discover the truth they will crush us, as we have no proofs if they take it into court."

"That's so," replied Amador, scratching his head; "they'd make us turn the pancake."

"You have deceived me about this," replied Adelaida, seized with the dread with which the result had filled her; "we must try to smooth it all out."

"Ah! if I have deceived you it was for your good," replied Amador, "and the thing isn't so bad, because the old man is greatly interested, fearing to lose the case. I'm certain that if I was to confess the truth to him he would give me a reward."

"There's nothing more to be done now," replied Adelaida, glad to see herself free from the consequences of the affair at so little cost.

"Don't be a fool," said Amador to her, in a tone of amicable confidence, "the old man offers money if we'll hold our tongues."

"I don't want money," replied Adelaida, proudly, "I want to get out of the quagmire into which you've forced me."

"Very well, I'll pull you out," said Amador.

Adelaida went away after extracting from her brother a promise to do what she asked him.

Amador calculated that when accepting the proposal which Don Damaso had made, he would ask for all the profit for himself that he could derive from the disgraceful catastrophe of his design. "My mother," he said, "will be contented with a little present, because she'll be annoyed when she finds she's been deceived, and I'll take the rest." Animated with this reflection he resolved to write to Augustin and ask for an interview. He was just sitting down and taking up the pen when Martin knocked at the door of his room. As Amador did not know the object of this visit he put on a very serious air when saluting Martin.

"I have come from Don Damaso Encina," said the latter, without accepting the seat which Amador offered him.

"He was here this morning," replied Amador, waiting till Rivas would tell him the message which he had brought.

"He has charged me to see you alone."

"Well, you have me here."

"In giving me this message, he said that I must have nothing to do with Doña Bernarda."

"He is quite right, you know my mother, she suffers no fuss on her shoulders."

"Don Damaso told me that from the little he saw of you, you appeared more reasonable than your mother."

"That is just my mother's way, he saw her here with mustard in her nostrils."

"My object is then to come to an agreement with you about this disagreeable affair with Augustin."

"What other agreement can there be than that which exists?"

"Don Damaso told me that he had represented to you the consequences of this act, if he brought it into court. You have no means of proving the validity of this marriage, and Don Damaso for his part can prove that this is an outrage which merits punishment. If, on the contrary, you confess the nullity of this marriage and offer some proof of security which will set the family of Augustin free from all annoyance about this matter, Don Damaso offers some indemnity for an amicable settlement, because he recognizes the fault of his son, although he could not have committed it without Adelaida's participation."

Amador remained thoughtful for some moments.

"If you had a sister," said Amador, "and any one came—making love to her—as you know, would you not try to punish him?"

"Without doubt."

"Very well, then, that's what I tried to do to Augustin."

"That's all very well, but you carried the thing too far."

"Well, he won't behave like that another time."

"You can finish the affair immediately," said Martin, showing Don Damaso's cheque. "Do you see?"

"What is it?" asked Amador, looking at the paper.

"Yesterday, you asked Augustin for a thousand pesos, and his father now offers you that sum in exchange for a letter."

"For a letter? and what does he want me to write in it?"

"What you have just told me, that you wished to chastise Augustin and got up a mock marriage."

Amador thought he had resisted sufficiently and resolved to end the matter and take Rivas' offer. The cheque for a thousand pesos was sufficiently tempting, and he calculated that if he was obstinate he would not be able to get any better offer than this, so he overcame his reluctance, frightened by the consequences of a law suit. "Very well," he said, grinning, "dictate the letter."

Martin then dictated a letter in which Amador explained the reasons which he had for punishing Augustin. When this explanation was finished—

"Whom did you employ to perform the marriage?" asked Rivas.

"A friend."

Martin continued to dictate, making use of the story which Augustin had told him of the event, with the explanations that Amador gave, besides the name and position of the man who had helped him in the representation of this farce.

"You promise me that there will be no consequences for this?" asked Amador, as he gave the name of the sacristan.

"On my word. You see that this letter is only a document to tranquillize Don Damaso, and that it cannot in any way injure you or any one else. Whoever may read it will see that it's an affair in which a good lesson has been given to a young man who was inclined to go astray."

Amador closed the letter and received the cheque which he devoured with his eyes. "After all," he thought, folding it, "it's not so bad, it has not cost me much."

Rivas returned to Don Damaso's house well pleased because he expected that the outcome of his mission could not fail to recommend him in the eyes of Leonor.

XXXV

Amador guarded, as one guards the relic of a saint, the document that made him master of a thousand pesos, and went to Adelaida's room.

"All is settled," he said to her, telling her of the interview which he had just had with Martin in all its details, except about the cheque which he had in his pocket. A thousand pesos appeared an enormous sum to the son of Doña Bernarda, and the facility with which he had gained it, far from satisfying his ambition, did not suggest to him anything more important than the following reflection which he made aloud.

"If we hadn't sold it, another cock would have crowed. I suppose it is Edelmira who has told it all to Martin."

Adelaida made no answer. She was quite contented with this peaceful issue of an intrigue, the participation in which she had quickly repented, and Amador's suspicions had no weight with her looking at the affair from its pecuniary aspect.

"Nobody could have done it but that fool of an Edelmira," continued Amador, "at, least so it appears to me."

"You'll undertake to tell my mother all that has happened," Adelaida said.

"We must let some days pass. We'll tell her after the 18th, at present it's too soon, and she would get very much annoyed." In this way Amador and Adelaida arranged not to disturb the pleasure that they expected on the annual *fête* days. They knew the violent character of their mother and they rightly supposed that the true account of the affair would annoy her so much, that she would deprive them of the amusements which Amador hoped to procure with the money he had received.

"If I tell it to her now," said Amador, "she will be angry with me, and as for you and Edelmira, not only will she be angry, but she'll shut you up for the 18th and not let you go anywhere." Those only can appreciate the importance of this argument who know the affection that all our social classes have for the civic *fêtes* which solemnize the anniversary of our Independence. "Not to see the 18th" (which is the usual name of the *fêtes*) is a punishment for every young person in Chili, and above all in Santiago, where the splendour and pomp which is given to this occasion attracts the presence of the inhabitants from all around.

But among the personages in the present history, the one who preoccupied himself least with the great day, and most about the advancement of his business, concerning the Hacienda del Roblè, was Don Fidel Elias. Resolved to accept the proposals which he had received through the medium of Don Simon Arenal and not contented with the mediation of a third party, Don Fidel paid a visit to Don Pedro San Luis and had a frank explanation with him about the business, and after a short time he gave his promise that his daughter should marry Rafael the same day that the new lease of Del Roblè was signed.

"You will not object," Don Pedro said to him, "to allow my nephew to visit now in your house."

"Why not? You are aware that it was only by the advice of Don Damaso that I deprived myself of the pleasure of receiving your nephew. When he wishes to present himself at my house he will be most welcome," said Don Fidel.

"It will be my duty," replied Don Pedro, "to pay you a visit, and Rafael will come with me."

In Don Damaso's house at this moment Augustin was waiting with impatience for Rivas' return. Leonor entered her brother's room and renewed the conversation which occupied the whole of the family about the affair of the marriage. Augustin, who had recovered part of his loquacity, told his sister the details of the affair.

"And the other sister, what is she like?" asked Leonor.

"She is extremely beautiful," Augustin replied.

"Didn't you tell me that Martin likes one of them?"

"Yes, this one, Edelmira," said Augustin, who in his gratitude for the favours that Rivas was bestowing on him, did not hesitate to name as a certainty that which was only a suspicion in his mind. Leonor remained thoughtful.

"Here is Martin," exclaimed the dandy, as he perceived Rivas crossing the courtyard in the direction of Don Damaso's study. Augustin called him, and Rivas entered the room. Leonor and Augustin asked him at the same moment—

"How did you get on?"

"It was quite all right," answered Martin. "I have here with me a letter which will calm all your uneasiness." As he said this he presented Leonor with the letter of Amador Molina.

"Am I to read it?" asked the girl, "is it not to be hidden from me? Tell me this," she added, looking at her brother, "why is this gentleman so reserved with me?"

"Hurry, read the letter, little sister," exclaimed Augustin. "Je tremble d'impatience."

"It appears your French is coming back to you," exclaimed Leonor, laughing.

"It is that Martin's news gives me *transportes de joie*," said the dandy, embracing her. Leonor began to read the letter, while at each paragraph Augustin exclaimed—

"Oh! perfecto, perfecto."

"They told me that this man was uneducated," said Leonor, after reading the letter, "but this letter is very well written."

"Yes, sister," replied Augustin, "I don't know how it has happened, because Amador can call himself *un sintique pur sang.*"

"Then you must have dictated the letter," said Leonor, laughing at Augustin's phrase, and then, looking at Rivas maliciously, she added—

"You have seen at the same time the Señorita Edelmira?"

"Oh! Ah!" exclaimed Augustin, whose gaiety had increased with the reading of the letter. "Either it is Mademoiselle Edelmira or some one who was very close to her; isn't that so, Martin?"

"Amador wrote in my presence," replied Martin, turning scarlet.

"That doesn't mean anything," said Augustin, "the principal thing is that *je redeviens garçon.*"

"How well you know the language," said Leonor to him.

The letter was carried by Leonor and Augustin to Don Damaso, who was talking to Doña Engracia, whilst Diamela was cutting capers on the carpet. During the reading of the letter Don Damaso's face was illuminated with joy, each phrase producing on it the same effects as the beams of the sun, when, in the morning, his rays spread little by little over the sleeping prairie. Doña Engracia in expressing her emotion had seized upon Diamela, whom she furiously squeezed each time that her husband gave a nod of approval.

"Papa," said Leonor, "I think that the letter has been dictated by Martin. Don't you find it well written?"

"You are right. Francisca is right in saying that she is fond of reading. Style is the man, as some one said—Finally nothing matters. Thanks to Martin everything is settled; that young fellow is invaluable. Look here, Leonor, you must make him accept some reward. I wouldn't deny him anything he wished."

"We shall see," answered the girl; "it doesn't seem to me very easy."

Augustin was then called by order of Don Damaso and received a severe reprimand for his conduct.

"What do you expect, papa," said the young man, confusedly, "youth must have its fling."

"That's all very well, but let it fling in some other way," replied Don Damaso, with the gravity of a Figaro. Then he added in a low voice, turning towards Doña Engracia, "The best thing to do is to try and get him married. Fidel's proposition arrives most opportunely."

La Señora gave Diamela a furtive squeeze, which expressed the sentiments of every mother when she thinks of her son entering the bonds of Hymen.

In the evening Martin hoped in vain for one of those conversations to the sound of the piano, which at the same time were his delight and his martyrdom, but Leonor played without calling him, and it was Emilio Mendoza who turned over the leaves of the music. There arrived a moment in which Augustin, who was seated beside Rivas, called his sister, who left the piano. "Come and help me to cheer up Martin," he said to her, "he seems to be broken hearted."

"Without doubt," replied Leonor, "he is beginning to feel the vexation of the promise that he made, probably without thinking."

"What promise, Señorita?" asked Rivas.

"That of never again entering the *Señorita* Molina's house," said Leonor, haughtily, her voice accentuating the word that we have put in italics.

"I made the promise to myself and I could break it without hurting any one," replied Martin, piqued.

"I don't believe it. How can you sustain such intentions?"

"What intentions are these?" asked Augustin, "I want to know; everything about this friend interests me now."

"One of his intentions is never to fall in love, for example," replied Leonor.

"Vraiment, mon cher?" said the dandy.

"Nevertheless it appears that the Señorita Molina has shaken his resolution," replied Leonor, in a mocking tone, before Rivas could answer Augustin's question; and with these words the girl turned her back and went to sit down beside her mother.

"That Leonor is full of perversity," said Augustin, as his sister withdrew.

"She is cruel," said Martin to himself, in deep depression; and he left the salon.

On that same night took place the visit of Rafael with Don Pedro to Matilde's house. The lovers conversed about the days that had passed when they were absent from each other. Don Fidel gave a cordial greeting to Don Pedro's nephew, all the more cordial on account of the benefits that he expected from the Del Roblè business, and Doña Francisca found some moments for a conversation with Rafael, in which she gave free rein to her romanticism, fed by the reading of George Sand. "The wife of modern civilization," she said to him under the influence of the theories of her favourite author, "is no less a slave than she was in pagan times. She resembles a flower which only lives when touched by rays of love," she added with enthusiasm, "man has abused his strength to restrict the liberty of her heart. You will understand this because you have given proofs through constancy of possessing a soul, superior to those that we meet with daily."

And San Luis, floating with sails spread over the sea of love's illusions, took this phrase seriously and went on with the conversation in the same romantic tone as his interlocutor. In another corner of the room San Luis' uncle said to Don Fidel, "Could we not have this union a month sooner?—in that case I could occupy myself with Rafael's future as he is to be a partner with my son." Thus it was arranged that the marriage would take place in the middle of the coming month of October; whilst the young people were forgetting the whole world in their love. After the visitors had left Doña Francisca lent her ear to the projects of her husband about the new works which he was going to undertake at Del Roblè, counting on the new lease. It was a great contrast to her poetic imagination to pass from theories about the emancipation of women to counting the stitches of her knitting. She had seized with such avidity the theories of her favourite author. She contented herself with recommending between two yawns to Don Fidel that he ought to pay a visit to her brother, and then retired with her daughter.

The following day Don Fidel arrived at Don Damaso's house just as the family were going out of the dining-room.

"Uncle, enchanté de vous voir," said Augustin, saluting Don Fidel. The latter called Don Damaso aside, and after some preface, told him the object of his visit, which disturbed the thoughts of his brother-in-law, whose mind was occupied with the idea of settling Augustin.

XXXVI

The first day of the great *fête* arrived, with its decoration of the houses, its flags on the street doors, and its salvos of artillery from the fortress of Hidalgo. The hearts of the citizens beat high at the idea of putting on martial clothes and showing themselves off before the fair sex. The hearts of the latter beat high with the prospect of the new dresses, the promenades, and the amusements. Let us think of the patriotic toasts that were drunk at the banquet in the evening when the national song resounded in all the streets of the city, and Santiago shook off its habitual lethargy and returned again to the gaiety with which they celebrate every anniversary of Independence. But the days of the 17th and 18th of this glorious month are no more than a prelude to the ardent enthusiasm with which the Santiagons appear to wish to recover the time lost during the rest of the year. Cannonades at the dawn of day, the national songs sung by the girls of every school (assisted by the strange-looking provincials who arrive at the capital intending not to lose a moment of the 18th), the formation of troops in the Plaza, and the blessing in the Cathedral, the procession to the Alemada, the fireworks and the theatre, are only the precursors of the great celebration of the 19th day—the Procession to the Pampilla. Santiago on this day is not the worthy daughter of the serious man who founded her, now she loses the affected Spanish gravity which characterizes her during the rest of the year, she is a mad city that with flying steps pursues the pleasures of the popular festival.

On the 19th of September, Santiago laughs, rides on horseback, wears extraordinary gay clothes, sings the story of the Independence, drives about in ornamental carriages and twangs the guitar, whilst quaffing copious libations. Old habits and modern customs elbow each other everywhere and regard each other as sisters, tolerate each other's respective weaknesses, and unite their voices to shout hymns to their country, the abode of Liberty. A minute description of the September *fêtes* would be too long a digression and would lose the attraction of novelty for Santiagons: the inhabitants of the provinces know it well enough from stories of travellers, and also because they themselves celebrate the festival in imitation of the capital. We shall omit, then, this description and confine ourselves to the incidents of our story. At the end of the speeches on the 18th, the waning light foretold the beginning of the fireworks. When one of these rockets went up very high it was saluted by the multitude assembled on the Plaza with a thousand exclamations of "las" and "los," "Oh! ilos," "Ah!" The sovereign public formed the chorus of admiration. One group was composed of the family of Doña Bernarda and her friends, discussing the merit of each rocket and prodigal of salutes to the passers-by with whom they were acquainted. Amador gave his arm to Doña Bernarda, Adelaida had taken that of a friend, and Edelmira, against her will, had accepted that of Ricardo Castanos, who took advantage of the occasion to speak to the girl of his undying love. Just then another group entered the Plaza, it was composed of the families of Don Damaso and Don Fidel. Leonor had a fancy to go to the fireworks and it was necessary to accompany her. Doña Engracia and her husband completed the retinue of her followers, having on their left hand a servant who carried Diamela in his arms. Further off, Matilde and Rafael walked together in loving conversation, Leonor and Augustin chatting on indifferent matters, and Rivas, who had given his arm to Doña Francisca, who was trying to get up a romantic conversation with him. Augustin, not content that only the people close to him should hear him, gave in a very loud voice a description of the fireworks in Paris. The company found themselves close to the place occupied by the family of Doña Bernarda.

"Oh! in Paris a '*feu d'artifice*' is a beautiful thing," exclaimed Augustin, just at a moment when four "trees" threw their burning rockets into the air at the same time.

"Oh! ah!" immediately exclaimed the multitude, as a signal of approving admiration.

"Aie! it's coming! Look after Diamela!" shrieked Doña Engracia, on seeing one of the rockets from the nearest tree arriving in their direction. The disturbance increased the confusion which the arrival introduced into the group of spectators, through whom it passed with the velocity of light.

"How they would applaud if they were to see the '*bouquet*' in Paris!" said Augustin. "It is something magnificent."

"Oh! let us get away from this," exclaimed Doña Engracia, on seeing the imminent peril which Diamela had just escaped. "Poor little thing," she added, taking the dog in her arms, "you are trembling like a bird."

In the midst of all this Doña Francisca did not abandon her intention of having a romantic conversation with Rivas.

"I never feel myself so much alone," she said to Rivas, "as in the middle of the jostling of a multitude. When one lives for the mind, all amusements seem insipid."

A terrible shower of sparks which passed over the heads of the family saved Martin the trouble of replying.

"Here you will have a little shelter," said Doña Engracia, hiding Diamela under her cloak. To calm the señora's fears the company went to a safer place, passing before Doña Bernarda and her belongings.

"Who is that walking with Rafael?" asked Doña Bernarda.

"It's the daughter of Don Fidel Elias," replied Amador; "how proudly he goes by."

"And doesn't even salute!" replied Doña Bernarda.

Adelaida turned pale on seeing Matilde and Rafael pass beside her. Rafael's story was well known to her, so she could well imagine the import of what she saw.

"Look, look," said Augustin to Leonor, pointing out Adelaida, "that is the girl they wanted to marry me to."

"And the other is the sister?" asked Leonor.

"Yes."

"She is one that Martin loves?"

"The same."

"She's pretty," said Leonor.

Martin passed with his companion, giving a slight bow to the Molinas, and Edelmira sighed as she replied to it.

"If I imagined that you liked this young Rivas," the official said to her, "I would have vengeance on him."

"Augustin didn't look at us either," said Doña Bernarda. "The little Frenchman wished to show his disdain."

The volcanos which burst out at this moment drew Doña Bernarda's attention to them. The fireworks terminated by the traditional Castle which was attacked by ships as usual. No incident occurred that relates to the persons in this story, some of whom went peaceably back to their houses, but others reflected about the encounter which had taken place. Doña Bernarda could not endure the idea that Augustin had shown such indifference and contempt for her family. "For very little more," she said, "I would publish everywhere that he is married to my daughter and set fire to Troy!"

Amador tried to calm her, assuring her that all would be set right after the *fêtes* of the 18th.

At the theatre, Martin, through an opera glass, was a witness of the admiration that the beauty of Leonor excited in the audience. Almost all eyes were turned to the box in which the girl displayed her wonderful beauty, dressed in luxurious elegance. The praises of Leonor's beauty from those who surrounded him, soothed his mind, which sank into a soft melancholy. He heard in the strains of the music and the murmur of the audience a certain friendly voice, child of his illusion, which prophesied the happiness of being loved some day by this being, so favoured by nature. Similar to those mirages of beautiful oases offered to the traveller's eyes by an optical illusion, this presage of love disappeared before Rivas when he tried to give it the form of reality, because then he was obliged to consider the distance that separated him from Leonor, and alienating itself from the present it dispersed itself vaguely and confusedly in the shadows of a distant future. When her first gratification at her triumph had passed, Leonor had thought of Martin. She had a certain proud satisfaction at the idea which occurred to her at this moment, of disdaining the admiration of all to devote herself to a poor and obscure young man, who could be so elevated by her love as to become the envy of the most fashionable and presumptuous men in this perfumed assembly. This thought naturally arose from her capricious spirit, fond of contrasts. Whilst abandoning herself to this idea, Leonor sought for Martin with her eyes and was not long in finding him. A look of fire responded to her glance and made her blush. Each beat of her heart which announced that love had invaded it was a surprise, as we have already seen, to Leonor's pride. The impression that Rivas' glance gave her was sufficient to make her proudly raise her head and look haughtily on the assembly as if defying its criticism. She still thought to herself at this moment that if she chose she could make Martin a happier man than any of those who were looking at her (without thinking that this reflection alone argued against her pretended independence). The first and the second acts passed whilst Leonor struggled without knowing it between her love and her pride. At the lowering of the drop scene at the second act, she turned and sought Martin's eyes and made him a signal to come to her box, a signal that the young man did not allow to be repeated. Leonor left her first seat and occupied one in the corner of the box, leaving a vacant one at her side, which she offered to Martin.

"It appears," she said to him, "that you are not amusing yourself much tonight."

"I, Señorita!" exclaimed the young man, "what makes you think so?"

"You seem thoughtful. Do you know what I imagine?"

"No."

"That you have repented of the promise that you made the other day in my presence."

"I don't remember any promise."

"That you would not go to the house of the Señoritas Molina."

"I'm afraid I must contradict you," replied Rivas, in the same laughing tone in which Leonor had spoken, "for I assure you that I had not even remembered that I had made such a promise, which is a proof that it cost me very little to keep it."

"I saw the girl in the Plaza, and I admire your taste; she is pretty."

"For such sincere praise of the beauty of a girl," said Martin, "one must be situated like you."

"Why?" asked Leonor, not following the drift of this remark.

"Because only those who are certain of the superiority of their beauty allow beauty in others," replied the young man.

"I see that you're going to learn the language of compliments," said Leonor, in a serious tone. Her pride spoke in this tone, for she had no desire that the young man should escape from his *rôle* of timid and respectful admirer. This very pride made her turn her haughty and queenly glance on Martin and ask him—

"Do you imagine that I am the rival of this girl?"

When Rivas received this glance his heart sank, and the thought returned to him that under her magnificent exterior of beauty, this strange creature hid a cruel and scoffing disposition.

"I had no such idea," he said, with melancholy dignity, "and I feel in my soul the interpretation that you have put on my words."

From the gallery in the theatre in which the Molina family occupied different seats, Edelmira had seen Martin come in and sit down beside Leonor.

"I'm certain that Martin is in love with that Señorita," said the official of police to Edelmira (he had not left her a moment).

Edelmira gave another sigh, thinking that in this observation her jealous lover was perhaps correct. At the same time Doña Bernarda said to her eldest daughter—

"Look, Adelaida, the next 18th you'll also be seated in that box with your little Frenchman."

After Martin's reply, Leonor remained thoughtful, and the young man retired after a few moments.

"I've been very severe," thought Leonor, seeing him go away, and proposing to efface the impression which her words must have left in Rivas' mind when they would be taking tea on their return from the theatre. But Martin did not return to her box, neither did Leonor find him in the salon when they arrived at the house.

"Has Martin arrived?" she asked the servant who carried in the tea-tray.

"He returned some time ago, Señorita," she replied.

When she lay down Leonor forgot the triumphs of the theatre, the flattering words with which the various young men had ministered to her vanity during the night, the overwhelming compliments of Emelio Mendoza, and the timid adoration of the wealthy Clementi Valencia: she only thought of the dignity with which Martin had replied to her glance of disdain.

"I've been very severe," she repeated to herself, "he has suffered, but he has not been humiliated."

Her proud temper could not refuse its admiration on encountering more dignity in the poor provincial than in the rich dandies of the capital; always ready to bow to her caprices.

XXXVII

D rawn by a yoke of oxen, a long low cart, with a bed coverlet hung instead of a curtain and an awning of "tortora," appeared upon the road to La Pampilla on the morning of the 19th of September.

In this cart, seated upon pillows and cushions, was the Molina family in happy chat with some of their friends.

Doña Bernarda leant her right hand on a basket of cold viands and her left on another basket containing bottles. Her daughters were opposite her, and reclining beside Edelmira was the official, Ricardo Castanos, who by special permission of his chief had obtained a holiday for the day; beside Adelaida was another gallant, and seated in the front over the "pertigo," with both legs hanging down, and a guitar in his arms, Amador Molina completed this picture so characteristic of the 19th of September.

The song which he sang was *apropos* to the occasion, and ended with the verse—

"Drive, drive, carman."

The others repeated this in chorus, imitating with their mouths and their hands the sound of trotting, whilst they swallowed repeated glasses of punch prepared beforehand by the clever hands of Amador.

We shall not follow the family of Doña Bernarda on its way, but when they arrived at the Campo del Marte they were stationed in one of the streets which are in front of the penitentiary prison, and surrounded by the numerous carts of families who arrived from the country on this day.

In the courtyard of Don Damaso Encina's house, two beautiful horses pawed the ground impatiently with their hoofs, and Rivas and Augustin mounted them at two o'clock in the afternoon.

The two young men arrived at the Alemada by the Calle de la Bandera and followed the crowd of carriages, foot-passengers, and riders, going in the direction of the Campo del Marte.

"You must cheer up," said Augustin to Martin, whilst he made his horse caracole to show his skill to the spectators who stood about in the doors of the street and in the windows of the houses of the Alemada; and this phrase with which Augustin tried to animate Rivas was only a continuation of the reiterated efforts with which he had conquered his friend's objections to accompany him to the *fête*.

"Are the family coming to the Campo?" asked Martin.

"I think not," answered Augustin, "mama is afraid to go out today."

Meanwhile the Molina family, seated, as we have said, in one of the streets with the long cars, entered ardently into the amusements of the day. The Zamacuecas succeeded one another and with them abundant libations which notably increased the patriotic enthusiasm of the dancers.

Amador was the life of the party, Doña Bernarda drank glass after glass to the health of the dancers; the official of police improvised gallant phrases in honour of Edelmira, and various inquisitive people who had surrounded the cart applauded each dance and drank with many compliments and loud laughter. In a word, animation was written on all faces except Edelmira's, who was unwillingly present at a scene so contrary to her delicate and refined instincts.

But Ricardo Castanos did not allow himself to be daunted by the indifference with which his beloved regarded the general gaiety, and as if in a rapture of love, he tried to take Edelmira's hand. Doña Bernarda caught him as she was swallowing a glass of mistela, and exclaimed between laughter and vexation—

"Look here, little official, if you take too much upon yourself I'll have you up in the 'plenipotentiary' which is opposite."

Great applause celebrated this threat, which Doña Bernarda accompanied by a gesture, pointing out the penitentiary prison to which the people commonly gave the name by which the señora had designated it.

This applause drew the attention of Augustin and Rivas, who at this moment passed the cart and who did not recognize the Molina family on account of the people who surrounded them.

"They seem to be amusing themselves here," said Augustin, pricking his horse.

Martin followed him closely.

Doña Bernarda saw on the moment the two young men, and called out to them—

"Here is the little Frenchman! Señor Martin Rivas, how are you? Tonight you are coming to us, we're going to have great fun; do you know our friends?"

"Is it possible, Señora," said the dandy, with feigned surprise, "I had not the honour of seeing you. Tonight, did you say?"

"Yes, yes, don't go on pretending," said Doña Bernarda.

"I give you my word of honour that—"

"Don't give me any words. Look here," she added, presenting him with a glass; and in a lower tone, "Drink the health of your wife. When is your papa going to acknowledge the marriage?"

Amador approached as soon as he saw the young men, and overheard his mother's words, but had not time to prevent Augustin replying.

"I understand that all that is settled, and papa thinks so also."

"Settled! what is the meaning of this?" asked Doña Bernarda of her son.

"Yes, mother," replied Amador, "we'll speak of this afterwards, but we are here for amusement now."

"Very well, then," exclaimed Doña Bernarda, slightly elevated by the wine, "so much the better; this little chap is one of the family, and he must condescend to amuse himself with us."

"I feel no desire to do so," said Augustin, to whom Amador was making signals not to contradict his mother.

"Whether you desire or not doesn't matter," said Doña Bernarda, seizing the reins of Augustin's horse, "are you of the family or not? Who are you, then?"

The tone in which Doña Bernarda uttered these words, showed Amador that his secret was in danger, and it was absolutely necessary to calm his mother, so that he could explain his arrangement with Martin about the supposed marriage under more propitious circumstances.

"Up to the present my mother knows nothing," he said in Augustin's ear, "and if you don't alight she is capable of making a row."

"I can't get down," said Augustin, who did not like to show himself in public with such company.

Those who had surrounded the group of the Molina family had almost all left when the dance ceased.

All this time Doña Bernarda had not let go the reins of Augustin's horse, and was insisting that he should get down.

"Oblige me by asking him to get down," said Amador to Martin, "do me this service."

Martin saw that to calm Doña Bernarda it was necessary to get down, and the words Edelmira said to him at this moment, contributed to his decision.

"Are you not ashamed of what is going on here?"

"Get down, little Frenchman," exclaimed Doña Bernarda, "if you don't get down I'm going to be furious."

Martin dismounted and Augustin followed his example and took the glass that Doña Bernarda presented to him.

At this moment Ricardo Castanos broke his glass on the edge of the cart because Edelmira was talking to Martin.

"You have forgotten us," said the girl to him with a glance in which could be traced the progress which love had made in her heart during his absence.

"I have not forgotten you," replied the latter, "but in order to tranquillize Augustin's family I promised not to return to your house."

"So that I shall have to suffer for the faults of others?" exclaimed Edelmira, ingenuously.

"You! why?" asked the young man, "why should you suffer?"

"More than you could imagine," replied the girl, blushing. "In these last few days I have learned to know you."

Martin had not time to reply, for his eyes opened in surprise at sight of a carriage which drew up in front of them.

In this carriage were Leonor and Don Damaso.

Augustin turned the colour of cochineal and did not know which way to look.

Don Damaso made him a signal to approach.

"You with these people!" he said to him.

"Papa, I'm going to explain it!" replied the overwhelmed dandy.

"Mount your horse and follow us," replied Don Damaso, in a severe tone.

Leonor leaned back in the carriage after giving Augustin a look of profound contempt.

At the same time Edelmira said to Martin, "You have told me that you have confidence in me."

"It is true," replied Martin, making heroic efforts to hide his shame and desperation.

"Do you love this señorita?" asked Edelmira, fixing on the young man an ardent gaze, and her voice trembling with emotion.

"What a question!" exclaimed Martin, trying to smile, "that would be looking very high."

"Come on, come on," said Augustin to him, "papa says we must follow him."

And after giving some entangled excuses they mounted their horses and followed Don Damaso's carriage at a gallop.

"I've got to know what it is all about," said Doña Bernarda to herself.

Edelmira repressed a tear which came to her eyes, and took the guitar which Amador presented to her that she might play a Zamacueca.

"Viva la patria!" exclaimed Amador, in order to distract his mother's ideas.

"Que viva!" responded the voices of those who surrounded the cart on foot and on horseback, and this patriotic ovation resounded in the midst of the quick-firing of the troops and the noise of the neighbouring "Chinganas," and sounded like a sarcasm in Martin's ears, who went away at a gallop, cursing his star for the disagreeable surprise which it had prepared for him.

In the midst of all this Edelmira, with death in her heart, mechanically sang the verses of the Zamacueca, and at the sound the dances and the gaiety began again, and laughter followed, and the libations continued until the retirement of the troops signalled to those in the carts that the hour had come to leave the scene of their annual festivities.

XXXVIII

The presence of Leonor in the Campo del Marte surprised the two young men the more, because in the morning she had said at breakfast that she was going alone to the Alemada.

Such had been in effect Leonor's intention on the morning of this day. After her conversation with Rivas in the theatre and her feeling that she had treated him with too much severity she felt a desire to be quite alone and to meditate over the state of her heart, a state peculiar to the new phase which had by degrees penetrated her mind, until now a slave to the frivolous occupations of the mechanical existence in which the greater part of the Chilian women must pass the most beautiful years of their life. On consideration we do not find the word "mechanical" misplaced as qualifying the kind of life led by our beautiful compatriot. Leonor, like the rest of them, without any further knowledge than that acquired at school, believed that the principal occupation of those of her sex was to be versed in accomplishments, and in the art of dress, only having the narrow outlook of a circumscribed and confined existence. Her natural haughtiness inspired her later with a desire to triumph in this arena and to shine in elegance as she already shone in beauty; she was the queen of fashion and the heroine of many *fêtes*. These triumphs were enough for her life as long as her heart remained unawakened to the exciting influences of its true destiny. But we have seen that satiety had struck, albeit gently, at her heart, and we have also followed step by step the metamorphosis of her being since she had known Martin. Leonor had arrived at the point of thinking of him in the morning after having done so the greater part of the night. It appeared to her that her plan of enslaving Martin was a cruel pastime, and she was convinced of many arguments which created the necessity within her of showing herself repentant for her sarcastic words. In these meditations, during which her mind was like a spider hanging on its threads, going up and down repeatedly, Leonor passed the hour after she had said she would not go to the Pampilla.

All strong minds are generally impatient, and Leonor found that it would be a century between her design and its execution if she had to wait until the evening to see Martin, and brighten his sadness with a look or a condolatory word. In love every delay is counted a century, the heart is so impatient when it is in the full flush of passion that it finds the ordinary mediums with which we understand time impossible.

So Leonor decided to efface this century. Her determination to go to the Campo del Marte was an order for Don Damaso, as were all the wishes of his daughter. So here we have the reasons why Leonor happened to meet Martin and her brother when they had dismounted from horseback.

When Leonor saw Rivas conversing with Edelmira she felt a new experience; that of a shaft of ice piercing her heart. With a firm intention of despising him and thinking no more about him, she thought of nothing else during the drive to the Alemada. Why did Martin appear more interesting to her since she had discovered that another woman, young and beautiful, loved him? Leonor could not explain this enigma. Meantime before her eyes passed the groups of people who come and go in the Alemada on the evening of the 19th September. The women decked out in their new clothes, the troops that march to the sound of martial music in the middle of the street, and the figures of the "civicos" of Renca and Nuñoa in the side streets. Her ideas were as mingled as the mass of human beings who passed before her eyes. She felt herself sad for the first time in her life, and returned home in a bad humour.

That night Martin was not at the theatre and Leonor heard with disgust her brother's explanation to Don Damaso of the scene at the cart. In the midst of a long conversation which took place in the theatre with Matilde and Rafael about the generalities of love she could not deliver her mind from the idea that Martin, breaking his promise, gave up the theatre for Doña Bernarda's house. When she lay down she had thought so much over this fact that her pride was not roused at the idea of having a girl of the lower class for a rival; so that the following day, having heard from Augustin that Rivas was going to breakfast with Rafael San Luis, she felt as if the very air of the dining-room where she had hoped to see him was frozen.

Martin had sought a pretext to absent himself because he did not dare to appear before Leonor after what had occurred in the Pampilla.

When Rivas had returned from Rafael's house, Augustin said to him—

"Leonor is the one who least believes in the excuses I've given; you must convince her, because whatever she believes my father believes, and this is a serious matter for me."

At the dinner that evening Martin had a real surprise which left him very perplexed for some moments as to what he was to think about it. This surprise was occasioned by the natural and amiable manner in which Leonor saluted him and spoke to him on several occasions. At the end of his reflections Rivas concluded by this sad deduction, common to a lover who does not think his love is returned.

"She looks on me with sufficient contempt, but is not in the humour to laugh at me."

"Now is the opportunity to justify me," said Augustin, as they went out of the dining-room.

"I hardly dare," replied Rivas, who, though desiring to talk with the girl, felt the necessity for some one to encourage him.

"Do me this favour," replied the dandy; "she quite likes you. Look here, this morning she asked me why you weren't at the theatre last night."

Saying this, Augustin brought his friend into the salon, where Leonor was playing the piano.

We have seen that Martin, in spite of his lover-like timidity, always felt his energy return in the presence of difficulties. On this occasion he recovered strength on finding himself alone with Leonor, since Augustin led him up to the piano and then went away to turn over the leaves of a book at the table in the middle of the room.

"I did not see you last night at the theatre," said Leonor, so quietly that the young man was completely tranquillized.

"I was somewhat tired after the day," he answered.

Leonor looked at him maliciously, but she said, "You were able to rest at the Pampilla where you found a good place to do so."

"Augustin told me that you did not appear to give much credit to the explanation which he gave of our motives for taking this step."

"Which you found sufficiently awkward, isn't that true?"

"Oh! what a bad opinion of us!"

"No, you may have full justice for I recognize the merit of your inventive powers."

"How so, Señorita?"

"Because, finding that the explanation given by Augustin was ingenious, I could only attribute it to you, and I naturally think it is yours."

"However flattering this may be to my capacity, I cannot accept it. Augustin has told no more than the truth about what happened."

"But there was something else that I saw, and that you have not explained."

"What is it?"

"A conversation, apparently a very tender one, that you were holding with the Señorita Edelmira."

"Since you do me the honour of remembering anything that concerns me, will you allow me to answer with entire frankness?"

"Is it a secret?" asked Leonor, with an indefinable air of repressed disquietude and simulated indifference.

"No, Señorita, an explanation of what you saw."

"I know beforehand that the explanation will be satisfactory, because I'm acquainted with your powers of invention."

"You will not be able to say that after you have heard me."

"Let us see."

"It is true that I was talking with interest yesterday, when you saw me beside Edelmira."

"Ah! now I see that you are going to place confidence in me and tell me your secrets," said Leonor, in a strained tone, and without looking at Rivas.

One would have said that these words left her lips after a struggle with the quickening beats of her heart. A beautiful pendant of cameos surrounded with pearls which encircled her neck by a fine chain, rose and fell like a little boat which is tossing on the waves, so plain was the oppression of her laboured breathing as she spoke.

"It is not a secret, Señorita, that I desire to tell you; it is, as I have said, a trifle—to be quite frank."

"Let us hear, then; I'm listening."

"The interest which I had and will always have in this girl, Señorita, owes its birth to the true appreciation which I have conceived for her character."

"Take care, you speak with too much warmth of this appreciation."

"I am strong in my likings, Señorita."

"Therefore I say, take care; they say that liking quickly changes into love."

"I'm not afraid."

"Why do you say so?"

"Because I know that I shall never love her."

"You are very presumptuous, Martin," said Leonor, in a grave tone, and looking at him with a smile at the same time.

"Why, Señorita?"

"Because you confide too much in the strength of your will."

"How much I wish I could struggle against it," replied Rivas, in a sincere accent; "if I could conquer my will I would be very happy."

Leonor avoided following the conversation over this ground as a flower-gatherer abandons the attractive beauty of the rose for fear of the thorns, and contents himself with the more modest flowers that surround him in the garden.

"Let us see," she said to him, "be as frank as you say you are."

"Put me to the test."

"Does this girl love you?"

Across the smile with which Leonor accompanied this question there was a look of anxiety in her appearance which could only have been guessed at by more expert eyes than Martin's.

"I don't think so, Señorita," answered Martin, in a decided tone.

"Are you sincere? for Augustin told me she did."

"I know nothing about it, and even with the fear of giving you a poor idea of my modesty, I can tell you that I would regret it if it was so."

"Why?"

"For the same reason that you have censured me with presumption, because I never could love her."

"Ah! you are looking higher, and think her of too inferior a position."

"That is not the case; I am an advocate for the independence of the heart. Before love social equalities are of no value."

"Then the reason why you don't love this girl is a mystery."

"No, Señorita, it is not a mystery."

Leonor resolved to abandon this side of the conversation because the rude question occurred to her mind which might explain the cause of which he spoke—

"Then are you in love with another?"

But she did not ask this question because, as it happened, a moment before she recalled something she had to do—a requital.

"Last night," she said to the young man, "I was not very amiable to you."

"I have studied much, Señorita," said Rivas, sadly, "how I may not be displeasing to you when I have the honour of speaking to you, and I confess that I have been many times unfortunate."

"Are you fixed in this idea?" said the girl, with studied surprise.

"They are incidents of much importance to me, Señorita," said Martin, in a voice of emotion.

The cameo pendant began again to agitate like a little boat on the waves.

At the same time Leonor began to play a bar of the waltz which she knew from memory, and fixed her eyes on the music before her.

"You have a sufficiently happy memory," she said, after many times repeating the bar—over which she stumbled.

"It is not the memory, Señorita, it is the constant fear of displeasing you."

"*Por Deos!* do you think I'm so bad-tempered?" exclaimed Leonor, pretending surprise to hide her agitation.

"It is only that I am distrustful of myself, Señorita."

"I can only repeat what I have said before, I see no reason for this want of confidence. If you really displeased me, would I not avoid all conversation with you?"

These words were accompanied by the last bars of the waltz which Leonor played before their turn came. Her hands trembled as she closed the piano, and without saying anything more she turned to the table beside which Augustin was seated turning over the leaves of the book.

Martin, more agitated than she, remained in the same place that he had occupied during the conversation. It appeared to him that a ray of light had suddenly come to illuminate his mind, only to leave it in more obscurity afterwards. His heart was afraid to interpret in favour of his love the light words which he had heard. He felt as if on the edge of an abyss. She was here, majestic and haughty as ever, ideally beautiful, rich, admired by all.

"What *madness!*" he said, with ice in his bosom, already oppressed by the violent beatings of his heart.

Augustin turned to Leonor.

"I hope that Martin has been able to convince you, little sister," he said, affectionately squeezing the girl's waist with both hands.

"About what?" asked Leonor, getting scarlet.

It would appear that this question coincided in a manner with something that was preoccupying her at this moment.

"That it was impossible to resist, and we were obliged to dismount," replied Augustin.

"Ah! yes, exactly," answered the girl, leaving the room.

"I'm glad," said Augustin to Rivas; "she will convince papa and make everything all right for me."

XXXIX

W hen the fumes of the liquor in Doña Bernarda Coldero's brain were dissipated after the *fête* at the Campo del Marte on the 19th, she began to reflect the following morning on Augustin's words. From these she clearly gathered that there existed some arrangement of the affair of the marriage, and this idea was corroborated by the evasive replies which Amador had given. What was this arrangement? and why were its clauses hidden from her—the mother of the girl? were the questions which arose in the mind of Doña Bernarda after much meditation, awakening her curiosity and giving rise to a firm determination to solve this seeming enigma and not to allow, as she said, "that they would make a fool of me and try to leave me with my finger in my mouth."

In effect she asked her son, who, desirous to smooth over as much as possible the explanation of the affair (thinking that the annoyance of his mother would diminish in proportion to the length of time that he was able to put her off), replied with evasive explanations which, far from disarming her suspicious, only increased them.

Doña Bernarda reiterated her questions many times; but firm in his ideas, Amador replied with new subterfuges, pretending all the time to speak plainly, but always vague about the truth of the affair. As some days passed without Doña Bernarda renewing her inquiries, the young man persuaded himself that a system of gradual explanation was the best way to inform his mother of what had occurred, so that the magnitude of the discovery would not irritate her temper, which he feared, with reason, might be roused if he revealed without a preface the deceit by which, in order to realize his plan, she had been made the victim.

But Doña Bernarda Coldero was not one of those whose curiosity can be satisfied with incomplete explanations, so that, far from contenting herself with what Amador told her, she resolved to strike a blow which she considered masterly, and which should serve effectively for the final settlement of the matter.

Wearing her mantilla she went out of her house one day in the beginning of October, resolved to have an interview with the father of the man whom she supposed to be her son-in-law. She had thought over this step for many days, and also thought over the words she would speak during this interview, and the firmness with which she meant to dispose of any other proposition for the future than that which was based upon the recognition of the marriage by the whole family of Don Damaso, who, being rich, should receive them in his house, and give them, as she said, "house and table."

Don Damaso offered her a seat, and Doña Bernarda began the conversation.

"I've come here, sir," she said, "about a little affair that you know of."

"Truly, señora," replied Don Damaso, "I do not know to what affair you allude?"

"What! you don't know? What other one could there be? The little affair then."

"Have the kindness to explain yourself."

"Do you tell me, Señor, that you have forgotten that your son is married to my daughter!"

"Señora," said Don Damaso, with surprise, "it is an extraordinary thing that you should come to speak to me of this affair."

"And what then? Who do you wish to speak to you about it? Am I not the mother? What nonsense! What do you expect, then?"

As may be imagined, Doña Bernarda displayed from the beginning of the conversation the energy and clearness with which she had determined to end the business.

"It's not a question of whether you are the mother or not, nobody denies that," replied Don Damaso, somewhat uneasy at the questions and explanations of his interlocutor; "it seems strange to me that you appear not to know that all that is settled and that I have nothing to say about the matter."

"I *diei pues!* I tell you this, if all is settled why are they not come together then? What are we jesting about?"

"Who do you want to come together?"

"These children! Goodness gracious, Augustin and my daughter! Who else do you think it could be?"

"But, señora, it appears that you don't wish to understand. I repeat that all is arranged."

"Well, then, Amador tells me the same thing, but what I want to know is what sort of an arrangement is it?"

"What! Don't you know?"

"I can only guess; I'm here to ask you."

"Your son, your own son has confessed that the marriage was a farce."

"What? And I! Why! did I not witness it? Before heaven, what a fool I am! And the curate who married them?"

"The curate was no curate, he was a friend of your son's."

"Who said so?"

"The same Amador."

"What a fool! I shall make him hear about it."

"He has confessed the thing."

"To whom?"

"To me."

Don Damaso in replying went towards his desk, and showed Doña Bernarda Amador's letter.

"Look here," he said, "here you have a letter from your son in which he confesses the truth of the affair."

"Let us see what the letter says," replied Doña Bernarda, who, not knowing how to read, did not wish to confess it.

"Here you have it," said Don Damaso, showing her the paper.

Don Damaso read Amador's letter aloud from the beginning to the signature.

This sudden revelation left Doña Bernarda stunned. The confused replies which on several occasions she had received from her son had not given her the least suspicion of the truth. She had always imagined that the arrangement to which Amador alluded was an agreement formed to induce the recognition of the marriage on the part of Augustin's family. The letter, the reading of which she had just heard, flung to the ground all her hopes, and tore from her eyes the veil which hid the picture of her shame. Her irritable character became exasperated at this occurrence, and her one thought was to return to her house and to discharge on her children all the fury of her rage.

"If this is the case," she said, trembling with indignation, "some one has got to pay me."

She left Don Damaso, and with quick steps returned to her house.

During the time that Doña Bernarda was forming the resolution of visiting Don Damaso, as we have seen (which happened at the beginning of October), no incident occurred worthy of mention to the other people who figure in our story. Happily and peacefully passed the days for Matilde and Rafael San Luis, who, absorbed in the devotion of a love which had no opposition, waited with tranquil minds for the day fixed for their union.

Numerous assurances about the renewal of the lease of Del Roblè which Don Fidel had received made him accept the repeated visits of the lover with the most affectionate benevolence, whilst Doña Francisca interested herself in her favourite authors, and held long and romantic conversations with her future son-in-law, who accompanied her with the complacency of a happy man in her excursions into the country of Romance, where Doña Francisca loved to wander, as a change from the prosaic life of Santiago.

The daughters of Doña Bernarda Coldero did not breathe the pleasant atmosphere of happiness with which Matilde and her family were surrounded. We have seen Doña Bernarda come out from her interview with Don Damaso full of indignation.

Adelaida had been living in silence, striving against the deep sorrow of the news of the approaching marriage of Rafael San Luis which had quickly spread in Santiago.

It was not strange that the news of the projected alliance of her former lover should reach the ears of Adelaida Molina. In the capital of Chili every rumour circulates with extraordinary rapidity and passes from mouth to mouth through the different circles and cliques of our society; besides Adelaida belonged to a social class which always wishes to know about the doings of the upper classes, and for this reason studies their movements, and amuses itself by commenting critically on their weaknesses. It is not strange, then, that the public voice, so loud in communities which, as in Santiago, generally occupy themselves with trifles, should bring to the ears of Adelaida that Rafael San Luis was going to abandon a condition in which he could have offered her a reparation for his fault.

At the side of Adelaida sighed her sister in the melancholy of an unrequited love.

Edelmira possessed one of those hearts to whom absence is a stimulant. During those days that Martin had left off visiting the house, her love had increased like the flowers on our hills, which receive no more watering than the rain from the sky. It was only upon her imagination, exalted by her characteristic sentimentality, that her love could feed.

Soon came to give her fresh anguish the remark that the official made in the theatre. The beauty and dignity of Leonor had astounded her. It appeared to her impossible that a man could see her without loving her, and Martin lived in the house with her. The young man now took in her eyes the gigantic proportions of a man loved by another woman; her longing for forbidden fruit was increased every day, although hers was a most ideal and platonic love.

To the misery of eating away her heart in lonely and melancholy meditations was added to Edelmira the daily annoyance of addresses which she hated. Ricardo Castanos endured her disdain with admirable constancy, and was upheld in his suit by Amador and Doña Bernarda, who looked upon him as an excellent match. Men are not always able to understand the disgust caused in a woman by the perseverance of an importunate lover, because there are fibres in the heart of a woman of a sensitiveness that is wanting in ours, which cannot be compared with hers, morally.

This obstinacy of young Castanos was an atrocious torture for Edelmira, since she had heard in her spirit the music of the song with which the heart celebrates the coming of its first love. To find an alleviation of her pain, Edelmira sought a means that many girls of strong imagination have found in the loneliness of their hearts. She wrote letters to Martin which she never sent, but they contributed strangely to feed her illusion. In these letters shone rosy gleams of passion, in the midst of the clouds of a phraseology copied from the most romantic periodicals which she had stored deeply in her imagination. All these Calypsos in the absence of their lovers think of a thousand enchantments to sustain them in the remembrances of happier days.

Edelmira wrote many letters before she found this pastime begin to pall, and about the beginning of October at which period this history has arrived they had ceased to give her pleasure.

Martin Rivas was very far from imagining that he was the object of such a passion. The interest with which Edelmira received him after his absence when he held the short conversation with her in the Campo del Marte, increased his liking for the girl, without his suspecting, or at least very vaguely that under her appearance of amicable solicitude was hidden a deeper sentiment. Martin did not carry his reflections on the matter further than the supposition that if he courted her perhaps she would love him.

He lived in too great preoccupation with his own love to divine the love of another, a girl whom lately he had hardly seen. Leonor's conduct influenced his dejected preoccupation because in the conversations subsequent to that which we heard in the previous chapter, a glimpse of hope had always been left behind, which at times seemed to Martin like a delirious dream and at others was clothed in the form of reality.

Leonor, neither by vanity nor coquetry, nor the studied intention of adding to Rivas' passion the anguish of doubt, had reduced him to this state. There was in her silence and at times in her least significant words as much serenity as if she had made a frank declaration of love.

The situation in which she found herself in respect to Martin was new and exceptional to her, she was accustomed to praise and social admiration, surrounded by rich and eloquent admirers, celebrated as worthy on account of her beauty to aspire to the most brilliant alliance. Leonor felt that before declaring her love for Martin she had to uproot ideas implanted in her mind from childhood. She felt herself under the necessity of measuring the worth of the man who had conquered her heart, before encountering the prejudices and violating the customs of the society in which she lived. Hence her frequent conversations with Rivas and the reason why at times she uttered words of hope which she thought were significant but which only served to perpetuate the doubts in which the young man had been living for some time.

XL

Let us return to Doña Bernarda Coldero as she went back to her house after hearing from Don Damaso the revelation of the secret which her son had hidden from her.

During her walk the irritation that this news had caused her increased, as may be well imagined. This revelation destroyed so many ambitious hopes, fostered by Amador, that, on seeing them vanish, her rancour against the deceit which had obliged her to relinquish them increased in proportion to the value that these hopes acquired when they were lost. It was thus that on entering her room she threw her mantle on a chair and called to her eldest daughter in a harsh voice.

Adelaida came immediately.

"Where is your brother?" asked Doña Bernarda.

"He is in his room," replied the girl.

"Call him, I have to speak to you both."

A few moments after they both arrived in the room where Doña Bernarda was waiting for them.

Doña Bernarda looked at her son with an expression of concentrated rage.

"So you have deceived me," she said, putting both her hands on her hips with a peculiar movement of her head.

"I! Why? What is it?" replied Amador, who like all those who have a guilty conscience on account of a fault, suspected on the moment the meaning of this question, and he turned pale.

"You don't know, then! Am I a fool that my children deceive me! Here is what is the matter. Is Adelaida married or not?"

"But, mother, have I not been telling you all these last days that everything is arranged."

"That for the arrangement! Have you nothing else to say? Truly! arranged treating us like negroes! What do you care if we have to wander in the street? Even little children will point us out."

"Are things as bad as that?" said Amador, dumfounded.

Doña Bernarda was exasperated at this exclamation, which in her state of irritability she found most disrespectful. It was the signal for discharging on Amador and on Adelaida all the force of her fury, breaking forth in satanic maledictions, horrible insults and terrible threats, which decency forbids us to transcribe. Adelaida, more timid than Amador, thinking she would free herself from this shower of curses which threatened to become blows, in a trembling voice gave this excuse—

"I am not guilty, mother."

To which Amador replied in a sarcastic tone—

"Indeed you were the guilty one! Don't you see that it was I who had to try to marry you off. Don't talk such nonsense to me!"

"And what, now?" exclaimed Doña Bernarda, "was it not you who came to talk to me of the marriage and made a fool of me about it, and you say you had no interest in it?"

"What interest do you suppose I had? That is a nice question!"

"And how is it that you say you are not the guilty one?" asked Doña Bernarda, pointing to her daughter.

"Yes, she says it, but it's not so certain."

"In the letter you say that you made use of a friend dressed up as a clergyman."

"In what letter?"

"In the one you wrote to Don Damaso."

"It is so; but I didn't do it for myself, I did it for Adelaida."

Doña Bernarda turned towards the latter with her face inflamed with rage.

"I am innocent," repeated Adelaida, replying to her look.

"She is not, she wishes to put the guilt on me," said Amador, stung, and replying to another look from his mother.

Then he added—

"If she's innocent, ask her why I did it?"

"Let us see, answer then," said Doña Bernarda to Adelaida.

"Why, how do I know? You may say to me what you like."

"I see," exclaimed Doña Bernarda, turning to Amador, "you may well say it, but you alone are the guilty one!"

With this exclamation the señora began a new hail of insults directed to her son, who was only able to interrupt her when he said these words—

"Look well, and first find out what has gone on in your house, and don't insult me without reason."

Adelaida gave him a supplicating look, which Amador could not see because his only thought was to calm his irritated mother.

"What passed in my house?" asked the latter.

"What does Adelaida say if it isn't for her that I did it? Nobody asked her to say that she is innocent. I have done nothing more than to help her to conceal what she did."

Adelaida knew the danger in which she was if her brother continued to speak, and interrupted him to take upon herself all the responsibility of the affair; but this resource came too late, as some suspicions of a new mystery entered the mind of the mother on account of what she had just heard. In vain Adelaida swore that she had incited her brother solely from the desire to marry a caballero; but Doña Bernarda's only answer was this question—

"Yes, but you have something that you're hiding in all this."

Amador would have been able to calm Doña Bernarda's suspicions if he had only confirmed his sister's assertions; but he took care not to do so, because he was afraid that he would find his mother's rage again turned against him.

Therefore, when Doña Bernarda kept on repeating the same thing and Amador held his tongue, she turned towards the latter and uttered the most awful threats if he did not reveal the truth.

"If you don't confess it," she said to him, shaking her fists in the height of frenzy, "I'll denounce you as incorrigible and have you taken away for a soldier, declaring that you are not yet twenty-five years old."

This threat was not a serious one to Amador because he could easily laugh at it and leave the maternal roof, but to maintain himself in any other place he would have to work for his living, and Amador was an inveterate idler. It appeared to him easier to confess the truth and give away his sister than to enter into a quarrel with his mother, who always provided for his necessities and even at times, by force of economy, helped him in many straits by paying his debts. The slackness of his habits had for a long time deprived him of all good feeling, for which reason he did not hesitate for one moment to sacrifice Adelaida and to draw on her alone the indignation of Doña Bernarda. Selfishness and his egotism alone spoke in his breast, and without hesitation he told his mother the consequence of the love-affair between Adelaida and Rafael San Luis, at the end saying a few words to soften the mother.

Doña Bernarda turned pale when she heard Amador's terrible revelation, and threw herself furiously on Adelaida, whom she dragged about the room, grasping her by the hair and uttering the most awful shrieks.

Edelmira and the servant ran at the sound, and, with Amador, interposed and joined all their strength to tear Adelaida from the hands of Doña Bernarda. Finally, to prevent the cries of the mother and the daughter, joined to those of the others who were interceding for her, reaching the ears of the people passing in the street, the servant ran into the courtyard and bolted the street door. Meanwhile, Doña Bernarda, showing extraordinary strength for her sex and age, not only beat Adelaida, from whom the pain drew lamentable cries, but gave several blows to both Edelmira and Amador who were trying to tear away her victim. A casual spectator of this domestic drama would perhaps have forgotten compassion in the comicality of the picture whose principal personage was Doña Bernarda showering furious blows with her right hand whilst her left was wrapped in the tresses of the unhappy girl. But, like everything on earth, this scene had to come to an end, as in effect it did when Doña Bernarda, aiming a blow at Edelmira, who with heroic intrepidity had tried to hold her arms, the left hand of Doña Bernarda had let go the tresses, and the impulse which her right gave was such that, not only did she hurl the compassionate Edelmira over a chair, but over-balancing herself when the latter fell, she rolled over into the centre of the room, where, from the rage in which she was and the blow she received in the fall, she remained without sense or movement.

Her children raised her up, even Adelaida assisting at this operation, and carried her to her room, where the servant rubbed her feet. Amador dashed water in her face, and the girls cried disconsolately in each other's arms.

Finally the señora recovered her senses and shed bitter tears over the dishonour of Adelaida. To the excessive agitation in which she had been, succeeded the physical and moral depression which comes after any extraordinary exertion, and she felt herself so feeble the following day that she was glad to remain in her bed to recover herself. All the gratitude which she had felt to San Luis for the help he had given her turned into hatred and a desire for vengeance, after the revelation of his conduct, and she employed the day in searching for some means of giving him a just punishment for his fault. But as her meditations did not give her any satisfactory result, she resolved to use a diplomacy which would carry happiness and honour to her family.

Satisfied with this new resolution, a few days after the scene to which it owed its origin, she directed her steps to the house of Rafael San Luis.

It was ten o'clock in the morning and Rafael was alone in his room. The unlooked-for presence of Doña Bernarda filled him with anxiety and agitating presentiments; nevertheless it was necessary for him to control himself and to receive her with affectionate urbanity. Of course the señora understood perfectly on her part the thoughts that occupied his mind, but she showed a tranquillity which she was very far from feeling. Seating herself with a laughing face on the sofa, which Rafael pointed out to her with an amicable smile, and throwing on another the veil which covered her head, she said in a tone of friendly accusation—

"We have missed you from our house lately."

"It is not my fault, believe me, Doña Bernarda," replied the young man.

"You have some motive, I don't know what. 'Loose horseshoe, you want a nail.'"

"What motive can I have? Absolutely none! You know my friendship for you."

"Certainly, and I also am fond of you. Look here, only the other day I said to Adelaida, where is Don Rafael, what has happened that he doesn't come?"

Rafael glanced at her the moment that Doña Bernarda named her eldest daughter, and with this glance his presentiments grew stronger, and he knew that this visit had some other object than the simple guise of friendship in which it appeared.

"I owe you thanks for your kindness," he replied.

"Very well, then, and why don't you come and see us?" asked Doña Bernarda.

"Almost every evening I'm occupied, and in spite of my desire to do so I don't know when I can go," replied Rafael, who above all things wished to discover the object of the visit.

"That is what we all say in the house—when will he come?—you must have found other and richer friends, and are ashamed to come to our poor house."

"Ashamed! You deceive yourself, Doña Bernarda."

"The proof is that you don't wish to come," replied the señora, in a tone in which could be noticed a falling off of the amiability with which she had spoken at the commencement.

Rafael noticed this and felt a slight access of impatience.

"I did not say I did not wish to go, but that I could not."

"It's the same thing, the case is that you will not come, and I know why!"

In this phrase her tone of discontent had increased.

"Because they say that you're going to be married."

"Have you heard that?"

"Only yesterday, Is it true?"

"It may be so."

"You don't say so!"

"It's a very old promise, dated before I had the pleasure of knowing you."

"It may be old; what do I know about that? But you forget that sometimes promises cannot hold good."

In saying these words Doña Bernarda fixed her gaze resolutely on Rafael whilst her features were stamped with a firm and determined resolution.

The young man turned pale to the ears; for although Doña Bernarda's presence alone gave him strange suspicions of what had brought her to his house, he did not expect that she would dare to attack him with so little ceremony.

"I don't know what you are referring to," he replied, pretending not to understand.

"How is it that you don't know it, and better than me even? It's better that we should arrange things in a friendly manner."

"Well, then, Señora, what do you want?" exclaimed Rafael, impatiently.

"That you marry my daughter whom you have dishonoured," replied Doña Bernarda, with spirit.

"Impossible," said the young man, "I have promised to marry a lady who—"

Doña Bernarda interrupted him furiously.

"And so, why should we be left out? My daughter is a lady also, and you deceived her with a promise of marriage; if you are a gentleman you'll keep your word!"

In vain Rafael sought for arguments and excuses to palliate his fault. Doña Bernarda always replied with the sentence she had just uttered.

"Finally," exclaimed San Luis, exasperated, "it's absolutely impossible that I could marry your daughter, and the best thing you can do for her is to accept the offer that I am going to make."

"What offer?" asked the señora.

"I have twelve thousand pesos which I inherit from my father, I promise to recognize my son and give Adelaida the half of this sum."

"I'm not asking for money," replied Doña Bernarda.

And she added to this a thousand recriminations which Rafael was obliged to support with humility. Finally she concluded with this threat—

"You don't wish to marry her! No! but I'll go before the judge and we'll see who'll lose. Every one will know the disgrace of my daughter because she must appear when I present myself. You wish for war, we'll give it to you, don't be afraid of that!" And she went out of Rafael's room leaving him the prey of mortal inquietude.

Rafael San Luis wrote to Martin begging him to come to the gateway, which in those days we called the old gate of Bellavista, to distinguish it from the gates of the Tagle and Bulnes Road.

An hour later found the two friends arrived at the appointed place and they took the road to the Alemada.

"I must have your advice on a serious matter," said Rafael, taking Rivas' arm.

"What is the matter?" asked the latter.

"In the midst of calm has appeared a cloud which foretells a tempest; you will never imagine who has paid me a visit?"

"Adelaida Molina?"

"Doña Bernarda! She knows everything, and she wants me to marry her daughter."

"She's right," said Martin, coldly.

"I know it," replied Rafael, uncomfortably. "I don't ask your opinion about that."

"Well, go on."

"I can't think of any means of parrying this blow, I have offered half of what I possess, and the cursed old woman isn't content with six thousand pesos."

"In that case give all that you can offer, the twelve thousand."

"She wouldn't take it; she will listen to nothing, if I don't consent to marry the girl. It appears to me useless to tell her that that is impossible; she would not consent to anything, even though she found me on the eve of my great happiness."

Martin remained silent, thinking that this phrase would save many unhappy girls on the brink of seduction if they could only hear it.

"What would you do in my case?" asked Rafael.

"Treat the matter as if it was finished, and since Doña Bernarda does not wish to speak of anything else but matrimony, deprive her of the occasion of even thinking about it."

"How?"

"Marry quickly."

"You are right, but there still remains a danger."

"What?"

"Doña Bernarda will bring me before the judge."

"Do you think that she will dare to do it?"

"I'm very much afraid of it, she is a violent woman, and capable of the deepest hatred. I think that to revenge herself on me she would not hesitate before the necessity of publishing the dishonour of her daughter."

"We must look for some means; although nothing seems secure."

"What means can we take?"

"Amador is greedy."

"More so than a miser in a play."

"We will pay him five hundred pesos to get his mother to promise to give up the idea."

"Will you speak to him?"

"With much pleasure."

"You do me a great service in this," exclaimed Rafael, gratefully, "you know how much I suffered before you found me, as now, at the gates of happiness. Doña Bernarda's threat makes me tremble. I would not be like this if my conscience was at ease; as you say, the poor señora is right, and my repentance is no help to her. Well, finally, we must do what we can; I owe you already immense thanks for having brought Matilde back to me, and if Doña Bernarda holds her tongue, I shall owe you still more. How can I ever repay you?"

"Let us speak of something else, are you not my friend?"

"Very well, let us speak of your love-affair; how are you getting on?"

"Always badly," said Rivas, with a smile, which did not succeed in hiding the melancholy of his face.

"I don't think so badly," replied Rafael.

"Why? You know something?" asked Martin, anxiously.

"Matilde tells me that her cousin speaks of you constantly. That is a good omen."

"She would speak of me among many others."

"Ah! that is the peculiarity; she speaks only of you. Let us see! Tell me, what have you said to Leonor? Perhaps this time I have more insight than you."

Thus urged to confidence Martin told him of the conversations that he had had with Leonor, mentioning the smallest occurrences and remembering the very words, with the retentive memory of those in love. He spoke with warmth of his recent hopes, and with anguish of his sorrow. Both hopes and anguish, thanks to the eloquence of a true love, appeared to Rafael like the light of the moon which in a cloudy sky shines suddenly and disappears afterwards behind thick clouds.

"If there was not something in all this on which to found a certainty," he said finally, "nothing on which to rest hope, I, in your case would commit an audacious act to find it out."

"What?"

"I would write to her."

"Never; I would never thus trick the confidence of those who give me such generous hospitality."

"Martin, my friend, you don't belong to this century."

Martin's sole reply was a deep sigh.

"That is to say that you resolve to love and doubt?" continued San Luis.

"Yes. Besides, I confess to you the dignity of Leonor deters me. The courage which at times I have had to reply to her with some spirit, abandons me when I am not with her and I feel the immense distance that separates her from me. Look at me, so obscure, so unworthy to aspire to her."

"Well, you must do what you think best."

The two young men got up from the chairs in the Alemada, where they were talking.

"When will you occupy yourself with my affair?" asked Rafael.

"This very day if I can, I am going to write to Amador; how much may I offer him?"

"You will arrange the affair as seems best to you; I am ready to sacrifice all I have."

They separated opposite the entrance gate of the street of the Estado, and each went to his house.

At this hour Amador was in his room with the official, the lover of Edelmira, who had just come in.

"Here I am, then, my boy," said Amador; "what can I do for you?"

"You know that I love your sister?"

"Something about it, my friend; we all love one another."

"But I fear she doesn't love me."

"A Dios! what better man could she have?"

"I have come to ask you what you think."

"According as it appears to me, she loves you sufficiently."

"And why doesn't she say so?"

"Who does not know what women are! Get out! You are like a boy; there's not a woman who doesn't pretend."

"Then you think that she would marry me?"

"I would swear it, my boy. Besides, I don't know anyone who wouldn't like to marry you; you've only got to say the word marriage and their mouths water."

"And your mother? Amador, what does she think of it?"

"It appears to her all right; who would not wish to marry her daughters—from the rich downwards?"

"Then will you speak for me?"

"Certainly, my boy," replied Amador, shaking hands with Ricardo.

"I have no genius for this kind of thing, and I trust to you. Amador will help me in the matter, I said to myself when I was coming."

"Well said! and this very night I'll speak to my mother; so cheer up."

A few minutes afterwards they separated, both contented, the official in the hope of marrying her whom he loved with all his heart, and Amador with the idea that the message with which he had been charged would serve to obtain his pardon from Doña Bernarda, who, from the moment that she had discovered the truth of his abortive intrigue, only spoke to him to abuse him.

He was sunk in these reflections when he heard a knock at the door of the room and went to see who was there.

A servant entered with a card. It was from Martin Rivas, who begged him to let him have a word with him at the hour of Oration in the Oval at the Alemada, to speak to him of an affair which interested the whole of Doña Bernarda's family.

"What answer shall I give him?" asked the servant, when he thought that Amador had finished reading the letter.

Amador answered by writing that he would meet him punctually at the hour and place indicated.

When he again found himself alone he was occupied with guessing the object for which Rivas wished to see him, and decided that it would be more prudent to wait until he had seen Martin before speaking of Ricardo's business to his mother.

Rivas arrived at the Oval of the Alemada a few minutes before the hour arranged to meet Amador.

Without preface Martin spoke of the object for which he came and offered him two hundred pesos if he would intercede with Doña Bernarda and cause her to abandon her threat.

"You said that Rafael offered six thousand pesos to my sister and that my mother wouldn't take it?" asked Amador.

"Yes," replied Rivas.

"I told you that my mother is obstinate and was furious with me on account of the letter, the thousand pesos that they gave me didn't pay me for all I suffered."

"I have three hundred pesos for you," said Martin.

"And they offer nothing for Adelaida and her child?"

"Eight thousand pesos; Rafael cannot give more than he has."

"I'll see, then."

"When will you give me the reply?"

"I don't know yet, who knows when my mother will give me a promise."

"As soon as you get it will you write to me?"

"Yes."

After this conversation Amador returned to his house and found his mother sitting with her two daughters.

"Mama," he said in her ear, "come into your room, I have to speak to you."

"What is it?" asked Doña Bernarda, when she found herself alone with her son in her bedroom.

Amador began by excusing himself for the past and assuring her that all had been done in the interest of the family.

"I would not have returned to this question," he added, "if I hadn't another good thing to tell you."

"Can anything be good at this present time?" said Doña Bernarda, somewhat pacified.

"Why not? Am I not always thinking of the family and you are always annoyed with me?"

"Let us see, then; what is it?"

"Would you not like to marry one of your daughters?"

"What a question!"

"What do you think of Ricardo?"

"He is very well."

"He wants to marry Edelmira."

Doña Bernarda's face lighted up.

"Ricardo is well off and will get on," added Amador.

"I think it is a very good thing," said the mother.

"Then you'll speak to Edelmira?"

"I'll speak to her tonight."

"You must be careful, Mamita, because Ricardo says she does not like him."

"Let her dare to be contradictory with me," said Doña Bernarda, in a threatening tone.

"That's so, because a husband like Ricardo is not to be had every day."

"Let her not be silly then."

"There's something else."

"What?"

Amador told her of his recent conversation with Martin and said, "He offered seven thousand pesos for Adelaida's son, provided Doña Bernarda desisted from the accusation."

"I was going to present myself to the judge," said Doña Bernarda, "I've been to see a lawyer whom I know, a friend of the defunct Molina, and he tells me that I can't get anything more than the child's keep."

"And besides," continued Amador, "we would have to go before the Tribunals to get even this, and seven thousand is much better."

Amador has spoken twice of seven thousand pesos instead of the eight thousand that Martin had finished by offering him. His calculation was only to mention the first amount, keeping a thousand pesos for himself besides his reward of three hundred pesos.

"Let us have the seven thousand pesos," he added, "and no one will know anything about it."

"It's very little importance who knows it," said Doña Bernarda in a doleful tone, "the very servant here knows it."

"Who told you?"

"I asked her, and she's told me all that she knows about it. She also knows who has the child, and every one knows it. Cursed business! It has cost us dear."

"But it's better, Mamita, that we make sure of the money."

"Well, go and arrange as you can," replied the señora, in disconsolate accents; and she went to look for her needlework, swearing between her teeth that Rafael would repent for the rest of his life what he had done.

Amador replied the following day that his mother promised not to go before the judge, provided that they gave Adelaida the stipulated amount, availing himself when giving this reply of what Doña Bernarda had said to him about her consultation with her friend the lawyer. Great was his surprise when instead of receiving from Rafael the eight thousand pesos of which he had hoped to reserve one thousand for himself, he found Martin empowered to give a donation in writing in Rafael San Luis' name to deposit the money in a house of business charged to remit the interest to Adelaida.

When this matter was finished Rivas went to Rafael's house to tell him about it.

"Notwithstanding all this," he said, "you must not consider yourself free from a fresh attack until you are married."

"I think so," replied Rafael, "and for that reason I have arranged with my uncle that he would shorten the time fixed with Don Fidel. I hope to be married within two weeks at the latest."

XLI

Doña Bernarda waited till the following day to speak to Edelmira of Ricardo Castanos' offer. Impressed by the conversation which she had had with Amador, and secure of her authority over her family, she did not hurry to speak to one of her daughters about marriage whilst she was still obliged to think how to revenge herself for the injury done to the other. She therefore put off to the following day the affair of Ricardo Castanos, and gave herself up to reflections as to how to punish Rafael San Luis.

The result of these reflections was probably satisfactory, because when she got up in the morning Doña Bernarda appeared more tranquil than on the preceding days, and when she called Edelmira her voice had lost the asperity with which she had spoken to every one in the house after the visit she had paid to Don Damaso Encina.

Edelmira came trembling at her mother's call, for she could not think that she would have anything pleasant to say to her, in the state of irritation in which she had been during the last few days.

"Sit down here," said Doña Bernarda to her, pointing to a seat beside her. "I've had a good offer for you," she added, after a brief silence.

Edelmira gave her mother a glance of timid interrogation.

"I see," continued the señora, "that your sister has been a fool in the past. I also have been wrong for letting into the house such cursed 'putres.' But you have had more judgment than the other, and for this reason God is now rewarding you."

Doña Bernarda made a pause in her moral exhortation to light a cigarette, a pause during which the heart of her daughter was overwhelmed with bitter presentiments.

"Ricardo," continued Doña Bernarda, "wishes to marry you."

Edelmira remained livid and trembling on her chair.

"He is a good fellow," continued the mother; "he is well off and will get on. We're poor, and when an offer like this comes don't refuse it."

Doña Bernarda waited for some moments in silence for her daughter's reply, but Edelmira answered nothing; she looked at the carpet with a dejected air, and appeared to struggle to suppress the tears which rose in her eyes.

"What do you think of it, then, daughter?" asked the mother.

The girl appeared to make an effort to raise her eyes to heaven as if she was evoking its aid.

"Mamita," she said, stammering, "I don't like Ricardo."

"What is this?" exclaimed Doña Bernarda. "We are cool! Are you a princess that you play the fool? What do I care that you don't love him? Who says that it's necessary to love? Perhaps my ears have deceived me, are you looking for a Marquis? Perhaps even that would not please you! Perhaps you're in love with some one else?"

"I? No, Mamita!" exclaimed the girl, frightened lest her mother should read in her eyes her love for Martin.

"Well, then, what more do you want? It all comes to the same thing."

"I don't want to get married, Mamita," said Edelmira, in a humble voice.

"That's all very well! But you can't go on living at your mother's expense. Good daughters! One. . . as is well known! . . . Blessed be God. If the defunct Molina had seen this! God did well to take him away; and now the other one doesn't want to get married, instead of relieving her poor mother! I hope you aren't mad, girl!"

Doña Bernarda finished these exclamations with a laugh which struck more terror into Edelmira than if it had been a threat. Also she couldn't bear the terrible look with which her mother accompanied it, and felt that she must bow trembling and submissive as a signal of obedience.

Doña Bernarda lit another cigarette to calm herself, and then turned to her daughter.

"What is the matter with you, then?" she said.

"I wasn't prepared for this," answered Edelmira, letting fall the tears which had gathered in her eyes.

"Did I tell you that you were to get married tomorrow? We're not in such a hurry. I spoke to you because I'm your mother, and know what's good for you."

These words brought a new horizon before Edelmira's eyes, she saw that an obstinate resistance would increase her mother's irritation to a point of exasperating her, and she knew that the only means allowed her at this critical moment was to gain time.

"This is what I beg of you, Mamita," she said, "give me at least a month to answer?"

"That is. . . to give him so little hope that he will get weary and change his mind. Do you imagine that within a month you are going to be more reasonable? Who gives orders here, then? I tell you that you aren't going to be married tomorrow, but the answer has got to be given now."

"But, Mamita—"

"What is all this, then? Do you imagine that I'm going to consent to let you lose this chance? Tell the saints that you want to take time!"

"I will do what you wish, Mamita."

"That pleases me, now you're speaking like a good daughter."

"But give me at least two months to prepare myself."

"You can have one month, and let me hear no more about it."

Edelmira bowed her head in resignation.

"And let me have no nonsense then, during this time," continued the mother. "When with him be polite, but no haughtiness, and let us have no afflicted hearts. Now go away, and be more happy than any one."

Edelmira went to her room after having listened to other admonitions which Doña Bernarda gave to her in the tone of authority which since the affair of Adelaida she employed to all her family.

On finding herself alone she threw herself upon a chair close to the head of her bed and wet with abundant tears her pillow, the confidant of her solitary love. In a flood of tears she said good-bye to her sentimental illusions, all the dearer the more hopeless they had appeared; she bid an eternal adieu to the unformed hopes, to the melancholy joys, to the sweet aspirations of this orphaned and unsuspected love, which she had so happily nourished as a recompense for the unhappiness of her life. Struck down by the very first blow of such unexpected sorrow she did not think of resistance nor of seeking any means to support the cruelty of her fate. She only thought of sobbing to herself, as children sob, to try to ease the pain of her heavy heart.

Doña Bernarda, for her part, assured after a fashion of the future of one of her daughters, now tried to undertake means of avenging the loss of the other's prospects, an idea which she had not abandoned for one moment since the fatal revelation of Adelaida's love-affair. Her rancour against the latter diminished in proportion as it increased against Rafael, and little by little she began to consider her daughter more unfortunate than guilty. The sight of her grandson, whom she had had brought to the house, far from quenching her thirst for vengeance, only increased it, until it became a necessity impossible to forego. Dominated by this idea she got into communication with the servants of Don Fidel Elias and in this way kept herself informed of the preparations which were being made in the house for Matilde's marriage; she spied on the doings of San Luis, who was absorbed in his love, forgetting the fears with which Doña Bernarda's threats had filled him, whilst she meditated on her vengeance in silence without telling her projects to any one.

In the meantime there was no more change in the situation between Leonor and Martin, than the incidents natural under the conditions which we have described, in which pride, half conquered, on one side and excessive delicacy on the other, formed a barrier. There passed between them those uneasy looks with which two lovers try to understand each other, those words which lips stammeringly pronounce when they touch upon the strange wonder which occupies their hearts. Those reticences in which in such cases they take refuge. Their timid approaches into the always flowery region of hope; the special atmosphere, balmy and warm in which lovers find themselves enclosed, when in the midst of others they live alone and find even in silence eloquent harmonies, delicious premonitions, in the whole of nature a secret agreement with the tremendous sentiment which agitates them. And nevertheless they were not happy.

Leonor saw the magnificent panorama of love unrolled before her eyes and was impatient of Martin's timidity. She was too proud to take the first step, and too reverent to ascend the pedestal on which she had placed her idol, and they both sighed. And in this state of discouragement in which the heart looks on hope as a miracle, Leonor, awakening her former pride, swore to forget Martin; and Martin, who had no idea of his power, prayed heaven to tear her image from him and with her his unfortunate love. But a glance defeated her proposition and made him forget his prayer, and they returned again to bathe their wings in the fresh light; butterflies, which away from its sweet warmth, cannot find the vital atmosphere indispensable to their life.

XLII

It having been arranged between the respective families to fix a much earlier date for the marriage of Matilde and Rafael, there was much going and coming in Don Fidel Elias' house on account of the approaching festival.

Matilde's relations were sending their presents to the bride.

Doña Francisca, descending to the prosaic details of life, studied models for dresses for her daughter.

Frequent journeys were made to the dressmaker to try on the wedding dress, and for luxurious garments fashioned by the ingenuity of the same artist.

They discussed jewels with warmth, opening and shutting caskets lined with velvet which came from a German jeweller in the Callé Ahumada.

Visitors arrived, and the conversation always began quietly; little by little it turned on dress and the tone of the voices became more and more crescendo as in the air of Don Basilio. They exhibited the presents, they praised one model and blamed another and heaped up observations about the cross of brilliants which every bride must have, until often the husband turns himself into another, much heavier to carry.

Visitors left, and scarcely had the presents been put away when others arrived, and they had to place again upon the table the things that they had just shown.

So passed the days.

To analyse the innumerable feelings which under these circumstances were agitating Matilde's heart, as they agitate the hearts of all those who marry joyfully (because there are a great number who marry from obedience or resignation), would be as futile as to describe the magnificent rising of the sun or the clearness of the sky in the springtime. The flowers of these imaginings open their trembling leaves to the endearments of the love which soothes their breast and embalms the gentle breeze which murmurs its divine promises in the ears of lovers. Thus for Matilde her past life and its duties were a dream, and the present was happiness, and the future irradiated such a brilliant light, that, like that of the sun, it dazzled her vision, and she preferred not to look at it.

"You who are not in love," she said, pressing Leonor's hands in sweet abandon, "cannot understand my happiness."

Leonor gave her a long look, such a look as is given mechanically when the mind is elsewhere.

"Listen," continued her cousin, "when I'm away from Rafael I find myself without words; sometimes a love like mine can find no language which can describe it fully. But you, what can all this matter to you?" she added, seeing that Leonor could hardly conceal her increased inattention.

"Why not?" answered Leonor, with a polite smile.

"You don't understand me."

"I understand you very well."

"Ah! are you in love?"

In the curiosity with which this question was asked by Matilde it could be seen that for the moment the woman conquered the lover—her curiosity took the place of her love.

Leonor answered with the same vivacity, but blushed a little.

"I! No, no, little girl!"

"You're telling me a lie."

"Why?"

"You're not the same Leonor that you were. When used you to be so thoughtful as you often are now? Tell me, and don't be so reserved. Do you know that sometimes I am almost guessing it. Which of the two is it? Clementi or Emilio?"

Leonor made no other answer than lightly pouting with her under lip in magnificent disdain.

Matilde then named many of the dandies in the capital and got the same reply; finally she exclaimed—

"It is Martin!"

"Oh! What madness!"

The cheeks of Leonor burned with the liveliest crimson.

"Why not?" continued Matilde. "Martin is interesting."

"Do you think so?" asked Leonor, pretending the most absolute indifference.

"I find him so; what does it matter if he is poor?"

"Oh, it isn't that," said Leonor, raising her head with consummate majesty.

"He has a good heart."

"Who told you so?"

"You did."

Leonor bent her head and pretended that she had pricked her finger with a pin.

"You have also told me that he has talents," said Matilde; "are you going to deny that also?"

"That is true."

"Don't you see I have a good memory."

"You praise him so much because you are grateful to him."

"Very well, but I only respect what I have heard from you."

"Also in our house we are indebted to him for many services."

"Which you are very grateful for."

"Certainly."

"Much more so than if any one else did them, since you talk to me always about him."

Leonor made no reply.

"Do you know I have got a right to be angry with you," said Matilde.

"Why?"

"Because you don't confide in me, though I have always told you my secrets."

"What do you want me to tell you?"

"That you are in love with Martin. Can you deny it?"

"I myself have not known it for a long time."

"At least you might confess it."

"It is true, I know I cannot leave off thinking of him," said Leonor, raising her beautiful head proudly.

"I am sure that he has loved you for some time."

"Who told you so?" asked Leonor, with lively interest.

"Nobody; but I knew it at the first glance."

Having conquered her natural reserve, Leonor told her cousin the history of her love, which we have seen gradually increase and unfold itself in her bosom. She spoke with a happy memory of all her conversations with Martin, as the latter had told his to Rafael San Luis, without omitting a single circumstance, nor a single one of the impressions she had felt when she thought Rivas was in love with another.

"Ah! then you are jealous?"

"Jealous! No; but if I suspected that he was in love with another, I would have sufficient strength of will to forget him."

"From what you tell me," replied Matilde, "he has never dared to speak to you of his love?"

"Never."

"And you have let him understand nothing?"

"I don't know; sometimes a word of mine seems to make him think; and then again the day I hope for seems to recede."

"Poor Martin!" exclaimed Matilde, after a short silence. "In your position you should be more compassionate to him."

"Do you think so?"

"Give him to understand what you want. What have you got to lose?"

"I have warned you that he is proud, and perhaps it is through pride that he does not speak."

"Or through delicacy; but you know him better than I do."

This observation made Leonor thoughtful; at the end of some minutes she looked at her watch, it was two o'clock in the afternoon.

Her curiosity satisfied, Matilde again renewed her favourite subject, and was talking of Rafael when Doña Francisca entered with a new garment for her daughter.

We shall leave Matilde, admiring the garment with her mother, to follow Leonor, who said good-bye to them. Entering the elegant carriage which was waiting for her at the door she ordered the coachman to drive home.

When the carriage drew up, she saw in the entrance a woman-servant, badly dressed, with a letter in her hand, who was asking for Don Martin.

This servant did not excite Leonor's particular attention as she entered, the only thing she thought was that the letter came from Rafael San Luis or from some other friend.

The man-servant at the entrance took the card to Martin, whom he found in Don Damaso's study.

Martin opened the letter and read the following, beginning at the date:—

"You are my only friend, and as I have often said to myself,
I have confidence in your word. For this reason I address
myself to you since those who could advise me abandon
or persecute me. In my sorrow I turn my eyes to you who
perhaps can give me words of consolation with which to
dry the flood of tears which flow from them, and therefore
I want to confide to you, Martin, what is happening to me.
My mother wishes me to marry Ricardo Castanos, who has

proposed for me. I was so far from thinking of him that until now I do not know how it happened. You have always shown me friendship, and will counsel me in this matter, counting upon which I will always be your grateful friend,

EDELMIRA

Martin read this letter twice without guessing that the natural simplicity of its words, the explanation of which he would find later, enclosed a world of timid hopes.

He called the servant after reading it the second time.

"Who brought this letter?" he asked him.

"A girl who said she would come back for the answer," replied the servant, with the almost imperceptible smile which those of his class give to show their masters that they know very well what the matter is about.

"Good. Come back in a few minutes for the reply," said Martin.

The servant left the room, and Rivas wrote the following reply:—

EDELMIRA,

"Your letter has given me much surprise, and I am infinitely grateful for the confidence which you repose in me. My surprise comes from the same source from which arises the agitation in which you seem to be, and I find myself very little prepared to give my opinion about an affair of this nature of which truly I have no experience, and am unable to advise you in a satisfactory manner.

"You ask me to advise you without remembering that it is a very delicate matter. Before offering advice I will confess that I cannot be an impartial judge in the present case, for I cannot tell you how much I reciprocate the sincere friendship that you profess. If you would ask me to offer a prayer for your future I would so truly and ardently pray for your happiness that my mind would remain contented with the idea that all are taken care of who can realize a just desire, praying to Heaven with the entire fervour of the heart. But your letter relates to advising you on a point which can decide your lot for ever, and I am wanting in strength to do it. No one is a better judge than oneself, Edelmira, in affairs like the one which now occupies you; consult your heart. The heart speaks loudly in cases like this.

"If, over and above this, my words have any power to calm the affliction of which you tell me, or you find me in the happy situation of being able to do you any service, do not hesitate to write to me, and honour me with the confidence which you offer me in your letter, and make use of me whenever you think I can be of any help to you.

Your affectionate friend,
MARTIN RIVAS

Martin closed this letter and gave it to the servant, charging him to give it to the person who would come for it.

At dinner they spoke of the approaching marriage which would take place in the family, and, thanks to Augustin's verbosity, Leonor was able to speak to Rivas several times during the general conversation.

On leaving the table Augustin took his friend's arm and both accompanied Leonor to the salon, where she, as usual, went to the piano whilst the two young men remained standing beside her.

"I was with Matilde today," said Leonor, continuing the conversation of the dining-room, "you can't imagine how happy she is."

"It is natural, Señorita," said Martin.

"The French," added Augustin, "say '*L'amour fait rage et l'argent fait mariage*,' but here love does both, *rage et mariage*."

"I think she is now the happiest girl in Santiago," said Leonor.

"Why don't you copy her, little sister?" said Augustin. "You can be as happy as she is when you like; have you not got two elegant lovers?"

Martin gazed at the girl and turned pale.

"Only two?" asked Leonor, laughing.

At these words Martin's pallor became a vivid crimson.

"When I said two," replied Augustin, "I spoke of those who visit you most. My *toda bella*, we know that you can have any one amongst the richest if you like."

"What do riches matter to me?" exclaimed Leonor, disdainfully.

"Would you rather have a poor man, little sister?"

"Who knows."

"I don't understand this century then; I am sorry for you."

"There are many things that are worth more than riches," said the girl.

"Grave error, *ma charmante;* riches are a great thing."

"And do you think the same as Augustin?" asked the girl, turning to Rivas.

"I think that, in certain cases, they are a necessity," answered Rivas.

"In what cases?"

"When a man, for example, considers money as a means to gain the woman he loves."

"You have a poor idea of women, Martin," said the girl, in a serious tone. "Not all are fascinated by the glitter of gold."

"Yes, but all love luxury," exclaimed Augustin.

"I put myself in the place of a poor man who is ambitious," replied Martin, with resolution.

"If this man is worth it in himself," replied Leonor, "he ought to have confidence and find some one who would comprehend and appreciate him; you are too diffident."

Leonor said these words rising from the piano. Augustin had already gone away.

"I am diffident," said Martin, "because I find myself as obscure as the man I took for an example."

"You see that, for me," replied the girl, in a voice of emotion, "riches are no recommendation, and I think much as you do."

One would have said that Leonor was afraid to hear Martin's reply, because she went away the moment she had uttered these words.

Rivas saw her disappear with a palpitating heart; like one, who in a dream, sees his happiness realized and awakens to seize it. When the girl had disappeared his mind strove to find the meaning of what he had just heard. At this moment a servant from Don Fidel Elias' house entered, asking for Leonor, for whom he brought a paper which contained only these words, "Come and see me, I want you, I think I am going to go mad with sorrow! I expect you at once.—Your cousin Matilde."

To know the events which gave origin to this letter, and which happened after Leonor had left, we must return to the house of Don Fidel Elias, where we had left Matilde with her mother.

XLIII

S hortly after Leonor had left the salon and had said good-bye to Doña Francisca and Matilde, Rafael, Don Pedro San Luis, and Don Fidel Elias arrived.

Whilst the last two talked with the lady of the house, Matilde and Rafael went over to the piano, at which the girl seated herself, and with a wandering hand began to play while she talked with her lover.

In this conversation they dwelt for a time in those castles in the air which true lovers build when they discuss the future. They spoke of themselves, only of themselves, like all other lovers, who are the greatest egotists in creation; they repeated to each other what they had already said a thousand times, and finally fell into silence in mute contemplation; their minds absorbed, their souls enraptured, with their hearts palpitating, their imagination drowned in the immense happiness which they felt.

This limpid and serene sky of happy love, this transparent atmosphere which surrounded them was quickly changed. A servant entered the room and approached the piano.

"Señorita," he said, in a low voice in Matilde's ear, "a lady wishes to speak to you."

"To me?" said the girl, awakening from the golden dream in which was she absorbed whilst gazing at her lover.

"Yes, Señorita."

"Who is it?" Ask her what she wants."

The servant went out.

"Some one is asking for me," said Matilde, once more gazing into the enamoured eyes of Rafael.

The servant returned just after Matilde had spoken.

Matilde and Rafael saw him returning and turned towards him.

"She says that she is called Doña Bernarda Coldero de Molina," were the words of the servant.

One would have said that a thunderbolt had struck San Luis, for he became livid, whilst Matilde repeated with surprise the name given by the servant.

"I don't know that lady," she said, consulting Rafael with a look.

He appeared petrified on his chair.

The blow was so unexpected, and with such suddenness all the consequences of this visit came to him, that surprise and perturbation choked his voice. But his intelligence was not choked in the same way, for on the instant he was able to calculate the desperation of the situation in which he found himself. Gifted, however, with a strong mind, he saw it was necessary to escape from the danger by taking at once a decided step; and putting on an air of displeasure at this disagreeable interruption, he said to Matilde—

"Tell him to bid her to come back another time."

Matilde noted the pallor of San Luis and the agitation which he tried to hide.

"What is the matter with you?" she asked, with loving solicitude.

"I? Absolutely nothing."

"Ask the señora what it is she wants?" she said, turning to the servant.

"She says, Señorita, that she wants to have a word with you."

The girl turned undecidedly to consult Rafael, and he repeated what he had already said—

"Let her return another time."

"Tell her that I am busy, and that she must come again," repeated Matilde to the servant.

The latter left the room.

"It is probably some poor widow," said the girl, with a smile.

"Probably," replied the young man, trying also to smile.

At that moment Rafael felt himself in a situation similar to that of a nervous person who expects firearms to go off; he breathed with difficulty, and all his nerves were strained to listen to any noise that might come from outside; with terrible uneasiness he calculated the time that the servant might take to give Doña Bernarda the message that he carried, the time that the latter would take to object, and the time that the servant or Doña Bernarda would take to arrive at the salon. This last hypothesis arose in the mind of the young man from the knowledge that he had of the tenacious and resolute character of Doña Bernarda.

Thus passed five minutes of mortal anguish for Rafael and inexplicable silence for Matilde, who sought in his eyes the continuation of the idyll which a moment before sang in their hearts.

Finally the door of the salon opened and the horrified eyes of Rafael saw Doña Bernarda enter, making bows and curtseys which were so low as to be grotesque.

Matilde and the others present looked at her with curiosity. The girl and her mother could not hide their astonishment on seeing the singular costume in which the widow of Molina presented herself.

It is necessary to explain that Doña Bernarda had attired herself with the idea of looking as like a lady as possible in the eyes of the people before whom she had determined to present herself. Over a dress of many colours which she wore at the last 18th of September, hung, apparent to every one, a lace petticoat bordered with colours, bought second-hand from a servant of an old lady who had worn it in its better days. Without suspecting that this article smelt of the hair-oil used by the lower middle classes, Doña Bernarda entered, convinced that it alone was sufficient to give an exalted idea of her personality to those who beheld her. For this reason she lavished extraordinary curtseys, in order that they might see, as she thought, that she knew the manners of good society, and that it was not the first time that she found herself amongst gentry.

"Who can this strange señora be?" Matilde asked Rafael, in a low voice.

The latter had stood up and with a pale and stricken face was fixing a strained gaze on Doña Bernarda.

"Which of you is Doña Francisca Engracia de Elias?" she asked.

"I, Señora," replied Doña Francisca.

"I am pleased to know you, Señora, and this gentleman will be your husband. No? This is your little girl. You haven't got to tell me, she's the picture of her mother. How is Don Rafael? This gentleman I have known since I don't know how long, we have been friends for years. Well, then, I'm going to sit down for I don't want to get tired. Years make a difference. What can be done? Are the whole family very well?"

"Very well," said Doña Francisca, looking in surprise at the others, and without being able to understand the apparition of this strange personage.

The rest contemplated her with the same astonishment as was depicted in the face of the lady of the house.

"Is she mad?" Matilde asked Rafael.

On looking at him she noticed so much anguish in the livid features of the young man, that her heart was at once seized with an inexplicable doubt.

Doña Bernarda, seeing that no one spoke to her, and fearing that if she remained in silence it would be taken as a mark of ill-breeding, quickly resumed.

"Now, Señora," she said, "I have to tell you why I came. For this reason I have called upon your little daughter, because I don't want to make a noise about it. Between polite people things are done quietly. The girl, however, sent me word by a servant that I should come back another day; that was not right, because I'm here, and I'm old and my house is far away. I nearly gave up the ghost! I have been sweating all the way down the road. How could I return home like a whipped dog with my tail between my legs without speaking to any one? Do you imagine that I have come here to ask for charity?

"Thanks to God we're not wanting for anything to eat! So I said to myself: This is the time to do it, before they get married, and so I came."

Doña Francisca took advantage of a pause in which Doña Bernarda took breath, to ask her—

"And to what, Señora, do we owe the honour of this visit?"

"The honour is for me, Senora. Since you ask me, I've come to tell you that I'm resolved. They tell me that your daughter is going to be married. Just look at her! she is the image of her mother!" she added ingratiatingly.

"That is so, Señora," said Doña Francisca.

"And to this gentleman? Is not that so?" said Doña Bernarda, continuing, and pointing to Rafael.

Rafael would have liked to have buried himself in the ground in his consternation and shame.

"Señora!" he said, in a tone of indignation, to Doña Bernarda, "what are you daring to do?"

"Here! I'm going to tell you."

"You ought not to allow this woman to go on with her ravings," said Rafael to Doña Francisca.

"Not ravings!" exclaimed Doña Bernarda, her face getting red, "we're going to see if they are ravings. Look, Señora," she added, turning to Doña Francisca, "tell the servant to call the girl who is waiting for me at the door with a child. We shall see if I'm raving!"

"But, Señora," exclaimed Don Fidel, in an authoritative voice, "what is the meaning of all this?"

"It's clear enough what it means," replied Doña Bernarda. "You are going to marry your daughter to a dishonourable man; wait till you see!"

Rising rapidly from her seat she went to the door.

"Peta, Peta!" she cried, "come here and bring the child."

They all looked at each other astounded, whilst Rafael leant against the piano, his hands clenched and his face distorted with mingling emotions.

Doña Bernarda's servant entered carrying a beautiful child in her arms.

"Now, then, here's the baby!" exclaimed Doña Barnarda. "Who says it's not Don Rafael's son? Who says that he keeps his word and hasn't deceived a poor honest girl?"

"But, Señora—" said Don Fidel.

"Here is the proof of it," said Doña Bernarda, "don't say that I'm raving, here is the proof. Don't deny that this child is yours and that you promised to marry my daughter!"

A profound silence followed these words, they all turned to look at San Luis, who advanced trembling towards the middle of the room.

"I have paid all I have to her daughter," he exclaimed, "and assured as far as possible the future of this child. What more does she want?"

Matilde had thrown herself on a sofa, hiding her face in her hands, and the rest remained in silence.

"Look here, Señora," said Doña Bernarda, "I appeal to you and ask you if it appears to you just that because a girl is poor she should be mocked at by fashionable people. What would you say if, though God forbid, that should be done to your daughter, or to any one? Even a poor girl can be honourable, and if a man gives his word, why does he not fulfil it?"

"We can do nothing in this matter, Señora," said Don Fidel; whilst Don Pedro San Luis turned to his nephew, and said to him—

"The most prudent thing would be for you to go; I'll arrange this for you."

Rafael took up his hat and went out, glancing at Matilde, who was stifling her sobs with difficulty.

Don Pedro San Luis turned then to Doña Bernarda.

"Señora," he said to her, in a low voice, "I charge myself with the future of this child and that of your daughter. Have the kindness to go away and come back to the house tonight. You will name the conditions."

Either Doña Bernarda found that the revenge which she had promised herself for so many days was more valuable than any offer of Don Pedro's, or that, firm in her position she wished in her plebeian pride to humiliate the aristocratic feelings of those who tried to stifle her voice with promises of money, but she looked for a moment at the man who spoke to her, and then lowering her eyes she said, in a most determined tone—

"I have asked nothing from you, sir, I have come here because I thought that this lady and this young girl are good-hearted and that they would not like to leave a poor girl who never has done them any harm, and this little angel of God, in shame; neither more nor less. Don Rafael can marry my girl when his rage is over and he sees that he has not behaved like a gentleman."

"But, Señora," said Don Fidel, "it appears to me that Rafael is free to do what he likes, and you had better come to an understanding with him."

"I knew very well what I would have to do when I came here," replied Doña Bernarda, in a still more threatening voice. "What I want to know is," she added, turning to Matilde and her mother, "if these ladies will consent that my poor girl shall remain dishonoured whilst they have wealth as well as honour; not like a poor girl who has no other wealth but her good name.

"How can one reconcile it with one's conscience," she continued after a long silence, "when it's only when one is poor that such things happen? Is this young lady going to want for husbands, well dowered as she is? God is just, Señorita, and those who are good are good. What more could I say? I know every one ought to be able to put their hand on their conscience, and declare it clear. Would you marry when you knew that through that you would bring shame upon a poor girl and a little child who is worse than orphaned?"

Doña Bernarda finished these words with her voice cut short by sobs, raising her eyes and her hands to Heaven and noisily blowing her nose, whilst she repeated several times the words of her last sentence.

"Look here, Señora," said Doña Francisca to her, in whose romantic imagination a favourable effect had been produced by the reasoning of Doña Bernarda, "you see how impossible it is to decide an affair of so much importance at once. We shall see Rafael when he is calmer and tomorrow in the morning or a little later we'll decide."

"You will have then to see him, Señorita," replied Doña Bernarda, "and above all she who was going to marry him thinking that her bridegroom was free, will have to decide. I ask you once more. What will my poor girl do who has been deceived, that is the lot of the poor, and thanks to God our family is a good one and Don Rafael has no reason to deny it. The defunct Molina, my husband, was in business and never owed any one a farthing."

"All will come right presently," said Doña Francisca.

"Very well, then, Señorita, I trust to you; you will bear witness in this I have acted like a lady, for I said to myself, it's better to go and see these ladies who are deceived than to present myself before the judge in which case the affair would be in every one's mouth. What could these ladies be guilty of that their names should have to appear in a court of justice? 'If they are ladies,' I said to myself, 'they would much rather arrange everything without noise, and they must be Christians like poor but honourable people.' It's much better to have friendly doings than enemies, of this there's no doubt, and a pretty and rich girl cannot want for a bridegroom, and she could get a hundred if she tried for them of the kind that don't go after poor girls and deceive them whenever they get a chance."

"Very well, then, Señora, we shall try and arrange this."

Then Doña Bernarda began (this time bathed in tears) to repeat her arguments, taking care to give a more precise form to the threats which she had just hinted at; with a certain mastery, manifesting that she felt disposed to follow the affair to its ultimate consequences; after which she went away leaving her audience in the greatest consternation.

XLIV

Matilde threw herself into her mother's arms, her voice broken with sobs.

"Come," said Don Fidel, "I hope we are not going to take the threats of this old woman seriously; she only spoke because she wanted to get something. What have we got to do with the honour of her daughter? Don't you agree with me, Señor Don Pedro?"

Self-interest spoke in these words from the mouth of Don Fidel. The idea of breaking the approaching marriage of his daughter with Rafael appeared deplorable to him, considering that on this marriage depended the lease of Del Roblè.

"I am going to speak myself with the señora, and try to appease her," replied Don Pedro San Luis to this question.

"That is a good idea, and I am grateful to you. What nonsense the old woman talks! Why should we be so quixotical as to try to repair the slips of her daughters? Why doesn't she take care of them as she ought to do, instead of coming here for payment for seduction? What virgins!"

"For God's sake be quiet," exclaimed Doña Francisca, scandalized by the social maxims expounded by her husband before Matilde.

"What is the matter, then? You heard what I said," replied Don Fidel, who was angry at any objection of his wife's. "This old woman is a mad woman, and who knows what else besides. As if I didn't know the world!"

"Pero hombre!" Doña Francisca turned to say, with an eloquent gesture and look, in which she begged her husband to respect the grief of his daughter.

Don Fidel was incapable of knowing that Matilde's heart was breaking, preoccupied as he was with the lease of Del Roblè; he only thought that her affliction came from the fear of losing her bridegroom, and he went to her, patting her shoulder affectionately.

"Don't cry, little girl," he said, "no one will take away your husband."

Don Pedro San Luis took advantage of this interruption in the matrimonial dispute just begun to assure them anew that he would cooperate as much as possible in the arrangement of this affair, and took his leave.

Don Fidel then, finding himself in the bosom of his family, gave reins to the true preoccupation of his mind.

"You," he said, "can do no more than Don Pedro in this matter, it's quite plain it's for me to do everything in this case."

"And what are we to do?" asked Doña Francisca, indignantly.

"What are you to do? Isn't it nothing? Be amiable, as I am; repeat, as I do, that we take no notice of this mad old woman, and don't pay the slightest attention to whatever she says. It will be a dreadful thing if the lease escapes me!"

"I'm not thinking about leases," replied Doña Francisca, indignantly, taking away her daughter and leaving Don Fidel to continue his reflections.

Matilde threw herself again in her mother's arms when she found herself alone with her; they had both retired to the girl's room, where they could give free course to their grief.

"Ah! mama, who would have believed it!" said Matilde, raising her eyes bathed in tears.

A long silence followed this sad exclamation in which the wounded breast of the girl exhaled the sorrow of such a bitter awakening.

Doña Francisca dried her eyes, and knew that her duty was to give courage to her daughter, whose first grief was taking the form of desperation in proportion as her mind threw off the torpor caused by the cruel and unexpected blow which she had just received.

"*Vamos hijita,*" she said, "calm yourself, for God's sake! All will be arranged."

"Arranged, mama!" exclaimed Matilde, rising with an energy that one would have thought her incapable of, "arranged, and how? Do you think, like my father, that I deplore the loss of a husband! That is to say that I did not love him! That is to say that I could love any man who could make me believe that I had always been his only love, when perhaps he is tired of some other, and would come wooing to me in order to set himself free from promises given to another! Ah! what does a husband matter to me when what I deplore is my love? When I lost Rafael the first time did you see me in despair as I am now? I suffered the blow with courage because I thought him worthy of a sacrifice; they separated me from him, but I never despised him! And now—what a difference!"

Sobs choked her voice which produced only inarticulate sounds, whilst the poor girl put her hands to her heart whose violent beating hurt her bosom.

"Don't weep, my daughter; calm yourself," were the only words that the mother could give, convinced at this moment that she had no consolation to mitigate such bitter sorrow.

"Could any one suppose that my love could endure the discovery which I have just made," continued Matilde, little by little becoming more tranquillized by the affectionate caresses of her mother. "Do you suppose that I can ever forget what I have just seen. Could I live tranquilly at his side? Everybody would have a right to accuse me of selfishness, and could I be happy knowing that an unhappy girl was living, sacrificed to me, whose only fault was being deceived? Was I not also deceived when I thought that he had never loved another? Look, mama! this is horrible, because the more I think of it, I see that it is a bottomless abyss; I do not love him now. I hate him.

"Who would be able to assure me that the reason he did not marry the mother of his child was for want of love? How far more likely it was because she was poor! Who can make me doubt that he only wished to marry me because my father was rich?"

This cruel supposition seemed to add a new and immense sorrow to the girl's heart, for she ceased to speak, looking with staring eyes around her, and slowly uttering despairing groans.

In vain Doña Francisca sought for the most comforting words to calm her desperation, in vain she strained her to her heart, adjuring her, for her sake not to abandon herself to this belief. Matilde did not hear her, did not feel her caresses, did not understand the sense of the words that came to her ears. Carried away by the last idea she had expressed, the hours of love came back to her memory, the vows, the sweet glances, and this idea guided her into the flowery fields of remembrance, cutting off at the root with an impious hand the illusions which enamelled them.

Some hours passed in this manner. Matilde spoke at times, following the thread of her reflections, and immersed in the violent sorrow which each new idea awakened, each as it came adding fuel to feed the voracious flame of her increasing grief. Grief, like happiness, finds the need of one single friendly heart in whom to confide; and thus it was that Matilde, to whom it appeared that her mother could not understand all that she felt, sat down at a table and wrote to Leonor the few words which the latter received, after having sown, as we have seen, a seed of hope in the mind of Martin.

XLV

Half an hour after receiving Matilde's letter, Leonor arrived at her house, accompanied by her father.

Leonor entered her cousin's room which Doña Francisca had just left, and Don Damaso remained in the ante-room where Don Fidel and his wife came as soon as they knew of his arrival.

The two girls embraced each other warmly without speaking a word, until Leonor, who was unable to understand the cause of Matilde's affliction, broke the silence.

"What is it? What is the matter with you?" she asked. "Your card has given me a shock."

Then Matilde, making an effort to dry the tears which had returned to her eyes at the sight of her cousin, related every particular of the scene in which Doña Bernarda had been the principal actor.

Leonor found herself overwhelmed at this revelation, and while pitying her cousin there arose in her mind an idea which showed the state of her heart.

"Perhaps Martin is in love with the other sister, he is such a friend of San Luis."

"What would you do in my place?" asked Matilde, believing that her cousin was only thinking of her sorrow.

"I? Truly, Matilde, I don't know what to say to you!"

"But put yourself in my place. What would you do?"

"Could you forgive him?" asked Leonor, without giving her cousin the reply that she had asked for.

"I could pardon him," the latter replied, "but I could not love him."

"It is very difficult to advise in such cases," continued Leonor.

"I am not asking you for advice. I am asking you what would you do if you were in my place?"

"I would scorn him."

"My father would not like us to separate. For nothing in the world would he break off this match."

"Then I would break it," said Leonor; "nothing would make me change from this decision."

"I think that a few words would be sufficient."

Matilde began to write slowly, on account of her feverish agitation. At the end of a few minutes she raised her head and read—

"Between you and me all is finished. It appears useless to me to enter into explanations concerning a resolution which is amply justified by many weighty motives in my mind. I write to avoid any other explanation which I am neither disposed to hear nor to read.

MATILDE ELIAS

"That is enough," said Leonor.

Matilde called a servant and told her to take the letter to its destination, without letting any one in the house know that she was going out.

"I felt I must see you," she said, "because you give me courage, although it is true I have neither wavered nor hesitated."

But this strength appeared lessened as she hid her face, and one could only see her body agitated with sobs.

"There is still time, if you like." said Leonor to her, "the servant can't have gone out yet."

"What! Do you think that I have repented? I am not weeping for that. Everything is finished."

Don Damaso heard the story of the affair from his sister's mouth, amid the constant interruptions of Don Fidel who thought he could explain the matter better.

"Well, did not I say," exclaimed Don Damaso, "that Rafael did not overlook money; this young man is a rake."

"But, *hombre!* Most men have done this," replied Don Fidel, "his foolish actions are all over now."

"Heavens, Fidel! what principles!" exclaimed his consort, scandalized.

"Look here, wife," he replied in a sententious tone, "women don't know the world as we do!"

"But they know morality."

"And who wants to say that I'm immoral because I'm a philosopher? I know the world better than you. You would say the same, brother-in-law."

Don Damaso, who was inclined to waver according to the Chilian fashion not only in politics but also in other cases, said—

"It is true that many people commit this class of faults, I do not deny it."

"Don't you see, don't you see," said Don Fidel to his wife, "when I tell you I know the world, it's because I'm certain of it. Rafael's affair is an insignificant peccadillo, and should rest in oblivion."

"I don't think that Matilde will forget it soon," replied Doña Francisca.

"She not forget it! Don't I know women? In about two days she won't remember anything about it."

"We shall see," said Doña Francisca.

"You'll see I do not make mistakes."

Whilst Don Fidel was looking for a match to light his cigar Don Damaso turned to his sister.

"I assure you," he said to her, "this young man is no good."

"And Matilde will not pardon him," answered Doña Francisca.

"So much the better, sister, so much the better; this man could not make her happy. In your place I would at once oppose the marriage."

"But you must aid me, then," said Doña Francisca.

"Oh! count on me," exclaimed Don Damaso.

They went over to talk to Don Fidel, and shortly afterwards Don Damaso sent for Leonor and they said good-bye to his sister and brother-in-law.

In the evening Leonor told Martin of the happenings in Don Fidel's house.

"Poor Matilde," she said to him, "is most unhappy, and begins to believe in theory, what you hold so firmly in practice; the theory of absolute indifference."

"Unfortunately," said Rivas, "one cannot always be master of one's heart, and this theory can almost always be counted amongst those which cannot be put in practice."

"Ah! you have certainly changed," exclaimed Leonor, "the Señorita Edelmira has much power over you."

"It is not the Señorita," replied Martin, "who has changed my purpose."

Leonor did not wish to prolong the conversation because the sincerity with which Martin had spoken destroyed the suspicion which she had conceived when with Matilde. The hopes the conversation of the evening before had raised in Martin abandoned him when he saw her leave her seat.

"It's all the same," he said to himself, "perhaps she will never love."

Shortly after he left the room and the house, and took the road to Rafael's dwelling, but Rafael was not at home.

"He went out an hour ago," his aunt said.

"I shall come early tomorrow, have the kindness to tell him so," Martin said as he said good-bye to the Señorita.

The very same night Don Fidel went to call upon Don Pedro San Luis.

"The proper thing to do," he said, after having expounded his theories about social life, "is to get this marriage over at once."

"But I think that we ought to let a little time pass, even if they themselves desire it otherwise; it is necessary to find some way to arrange with this old woman, who otherwise can make it very disagreeable for us."

"Those young people must see each other tomorrow," continued Don Fidel, who could only see the delay of his lease in any postponement of the marriage.

At this moment Rafael entered the room. The two who were talking could not suppress a movement of surprise on seeing him. His insolent face, disturbed look, the distant salute which he made to them, and the air of surly melancholy with which he threw himself on a chair, left Don Pedro and Don Fidel mute for a time.

The latter was the first to break the silence, and turning to Rafael—

"Frankly," he said, "I am here with Don Pedro arranging that now it is better to hasten on the marriage. I am speaking for the happiness of my daughter; what do you think about it?"

"It is useless, Señor," replied the young man, in a hopeless voice.

"How useless?" exclaimed Don Fidel, getting up.

Rafael drew a letter from his pocket and passed it to him, saying—

"Read, and you will see."

Don Fidel rapidly read Matilde's letter, for it was her letter, which he held in his hand, and, folding it, he exclaimed—

"Bah! foolishness! You know that her love is stronger than these words, torn from her in surprise. Let us go together to the house and you will see how different she is."

"No, Señor, I shall never go," said Rafael, in a sombre tone.

"What nonsense! Look, Señor Don Pedro! this is what lovers are like! They're just like glass, anything breaks them."

Don Pedro took the letter from Don Fidel's hands and read it.

"The letter is serious," he said.

"You do not know girls, Señor Don Pedro," he said; "don't you see that she only wants to be coaxed. Let Rafael come with me and you will see."

"I shall not go, Señor," said San Luis. "This letter, which it appears Matilde has written without your knowledge, tells me clearly that all is finished."

"That cannot be, I shall arrange everything. Would you pay any attention to a silly girl; I am certain that at this moment she's sorry for having written it."

"I thank you for your interest," said Rafael, "but I beg you to leave Matilde entirely free. If she was able to write me this letter, what use would it be to throw myself at her feet?"

"What I desire is," said Don Fidel, following up his idea of the lease, "that both of you must never forget my opinion of this affair, and my desire to see my daughter married to you. If unhappily the marriage does not come off, I hope that you will both be witnesses to the efforts and goodwill I have shown to arrange it."

"Oh, we don't require you to say anything about that," exclaimed Don Pedro.

"I prefer formality in business matters," continued Don Fidel, "and for this reason it is that when I make a promise I do not break it, even if it's against my inclination."

"I also do not forget my obligations," said Don Pedro.

These words gave Don Fidel indescribable comfort after the inquietude which Matilde's letter had caused him. He found in them a formal promise of carrying forward the lease and looked upon the rest as secondary.

After having forced a new promise with reference to Del Roblè (by means of energetic protestations against the want of formality in business matters) Don Fidel left the house and returned to his own, with the intention of interposing his authority, so as better to secure the lease by means of a retraction from Matilde of the letter which he had just read.

But Matilde, as we have seen, had recovered from her weakness, and, although it was with tears, yet she was able to resist the imperious voice of Don Fidel, who again left his house consoling himself that the lease of Del Roblè was in any case assured.

With the conviction that it would be impossible, short of violence, to bring about the marriage broken in such an extraordinary and unforeseen fashion, he took the road to Don Damaso's house, congratulating himself on an idea which had just arisen in his mind and which he was now going to try to establish.

To be certain of the lease and to marry Matilde to Augustin, he thought would be a master stroke, and when he entered the salon he called Don Damaso on one side.

"What I told you today before my wife is not what I really wished," he said, "but I was obliged to say it because in another way it was of use to me. To my sorrow, and to please Matilde, who had become very obstinate, I had to compromise with Don Pedro San Luis; but now all is changed."

"How?" asked Don Damaso.

Then Don Fidel told him about Matilde's letter, and the resolution his daughter had made.

"Magnificent!" exclaimed Don Damaso.

"All my desire is that she should be Augustin's wife," said Don Fidel, "but as I don't wish to annoy her—"

"Since she has broken it off herself the matter is different."

"That's what I think; but it is necessary to let a few days pass."

"Ah! I suppose so."

Don Fidel went to bed that night giving thanks to Doña Bernarda for what he had called in the morning her most unseasonable visit.

XLVI

M artin waited with great impatience the coming of the following day. His uneasiness about Rafael deprived him of his night's sleep. To this uneasiness was also added the trouble which we have seen he was in after his last conversation with Leonor, and these two preoccupations during many hours divided between them the dominion of his mind, until, overtaken by sleep, he dozed a little before the dawn. On account of his insomnia he left his bed at six o'clock, and, as was his custom, studied for two hours.

At nine o'clock he was at Rafael's house, and finding that the rooms of the latter were shut, he knocked at a door which led to the interior of the house occupied by Doña Clara, Rafael's aunt.

On hearing the knocking the señora presented herself; she had only a few moments before returned from the church.

"Rafael has gone out early?" asked Martin, after saluting Doña Clara.

"Don't you know what has happened?" asked the señora, clasping her hands with an air of consternation, "Rafael has gone away."

"Where?" asked the young man, anxiously.

"To the Recoleta Francisca," replied the señora with a gesture which in the midst of her sorrow still showed somewhat of satisfaction.

"To the Recoleta!" repeated Martin. "When?"

"This morning, very early."

"And why has he taken such a terrible resolution?"

"Then you know nothing?"

"Something happened yesterday at the house of Don Fidel."

"Very well, afterwards Rafael received a letter from the girl, saying that he was not to think of her any more, and I don't know what else! Poor thing! if you had only seen him last night! He cried like a little child. God! how he cried! It broke my heart."

"Poor Rafael," said Rivas, with genuine sorrow.

"The poor fellow told me everything last night. *Hijito!* How do young men live now! For this, mark you, he felt so deeply that he has been obliged to go to the Recoleta. It is necessary to be reconciled to God. How can one hope to be happy and live in such a fashion!"

The simple piety of the señora impressed the noble heart of Martin, but he wished to defend his friend.

"You know how he thinks about it now, and how he will repent his fault as long as he lives."

"That's true—*Hijito!* Poor Rafael!" said the señora, in whose eyes tears had gathered.

"I am going to see him today," said Martin, rising from his seat.

"He has told me that it's useless, he will see no one."

She turned as if a remembrance had come to her, and added—

"Ah! I was forgetting, he gave me a letter for you. here it is."

The señora gave Rivas a sealed letter, and he said goodbye to her in order to read it in private. On arriving at his house the servant gave him another letter.

"That girl of the other day brought it and is coming back for an answer," he said with a semi-smile of intelligence.

Rivas went up to his room and opened Rafael's letter, leaving the one that the servant had just given him on the table.

San Luis' letter was as follows:—

DEAR MARTIN,

"When you come to look for me tomorrow my aunt will tell you of the resolution that I have taken. It is night, and in the silence I have been able to meditate over the terrible events of this day—I have lost her! Can you imagine my sorrow? I cannot describe it. Do you remember that one day when reading the life of Martin Luther, I said he was a coward, because the terror caused him by the death of a friend who was killed by a thunderbolt at his side, decided him to become a monk? This judgment was the vain arrogance of youth, which spoke by my mouth, you who absolved it will understand the shock which my mind has received from a blow which has almost stunned me. It is a thunderbolt from heaven, it has come to strike me in my love, in the very centre of my heart, burning down to the roots of hope. The last of those ephemeral blessings with which man may charm life. Only once, beside the body of my father who died in my arms, have I felt my soul frozen as I feel it now. It is the realization of utter abandonment of a heart by love, which love alone was sustaining, and nothing in the world will ever be able to console me.

"Only three lines, Martin, only three lines in her letter, but three lines which have poured like burning lava over my bosom, devastating everything except my immense love. In a few words, without anything to mitigate her harshness she struck me on the face with her terrifying scorn. Nothing which speaks of the past, of yesterday, palpitating today, shows itself in these lines. Nothing which leaves a hope of the pardon which all noble souls inspired by God keep for us miserable transgressors. She, with the heart of an angel, with her soul bathed in divine purity, scorns me, Martin, and abhors me. How can I struggle against this dreadful conviction! Until today I thought that my will was capable of facing every fate, but I did not count on this, because I thought that to lose one's life was the most dreadful fate that could threaten any one, and against death I felt courageous.

"I have passed some hours, Martin, thinking as well as I was able on what I ought to do. And one idea returned every moment to my mind with most incredible persistence! It is a chastisement from God! What right have I to aspire to felicity when I have trampled without compassion upon another being innocent and frail! If the justice of heaven sometimes intervenes in the sins of the world it must punish the facile morality with which we accustom ourselves to ridicule those as cold-blooded who are chaste in this world, and we should prostrate ourselves on our knees before the infallible justice of God. The weight of this truth, which is daily mechanically repeated in the churches from the pulpit, oppresses the mind when in trouble and terrorizes the soul, whilst in the midst of happiness it is heard with neglect. I yield then to the weight of this idea, its strength deprives me of mine.

"But do not think that, carried away by the impression of such tremendous sorrow, I am going to consecrate my life to penitence, give myself up to a cloister with indissoluble vows. I want to find calm in silence, I want to fortify myself with the examples of virtue, I want to see if it is possible to tear her beloved image from my breast, to mourn as if she has ceased to exist. Then, when time may have tranquillized my mind and converted into a bearable melancholy the atrocious grief which I suffer, who knows what I may do. I have lived so much in my love that I scarcely know of anything else; for this reason no one can prophesy what I shall do.

"Do not believe also that I have ceased to think of Adelaida; neither her nor her mother can I blame for my misfortune. I pardon them, and I hope that they will pardon me. I could, I know well, repair my fault in the eyes of the world and give her back the honour that I deprived her of, but you are not ignorant, Martin, that I do not love her. It would be a monstrous union which could only be ended by suicide, and this also would be a disgrace to her. I know that I could give her my life, but not happiness.

"In my retirement I will receive no one, not even you. I shall write to you when I feel the necessity of doing so. My aunt is empowered to receive my letters and will send on to me all that are addressed to me. A priest, an old friend of my family, has made this retirement easy for me; he will be my advisor.

Your friend,
RAFAEL SAN LUIS

Martin threw San Luis' letter on the table, and leaning his forehead on his hand, gave himself up to the sad meditations which the reading of it caused him.

He was called to breakfast while he was still thinking of Rafael's misfortune, and had forgotten the other letter which he had received on his return. He took it up before going out to the dining-room. On crossing the courtyard he opened the letter but only had time to read the signature. It was from Edelmira Molina.

To explain it, before letting its contents be known, we must go back to the day before Edelmira had written the first letter to Martin which we have seen him read.

We said that Edelmira, before her last talk with Doña Bernarda (in which from terror she had agreed to marry Ricardo Castanos), had written to herself letters which were supposed to be written by Rivas, and which she guarded with the affection and all the illusion which impassioned hearts possess. The peremptory command of her mother deprived the girl of this dream of love, in which she had so often fashioned herself a happy future. But by dint of fostering this illusion Edelmira had arrived little by little to looking at it as a possibility, and that which had at first appeared to her as madness began to convert itself into hope. In this state of crystallization, to make use of the picturesque theory of Stendhal on the subject of love, Edelmira thought that, being obliged to give her hand to another, was to tear violently from her her cherished hope, without giving her any time to try to realize it. Her will protested in silence against this violence done to her silent love. From this protest to the desire of defying the oppression of the power which moved her, was not more than a hair's breadth. Hence arose her resolution to write to Martin, a resolution which had nothing strange about it if one thinks of the education which Edelmira received in the social class to which she belonged. Although in this class modest women have the same instincts as in the elevated and cultured class of society, their habits of life, of which we have shown some pictures, little by little conquer that timid modesty, which, like a frightened bird, is instinctive in a woman in love. Less refined amongst the middle classes, the language of gallantry must naturally conquer by force of habit the susceptibility of the ear, and also do the same with the impressionability of the heart.

In the social circle in which Edelmira moved the coarse jests and the crude love-making give women different ideas about the relations of the sexes than those which prevail in the minds of girls born in what are called good families. It was for this reason that Edelmira, whilst more cultivated than those of the majority of her class, found nothing strange in the means that occurred to her for sounding Rivas' sentiments. On the other hand, this step is taken in all social classes, although sometimes in a more delicate manner, particularly when the heart is on fire and nourishes a solitary love; because there are moments when every woman finds strength to conquer her timidity and to seek in the heart of the man whom she loves, an echo of the powerful voice of the sentiment which agitates her own.

We saw that the first letter which Edelmira addressed to Rivas might be considered as looking for the alleviation of distress that all seek for from a friend when they find themselves overcome by some sorrow. On reading Martin's reply she saw that it contained sincere expressions of friendship which her mind, dominated by one idea, could well interpret in the sense of her aspirations. It was thus that, although Edelmira did not dare to say to herself that Rivas was veiling the expression of his love in words of friendly counsel, she thought at least it was vague, and she received much consolation, because these words offered her help in case of necessity and strengthened her resolution of not obeying her mother in this matter.

Animated by the success of her first step she determined in consequence to take a second, and wrote to Martin the letter which we saw him open as he turned towards the dining-room where Don Damaso's family were assembled.

At table they spoke little, as Don Damaso wished to respect the friendship that Martin had for San Luis, in gratitude for the services which Martin had given him in the direction of his business affairs. But on going out of the dining-room Augustin called Rivas who was about to enter the study, whilst Leonor sat down before an embroidery frame on which she was working.

"And what is Rafael going to do about this?" asked the dandy, lighting an expensive cigar and offering another to Martin.

"He went this morning early to the Recoleta," said Rivas.

"How romantic that is; I pity him with all my heart," exclaimed Augustin.

"He wrote me a letter, he was in a state of desperation," added Martin.

"I do not understand this desperation," put in Leonor, "when he could distract himself with other love-affairs as he has already done."

"Little sister, there are love-affairs and love-affairs, and one must not mix them up."

"Ah! I did not know," replied Leonor.

"One could love for taste or for passion," continued the dandy.

"What I find," said Leonor, looking fixedly at Martin, "is that there is not one man capable of loving."

Rivas protested with a look, while Augustin exclaimed—

"Ah! for example, my beauty, you're wrong. Without speaking of Abelard, whose tomb I have seen in Père Lachaise in Paris, there are a crowd of others, who have passed their life in loving."

"You, you are so silent; are you thinking the same although you think it in Spanish?" said Leonor to Rivas.

"I think, Señorita," replied Martin, "that you judge men with too much severity."

"And the example of your friend San Luis, does it not justify my opinion?" asked the girl.

"But there are exceptions," replied Martin.

"Why not?" said Augustin, "exceptions undoubtedly there are. As I said before, look at Abelard in Père Lachaise, without counting the rest."

"Exceptions," said Leonor, at the same moment, without paying any attention to her brother, and turning to Martin. "Where are they? How can one know them?"

"Trust to me for that, little sister," said the dandy. "I know them. Martin is one of them."

"Ah! you count yourself amongst the exceptions?" Leonor asked with a smile, whilst Rivas felt his cheeks burn.

"Señorita," he replied, "there are things in which it appears one can praise one's self, and without doubt this is one of them, I think that I may consider myself amongst the exceptions."

"You think so, but you are not certain."

"I am quite certain," replied Martin, giving the girl such an ardent glance that she was obliged to lower her eyes.

"Tell us, Martin, are you in love?" questioned Augustin; "come on, then, tell us all about it, my friend?"

"You are going to make him tell lies," said Leonor, conquering with a smile the agitation with which she had put some stitches in her embroidery.

"Why, Señorita?" asked Rivas, in the same tone of raillery.

"You cannot compromise the one you love," replied Leonor.

"Unfortunately there is no talk of being able to compromise her," replied the young man, with resolution, "she is placed in a station so much higher than I am that my voice cannot reach her," he added, taking advantage of the moment in which Augustin had gone out to smoke his cigar in the patio.

"Loud speaking can be heard from afar," replied Leonor, with another smile which badly hid her agitation.

"In that case," said the young man, "when you ask me the same question as Augustin I shall not lie to you."

Leonor bent her head over the embroidery and Augustin returned to his seat.

A few moments afterwards Martin entered Don Damaso's study, and a long time passed before he remembered Edelmira's letter, which he had in his pocket.

XLVII

L eonor's reply had opened a new horizon in which Martin's imagination wandered with the jealous eagerness of one who, for the first time, feels that there is a hope of finding his love returned. The story of the boy who amused himself by building castles in the air when he went into a crowded neighbourhood to sell his basket of fruit, perfectly depicts the brilliancy of these first hopes. Many of them vanish like the castles of the boy, and roll on the ground like his basket. Happily for Rivas there was nothing on this occasion which could cloud the horizon in which his imagination revelled. Leonor's words and the agitation which accompanied them, the expression of her eyes, all supported him in his adventurous dreams.

It was only after half-an-hour that Martin remembered that he had in his pocket a letter which he had not read.

He opened it, and read the following:—

Dear Friend,

"Your kind letter consoled me greatly, and I owe you many thanks for it. You are my only confidant because my family do not lend me any support against the fate that threatens me, so that when you offer me your friendship now that I am so sad, without friends or relations to whom I can apply, you do me a great service. I would have had still more to thank you for if you had given me the advice which I begged for in my last letter. Reflecting in my mind about what I said to you, in order to find out why you did not give me this much needed advice, I think I ought to be more frank with you and tell you everything, since you are my friend. My repugnance to the marriage into which my mother wishes to force me, is not only that I have no affection whatever for Ricardo, but also for another reason, which I must tell you, and it is that my heart is not free and I can never be happy without him whom I love with all my soul. When you know this, Martin, you can give me advice—because the time is passing quickly—and every moment I am sadder about it and I can never accustom myself to the idea of marrying one whom I do not love.

"Forgive me if I trouble you, but I have no other friend than you, and I can never forget your kindness.

EDELMIRA MOLINA

"Poor girl!" said Rivas, as he took some paper to reply to her letter. From his reply one can imagine the exaltation of his mind since his last conversation with Leonor.

DEAR FRIEND,

"You are in love and you think yourself unhappy; do you not find in your mind sufficient resolution to resist! Seek for strength in this very love and meet it valiantly. When I thought it only was an affair of conquering what perhaps might be but a caprice, I thought that I ought to limit myself to offering you my friendship, avoiding taking part in a determination which might influence your future; but you love another 'with all your soul,' and you ask me if to obey your mother, you ought to abandon this love, and give your hand to one to whom you never can give your heart. I think, for my part, love is so exclusive, so severe is the allegiance that we owe to it when it is pure, that I would consider it a weakness to suppress it under the weight of any obedience whatever. Its laws, besides, cannot be loosened in life, and whoever cannot keep their faith, can never expect any other future than tears and sorrow. Why don't you throw yourself at your mother's feet and speak to her from your heart? She has also been young and will understand you. If you have not the courage for this send for me, and I will speak to her. My friendship for you is so sincere that I think I would have power to gain her to your cause and to soften a heart which cannot wish for more than the happiness of her children.

"On the other hand, Edelmira, a love like that which I consider you capable of feeling ought to abandon mystery and find strength in its innocence.

"The heart of a mother is a pure sanctuary in which you can confide your secret until you can show it to the eyes of all. Have, then, confidence in it, and do not waste any tears on a passion which ought to be the pride of a noble heart like yours.

"You ask me to excuse you—for what? I beg for your confidence. I demand it in the name of our friendship. Let me be the depository of your secrets, give me some title to serve you as I wish, let me contribute to your happiness as I ardently desire. Make use always of

Your affectionate friend,
MARTIN RIVAS

Edelmira received this letter in the evening from the hands of the servant of the house, who understood that it would pay her to carry on this correspondence with Martin. The theories which the young man made plain in a few words about love, kindled the heart of Edelmira, lighting in it the fire of a vital passion. She thought that the love of such a man was a treasure and felt her love increase for him. Sentimental and romantic ideas came to her mind. Her longing increased for a happiness which it was necessary to obtain at all costs, and with this conviction—which Martin's words of friendship increased—the delicate expression of a love which longed for hope augmented little by little until hope became almost a certainty.

Plunged in this sweet speculation, thrilled by the hope which she entertained for the realization of her desires, Edelmira let several days pass without writing.

During these days Leonor had not offered the young man any occasion of renewing their scenes of reticence (in which many lovers excel for some time before giving the decisive attack). To console himself Martin had worked hard in Don Damaso's business. The latter had little by little left to him all the burden of his commercial affairs. Also a great part of his time was occupied by the studies which he had for a time discontinued, and following the practice of Chilian students it was necessary that he should make great efforts by application to recover the time lost before the 18th September, the term which the Colleges allow for ending the voluntary holiday, to give itself up to the examinations for the rest of the year. Besides these occupations Martin found time in his *rôle* of lover to speak of his love in long letters written to Rafael San Luis. In them he repeated the eternal theme in the infinite variety of forms in which the imagination clothes the impressions caused by the loved one, and which the heart in its turn knows how to multiply with inexhaustible fecundity.

But the days passed without Rafael making any reply.

ALBERTO BLEST GANA

Finally, at the end of ten days the servant entered the room bringing a letter with a knowing smile. It came from Edelmira.

"Your letter," she said, "has consoled me, but notwithstanding how much I esteem your advice I can never dare to speak to my mother as I speak to you. I must confess that I am afraid, and I think also that she would take it very badly; she likes to be obeyed without question, above all since what has happened about Adelaida.

"You tell me to seek strength in my love, and it is true that I need it to help me to decide to suffer anything before marrying against my will. But this is the limit of my strength; since I do not dare to confess to my mother that I am in love with another. It may be that this is on account of another thing that I did not tell you in a former letter; and it is that I love some one without my love being returned; and I do not know if it ever will be returned. I have let many days pass without writing to you in order not to trouble you, and also because I did not dare to make the confession which I now make. Now you know everything; I have told you all; you know my heart as I know it myself.

"I hope you will always help me with your advice. I assure you that this is my only consolation, and the only thing that can give me courage in my affliction; with it I shall be able to wait until the day arrives on which I must answer my mother."

This letter from Edelmira, like the others of which we have given the substance (with a few faults eliminated which would have marred the reading of it), deeply roused Rivas' sympathy, because he found a great resemblance between his situation in respect of his love-affair and the way in which this girl was placed. He and she both suffered from an unhappy passion, and they had no other pleasure than entwining it with hopes. This eulogy made him sympathize still more with Edelmira in her fate.

"Be persuaded, Edelmira," he replied, "that the sad fate of loving without hope cannot come to one who, like you, is beautiful and has a noble heart, whose love would fill any one with pride. After your confession what can I say to you? Neither do I dare to ask the name of the man who does not know that you love him. But I am certain that he is a man worthy of you, capable of understanding you and of sheltering in his breast the treasure that you consecrate to him. Am I mistaken? I don't think so, and under this persuasion I can only advise you to keep your love intact, because it will be the guardian angel of your purity. I don't know why, but I have a presentiment that heaven reserves a recompense for those who harbour such beautiful sentiments without leaving the paths of virtue.

"Meantime I think that you, notwithstanding your timidity, ought to make up your mind to confide this secret of your heart to your mother. The day in which you have to decide definitely is not far off and it is better to mention your intentions in time, in place of causing a surprise which might be fatal for you. To confirm this advice I repeat my previous offers. Make use of me and believe that it will give me infinite satisfaction to do anything that may contribute to your happiness."

Edelmira gave a deep sigh when she read this letter, she was at the end of her resources, and had arrived at the necessity of naming the man that she loved.

Although, as we have said before, she thought vaguely that some phrase in Martin's replies, or some unforeseen incident similar to those which lovers—those blind believers in chance—always look for would give her an opportunity to reveal to Martin the whole of the secret which she had half confided to him. But his replies had destroyed her illusion and accident had not realized the impossibilities which each time she had hoped for. What was to be done? A deep sigh was the only reply to this vexed question. The letters that she read and re-read a thousand times showed her that Martin possessed a warm and noble heart. What a sight for a girl in love! Was it not to have a glimpse of Paradise without being able to pluck one of its flowers?

Edelmira saw them display their gay colours, rocking in the balmy breezes and blowing towards her, their perfumes wrapt in their fluttering folds. These perfumes gave her burning vertigoes of insomnia during which this question—what is to be done?—presented itself like the angel with the flaming sword to drive her from this Paradise. Her mind was controlled by her natural prudence on one side, and on the other by her firm resolution to resist her mother, so that in the midst of this long and restless insomnia she could think of no other means of salvation than to leave her destiny to time.

One circumstance now contributed to determine her in this resolution; Ricardo Castanos proposed to Doña Bernarda to put off the marriage until he had obtained the rank of captain, which the chief of the corps had offered him. This would take place at the end of November, and he could then fix the marriage for the end of December.

Edelmira communicated this happy news to Martin in a letter to which Rivas replied congratulating her, but repeating his advice to tell Doña Bernarda the secret of her love, if Edelmira did not give up her idea of resistance. But the girl received this advice with her former objections, and preferred to leave to time the solution of the problem.

Whilst her fears were sleeping in such groundless repose they were all dispersed one day by the same Ricardo announcing that the formalities for his new rank were over and all would be finished at the end of five or six days. The conversation at which Ricardo gave this news took place on the 29th November, consequently there remained very few days for the preparations for the marriage, fixed for the 15th December.

Then returned to Edelmira all the agony of a desperate struggle between her fear of her mother and her aversion to the young Castanos who thought that with three stripes upon his sleeve he was offering a kingdom to his disdainful lady-love. Edelmira saw that she had hoped in vain for time and that it was necessary at once to take a decided step, under the penalty of giving her hand and renouncing her happiness for ever.

XLVIII

Without considering himself entirely happy during this time Rivas had curbed his impatience and strengthened his will by his decided devotion to his studies and his work as secretary to Don Damaso. With secret pleasure he announced to his family at the beginning of December the happy result of his examinations which left him free until the following year; telling his mother that for reasons of economy he would be obliged to give up the journey which he had meant to take during the vacation in order to see her. But besides this reason, his love was the most powerful agent in fixing him in Santiago, since he thought that absence might make him lose the chance of being loved; the possibility of which was every now and then indicated by Leonor's manner. We have seen how this girl had been little by little accustoming her pride to loving a man who occupied a social position so inferior to that of others who almost every day proposed for her hand. Her pride conquered, distrust now took possession of her— distrust, the child of the same pride which made her fear for Martin's love, the sincerity of which she doubted at times because she could not explain to herself the timidity of the young man who she saw display strength of decision in all the other acts of his life. Hence came her reserve which went badly with the frankness and resolution which characterized her; hence also her design to advance no further in the path in which she was walking until she had irrefutable proofs of the love of Rivas. Without understanding the delicacy of the young man who never ventured to take advantage of the different occasions on which he could have declared himself, Leonor contented herself with conversations such as we know of, and talking continually of her love to Matilde Elias. Matilde received the confidence of her who had been the depository of her own hopes and was now the depository of her sorrow, without ever rousing herself from the weight of her grief, but wishing at the same time to repay Martin in some way for the slight services that she owed him.

All the family had admired the courage with which Matilde had recovered herself from the weight of the blow which had so quickly and so unexpectedly destroyed her happiness. Some words of hers to Leonor explain the firmness which no one had expected in the meek and timid creature whom the least trouble had until now overwhelmed.

"If I had been able to preserve my respect for Rafael nothing would have consoled me, but whilst I pardon his deceit, I bewail not his loss, but the loss of my love which has died."

In effect there arose in her heart a mourning for her love and a pardon for him who had destroyed it. Once she said to Leonor—

"Martin has an upright mind which abhors deceit; he also condemns Rafael's conduct. If ever he tells you that he loves you, you can believe it before any one else's oath."

With the arrival of the summer, preparations were being made by Don Damaso's family to go into the country. It had been arranged that Matilde would accompany her cousin during the stay of Leonor's family in a Hacienda of her father's on the neighbouring coast, which was frequented by the people of Santiago as a bathing place.

This gave occasion to Martin to write San Luis a long letter with the motive of speaking of his happy expectations.

"WE SHALL HAVE A ROOM where we can work, Don Damaso has told me, and at other times I can see her. Perhaps we can go together to some places which, if they are not picturesque, I have enough imagination to adorn and I shall return, my dear friend, to days of confidence and tranquillity. Do you not think that an occasion may present itself in which I can tell her how much I love her and speak to her of the thoughts which have held me for so long a time. All this makes me giddy, I can hardly contain the beatings of my heart, which I have sought with such earnestness but in vain, to teach to conquer itself. It conquers *me*, and my lectures are lost in the sound of its beating."

Destiny nevertheless reserved for him something very different to these happy plans which he entertained himself in forming.

We have said that the day fixed for the marriage of Edelmira and Ricardo Castanos by Doña Bernarda was the 15th December.

On the 14th Edelmira resolved to summon all her courage and to throw herself at her mother's feet, begging her in the name of heaven not to oblige her to give her hand to the man whom she could not love.

"Now just look at this!" exclaimed Doña Bernarda, raising her hands to heaven. "You expect a great deal too much. What do I say! What a disgrace! A captain in the police wishes to marry her and the lady doesn't think it good enough. We shall have to turn some major into a widower, so that he shall come and offer you his hand!"

"But, mama, I cannot be happy with this man," said the agonized girl.

"Then are you a prophetess that you don't know that you're going to be happy! Do you think you know better than your mother? If you don't like him then you've *got* to like him because he will be your husband. I'm not going into the streets to look for some one to marry you; nor are you going to live all your life at my expense. I'm going to have some comfort from one of my daughters. I also didn't care about the defunct Molina when I married, it was enough that I liked him afterwards, and I don't want to talk any more about it, and so I tell you."

In vain Edelmira sought the help of Amador, but he refused to intercede in her favour.

"My mother wishes it," he answered, "and when once she gets an idea into her head nothing will change it. Don't be so foolish, what more do you want than a captain?"

The inflexibility of her family made Edelmira again think of the only support she could count upon. She turned her thoughts to Rivas.

"If all abandon me," she thought, taking up her pen, "he will save me."

Edelmira was seized at this moment by the agitated fluctuations of desperation; she saw herself conducted to the altar by Ricardo under the imperious gaze of Doña Bernarda, saying good-bye for ever to peace of mind and to her chaste love for Martin. This picture had been her nightmare for nearly two months, but now it was taking the form of reality and nothing offered her any escape from those who were driving her to this horrible destiny.

Under these impressions she wrote to Martin relating the useless supplications which she had addressed to her mother and her brother. She depicted her desperation with the eloquence of truth, and reminding him of his repeated offers to help her, begged him for his support in putting into execution a plan which she had conceived and which was the only one which could save her. Her plan was to fly from the maternal roof and to take refuge with the aunt at Renca who had given hospitality to her sister, when she had been obliged to hide her condition from Doña Bernarda.

"This aunt," continued Edelmira in her letter, "has a good deal of influence over my mother, and has been very useful to her, above all in money matters, because she has a very good estate in Renca; so my mother denies her nothing. I would have liked to have asked my aunt to come to Santiago, but besides that she never cares to go anywhere, she became a widow here and she was very fond of her husband. My mother would have talked her over, but going to her with the resolution that I have taken, she will defend me. As she is much younger than my mother, she is like a sister to us, and is very fond of us, and I am certain she will receive me favourably."

To these explanations Edelmira added protestations of an irrevocable resolution, and begged Martin to provide a carriage for the next day at 7 o'clock in the morning, the hour at which, under the pretext of going to confession, she would be at the church of Santa Anna with a servant from their house.

Martin received this letter the day after he had written to San Luis speaking of his prospects of travelling into the country with Don Damaso and his family. After begging Edelmira to weigh well the resolution that she had announced, he added—

"If you persist, tomorrow the carriage will be punctual to the hour and in the place that you have indicated. You must permit me not to leave you to the mercy of the coachman, and allow me to accompany you to your aunt's house. It will be a pleasure for me to do you this service. You can come out of the church at the hour arranged and will find me there; take all the precautions that you think necessary, and above all do not deprive me of the satisfaction of accompanying you."

Edelmira kissed this letter when she found herself alone at night, and was careful to give no suspicion of her intentions. After making her preparations for the journey, she hoped that Adelaida and all the others in the house would be sunk in sleep. In these preparations her first care was to make into a package and attach to her belt the letters of Rivas, which were a treasure to her.

Then she gave herself up to thinking over her lot, and waiting for the hour on the following day when she was to go to the church.

XLIX

At half past six on the morning of the following day Edelmira set out from the house with a servant and shortly afterwards arrived at Santa Anna.

In the Plaza before this church could be seen a post-chaise with a horse in the shafts, held by the reins by a postilion who was mounted upon another horse of the well-known race of Cujo to which both belonged.

The postilion, cracking his whip from time to time, hummed under his breath a popular tune in a nasal and monotonous voice.

Edelmira felt an involuntary tremor on seeing the carriage in which her flight was to be made, and, without thinking, stopped a moment to look at it.

It appeared that the aspect of Edelmira and her servant roused the gallantry of the postilion, who interrupted his humming to say to them—

"What are these morning stars seeking? Here I am to serve them."

"Why do you trouble yourself, when there is no necessity?" replied the servant.

Edelmira came out of her day-dream at these words and turned her steps to the door of the church.

"*Adios!*" exclaimed the postilion on seeing them go away, "they go away and leave me in darkness! Such severity with such beautiful eyes!"

"Just listen to him! As cool as you please," replied the servant, whilst Edelmira, frightened at this dialogue, hastened her steps. The girl and her servant had hardly arrived at the steps before the front of the church when Rivas presented himself, he having doubtless, from some neighbouring spot, seen Edelmira arrive.

She became livid on seeing him so near, and stopped in agitation.

To prevent any suspicions on the part of the servant Martin appeared surprised at this meeting and exclaimed—

"Señorita! You here at this hour!"

Edelmira replied in a stammering tone, and moved away from the servant, who did not appear to be displeased with the gallantries of the postilion, in whose direction she frequently turned her head.

"I see you are punctual," said Martin to Edelmira in a low voice; "are you determined?"

Edelmira looked at her interlocutor as if she had forgotten her fear on the moment, and the grief which had hollowed her cheek.

"Quite resolved," she answered him.

"And you permit me to accompany you?"

"Why should you put yourself out for me?" she asked, in a sad tone.

"It is what I most wish," replied Martin, "and, as I told you in my letter, I cannot consent to leave you to the mercy of a coachman whom we do not know."

This observation about the coachman had much weight in Edelmira's mind, already frightened by the compliments the postilion had been paying her.

"Besides," added Rivas, "you've given me the right of friendship, which gives me power to make it effective. Far from it being a trouble to me to accompany you, it is a pleasure."

Edelmira heard with esctasy the kindly words of the man on whom her thoughts for so long had been centred.

"Have you not enough confidence in me?" asked Rivas.

"Oh!" said she, "in you more than in any one."

"Then I'm going to expect you in the coach. As you. see, I can perfectly well remain there without being seen."

"I'll endeavour to come out as quickly as possible." replied the girl, turning towards the church.

The servant did not see this movement of her mistress as she was replying with generosity to the fusillade of sheep's eyes made by the gallant postilion.

When she saw Martin pass she followed Edelmira discontentedly; the latter had now entered the church.

"Wait here for me," Edelmira said to her, pointing to a chair, "I am going to look for the confessor, and will soon come back."

Martin in the meantime had entered the coach and begun to wait.

Edelmira spread her carpet before the altar, and went down on her knees in prayer.

After having fervently begged the protection and support of Heaven, and after having prayed for courage in the decisive step which she was about to take, she got up, folded the carpet, and went towards the confession box whence she could see the servant whom she had left waiting for her.

The servant passed the time in looking at the saints on the altars, and occupied herself, like the generality of the lower classes, in thinking of nothing. Then Edelmira took advantage of this inattention to leave the confession-box, and, still looking at her, directed her steps to the door of the church.

The pious people were all beginning to arrive. Dressed in the upper petticoat worn by Spanish women and in mantle like that worn by Edelmira, they favoured her safe exit by their movements in going and coming across the church, which most of them looked upon as a meeting place.

Edelmira found herself in the plaza with her heart beating, and her body trembling. As those who were passing by and those who were entering the church looked at her with curiosity, she judged that it was more prudent to act with resolution and went straight to the coach.

Opening the door Edelmira got in, and Rivas said to the postilion— "Go on."

The horses hearing the sound of the whip set off at a quick trot.

Edelmira's servant, tired of looking at the altars, looked at this moment at the lay brother who was lighting some candles, and thought that the postilion was a much finer man than the lay brother.

It appears that the postilion, who so quickly captivated the preference of the servant, gifted with the instinctive malice of the majority of our common people, had strong suspicions about the pair that he was driving, so, improvising a variation upon a well-known song, he sang, accompanying himself with the whip—

> *"Me voi, pero voi contigo*
> *Te llevo en mi corazon;*
> *Si quieres otro lugar*
> *Aqui en el coche cabimos dos."*

> *("Behold me but thou art with me*
> *I carry thee in my heart;*
> *If you prefer any other place*
> *There is room for two in the coach.")*

Edelmira had hidden her face in her hands, and was striving to control the sobs which rose in her throat.

Martin waited until this paroxysm of grief, which he respected, should pass, and only spoke when he saw that his companion on the journey was more tranquil.

"There's yet time to return," he said to her; "command me, Edelmira, I am at your service."

"Don't think that I repent," replied the girl, wiping the tears from her eyes; "I weep at seeing myself obliged to leave my own house."

"If you have confidence in your aunt," replied Martin, "I expect that everything will be arranged as you wish."

"As I wish, no," said Edelmira, fixing her eyes on Rivas with a singular expression, "but I shall escape the marriage."

"The other may come afterwards."

"Who knows?"

This exclamation of despair was accompanied by a sigh.

"You appear to be passionately in love," said Rivas, deeply interested in Edelmira's love-affair, which, as we have said, he found analogous to his own.

Edelmira's cheek became covered with blushes.

"I told you so in my letter, then," she said, lowering her face.

"And without hope?" asked Rivas.

"Without hope," said the girl, sighing.

At this moment could be heard more clearly the voice of the postilion who repeated, cracking his whip—

"Si quieres otro lugar
Aqui en el coche cabimos dos
Cabimos *dos* guayayai. . ."

and his voice mingled with those of the strawberry sellers who at this hour enter the capital to sell the celebrated strawberries of Renca.

Edelmira and Martin remained silent, listening to the voice of the gay postilion.

"Do you remember having heard this song?" asked the girl.

"Your brother sang it the night that I had the pleasure of knowing you," replied Martin, "but Amador didn't adorn it with this last verse."

"I see you have got a good memory."

"Had you forgotten the circumstance?"

"Oh no! I remember much of that night, but above all I remember all that I spoke of with you."

"Perhaps because *he* was there," said Martin, smiling.

"Who?"

"He of whom we have been speaking."

"Ah! no. Then I didn't care for any one."

In spite of the innocence of this observation, there was so much sadness in Edelmira's voice that Rivas said to her—

"Until now you had confidence in me, are you sorry for it?"

"Am I sorry for it? No."

"I ask you this question because I want to serve you in every way."

"What more could you do for me. I have troubled you enough already."

"I could do still more perhaps if you would tell me the name of him you love."

"No, no!" exclaimed the girl, excitedly, "never!"

"Do you think that I asked you this question from curiosity?"

"No, but—"

"Come, I'll not insist; but believe me it was not from curiosity, but from the hope of being able to help you."

"I believe you, Martin, forgive me if I don't answer it, but it's impossible now," said Edelmira, in feeling accents; and then she added, giving to her voice that tone of sweetness which we employ to a person whom we fear to have offended, "I might tell it to you another time, perhaps."

"Tell it to me only if you think it would be useful to you for me to know it."

"Very well."

"But we can speak of him without mentioning his name," replied Martin, thinking that there could be no other conversation more agreeable than this to Edelmira.

"That is so," she replied with a smile.

Then they chatted happily about the recollections of her love. Edelmira appeared to forget the situation in which she was and depicted with simple eloquence the birth of this passion without explaining its origin, which she herself did not know. Martin was a good judge in appreciating the merit of the picture which the girl drew for him, and found touches of admirable truth which he compared with his own numerous recollections of solitude and love.

Thus they arrived at the aunt's house, and she, after hearing Edelmira's explanations, lavished attentions on Martin.

"If you wish to do penance," she said, "I beg you will breakfast with us."

Rivas accepted with pleasure, and breakfasted pleasantly with Edelmira and her aunt.

In the dishes which were presented to him, in the great basket of strawberries which spread their aromatic odour over all the room, in the furniture which decorated it, in everything, the young man found a pleasure which enchanted him. In this frame of mind he accepted the offer which the widow made him of a horse to ride, with which Martin amused himself for hours, galloping at times, pulling up at times to look at the view, some landscape in which in imagination he was with Leonor, he lying at her feet, forgetting the world, speaking to her of his love, praising her beautiful hands.

On saying good-bye in order to return to Santiago, Edelmira accompanied him to the coach.

"Whilst you were out riding I kept my promise," she said, handing him a letter, "here is the name that you asked me for on the way."

Rivas took the letter and went away without remarking the agitation with which Edelmira had given it to him.

"Don't open it until you are gone," said the girl to him when the carriage was about setting out.

Rivas saluted her again in farewell, and went away.

The ride on horseback which he had had, and the satisfaction of being of service to Edelmira put Martin in a very good humour. Leaning back in the coach, which was going quickly enough, he gave himself up for a long time to the ideas which offered themselves about the projected journey into the country with the family of Don Damaso, and he only thought of opening Edelmira's letter when he felt himself somewhat far from the house where he had received it.

The letter contained the following:—

"Martin, you know the history of my love, but you have never heard it all, because I did not dare to tell you on our journey the name of the man I love, but you will find it at the beginning of this letter.

EDELMIRA MOLINA

"I!" exclaimed Rivas, in surprise.

Then after reading the letter a second time he said with true feeling, "Poor Edelmira."

Truly for the rest of the journey he could only think of the revelation made by the paper which he held in his hand, and he arrived at Santiago full of sadness at having been, although involuntarily, the cause of the difficult position in which Edelmira found herself.

He left the coach in the Plaza de Armes and went on foot to Don Damaso Encina's house. As he was going up to his room he heard the voice of Augustin, who called him from his chamber.

"Hombre!" he said to him excitedly, "where do you come from?"

"I've been away from Santiago, why do you ask me?" answered Rivas, uneasily.

Augustin shut the door of his room which opened upon the other courtyard that communicated with the interior apartments, and then approaching Martin he said to him in a tone of the greatest mystery—

"I am going to tell you what has happened!"

L

To understand what Augustin then said to Rivas we must revert to what happened during his absence.

The servant whom Edelmira had taken with her in the morning to Santa Anna had got tired of making comparisons between the lay brother who was arranging the candles on the altar, and the gallant postilion who had thrown such captivating glances at Edelmira or herself.

The servant was inclined to think that it was she who had captivated the gallant postilion, and certainly, as we have already said, she found him much more interesting than the lay brother who lit the candles.

But as after a time the latter went away and the servant had nothing to make comparisons with, she amused herself by counting the altars and the candles which each held, and as at the end of three-quarters of an hour, remembering that she had not said any prayers, she repeated some "Salves" and some "Pater Nosters."

The hour passed; she began to think that the number of Edelmira's sins could not be a very small one since she took so long to confess them, and tired of thinking of this she gave up thinking and went to sleep.

A sister of mercy woke her half an hour afterwards to ask her if the Gospel of the Mass which was said at this season was over.

The servant contented herself with answering—

"I haven't seen it, it hasn't passed by here."

The Sister of Mercy went away saying, "God bless you," and the servant yawned several times.

Tired of waiting, she went to all the confession boxes and then all over the church in every direction, looking at the faces of the devotees, which could be seen beneath their veils.

Not finding Edelmira in the church she went out into the Plaza. Neither was Edelmira there, and she noted with regret the absence of the amiable postilion.

She returned more quickly to the entrance of the church and looked at the devotees, and then went out again into the Plaza full of inquietude.

The first person that is always seen in every plaza in Santiago is a policeman; the servant turned towards one who was playing terrible variations on his whistle in the ears of the passers-by.

"What hour might it be?" she asked him.

"It has just struck ten o'clock," answered the policeman.

"Ten o'clock! Good gracious!" exclaimed the servant, hastening to walk quickly back to the house.

But it was a quarter past ten o'clock when she arrived there, where Doña Bernarda was waiting impatiently for her breakfast.

"And Edelmira?" she asked, seeing the servant enter.

"Has she not come back, then?" asked the latter.

They looked in vain for Edelmira all over the house; and afterwards the family gathered together to consider where they could look for her. An hour passed in making a thousand guesses; when this hour was over the family sat down to breakfast, and after breakfast they waited for two more hours without having any suspicions that Edelmira could have run away.

But as Edelmira did not arrive Doña Bernarda called the servant and asked her about the walk to the church. The servant showed so much confusion in her narrative that she omitted the meeting of Edelmira with Martin. This confusion raised vague suspicions in Amador's mind, which he communicated to his mother, to whom he proposed the medium of threats, and even violence, to tear the secret of this mystery from the servant, in case there did exist a mystery.

"These 'chinas' are made for evil," said Doña Bernarda, sententiously, "and it's necessary to treat them as such."

Consequently the servant appeared again before the tribunal of the family, and was very shortly involved in the net which Amador extended skilfully. Threats had such an effect on her that in less than half an hour the servant had related all the circumstances of the morning excursion.

"Mother," said Amador, when he was alone with Doña Bernarda, "I shouldn't be surprised if she has run away with Martin."

"Deos la libre!" replied the señora, clenching her fists, "for I'll send her straight to the Corruption."

By this name she designated the House of Correction for Women.

At this moment Ricardo Castanos arrived, and being informed of the event, was of the opinion that he would go to Don Damaso's house, an opinion accepted by an unanimity of votes.

Amador and Ricardo arrived at half-past three o'clock in the afternoon at the house which had given hospitality to Martin.

The servant told them that Rivas had gone out before seven o'clock in the morning.

The hour was suspicious, and the two young men looked at one another.

"Shall we go back?" asked the official of police.

"It would be better that we should see the master of the house, and tell him of the affair."

This advice prevailed after a short discussion, in which Amador held to his opinion; with the hope of meeting and assaulting Martin, to revenge himself for Martin's participation in Adelaida's affair.

"If he is not mixed up in this," he said, "what brought him so early to the church, and what a coincidence also that he should arrive at the same time as Edelmira."

This reflection awakened the zeal of Ricardo, who, as if he was taking charge of his companion against an enemy, said resolutely—

"Go slowly."

"Don't interfere in this," Amador replied, "I'm taking the lead."

Don Damaso Encina was in his study reading an article in the Opposition newspaper.

Amador and the official saluted him with great ceremony, and the son of Doña Bernarda was the spokesman, and told him the object of the visit.

"I do not think that Martin would be capable of such a thing," said Don Damaso, when Amador concluded the story of his suspicions.

"You don't know him, señor," replied Amador, "he doesn't look capable of breaking an egg, but he is in reality quite the contrary."

Don Damaso called his son to investigate before the two men all that he knew.

Augustin heard the story and said—

"It's an insult, I don't believe it."

"And why did Martin go out so early?" replied Amador.

"He can go out early without going out to steal girls," replied Augustin, taking advantage of the opportunity to scoff at him, who had made him suffer so much shortly before with his plot of the mock marriage.

"We haven't come here to be mocked at," said Ricardo Castanos, angrily.

"I say what I think," answered Augustin, "and if you're certain that Rivas has run away with the girl, the best thing you can do is to go and look for him elsewhere."

Don Damaso interposed his authority and said that if Martin had taken any part in her escape he would have justice done to him for the honour of the house.

Amador and the official then retired.

"Papa, they wanted to get money from you," said Augustin.

"That's what I think," replied Don Damaso, "the fact is that they have reason to suspect Martin, but if it is true, I'll not permit a young man who sets such a bad example to remain in my house."

Augustin retired, leaving his father much satisfied at the judgment he had shown in this affair, and went to Leonor's room.

"Hermanita," he said, "do you know what has happened?"

"No."

"They have come to accuse Martin of running away with Edelmira Molina, your ex-sister-in-law."

Leonor let fall a book which she was reading, and stood up as pale as a corpse.

Augustin related to her what he had just been told in his father's presence.

"And you, what do you think of it?" asked Leonor, with anxious disquietude.

"Upon my word, I don't know what to think," answered Augustin, who, as we have seen, thought there was a love-affair between Edelmira and Martin.

Leonor felt a violent longing to burst into tears, but found strength to contain herself.

"Martin has always denied that he was in love with this *muchacha!*" she exclaimed, giving a strong accent of contempt to the word *muchacha*.

"What can you expect? *Mi bella*, every one has his little secrets in this base world."

"It's an unpardonable piece of hypocrisy!" exclaimed Leonor, with badly suppressed rage.

"Hypocrisy, Hermanita! As much as you like, but you must remember that the poor boy is a man after all."

"And why does he deny that he is ever in love?"

"*Pourquoi?* that's good. Truths are not always to be told, *Bella Hermanita.*"

Leonor let herself fall back on the sofa where Augustin had first seen her.

"Observe," he added, "we're not very indulgent with poor Martin, who has rendered us so many kind offices. You are not kind, Hermanita, you don't behave like the beautiful proverb which says—the heart of a woman is all generosity—"

"And what *do* I say!" exclaimed Leonor, impatiently.

"I don't know, but I can see that you treat this affair *très serieusement*—"

"You're wrong," replied the girl, with well-feigned serenity; "what does all this matter to me?"

"Those services of which you speak are such that it makes me feel this greatly, because papa and mama cannot regard all this with indifference."

"Ah, now I'm glad to hear you, you speak like a book. You will punish me if I smoke here, so I will leave you."

Augustin left Leonor's room lighting a large cigar, and went to his quarters.

A few minutes afterwards Rivas arrived, to be met and questioned by Augustin, as already related.

"I'm going to tell you what has happened," he said to him after having closed the doors of the room with a mysterious air.

"What is it?" said Rivas, sitting down.

"Amador and the lover of Edelmira have just left the house."

"Yes?" asked Martin, slightly changing colour.

"They have come to tell papa that you've run away with the girl."

"Blackguards!" exclaimed Rivas, between his teeth.

"I said the same, I must confess that I found it amusing. But I defended you warmly, have no fear about that; but I assure you they were furious. What we have to do is to dispel all papa's suspicions."

"And how?" asked Martin, coolly.

Augustin looked at him thunderstruck.

"Par example," he exclaimed, *"c'est un peu trop fort!"*

"I don't see why."

"You don't see why? Caspita! it's not enough that he isn't certain, it's absolutely necessary that papa should be convinced of your innocence."

"It will be rather troublesome to make him believe it."

"How troublesome?"

"What Amador says is half true."

"What! You've run away with Edelmira!"

"I have accompanied her."

"Where?"

"To Renca."

Augustin got up, put on his hat, and saluted Rivas.

"I bow before your talents," he said. "If you had only done the same with Adelaida you would have saved me much annoyance. You're a man of strength, my friend, I bow before you, you are my master."

"How?" asked Rivas, laughing at the comic gravity of his friend.

"How! It appears a small thing to you to run away with a young girl as beautiful as a flower. You are extraordinarily modest, my friend."

"I didn't run away with her, I accompanied her."

"Really! But you've got to tell that to papa."

"I don't understand," replied Martin.

"You understand very well on the contrary. Happy mortal!"

Then Rivas explained to him what had happened, with the exception of Edelmira's affection for himself.

Augustin lit his cigar which had gone out.

"The aspect of the thing is changed," he said, "you have sacrified yourself to friendship."

"I don't see in what the sacrifice consists."

"Look here; girls can be very malicious, and also be mistaken. Just imagine! Leonor is furious."

"Ah!" said Rivas, agitatedly, "does she also know it?"

"All, and she believes what I believed, although I tried to excuse you."

At this moment they were called to dinner.

"But you are going to deny everything to papa," said Augustin to him.

"I haven't committed any crime that I should hide my actions," said Rivas, with dignity.

"You are free to do whatever you please," said Augustin, opening the door. "I give you my opinion."

They walked together into the dining-room.

Augustin felt distressed, because he had a true affection for Rivas.

Rivas appeared calm, although his heart was beating violently. All he feared was Leonor's disdain.

When they entered the family were seated round the table.

LI

A great silence reigned in the dining-room when the two young men sat down. Don Damaso took his soup with an air of affected gravity and Doña Engracia gave a piece of chicken to Diamela, Leonor fixed her gaze on one of the windows of the room from which hung a rep curtain over another of fine white lace.

Martin sought her eye in vain and thought he read his sentence in her face; for the girl held herself with a singular haughtiness.

Nevertheless this silence was too embarrassing to last much longer and the weakest in character found it necessary to break it.

Don Damaso relaxed little by little the gravity with which he had replied to Rivas' salute, and finally decided to say a word to him, particularly as nothing broke the silence which was worrying him.

"Have you been out?" he asked.

"Yes, Señor," replied Martin.

No other question occurring to Don Damaso he became silent. But Augustin was not one of those who can remain long in silence, and it appeared to him that he ought to follow his father's example.

"We've got no places here made expressly for picnics into the country as in Paris," he said.

And he plunged into a description of the Lake of Enghien, of the Park of Saint Cloud, and various places in the suburbs of Paris. As the others found themselves very little disposed to interrupt him, he was able to continue his dissertation during almost the whole meal, launching into a host of Gallicisms and Frenchified phrases with which he tried to give a local colour to his description.

"That's the place where one can amuse one's self," he exclaimed with enthusiasm at the finish, "and not here where the environs of Santiago are so hideous. No parks; No châteaux, and nothing."

The dinner ended without Leonor having appeared to see Martin's presence at the table. On getting up, Doña Engracia said to her husband—

"I hope you are going to speak to Martin, because it can't remain like this."

"There's plenty of time, I'll speak this evening," replied Don Damaso, who, paying much respect to his digestion, took advantage of this pretext for not having a serious explanation with Rivas about the affair of Edelmira.

"Very well, then, but don't forget to do it, there must be no scandal in this house," replied Doña Engracia, giving a pat to Diamela, as if to make her a witness of what she said.

The little dog replied with a growl, and they left the ante-room in which they were speaking.

Behind their parents came Leonor and Augustin. Rivas was the last to leave the dining-room and he went straight up to his room.

"Do you know that there's something true in what they say about Martin?" said Augustin to Leonor when they were alone.

"Who told you so?" asked the girl, who in her own mind was imagining that Martin would free himself from the accusations hanging over him.

"Martin himself," replied the dandy.

"Is it possible? Did he dare not to deny it?" exclaimed Leonor, with an expression of anger which in itself seemed to speak of revenge.

"But he did it out of the purest kindness."

"Oh, indeed!" said the girl, with a sarcastic smile.

"Imagine! the old woman wanted to marry this girl off against her will."

"And Martin from the purest kindness, as you say, made himself her champion; is it not so? This excuse appears to me a very poor one, it belongs to the age of Don Quixote."

"Bother!" exclaimed Augustin, who had inherited from his father the facility to change his opinion every moment, "do you know that you have given me something to think about, it may be that you're right."

"And you believed him?" added Leonor, with an expression of badly suppressed rage, "you have an admirable facility for believing everything. Look here, what would you have done in his place? Would you have confessed a sin? for this is a very grave sin, What does it matter if the girl is poor, if she is virtuous?"

"All that you say appears to me as true as Gospel, *mi bella*, and I'm no better than a fool: Martin can turn me round like the sails of a windmill! And I believed every word he said without doubting him for a moment!"

Still exclaiming, Augustin went away, and Leonor went to her room. She did not wish to confess to herself that she was furious, and to distract her thoughts she began to try on a hat which she had bought for the country. Whilst she was looking at herself in the glass, two large tears ran down her fresh cheeks which were burning with rage.

In the evening Don Damaso saw that Martin did not come into the salon, and instigated by his wife, he sent for him, and whilst the others were conversing he shut himself up with Rivas in the ante-salon.

On looking at both their faces, one would have thought that Don Damaso was the culprit, so much difficulty did he appear to find to open the question. Martin, unaffectedly calm, waited until Don Damaso would break the silence. Seeing at the end of some time that he waited in vain and that Don Damaso was trying in a thousand ways to hide his agitation, he decided to get him out of the difficulty.

"I have been speaking with Augustin, Señor," he said, "and I know from him the accusation that has been brought against me."

"Ah! you know it; well, my boy, that pleases me. Just imagine! Those two men presented themselves and told me what you know. You can imagine I did not believe such a thing, but the señora—"

"Before you continue, Señor," said Martin—taking advantage of a pause in which he appeared to be looking for words—"I must tell you that the accusation is not altogether groundless."

"What do you say?" asked Don Damaso, thinking that he did not hear distinctly.

"I was saying, sir, that the story that you have heard about me is not entirely without foundation; there is a certain amount of truth in it, although it is natural that my accusers are wrong in many things."

"I am perplexed," said Don Damaso.

Martin told him the same story that he had told Augustin before dinner.

"You can well imagine," said Don Damaso, "that for my part I absolve you; but, you see, in this house I have my family: the señora is very strait-laced, my boy, and is easily shocked, I'm not, and above all—"

"I thank you very much, Señor, for your pardon," replied Martin, "my conscience is so clear that in this case it is not necessary. From the little that you have said to me I think I understand that the señora is alarmed and it shall not be I—who owe so many favours and attentions to you—who would be the one to destroy the tranquillity of your family. I understand what I ought to do and tomorrow you will allow me to leave your house so that the señora's mind may be tranquillized."

"*Hombre!* don't speak of that!" exclaimed Don Damaso. "But you understand my embarrassment. No? The señora will say that it's not true, and soon—"

"I have never given her occasion to doubt my veracity," said the young man, with dignity.

"Of course not, and nobody doubts it; but you know the señora and—"

Martin was firm about what he had said and Don Damaso involved himself in his own excuses without saying anything decisive.

"If he goes I shall miss him greatly," he thought, whilst Martin left his seat and entered the salon where all the ordinary visitors of the house were assembled.

Leonor was talking to Matilde. She came rarely to the house of her aunt since her marriage was broken off.

When Rivas entered the salon his face showed a very different expression from that which he ordinarily wore in Leonor's presence: the aspect of the young man showed firm and fixed resolution. As they hesitated, he went straight to the place where the two girls were seated and his glance was as certain as his bearing.

Leonor turned very pale on seeing him approach her with this air of resolution, and gave him a glacial look.

But this look did not intimidate Rivas, who appeared dominated by a fixed idea.

This idea was to be found in a reflection which he had made on leaving Don Damaso.

"If she does not believe me, what is to be done? But I am determined to speak to her."

With this firm design he sat down beside Leonor, doing it, however, in such a manner that the others could not see anything premeditated in the action.

Leonor turned her head towards her cousin with insulting affectation; but Martin was not discouraged by this.

"Señorita," he said in a firm tone, "I wish to speak to you."

"To me!" said Leonor, in whose accent might be found a slight tremor.

"Didn't you speak to my father?" she added, with the air of majestic arrogance which formerly intimidated Martin.

"For the same reason that I have spoken to him," he replied, "I now desire that you do me the favour of listening to me."

"Truly, the tone in which you speak to me surprises me," said the girl to him, feigning astonishment and the height of indifference and disdain.

"Perhaps I am agitated: forgive me. What has just happened to me is so important for my future that it is not strange if I am disturbed."

"What has happened to you?" asked Leonor, with a smile which contrasted with the seriousness of the young man.

"You know what has happened, Señorita."

"Ah! the affair of the Señorita Edelmira! I would not have believed it."

"Augustin must have told you the story which he heard from me just now."

"Yes, Augustin told me something about a service that you had done this señorita; a bad excuse, an invention of Augustin's at least."

"Señorita, that which you call an excuse is the truth."

"Truly! Forgive me, I thought that it was a story invented by Augustin to amuse me."

"Do you think then that there's not a man existing capable of doing such a service as this?"

"Most certainly there is one; you are he. Since you tell it to me I must belive it."

"You speak to me in a tone which contradicts your words."

"Do you think that I'm taking the trouble to pretend?" said Leonor, proudly, raising her beautiful head.

"I don't think that it's necessary for you to take either this or any trouble for me," replied Rivas, with true dignity, "but I would like to find more sincerity in your words so as to appreciate the opinion that you may have of me."

"Holding so much appreciation of my opinion why did you not consult me about your elopement? You may call it as you like, but perhaps I would have been able to make a plan more easy to carry out than yours."

There was so much sarcasm in Leonor's tone that Martin felt the blood flow over his face.

"You are cruel to me, Señorita," he said with bitterness. "You humiliate me. Besides, if, like your mother, you believe that in doing a service—which I would do again if it were necessary—I have failed in the respect I owe to the family, since I come to justify myself, you might be more indulgent."

These words produced some impression in Leonor's mind, for she had counted on Rivas defending himself with trivial excuses.

The young man continued—

"Your mother has confined herself to letting me understand through Señor Don Damaso that I must leave her house. Certainly it was not necessary to give me this hint to do so. I had incurred enough already from your displeasure. As my resolution was made about this, I did not wish to leave without telling you the truth of the matter and justifying myself in your opinion. Now you receive me with sarcasm. Why do you not let me take away with me the impression that I have always had of you? It would be more pleasant to me to remember you with pleasure than with pain, because in any case I must always remember you."

Leonor felt disturbed as she looked at him; the melancholy voice of the young man saddened her.

"My father must have explained himself badly," she said to him, in a voice which sounded more timid than proud.

"I don't know, I did not inquire," replied Martin. "My principal desire is to justify myself in your eyes."

"You have completely done so," she said. "This girl was your lover, and you were quite right to serve her."

Martin could not know whether these words were sincere or not, and he perceived that with them, Leonor wished to end the conversation.

"Perhaps some day time will justify me," he said to her.

"And can you not do yourself what you leave to time?" said Leonor, looking at him fixedly.

"I cannot, Señorita, it is the secret of another which I must respect."

All her suspicions at once returned to the mind of the girl, and she believed that this was only a *rôle* well acted by Martin.

"It's always the secret of a friend, is it not so? What's to be done? Let us wait for the justification of time."

Sarcasm had returned to her voice, and pride shone in her eyes.

"I flattered myself with the idea that you would believe my word of honour," he said to her.

"So it appears," she replied drily.

"How can I go on? It's impossible!" Martin thought when he heard this answer.

Then Leonor, as if to finish the conversation, turned to Matilde, who at the moment was talking to Augustin.

He would have liked to throw himself at Leonor's feet and there breathe his last breath, praying to Heaven to justify him without it being necessary to stain his honour by making use of Edelmira's letters which might save him.

Meantime Leonor continued to talk to Matilde, and Rivas left his seat.

When he had left the salon and found himself alone in his room he threw himself on a chair sobbing like a child. At the end of a quarter of an hour he remembered Edelmira's letter, which he took out of his pocket.

"Poor girl!" he said, returning to the resemblance which he found always between her lot and his own.

At the same time he remembered that shortly before he had thought that Edelmira's letters would dispel Leonor's suspicions, and taking them all out of a box on the table on which he was leaning, he burnt them in the light of the candle, together with the one he had received that day.

On seeing them consumed he felt justified in his mind, saying to himself, "Thus I am free from temptation."

He fixed his eyes on the light with the expression of a man whose brain is stunned by one of those mortal blows which paralyse beyond tears, the senses almost leaving the sufferer.

The night was for Martin a night of martyrdom. To distract his trouble he employed some time in arranging his luggage, which, not being very voluminous, was soon prepared for the journey. His preparations concluded, he spent a long time leaning his forehead on the panes of the window which looked upon the court. From there, although he could not with his own eyes see Leonor, he recalled to his memory the incidents of his life since the time that, poor, but free from care and full of hope, he had first crossed this courtyard. In this elegy which almost every one sings to lost hopes, Rivas bade farewell to the golden dreams with which love enchants the flowery years of youth: but endowed by nature with solid energy, far from being cast down by the prospect of his sad future, he found in his own suffering the strength which is wanting to many in these cases. He thought of his mother and his sister and remembered that he owed to them the consecration of his strength. Fortified with this remembrance he sat down at the table and wrote to Don Damaso a letter giving him thanks for the generous manner in which he had shown him hospitality, and another to Rafael San Luis, in which he gave him an account of the affair and his determination to go to his family until the opening of the National Institute, where he would go in order to continue his studies the following year.

After having written these letters he thought of how to reply to Edelmira. He thought for a long time over this, because, although it appeared to him harsh to tell her the truth, his moral rectitude warned him not to foment a passion which he could not return. Finally his right feeling triumphed and he wrote to Edelmira telling her the story of his hopeless love from the time of his arrival in Santiago. Although in this letter he did not mention Leonor, her name could be guessed in every page. Rivas finished his letter to Edelmira without making the least allusion to the day's happenings, telling her only his project of being absent for two months from the capital.

At six o'clock in the morning of the following day Martin brought his luggage to the inn at which he had put up on his arrival at Santiago.

On leaving he gave Don Damaso's servant the letters to post which he had written during the night, remunerating him generously at the cost of his savings to assure his attention.

After that he soon found a coach which had a seat unoccupied, and at ten o'clock in the morning he was on his way to Valparaiso.

LII

In the beginning of January in the following year the family of Don Damaso were all at his hacienda.

As had been arranged, Matilde had made one of the party, and occupied with Leonor a room, the windows of which looked out on the orchard of the house.

Augustin and his father went out daily on horseback in the morning and joined the family at breakfast time, after which Leonor played the piano, and Augustin—not having anything better to do—paid his addresses to his cousin.

Doña Engracia saw with satisfaction the attentions that her son paid to Matilde, for whom all in the house felt a sincere affection, and with no less satisfaction the señora assured herself that the country air suited Diamela very well.

Don Damaso, on his part, read the newspapers that arrived from Santiago, leaning sometimes to the Ministry and sometimes to the Opposition, according to the impression which each article produced, and when sending off his letters he continually missed Martin, who with so much expedition knew how to interpret his thoughts and saved him this work.

The solitude and monotony of this country life, in which weeks passed by without any incident worthy of mention, had worked in a different manner in the minds of the two cousins, who, although living in the greatest intimacy, kept each her secret thoughts.

Matilde had wept for her bitter disappointment, as we have already seen, but this disappointment had destroyed her respect for Rafael San Luis, and with the want of respect love had died in her breast.

Time, and the absence of those surroundings which had witnessed her happiness, little by little healed her wounded spirit, leaving only that melancholy which precedes the complete cessation of pain. In this condition, the attentions of Augustin, who pleased her with his youth, his quickness, and his elegance, succeeded in making Matilde first forget her former love, striving to console herself after the violent blow, which, on the portal of happiness, had overwhelmed her with sorrow, and she ended in taking pleasure and a liking for the animated conversations with which her cousin entertained her.

The state of mind of Leonor was completely different. That which at first appeared certain with regard to the existence of a love-affair between Martin and Edelmira, was transformed little by little into a doubt through the continual meditation to which solitude condemned her. Then returned to her memory the recollections of past conversations, the looks with which Martin had told her of his love, although he had not dared to do so in words, and these recollections gave the appearance of truth to the reasons with which the young man had explained his conduct. Ingenious as the mind always is in finding reasons in support of what the heart desires, Leonor's recalled the frankness with which Rivas had confessed his participation in Edelmira's flight, and decided in favour of his cause, alleging that if he had been guilty he could have shielded himself more securely by denying everything. As is logical, from these reflections was born in Leonor the feeling of regret for having treated him with such asperity and for having replied with bitter sarcasm to Martin's sincerity. At this distance all those ideas came back to the memory of the girl in alluring colours, so that very shortly before the family returned to Santiago, at the end of February, Martin— without defending himself—had regained his place in Leonor's heart; with the additional advantage for him that the girl now accused as idiotic the pride with which she had always frozen the words of love on Martin's lips which he appeared about to speak.

The victims of this gradual reaction in favour of Rivas were several of Leonor's admirers, including Emilio Mendoza and Clementi Valencia, who at that time arrived upon a visit at the hacienda of Don Damaso. It should be said that Leonor took pains to observe a scrupulous fidelity for her absent lover and fled from declarations which formerly she received with laughing disdain; for she carefully avoided occasions to find herself alone with any of these young men; and frequently, when gaiety reigned in the salon, she, hidden amongst the trees of the orchard, recalled to her memory past days in Santiago and thought she felt presentiments that the former scenes would be renewed.

At this time Rafael San Luis wrote to Martin—

DEAR FRIEND,

"After two months of solitude and silence, of meditation and tears, I am the same as I was; I love as much as ever. I have prayed to heaven to tear this love from my breast, I have striven to forget it in mystical contemplations, in beautiful examples of virtue which present the force of the spirit overcoming the heart; nothing holds the charm that fables give to the waters of Lethe; I cannot forget. I do not say, like the fatalists, 'Thus it has been written!' But I ask myself always with my mind surcharged with terror—Is it a chastisement of God? Why arises in my memory the remembrance of the days of vanished happiness; and at every hour why arises her image, at times to my sorrow loving me, and at others repeating to me the cruel words in which she condemned me in her letter? In this state what can I do?

"The solitude of the cloister, far from calming the ardour of my love, has given it nourishment. Neither prayers nor studies have held for me the balm with which they console the cares of others; in this atmosphere of ice my forehead always burns with heat, the anxiety of my mind cannot breathe in this air, and my youth and sorrow contend in my soul, praying me for more space and more light and more air; another life in fact, which agitating the strength of the body, acts also on my mind.

"As on coming here I did not wish to make any violent resolution, so also I did not wish to relinquish the period of probation which I have described to you by abandoning my retirement. I think now as I thought then. At the end of only one month of seclusion, and only after this second month of probation have I determined to return to my poor aunt, who with the greatest delight thought my feet set in the path of religion.

"So I shall leave here tomorrow and I shall occupy myself as I can. I have in prospect a certain occupation which may suit my character better and which will be more efficacious towards mitigating the intensity of my grief. When we meet again perhaps you also will seek in it an alleviation of the pain which I imagine afflicts you. Come, then, and perhaps you may follow me into the life into which I am going to enter, if so, before we do it, let us sow no seeds of hope in the country of the future, let us cut up by the roots those flowers which this seed has left us. For me the sun of happiness begins to shine with more brightness and withers those poor flowers; but do not forget that we must not weep for ever. I will show you a future to which to consecrate the strength of our minds.

Rafael San Luis

Just at the time that Rivas received this letter, another from Edelmira Molina arrived which ran as follows:—

DEAR FRIEND,

"I shall not tell you the sorrow your letter caused me in telling me that you loved another without mentioning her name. Whoever she may be I assure you that I shall pray to heaven that she will repay you with the love which you merit, and although I have bewailed my unhappiness I do not complain, because I owe to you too much for me to have any other aim than your happiness. What I also pray to God for is to grant me one day the opportunity of proving the disinterestedness of my affection, and giving me the power to do you some service in return for those which you have done for me with so much delicacy.

"I write this from my aunt's house where you left me, and I am going to tell you how it is that I have not returned to my mother's roof. Two days after you had brought me here Amador arrived looking for me; but my aunt opposed my going away, and wrote to my mother saying that I would only return when she promised to leave me free to marry whoever I chose; and although my mother has promised that she will do as my aunt asks, the latter has kept me here to spend some more time with her.

I say good-bye, wishing you the most complete happiness, and telling you that you will always have a grateful friend in
                                                    EDELMIRA MOLINA

These two letters and the explanations which precede them are enough to make known the situations of the principal persons in this story at the time of Martin Rivas' return to the capital at the beginning of March, 1851.

LIII

I n these first chapters we have given a slight sketch of the political spirit which then held apart all social classes of Chilian families, and especially the inhabitants of Santiago, and which was the focus of an active liberal propaganda whose voice was first heard in the Society of Equality. Without entrenching on the domain of history we must give a rapid glance at the political situation, where a great public event was in preparation; an event of great importance for some of the people with whom we have been already concerned.

The tension of feeling, maintained by bloody disputes which the Press on both sides had fostered in the public, arrived at its culmination at the news of the popular mutiny which took place in the Aconcagua on the 5th November, 1850. Foreseeing minds trembled at that which they felt was the precursor of new and more bloody disturbances. The more excited prepared themselves for the strife, and the Government increased its vigilance at this highly significant intelligence. From that moment the fury of the Press increased, fed by the burning enmity of faction, and the rancour of party planted in manyminds the profound roots which sprout at the present moment, ten years afterwards, with the vigour of the first days of the battle. The Liberal Press, defending the right of insurrection and the public voice (which unites isolated opinions, condensing them into one voice which often has the gift of prophecy), had aroused in many minds the belief that the movement in San Felipe would have a terrible reverberation in Santiago. Even in February they spoke of the imminence of a revolution, in which would be found amongst the rebels against authority almost all the forces of the line which then garrisoned the capital. They reckoned that immense masses of people would rise at the first call of certain chiefs, and hoped at the same time that the Civic Force would fraternize—according to the prevalent expression—with their brothers of the people in the crusade against tyranny.

Such was, in effect, the situation in Santiago in the beginning of March, 1851, when Martin Rivas arrived at the inn from which, two months before, he had issued on his journey to Coquimbo.

He dressed quickly and, leaving the inn, took the road to Rafael San Luis' house. In a quarter of an hour the two friends had given a long and affectionate embrace. On sitting down each sought to find in the appearance of the other the traces of the grief which each had experienced during the time that they were separated. San Luis found in Martin's face the youthful and at the same time thoughtful expression which he had always known; the same purity in the dark complexion, the same strength in the deep penetration of his glance; the same nobility of forehead: it was impossible to read in this serene face the revelation of any secret sorrow.

Rivas, for his part, found that Rafael's appearance, his pallid cheeks, the contraction of his eyebrows—something indefinable in his whole expression spoke of the heartbreaking struggle through which this young man had lived for so long a time. In both this involuntary inspection lasted but a moment.

"Well, how have you been?" asked Rafael, affectionately.

"You can imagine," replied Rivas, "except for the pleasure of seeing my mother and my sister, all the rest was sad."

"Have you forgotten *her?*"

"Not for an instant."

"Poor Martin," said San Luis, taking his hand. "You remember my prophesies since we first knew each other."

"Yes, very well; but now it's too late."

"Did you receive a letter from me?"

"Yes, I gathered from it that you have put a final end to your life of a hermit."

"In that letter I spoke to you of an occupation which I was thinking of undertaking?"

"Yes, what is it?"

"A new love," said San Luis, with a melancholy smile.

"That means you have forgotten Matilde?" asked Rivas.

San Luis approached his friend. "Look," he said, pointing to his black hair, "don't you see some grey hairs?"

"Certainly."

Rafael sighed deeply, but without any affectation of sentimentalism.

"My new love," he said, "is politics."

"Ah! I remember; when I first knew you, you were much occupied with them."

"I have returned to them, in this way. A few days after I wrote to you to the North I received a letter from two friends with whom I was leagued by the Society of Equality. Here it is," he added, reading—

"'We hope that your love fever is calmed; the country has need of you, and the moment to prove that you have not forgotten her is at hand. Will you let her believe that your heart is unworthy of the faith which you formerly professed? We expect you in the place which you know of.'

"This," continued Rafael, "helped to decide me to conquer the repugnance which, notwithstanding my horror of loneliness, I felt in returning to my former life. On coming out my first visit was made to those who thus offered me a new field in which I might find a chance, if not of forgetting my sad memories, at least of depriving them of their most searching bitterness. The old *régime*, full of resistance, of exclusivism and of force on the one side; the other begging for reforms and assurances. I believe that the man who feels in his breast anything of what may be called by the name of patriotism, cannot hesitate in his decision: I embrace the new *régime* and I am ready to sacrifice myself for it."

He then gave a minute sketch of the state of politics in Santiago which we have already slightly described, and unfolded his theories on the subject of Liberalism with the warmth of a passionate soul, full of faith in the future. The fire of his conviction quickly spread to Rivas' mind and germinated in his noble nature.

"You are right," he said to San Luis. "Instead of sorrowfully weeping like women, we must consecrate ourselves to a cause worthy of men.

"Tonight," said Rafael, "I shall present you to our reunion and tell you about our aims: for my part I am persuaded that the time has completely passed for peaceful efforts. At present it is war, I do not know what those that lead us may be thinking of I, as a soldier, must resign myself to hope, but with impatience."

During this conversation all vestige of grief had disappeared from Rafael's face, his cheeks were flushed and his large eyes shone with enthusiasm.

After a long conversation the two friends separated, making an appointment for the night.

Martin was punctual at the rendezvous: he wished to be rid of the thoughts which his visit to the streets of Santiago had recalled to his mind, and he found it necessary to use much strength of will not to pass through the doorway of Don Damaso's house, which he saw for a moment from a distance.

At the reunion to which San Luis brought him, Martin heard hot speeches against the Government, and the accusations which had been brought against it for some time by the Opposition.

There were to be found other enthusiasts, dandies, converted into tribunes desirous of consecrating their strength to the country and calling for the hour of peril in order to offer their lives to her.

In the state of his mind Rivas waited for no advice, feeling his heart beat at the idea of also contributing to the realization of the beautiful political and social theories which these young men professed and hoped for the country.

On leaving the reunion at eleven o'clock at night Rafael took his arm.

"I am going to ask you a favour," he said.

"What is it?"

"Since I have known you," continued San Luis, "I have had a sincere affection for you. We have since lived in intimate confidence; but, in spite of my desire of being always with you, I did not dare before to propose that we should live together, because I knew that nothing was so precious to you as the house where you could see Leonor so frequently. Now you are alone why don't you come to my house? You know my aunt—she is a saint, and she loves you because you are my friend. You will be just as if you were at home, and we shall look after you like a spoiled child."

The sincerity of this offer decided Martin immediately, and he gratefully thanked his friend.

"Good," said Rafael, joyfully, "we shall begin from tonight, I'll give you up my bed and tomorrow we shall send for your luggage."

"I have a project for a little journey in the morning," replied Martin, "and I would prefer, in order to get a carriage early more easily, not to go to you until tomorrow afternoon."

"Just as you like. Where are you going to?"

"To Renca, to see Edelmira."

They said good night and separated.

At ten o'clock in the morning on the following day, Martin once more took the road to Renca, and the journey recalled to him once more the hopes with which he had seen it for the first time.

Then he had seen, in the landscape which presented itself to his eyes, the promises of happy days spent in the country with Leonor. Now far from the image of the beloved girl all had disappeared, condemning him to grief before having known joy. On seeing the house at which he had left Edelmira this preoccupation was dissipated and replaced by reflections as to the fate of this girl for whom he felt a sincere friendship.

He got down in the courtyard and went up to the house. Edelmira had seen him from the window of the room in which she was and came running to receive him.

The sincere affection with which Martin saluted her caused to disappear from Edelmira's cheek the rosy tint which covered it when she found herself near the young man, and both began a conversation principally about the life which each had led during the last two months.

"However much I desired to return to my mother's side," said Edelmira, "I wished to pass some time longer here to make certain that Ricardo had given up coming to our house."

Not a single word was spoken as to Edelmira's last letter during this interview, in which the aunt of the girl took part, overwhelming Martin with attentions. Two hours afterwards, when Rivas was saying good-bye, Edelmira rose with the expression of a person who has made a resolution after having hesitated for some time.

"I have something to say to you," she said, taking advantage of a moment when her aunt had gone out.

"I am at your orders," replied the young man.

"You must answer me as I wish," continued Edelmira, getting scarlet. "Do you remember the frankness with which I spoke to you?"

"I remember it well, and I swear to you—"

"Don't swear anything, but reply to what I am going to ask you. Is it not Leonor whom you love?"

"Yes."

"I thought so, and as my brother has told me a little about the visit which he paid with Ricardo to the father of this lady, I have seen that the service that you did me must have harmed you."

"It may have been so," said Martin, trying to smile.

Edelmira's aunt entered and the young man said goodbye to both.

Edelmira accompanied him out of doors as she had done the first time, and remained for a long time looking after the carriage in which Rivas was travelling. When this was lost to sight at a turning in the road, Edelmira entered the room, and said to her aunt—

"Did I not tell you? Martin has lost his happiness through me, but I'll do all that I can to give it back to him; so that thus I may be able to repay his generosity."

LIV

O n the 15th of April Matilde and her mother entered Leonor's house. They were both dressed in mantles and veils. It was nine o'clock in the morning and they were coming from the church. Doña Francisca entered her brother's room and Matilde Leonor's.

"What are you doing?" she asked the daughter of Don Damaso—who, with a book in her hand, was looking out of the window instead of reading.

"Nothing; I was reading."

"Do you know why I came to see you at this hour?"

"I can't imagine."

"On coming out of San Francisca I had a meeting."

"With whom?"

"Guess."

Leonor felt Rivas' name tremble on her lips, but she answered—

"I can't imagine."

"With Martin," said Matilde, "he knew me on the moment and saluted me."

Leonor did not endeavour to hide the perturbation which was depicted in her face.

"He is here!" she exclaimed. "Papa has had him sought for everywhere hoping that he might return. How did he look?"

"Very handsome; he appeared to me even better looking than before."

"Was he alone?" asked Leonor, anxiously.

"He was alone, and even if he had been with Rafael I assure you that it would not have mattered to me. You know that that is finished."

A few moments afterwards Doña Francisca came to fetch her daughter and they said good-bye to Leonor.

The latter remained thinking about the news which her cousin had just brought her. She knew that if she announced Rivas' arrival to Don Damaso he would do everything possible to make him come back to his house, but the joy that the idea gave her of seeing Martin as before, in the intimacy of private life, was dispelled at the remembrance of the motives which had caused him to leave their house.

"How do I know if he loves me?" said humbly to herself the haughty beauty, to whom the most distinguished men of the capital were continually paying homage.

Love during this time had done the work to her pride which a drop of water makes when it falls constantly on a stone. It had conquered her proud resistance. Her vigorous moral organization yielded to the law of passion because she was a woman before being the spoilt child of her parents and of Society, which had cultivated the germs of haughtiness in her disposition. This superb beauty who had played with the hearts of so many submissive admirers, now frankly accepted the part of a forsaken lover, and experienced an irresistible pleasure in consecrating her heart to one whom she had at first looked upon as an insignificant person. Under the dominion of the gradual transformation which operated on all her being, the pale flowers of sentiment had opened their melancholy blossoms in her mind, which a short time before was laughing at the slavery which love, sooner or later, must impose upon those who are gifted by Heaven.

After lunch Leonor evoked the remembrances of her conversations with Martin, all those trivial incidents which compose the world for lovers, trying at the piano pieces which in those days she played much more frequently.

In this occupation she was found by a servant-maid who approached her and said to her—

"A lady is in the courtyard and asks for you."

Leonor cut short the strains of a waltz and looked into the courtyard. There she saw a girl dressed in a mantle and veil, whose youthful beauty suggested to Leonor this question—

"Where have I seen this girl?"

The mantle covered part of the face of the unknown girl and lent in this fashion an expression to her features which can well explain the difficulty in recognizing her which was felt by Leonor.

"Ask her her name," she said to the servant, who went away with the message and brought back the following reply:—

"Tell her that I am Edelmira Molina and that it is most important that I should speak to her alone."

"Edelmira!" exclaimed Leonor, when the servant had told her the name.

She appeared to reflect for a few moments, and then, raising her head, she said—

"Take her into my room."

When the servant again went into the courtyard, Leonor glanced into one of the mirrors in the salon in which she was, and, almost without thinking of what she was doing, arranged her hair—divided into two long and heavy plaits; this done, she turned to her room which Edelmira had just entered.

Leonor carried herself with the haughtiness of a queen to the girl whom she believed to be her rival.

"Señorita," said the latter with a slight embarrassment, "I have come to accomplish a duty."

"Be seated," said Leonor, who saw the efforts that Edelmira was making to conquer her agitation.

Edelmira took the seat which was pointed out to her, and said—

"I owe a great debt to a young man who lived in this house last year, and as it is only since the last few days that I learnt the reason for his leaving it, it is only now that I have been able to come. My brother," she added, "has brought me here and is waiting for me at the door."

"And what can I do in this affair?" asked Leonor, in a dry voice.

"I have addressed myself to you," replied Edelmira, "because I have not dared to speak to your mother; and I saw that it was absolutely necessary to take this step to justify Martin."

The name of the young man for whom the heart of both those girls was beating seemed to echo for some seconds in the room.

"I knew," continued Edelmira, "that here it was believed that Martin had run away with me from my own house. Your father was made to believe this by my brother, and the other young man who was here with him, the same day that I fled from Santiago to Renca, where I have lived until now."

"Did you run away alone?" asked Leonor, with a certain irony mixed with anxiety.

"No; Martin had the generosity to accompany me," answered Edelmira, trembling. "For this reason they believed that he was in love with me, and took me away from my house, but this is not true. I ran away from Renca because they wanted to marry me to the young man who accompanied my brother here that day; Martin had the kindness to accompany me, and without him I would have been miserable today."

"Truly, Señor Rivas has been very generous and disinterested," said Leonor, "as since you don't love him he acted in this manner."

"I have not said that I do not love him," quickly replied Edelmira.

"Ah!" exclaimed Leonor, in whose eyes shone rays of hatred.

This look made the other girl sigh, because she learned by it enough to convince her that Martin's love was responded to by Leonor.

"I am not concerned in this," said Leonor, haughtily, "what do you think that I can do in this affair? If you love Martin it would be better to tell him so yourself."

"Yes, Señorita, I love him," reiterated Edelmira, in humble but impassioned accents; "but he does not love me, and he has never loved me."

"I don't know whether to praise your frankness more than your modesty," said Leonor, in a sarcastic voice, "and I regret that Martin is not here for me to intercede with him in your favour."

"I have not come here to beg for any service whatever," replied Edelmira, with pride, "I have come here to justify Martin, because I have probably been the cause of his misery."

"Ah! He is miserable?"

"Yes, I know it from himself; he told me so two days ago."

"Where did you see him?" asked Leonor, forgetting her *rôle* of indifference.

"He came to see me at Renca."

"That sounds well," said Leonor, in a bitter tone of mockery. "How can you say that he does not return your love?"

"He did it because he is of a noble nature and he has promised me his friendship."

"Don't be downhearted; friendship and love are not far apart."

"No, Señorita! He is only a friend, and I have proofs of what I say."

"Proofs!"

"Yes, I have proofs and I bring them here, because, as I said just now, my duty is to clear one who has served me so generously."

Edelmira took out all Martin's letters which she had kept, and presented them to Leonor.

"If you take the trouble to read these letters," she said, "you will see that what I have told you is the truth."

Leonor opened the first letter which Edelmira handed her and began to read it with a smile of contempt.

"But this appears to be a reply?" she exclaimed, when she had glanced over some lines.

Edelmira explained to her what she had written to Martin, and Leonor continued to read, if not with lively interest, certainly not with an air of contempt. In this way she learned the truth of the friendship which existed between Edelmira and Martin and the loyalty with which the latter had acted in this affair. On reading the letter which Martin had written to Edelmira before undertaking this journey, Leonor had a difficulty to hide her joy. She could not find there any doubt but that she was the mistress of the heart whose nobility was revealed in the letters which she held in her hands.

On looking at Edelmira after reading, the expression of her face had completely changed. The ironical inflexibility of her eyes was replaced at this moment by the most affectionate kindness.

"These letters," she said, "don't leave the slightest doubt, and above all they are an honour to your generosity."

"Señorita," replied Edelmira, enthusiastically, "no sacrifice would be painful to me that had to do with Martin, and I don't speak thus because I love him, for you have seen by these letters that I can never hope for a return, but because my gratitude is great: it is thus that I can alone accomplish my duty, by telling you the truth."

"I owe you thanks for the confidence that you have shown me, not thanks alone from myself but from my family, because we are indebted to Martin for many important services, and my father will be very pleased to go and see him. Do you know where he lives?"

"In the house of young San Luis, his friend."

On saying good-bye Leonor accompanied Edelmira to the courtyard and kindly pressed her hand. This display of affection decided Edelmira that she was right in her surmise that Rivas' love was returned.

After this Leonor went into Augustin's room and found him in the serious occupation of dressing.

"I'm making my *toilette, et je suis à toi, immédiatment*," the young man said to her.

Shortly after he opened the door and Leonor entered the room.

"I bring you good news," she said.

"Have you seen Matilde?" asked the fop, thinking the news had to do with his cousin, for whom every day he felt more affection.

"No, it's another kind of news. Martin is in Santiago."

"I was not thinking about him. That good friend; I have missed him. Where does he live?"

"In San Luis' house."

"That is serious."

"Why?"

"Because, who knows, he may be the successor of San Luis in my cousin's heart."

"No matter, your duty is to go and find Martin!"

　　　　　　　　　　ALBERTO BLEST GANA

"Caspita! little sister, you are peremptory."

"You forget how Martin left this house."

"No, no. The fault was papa's. He paid attention to base slanders."

"For that reason we must try to repair the wrong, and take from him the right that he has to believe us ungrateful."

"You have not been talking like this lately, little sister."

"No, but now I have changed."

"*Le roi galant a dit, 'Souvent femme varie,'* this occurs in all French books, and is true."

Then it was arranged that Augustin and Leonor would speak to Don Damaso about the affair; and when later in the evening they did so the latter received the news with great pleasure, saying that he missed Martin more every day. The dandy went that night to Rafael's house.

The latter and Martin had gone out, so Augustin decided to return the following day.

Much that is important has to be related about this following day, which was the 19th April, 1851.

LV

Martin and Rafael returned home at midnight on the 18th of April. In both of them it was easy to recognize the excitement raised by political passions, for their talk was animated, and their gestures and glances were animatedly supporting their liberal dissertations upon the charges which the opposition was now formulating against the Government (which was now at the end of its second period) and against those who were endeavouring to reinstate it.

Martin had warmly embraced the cause of the people, and in consequence had uprooted from his mind the profound melancholy which had preyed upon it during the last two months.

He was able to stifle the voice of his love beneath the noise of political passions, and had by this time acquired sufficient self-command to enable him to regard Leonor as one who would live in his memory as a sweet remembrance and not as a constant sorrow, and had conquered the anguish which destroys the spirits of those who let themselves be overcome by grief. In order to keep himself in this frame of mind Rivas lived amongst his books during the day, and politics during the night.

Rafael, who was not studying anything, lived immersed in occupations of which he gave no account to his friend. Sombre and silent at times, he appeared on other occasions wildly excited. He conversed frequently in secret with people who came to see him, and often went out alone from his house after returning to it with Martin from the Club which they frequented. There was something in his mysterious conduct which drew Rivas' attention, but up to the present he had abstained from all questioning.

The names of Leonor and Matilde were hardly ever mentioned by the two young men, it appeared that each of them wished to hide from the other the shrine at which—to his sorrow—he worshipped in silence.

They arrived, as we have said, at Rafael's house at midnight.

On lighting the lamp they saw placed upon the table a card which San Luis glanced at and then passed to Rivas.

"Augustin Encina," was on the card, and lower down, written in pencil, was, "I shall come back tomorrow at eleven o'clock."

Martin remained thoughtful while San Luis lit a cigar and began to walk up and down. The vivacity with which they were both speaking when they entered the room seemed to disappear upon reading the card. At the end of a few moments Rafael broke the silence.

"What do you think of this visit?" he asked, coming to a standstill before Martin.

"I did not expect it," the latter replied.

"But you are pleased at it?"

"I don't know."

"He came to ask you to go back to their house."

"I don't think so."

"Supposing it was so, would you go?"

"I would not accept the offer."

"But if it was made to you not alone by the parents, but also by the daughter?"

"I would give the same answer."

"You would do well," said San Luis, resuming his promenade.

"I do not deny that it is a family to whom I owe much gratitude," continued Martin, after a short pause. "I arrived at Santiago poor and without friends; they not only gave me hospitality, which many people offer as alms to their nearest relations, but they gave me more than this, a place in the private life of the family, and in that I appreciate the kindness which they have done me."

"Do you count for nothing your services to Don Damaso in having saved his son from the trap into which he had fallen?"

"I have been able to do more than one service to him, but I am for this none the more free from the gratitude which I owe them."

"Then return to their house," said Rafael, bitterly.

"I have said that I will not return," said Martin, drily.

Silence reigned again, but was for the second time broken by San Luis, who resumed the interrupted conversation on politics. But Martin did not take part in this with the same animation which he showed before having seen the card, so that San Luis, noticing his preoccupation, said good night to him and retired.

Augustin was punctual at the appointment on the following day, for at eleven o'clock in the morning he entered Rivas' room. The two young men embraced each other warmly.

"I come to carry you off," said Augustin, "and to bring you the kindest regards of everybody in the house, from papa who desires to embrace you, down to Diamela who ardently longs to bite your heels."

"My dear Augustin," said Rivas, "how can I thank your family for their kind messages? I can never forget it, but, as you see, it is absolutely impossible for me to accept their kind offer."

"I ask you why?"

"Because I would never forgive myself for leaving Rafael alone."

"Your first home in Santiago has been ours," replied Augustin.

"I know it, and I shall always preserve for your family a profound gratitude for their kindness."

"That is all very fine, my son, but if you do not come they will call you ungrateful in every possible tone of voice."

"But I shall not be so; I refuse your offer at great pain to myself," said Rivas, patting the dandy affectionately on the shoulder.

"Now, look here, no *pas de façons* with me, come along! Look here, I've promised one person especially that I will not return without you."

"Whom?" asked Rivas, with a most lively interest.

"Leonor. We learnt from her that you were here; I don't know how she found it out, but that shows that the French are right when they say *'ce que veut la femme dieu le veut.'*"

"Tell the Señorita Leonor how much I thank her for her interest," said Martin with emotion, "and how deeply I feel my inability to accept the generous hospitality offered me by her family."

"Yes, she'll give me a nice reception!" said the dandy. "When Leonor wishes for anything it's understood that it is an order, and she has definitely commanded that it is the duty of all of us to make reparation for our offence against you in putting a bad interpretation upon an action which was all the time a proof of your kindness."

"Ah! you are doing me justice," exclaimed Rivas, eagerly.

"And why not," exclaimed Augustin in the same tone. "At home our opinion is unanimous, except in politics. There is no managing papa, today he is in opposition, and tomorrow ministerial. However, don't let this stop you, come in full confidence. Papa says that he has much need of you."

Martin again began to excuse himself, alleging his duty to himself, alleging his duty to San Luis.

"Well! you've got to come to the house in person to explain yourself," Augustin replied. Then he added, "When will you come?"

"I shall try to come tonight," said Rivas.

Having obtained this concession, Augustin launched forth with his usual loquacity into confidences, referring to his flirtation with Matilde, and the hopes that he had of his love being returned. At the end of an hour he took himself off, leaving Martin deep in the reflections caused by what Augustin had told him about Leonor. The remembrance of past scenes in the girl's house, and the light manner in which she had treated him, restrained the force of the desire to see her which had seized upon him, thanks to Augustin's words. In the midst of these meditations, and without having made up his mind how to act during the visit which he was to pay that evening, Rafael met him at four o'clock in the afternoon. Rafael appeared happy and animated, and with a smile he asked Rivas—

"Did Augustin come?"

"Yes, he paid me a long visit."

"Did he try to take you away to his house?"

"He tried hard."

"And what did you answer?"

"I replied that I would call there this evening."

"You did not do well," said Rafael, in the tone of authority which Rivas had known him to employ to his fellow students in college, but which he had never used to him.

"I can be the sole judge of that," replied Rivas, whose proud spirit resented all tyranny.

"In the intimacy in which we live I may well give advice," replied Rafael, softening his tone.

"Let us hear the advice?" said Martin.

"I believe that you ought not to go to that house, at least not now."

"And why?"

"Because you run the risk of again entering upon the career of suffering in which I found you when I first knew you; you have too good a heart, Martin, to leave it to be trampled under the feet of a proud girl full of inexplicable caprices; she would trample upon it without pity, for the pleasure of having one more victim sacrificed to her beauty. On the other hand, there is no advantage to be gained by paying a visit there this evening, because, timid as you are with girls, if you run the risk of looking at her, she will find a pretext for again enslaving you."

Here San Luis paused. On seeing that Martin made no reply, he continued—

"I can give you some news which might decide you to take another step before arriving at a conclusion in your already sufficiently romantic love affair."

"What news?"

"I shall ask you one thing before telling it to you."

"What is it?"

"The opinions which you have expressed in our secret conclaves, were they really sincere, or only hasty utterances?"

"If they were not sincere I would not have uttered them."

"That is to say that you have committed yourself to our cause with all its consequences?"

"With all," said Martin, firmly.

"And you look upon as binding all undertakings which you have contracted there, to place yourself at the orders, which I assure you, come from our chief?"

"I look upon them as sacred."

"Not even Leonor will make you break your word?"

"Neither she nor any one else."

"You are the man I have always known you to be," said San Luis, seating himself opposite his friend.

"I'm waiting for your news without so many questions," the latter replied.

"My news is this—everything is ready, and tomorrow the Revolution begins."

Rafael had lowered his voice in saying these words.

"Very few," he continued, "possess this secret. In our club only four know it, and between us we have distributed posts to the others. I have chosen you to be my lieutenant if you will accept it."

"You have done well," said Martin, with animation.

"Now you see," continued San Luis, "why I opposed your visit to Leonor; I was afraid of her power, and I did not want our friends to think you were a coward."

"You are right, I shall not go to see her."

"Many people think that no fight will take place, and that the forces of the line will melt away before our standard; I do not think this, but I have faith in our success."

"Upon how many men can we count?" asked Rivas.

"The safest is the Valdivia battalion; to this corps we may add a part of the Chacabucas and perhaps some batteries of artillery. As for me, the only one that I am sure about is Valdivia, with which, well directed and aided by the populace whom we have armed, we can seize upon all the barracks, beginning with that of the artillery where we can find the ammunition that we require: Bilbao and several others whom you know will take part in the expedition and have promised that they will be on our side."

"I owe you thanks for the good opinion that you have of me," said Martin, pressing his friend's hand, "and I will take care that you do not lose it."

"Before going further, and as we have all the evening to talk about this," continued San Luis, "I am going to tell you now what I have thought that you can do instead of going to see Leonor."

"What is it?"

"I am certain that if you were again to remain in the same house with her, nothing would prevent you from declaring your love."

"If she were not so rich, and that I did not owe so much gratitude to her father, perhaps I would dare to confess it," replied Rivas.

"I founded my opinion upon these very reasons and as they are correct, I will tell you the truth. Do not dare to declare it. It might be that she is proud enough to give you her hand and to say to you—I have sounded the depths of Martin's heart, because mine contains the same feelings. She is besides most ideally beautiful."

"That is so," explained Martin, sighing.

"Do not be diverted from the path, and let the exceptional situation in which you are placed be my excuse in your eyes for the counsel I shall give you."

"I am waiting for your words with impatience."

"My idea is that you will write to her telling her that you love her, and that your letter shall reach her tomorrow."

Martin remained thoughtful.

"Do you wish that she shall never know of your love?" said Rafael.

"No," replied Rivas hotly.

"Very well, then, you will never have a better opportunity than the present to tell her so: the proximity of peril will excuse your audacity, and if she loves you she will pardon you with all her heart. If, on the contrary, she does not reciprocate, nothing is lost, since you have not presented yourself at the house, and no one can accuse you of disloyalty."

San Luis required to argue but little further in order to convince Rivas, who forgot the peril which the following day might hold for him, in his thought of the avowal which his heart for so long had desired to make.

In the evening Rafael said good-bye to Rivas.

"Here I leave you," he said to him; "I am going to receive the final orders and I shall try to get back before two o'clock."

He shut the door and Martin seated himself at a table to write the letter whose phrases were shining in his mind in letters of fire.

LVI

For Martin it was the most solemn occasion in his life. He was going for the first time to speak of his love to the woman who reigned in his heart, and he was on the eve of commencing an undertaking in which his life was at stake. Without a sensation of fear, he nevertheless felt an uneasiness which the idea of approaching death gives even to the most courageous minds, when healthy vigour appears to seize them with a greater force through the natural instinct of preservation. In this state he took a pen and wrote:—

SEÑORITA,

When you receive this letter it may be that I have ceased to exist; or I may be in great danger of death; it is this conviction alone that gives me courage to write it. Is the love with which you have inspired me a secret to you? I do not know, on account of the timidity with which you have always imbued me, on account also of the consideration which I owe to your family which has always treated me with such generosity, but I think I have not always had sufficient strength to hide my secret. I make this confession to you unpretentiously and with all the sincerity of my soul. You have been my first and my only love in life. The counsels of reason opposed the dominion of this love, but I had not sufficient power to vanquish it, and my heart has yielded to its imperiousness without strength to resist, although without hope of ever seeing it returned. After having struggled with it and endeavoured with all my power to hide it from you and every one, I cannot deprive myself of the consolation of speaking of it, when perhaps tomorrow life shall have left me. Pardon me such audacious weakness, it is perhaps the last farewell of a dying man, perhaps a message from one who tomorrow unhappy fate will force to travel far from you; in any case it is a secret which I have confided to your loyalty and which I pray you will not hear with disdain nor treat with mockery; since it comes from a heart which believes it is worthy at least of your esteem, and which has not worshipped any star than that of your love.

"Moreover, Señorita, since I left your house, I have not told you anything until now, to clear myself of an unjust accusation which perhaps time has exposed. And if I had strength sufficient to resign myself to suffer the pain of unmerited dishonour, still, I have had the hope of being able to justify myself. Now that perhaps the occasion for doing so may never come again to me, I would like at least to repeat to you that the reasons I formerly gave you for my conduct were true and sincere, and I would like to have the consolation that you believe me now, considering the solemnity of the moment in which I recall this to you."

Martin added to this letter a few words about the gratitude which he had to Leonor's family, and avoided in the same way as he had done throughout the letter, the romantic phrases so much in vogue at the time—as portrayed by novelists in their amatory epistles—in addressing himself to the girl who even in the familiar scenes of life still remained as a goddess in his eyes. Rivas found no other expression than that given him by the profound love which filled his heart, nor could he display the fire of an exalted imagination and the overflowing phrases which boil from the pens of lovers. Nevertheless, after having read his letter over several times, he felt himself as it were relieved of a great weight by realizing that he would not die without Leonor knowing his feelings towards her and giving him at least her esteem, in return for the love which he laid at her feet as an offering.

At eleven o'clock at night San Luis entered the room.

"All goes on perfectly," he said to Martin. "Here we have our weapons." Saying this he took out two belts, each with a pair of pistols, and two swords which he carried hidden under his cloak. "Here you are," he continued, handing Rivas a belt and a sword, "you are armed to defend your country in the name of which you carry these arms, and to fight for her."

The two men looked over the arms, divided the cartridges prepared for the pistols, and tried the swords, hiding their mutual preoccupation beneath a smiling exterior, and laughing phrases about their sudden appearance as warriors.

After this Rafael explained to Martin all that he knew about the plan of attack and the elements they could count upon to aid them to conquer. During this conversation, which lasted until two o'clock in the morning, they started at every noise they heard in the street, remaining at times silent for a long interval as if they were expecting to hear in the middle of the night some movement in the sleeping population.

"The hour of going to our post approaches," said Rafael, looking at his watch which was pointing to three o'clock. "Have you got your letter?"

"Yes," replied Martin.

"I paid a peso to Don Damaso's servant to wait for me," added San Luis, "promising him eight more for delivering your letter."

On saying this he left the room and returned in a few moments; his face was pale and agitated.

"Poor aunt," he said on entering, "may she sleep tranquilly."

He looked round the room, witness of so many of his joys and sorrows, and as if he wished to throw off the weight of his remembrances, he exclaimed—

"Come away, perhaps we shall return here victorious."

They went out into the street, hiding the arms under their cloaks, and went in silence to the Plaza de Armas, which they crossed, turning thence to the house of Don Damaso Encina. On arriving there San Luis said to Rivas—

"Wait for me here." He turned to the street door on which he knocked gently, it was immediately opened by the servant.

"Take this letter to the Señorita Leonor," he said, handing him Martin's letter, "it is absolutely necessary that you put it into her own hands as soon as she leaves her room. Here is your money," he added, at the same time renewing his directions to the servant, who promised to carry them out faithfully.

Then he and Rivas continued their walk until Rafael directed their steps to an old house whose door opened easily, and followed by Rivas entered a dark passage, closing the door of the street after them.

A few moments afterwards groups of two and three men began to arrive; they were armed with pistols which they hid under their coats, and as the moments passed the door opened and new groups arrived in the courtyard. San Luis approached them and divided them into two groups as nearly in military formation as possible, giving the command of one group to Martin and the other to another young man, reserving the office of commander-in-chief for himself. Some other young men of the club to which Rivas and San Luis belonged were given subaltern posts, and drawing them all up in order of battle, Rafael made a short speech calling upon their Chilian courage. After this he ordered one of his officers to go to the Plaza and find out if the forces of the line had arrived which were expected there. The messenger returned after ten minutes saying that the Valdivia battalion had arrived.

San Luis then gave the signal to start, and they all marched in good order to the meeting place at which they arrived a few moments after the Valdivia battalion—this statement may be confirmed by reference to the newspapers of the 20th April—San Luis joined Colonel Don Pedro Urriola, prime instigator of the mutiny, and conferred with him and the other chiefs who had joined the movement. The opinion that the forces of the line and the civil population would take part in their favour prevailed amongst them all, and Rafael was one of those who advocated the imperative necessity of taking action immediately and seizing the barracks to arm the people.

The swift passage of time hastened their decision to attack, especially as by 5.30 in the morning the revolutionary troop had increased but little, although it had been in the Plaza de Armas an hour and a half.

They decided then to begin the attack, and a picket was ordered to march in company with San Luis' forces to seize upon the Bomberos barrack.

The soldiers of the line and the peasants set out in marching order to kindle the first sparks of a combat, which on account of the time lost in coming to a definite resolution, must have been one of the most bloody that history relates of the capital of Chili.

LVII

From a publication printed the day following the battle, we will quote two paragraphs which describe the commencement of the combat of the 20th April.

"Colonel Don Pedro Urriola turned to the Plaza," said the paragraph, "and succeeded in surprising the capital which only held three men, who, guarding the entrance, were standing at ease as usual. Then the quarter of Bomberos was seized, and the arms of the barrack were given out to the people and to the rebels amongst the soldiers of the guard; the same was done with the soldiers of Chacabuca who were in the citadel."

The quarter of Bomberos in effect had opposed very slight resistance to the attack of the mutineers, who seized upon the arms and returned to the Plaza more numerous than ever. There unexpected news awaited them: two sergeants from Valdivia who had marched with two pickets of this corps to seize the quarter which was occupied by battalion No. 3 of the National Guard, had revolted against the officers who commanded this force and had fired at each of them, killing one, and severely wounding the other, after which they had turned with their pickets to swell the ranks of the Government. When this news arrived at the Plaza, fatal presentiments spread amongst the revolutionists. This example of defection might be contagious and might spread to the Valdivia battalion, the only veteran force which until now had taken part in the rising.

In the meantime the news of the mutiny had spread to the farthest ends of the city, and the people ran in troops to the Plaza de Armas where the heads of the Revolution were preaching mutiny, without having any arms to offer to those who wished to take part in it. The same news was also made known to the Government by others, with the result that the administration were able to take advantage of the precious moments for defence which the Revolutionists had lost in useless disputes and vain expectations. The drums were beaten in every quarter, artillery were got ready for resistance, the companies of the Civic Corps under arms united in the Plaza de la Moneda, and the Forces of the Government seized the Hill of Santa Lucia, dominating the neighbouring streets.

During this time the rebels in the Plaza, seeing that no new force was coming to join them, and lacking arms to give to the people, resolved to attack in the artillery quarter a storehouse of arms and ammunition; consequently a point of great importance for the success of the enterprise.

"The artillery barrack," says the paper, already quoted, "is situated at the foot of the Hill of Santa Lucia, near the Cañada, in a hired house; a bad military position, making an angle between Angosta de las Recojidas, and the Cañada, with an immense open space on its front and sides. There was a cross-street eight yards from the principal door which exposed to view the guns which could be brought out on opening the door. Almost opposite this principal door is the street of San Isidro, whence the door could be swept by the fire of superior forces."

To arrive at the quarter the position of which has been described, the Revolutionists went by Estado Street to the Cañada.

Before describing the sanguinary combat which took place at this point we must relate what was passing at this hour in the home of Don Damaso Encina.

This house was situated in one of the most central streets of Santiago, and the news of the Revolution arrived to rouse the family in the midst of their slumbers in the early hours of the morning.

Don Damaso jumped from his bed, on hearing the word "Revolution" uttered by the servants in the rooms close to his bedroom. This jump was imitated by Doña Engracia with admirable agility when she heard her husband in horrified accents shouting whilst looking for his pantaloons—

"Revolution, wife! Revolution!"

The want of light increased the terror of these words, which not only astounded Doña Engracia but augmented Don Damaso's own fright, who did not intend to give them such a fatal significance when he uttered them. Under the influence of such sudden terror the couple began to run about the room, frantically looking for articles of clothing which they were already holding in their hands, without knowing it.

"And my boots, what has become of them?" said Don Damaso, in desperation, rushing all over the room in search of them.

"Look, man! you're running away with my petticoat," said Doña Engracia, who, having lighted a candle, found herself at the foot of the bed modestly crouching in the very scanty robe that failed to cover her.

With the aid of the light Don Damaso saw—without knowing how—that he had covered his shoulders with his consort's petticoat, and, wishing to get rid of it with the greatest possible speed, he inadvertently flung it at the head of Doña Engracia, who, trying to catch it in its flight with one hand, whilst with the other she endeavoured to hold the folds of her chemise over her bosom, gave a blow to the candle which again plunged them into darkness.

To the exclamations which the frightened couple gave at this incident were united the yells of Diamela, increasing the turmoil and disorder in the room, in which each of them seemed to wish to drown the other's voice.

Finally, after again lighting the candle, Don Damaso found his boots, Doña Engracia put on her petticoat, and Diamela, becoming calmer, curled up in the bed which had been left by her mistress.

"It is necessary to dress quickly," said Don Damaso, giving an example of activity but not of dexterity, because each article appeared to have hidden itself at this critical moment.

Then they heard loud knocks at the door.

"Who wants to come in here?" exclaimed Don Damaso, turning livid.

"Papa!" called the voice of Augustin. "Get up! There is a revolution!"

"I know it," answered Don Damaso, opening the door to his son.

Whilst finishing dressing, Don Damaso and Doña Engracia directed a fire of questions about the revolution to the dandy, and as Augustin knew nothing about it he merely kept repeating the questions put to him.

"And Leonor?" at last asked Don Damaso, seeing that his son could neither satisfy nor calm his anxiety in any way. The three went off to Leonor's room where they found her dressed and seated quietly beside a table.

"Daughter! There is a revolution!" said Don Damaso to her.

"So they say," replied the girl, serenely.

"What are we to do?" asked the father, astonished at Leonor's courage.

"What do you want to do?" she asked, "it appears to me the best thing is to wait here."

But Don Damaso could not remain quiet and could not understand how at such a moment any one could sit down. So he rushed out of the room and called the servants, ordered them to bolt the doors, and then returned to Leonor's room, saying—

"This is the fault of those villains who go out preaching to the mob; cursed Liberals! As they have nothing to do they make revolutions. Ah! if I were Governor I would shoot them all on the spot!"

Some shots that were heard in the distance cut short his speech and flung him almost inanimate upon a sofa.

Doña Engracia, also overcome with fear, threw herself into the arms of her husband without thinking that in embracing him she was holding Diamela, who uttered piercing yells at such cruel and unexpected torture.

"Papa! Mama! Let us be men! Oh, hold your tongue, Diamela!" said Augustin, pretending a serenity which his trembling limbs contradicted.

The only person who appeared unmoved was Leonor, who exhorted them without affectation to be calm.

In this way the moments passed till the light of day appeared, which had the effect of calming the agitation from which every one in the home was suffering except Leonor.

A servant entered the room, and in a voice choked by fright, said—

"Señor! They are knocking at the door!"

One would have thought that in these words he was announcing to Don Damaso that a shower of bombs were about to fall on the roof of the house, for he took his head in his hands and exclaimed:—

"They are coming to plunder! They are coming to plunder."

Leonor, without paying any attention to her father's groans, said to Augustin—

"Why don't you go and see who it is knocking?"

"I! It's easy to say that! And suppose they are armed rabble? I! No! I'll defend you; but don't let us open the door."

"An original manner of defending us," replied the girl, leaving the room and going towards the street door, where the blows were being redoubled in an alarming manner.

Those who knocked were Don Fidel Elias, his wife, Matilde, and some children of the family: they all entered the house, talking at the same time about what they had seen in the street. As soon as they had gone into the inner rooms the servant who opened the door came to Leonor.

"Señorita," he said, "some one has given me this letter for you."

The girl took the letter and opened it mechanically.

On reading Martin's signature she raised her eyes and said to the servant in a choking voice—

"That's all right, go back to the door and tell me if any one knocks."

Whilst saying these words her face had recovered its firm tranquillity and only a slight pallor indicated that she was labouring under strong emotion.

Instead of going to the room where Don Fidel and his family were, she entered another where she was alone, and after shutting the door she opened the letter which she had hidden in a bag.

On reading it the girl lost all the courage which had distinguished her from the others in the house, her face was absolutely without colour and her eyes were full of tears, whilst her agitated breathing showed the quick beatings of her heart.

"What is to be done! My God!" she exclaimed. In this exclamation was summed up all the anguish which she felt at the idea of the peril in which Rivas might be at that very moment.

Then she got up suddenly as if a new and more terrible blow had struck her to the heart.

"Perhaps he is already wounded, or dead!" she added, casting up to Heaven those most beautiful eyes wet for the first time with tears of love.

Then she prayed God earnestly for Martin's life: a sublime prayer, brokenly worded, but most warmly eloquent, with the eloquence of a loving heart; and then—as if confessing for the first time all the impotence of pride, the sterile vanity of beauty—she wept like a child with an absolute forgetfulness of everything except what related to her lover.

After passing some moments thus, she made a great effort to calm herself, and after arranging the disorder which a moment of infinite desperation had given to her attire, she left the room, carrying Rivas' letter next her heart.

The arrival of Don Fidel had now given a new direction to Don Damaso's thoughts, and almost completely calmed him. On entering, Don Fidel recounted the news which he had heard in the street, news which supposed that the Revolutionary force was coming from all quarters and going to the Casa de Moneda, the last defence of the Government.

"Perhaps by now," he said finally, "all is finished."

Then they all went out of the room in which they were talking and mounted to the upper part of the house to observe from the balcony the movement in the streets.

"Men, what is going on?" called Don Fidel to two men who just then were running past.

"The people have won and Colonel Urriola has seized the artillery," said one of them.

"Long live the people!" cried the other.

"Long live the people!" repeated Don Damaso, who was always on the winning side.

Then, as if to justify this seditious exclamation—

"Sometimes" he said, "these poor oppressed people are obliged to justify themselves."

ALBERTO BLEST GANA

"That is no reason why they should oppress us," replied Don Fidel, who had a horror of the mob.

"It is only proper that the people should recover their just rights," said Don Damaso, with an admirable patriotic intonation in his voice— quite forgetting that half an hour before this people did not exist for him except simply as a rabble.

Whilst they were thus discussing and wondering what would happen next, Leonor found herself in the room which Rivas had formerly occupied; she went there that she might pray even to the furniture to tell her about the absent one, implore Heaven for him, and clutch passionately the letter which was hidden in her bosom.

Now the noise of firing could be heard from the artillery quarter, which caused the others to leave the balcony and descend the stairs in a body to seek shelter in case of any unforeseen accident.

In place of following them we will go back to the scene of the battle where some of the personages of this story are figuring among the combatants.

LVIII

We left the Revolutionary Column marching towards the Alemada by the Street of Estado.

San Luis marched at the head of his troops, whose ranks had much increased on the road, although many of those who arrived had no fire arms.

Martin calmly, as if he was marching on parade, endeavoured to preserve order amongst his men, exhorting them to observe military formation. The people were crowded together in the Alemada, in the streets, and even on the foot paths, cheering on the Revolutionaries, who marched along in splendid order and counted upon an early conquest of the artillery quarter.

But before arriving there the Revolutionaries perceived various pickets of the battalion of the Chacabuco infantry posted at different places on the neighbouring hill of Santa Lucia.

As the forces on this Hill dominated the quarter which they intended to attack, it was necessary to begin by dislodging the Chacabucas from their position. With this view the Revolutionaries rushed to scale the hill, but the soldiers on it instead of offering resistance abandoned their positions and fled down to the Cañada by the Southern fort, quickly entering into the Artillery barrack, which opened its doors to them and which by this means received fresh forces to add to the reduced number of the defenders of the barrack.

On account of their swiftness the Revolutionary force could not frustrate this rapid movement and only arrived at the barrack when its door was shut behind the soldiers of the Chacabuca.

The chief of the Revolutionists then gave the order to attack the barrack, and the troops took the offensive, commencing the attack in the midst of the clamour of the people—of whom the greater part observing the scene abstained from taking part in it; in some cases for want of arms and leaders, without whom nothing can be done in taking the initiative by the masses, who always require to be led by the Caballeros, who—notwithstanding the propaganda of equality—they always look upon as their natural superiors.

Rafael San Luis led the attack of his troop on the flank of the barrack whilst the front was assaulted by the Valdivian troops. The combat now became general, although the besiegers economized their shots in order to make them the more telling by taking good aim. Whilst the veteran troop was directing a strong fire upon doors and windows those of San Luis and other popular chiefs threw stones from the roofs and tried to smash the principal door. In the midst of the most lively fire a party of men led by Martin Rivas succeeded in crossing the threshold of one of the doors which looked upon the street of the Recojidas.

"Forward, boys!" shouted Martin, brandishing a sword in one hand and a pistol in the other.

Thus saying, he tried to penetrate into the barrack followed by his men, but they were met with such a murderous fire that almost all those who followed Rivas rushed back. In vain by speech and example he endeavoured to lead them on, but, at that moment were heard the first discharges of a piece of artillery which the Captain of the besieged had placed in the cross-road. Rapid and incessant firing then took place, the ceaseless noise of the fusillade stunning the ears of the people, and the repeated discharge of the cannon which barred the street, decimating the Revolutionary ranks.

It was the noise of these discharges which had made the families of Don Damaso and Don Fidel come down from the balcony. At the moment when Leonor was invoking the mercy of Heaven for Martin, the latter, like the knights of old, had rushed into the thickest of the battle bearing in his bosom the image, and on his lips the name of Leonor.

Notwithstanding his courage the besiegers saw themselves in great danger from the sustained fire and the brave examples of the besieged, when there appeared at the entry of the Street of Augustinas a body of soldiers "with Colonel Gracia at the head," as the aforesaid newspaper mentions.

This column, composed of as many of the National Guard as the Government had been able to gather together, advanced down the street and soon found themselves between two fires from a detachment of Valdivians, whom the Revolutionary leader sent to attack its rearguard, and the rest of the mutineers who were firing against its advance at the same time. The noise of the combat was still terrible at times and the courage of the Revolutionaries rivalled in daring that of the chiefs and the officials of the Government, for guns were showering upon them a hail of bullets on every side.

Rivas and San Luis matched each other in courage and coolness. Not content with cheering on their own men, each of them armed himself with a gun, and leaving their swords hanging in their belts, fired like the soldiers upon the enemy. The voices of the soldiers (drowned by the detonating sound of the guns mingled with the groans of the wounded and the curses of those who were forced back instead of advancing) were lost in the murderous discharge of the enemy's guns.

In the midst of the combat a bullet struck Colonel Urriola, the leader of the Revolutionaries, who fell, saying, "I have been deceived!" Words which history quotes as a proof that the Revolutionaries did not count upon the obstinate resistance with which they were met.

The news of the death of the chief spread through the ranks of the mutineers, and soon its moral influence was felt in the combat as the fire grew calmer, and passing from offensive to defensive they all fell back to the Cañada opposite the principal door of the quarter. Reuniting in a compact body the Revolutionaries here renewed their fire with more ardour than before. These moments were the most bloody of the fight. Then they took shelter against the walls to make room for two pieces of artillery which were discharging a lively fire against their enemies.

In a group gathered at the entrance of the street of San Isidro Martin and Rafael with their men fired a volley upon a troop which had just come out from the barrack, and shouted to those who were not armed to take the arms of those who had fallen. This was without doubt the most critical moment of this bloody fight. The belligerents divided only by a few paces from one another, defying each other with voice and gesture, were able to fire with certainty and to see the effect of it upon their opponents. The noise was stunning, and men fell on both sides in horrifying numbers. Curious onlookers, who from the dawn of day had been in the vicinity, had fled from this awful sight, leaving the victory to be disputed by the combatants, who in their feverish enmity appeared to have forgotten that each shot was watering the Chilian soil with the generous blood of one of her sons. The most daring courage in the presence of danger, obstinate tenacity in defence and ferocity in attack, indomitable ardour and heroic coolness were attributes of the national character displayed on both sides at this supreme moment. The two pieces of artillery, upon which Rivas and San Luis and their men directed a murderous fire from the entrance of the San Isidro, were discharging less and less frequently, because the showers of bullets which fell upon them had placed *hors de combat* the two officers who had successively commanded them and the greater part of the men who had served them. The chief of the quarter had put new officers in command of these guns in place of the two who were severely wounded in serving them. Of these two, one was his own son. But on the arrival of the leader a furious discharge felled almost all the artillerymen who yet remained on foot, and the Revolutionaries advanced through the smoke of this volley in order to seize upon the two cannon which death had left without defenders. Martin and Rafael arrived together and were the first to lay their hands upon the guns, which had caused such ravages in the ranks of their men.

"Victory, victory," shouted San Luis.

And his shout was repeated by all as they dragged the cannon from the posts which they had occupied.

But the shouts of victory had hardly ceased when the principal door of the fort opened anew and a horrible fusillade was directed upon the rebels, causing the most frightful butchery amongst them. San Luis gripped Martin's arm forcibly when he found him beside him and he shouted to his men—

"Fire, fire, the enemy is at the last gasp!"

A sentence that was stifled by the sound of fresh fusillades whilst the young man who had uttered it threw both his arms round Rivas' neck saying—

"I cannot stand on my feet, I am wounded."

Martin took him round the waist, dragging him through the ranks of the combatants, and carried him to the door of a house which he opened with a kick and entered carrying Rafael, whose coat was now bathed in blood.

Two women and an old man were in the room when Martin entered carrying Rafael.

"Señora, this is a young man for whom I implore your help," said Rivas to the woman, who seemed the elder.

The two women, the old man, and Martin, took off Rafael's coat and found his breast had been pierced by two bullets; when he breathed, torrents of blood flowed from the two wounds.

San Luis took his friend's hands.

"Do not leave me," he said to him. "It's impossible to save me, and I feel that I have but a short time to live."

Martin's eyes, which a few moments before were blazing with the fire of battle, filled with tears.

"You are also wounded," exclaimed San Luis, seeing that little by little the blood flowed from one of Martin's hands.

I don't know, I have felt nothing," he said.

The same discharge which had wounded San Luis had also hit Martin on the right arm.

"Victory is almost certain," added Rafael, every moment speaking with greater difficulty. "Listen to the guns, the fire from the Fort is dying down."

Each word was spoken with a great effort; his voice sank by degrees whilst the bleeding from his breast continued, in spite of all the care that Martin and the others took to stop it with cloths and improvised bandages.

After a pause, during which San Luis appeared to be trying to hear what was going on at the seat of the fray, he pressed with feverish ardour Martin's hand, and making an effort to rise—

"Say farewell to my poor aunt," he said, in a failing voice. "If you can see Adelaida ask her to forgive me, and you will not forget me, Martin, because—"

The effort which he made to finish this phrase appeared to exhaust the last breath of life which remained in him, for the words died upon his lips, and his head fell upon the poor pillow, which the woman had placed for it.

"Dead! Dead!" exclaimed Martin, holding him in his arms and weeping like a child. "Poor Rafael!"

For some moments he gave free course to his grief and then, raising himself, he kissed many times the already' livid forehead and cheeks of San Luis: he promised the women that they would be well rewarded if they would convey the body to the house of Don Pedro San Luis, and left the room, exclaiming—

"I will avenge thee."

His eyes at this moment shone with a sombre light, and with his right hand he clutched his sword, which he drew as he went out.

When Martin arrived at the place of combat the greatest confusion prevailed there; the Revolutionary force was disorganized. One of the officers of Chacabuca, made a prisoner at the beginning, taking advantage of the disorder which prevailed, took flight to the artillery quarter, and several soldiers followed his example, and the contagion was communicated to others around them. At this, little by little the fire of the Revolutionaries ceased, and when Rivas arrived opposite the Fort, they were entering—believing themselves victorious—and there fell into the hands of their foes.

Martin also entered under the same delusion, and met at the entrance Amador Molina, who having hidden himself during the fray, was at this moment shouting in favour of the Government and against the Revolutionaries—whom in the beginning he had appeared to support.

A man who had fought with Rivas approached him.

"We are lost," he said, "the troops are leaving us and we must fly."

At this moment Amador shouted—

"Ricardo, here are two Revolutionaries."

"Coward!" said Martin to him, taking him by the throat, "you are a traitor, but I will not kill you!"

In saying this he hurled him violently against a wall.

"We must fly, it is absolutely necessary," the young man who had just spoken said to Martin, and he dragged him out of the room at the door of which several inquisitive people were looking in.

Martin resisted for a short time, during which Amador had run into the courtyard, calling the Police officer, who with some troops at his command formed part of the Civil Division which had gone to the aid of the Fort.

When Rivas had decided to fly Amador was rushing back to the place with Ricardo Castanos and some soldiers.

"Quick! quick!" said the young man to Martin, "do not give them the pleasure of taking us prisoners."

"Adios!" said Martin to him, pressing his hand; and he took to flight in the direction of Don Damaso's house, whilst Amador and Ricardo were looking for him amongst the people who had arrived at the entrance.

This circumstance gave him an advantage over his pursuers, who ran into the street when he had already gained the distance of a square of houses from the Fort.

"Let us seek for him in Don Damaso's house," said Amador to the officer, "and if we don't find him there we shall have to search the city for him."

LIX

We have mentioned the principal events of the sanguinary combat which took place in Santiago on the 20th of April, 1851; endeavouring to confine ourselves to the official paragraphs of the newspaper to which we have previously referred.

We must now occupy ourselves with the persons of this story.

Leonor and the others in the house had passed some hours in mortal anxiety. The sound of the combat struck to their hearts, arousing a fear in almost all and giving Leonor the most anxious inquietude.

Doña Engracia had called all the inhabitants of the house into one room in which they were reciting the rosary in turn. Don Damaso and Augustin said the "Ora pro nobis" with exemplary devotion, whilst Leonor, leaving the room, went to the top of the house.

There, leaning on the balcony and listening to the noises which came from the city, she prayed to God for Martin and strove to divert her thoughts from the fatal presentiments which oppressed her at the sound of every shot. She did not dare to question the people who passed by in the street for fear of hearing the fatal tidings that her heart was anticipating.

Keeping her eyes fixed in the direction of the battle she saw a group of men who were running towards the house. On arriving under the balcony one of them stopped as if to take breath.

"Señorita," he said to Leonor, "they have conquered us, the Valdivians have gone over to the Government."

Saying these words, he followed the others, who were calling him from the distance.

Leonor felt an icy current steal through her veins at the thought of the battle being lost. Martin was either dead or a prisoner. Raising her thoughts to Heaven with renewed fervour, without knowing what she was doing, she began to pray aloud, mingling the name of Rivas in the fervent words of her improvised prayer.

At this moment she saw not far away a man who was running towards the house. For an instant she thought that she was under the influence of hallucination, and a minute afterwards gave a cry of joy, and rushed down into the courtyard. She had recognized Martin!

There was no one in the courtyard, and the door of the street was fastened with a key and an enormous bolt. Leonor turned the key, and pulled back the bolt as easily as if it had been as light as a feather. This took a few seconds only and then she opened the door.

Martin arrived at this moment, and found himself face to face with Leonor, more beautiful than ever in the disorder of her dress and the pallor of her face.

The young man, who had just faced with calmness all the dangers of four hours of fighting, was dismayed in the presence of this girl, who looked at him with such an expression of joy, her large eyes full of tears.

"Señorita," he said, "I have come—"

But he could not continue, because Leonor took his hands in hers, saying—

"Come in, come in quickly, that I may look at you."

And Martin obeyed the soft pressure of those hands and the sweet imperious tone with which the girl accompanied the movement.

Leonor then bolted the door with the same force and swiftness that she had employed to open it, and said to Martin—

"Follow me."

They crossed the courtyard, and, instead of entering the rooms in which they were reciting the rosary, Leonor opened the door of Augustin's quarters and turned to the second courtyard to enter her own suite, the door of which she bolted after Martin.

"No one has seen us yet," she said, with the breathlessness of one who has been running a long distance.

Martin remained standing in the middle of the room looking at Leonor; it appeared to him that all this was a dream. This beautiful girl whose name he had been invoking so often in the midst of the fray was now at his side in the mansion which he had always looked upon as a shrine, and the haughty beauty of proud mien and disdainful glance was now approaching him with a sweet, although agitated smile, and was looking at him with love in her eyes.

"Seat yourself here," she said, pointing to a chair. "I received your letter this morning," she added, looking at him tenderly.

She was going to continue when, giving a choking cry, she quickly approached the young man.

"Ah! you are wounded?" she said, taking his arm, the hand of which was bathed in blood.

"It cannot signify anything, because I feel no pain whatever," replied Martin.

"Let me see; take off your coat," she replied, in a tone of authority.

The sleeve of the shirt was covered with blood which was sticking to the wound, and had staunched the blood.

"It's no more than a scratch," said Martin.

"No matter, we must see to it," replied the girl. And, drawing from her neck a fine handkerchief of batiste, which she wore as a kind of cravat, she bound it round the wound, after having turned up the sleeve of the shirt.

"You have made me suffer this morning more than I have ever suffered in all my life," she said to him, as she bound the wound with the handkerchief. "Why did you not come last night as you promised my brother?"

"Señorita," replied Martin, now finding courage to allude to what he had said in his letter, "I did not dare to come. Notwithstanding the cause for which I have exposed my life, notwithstanding the time I have passed far from you, my love for you would have mastered me, and I know that if I had come last night I might have faltered had I thought of today."

"How could you expose your life in this manner?" said Leonor, in a tone of reproach and lowering her gaze. "Why have you never spoken to me with the frankness that you used in your letter?"

"Because I never had sufficient courage to do so. Besides, did you not condemn me by appearances?"

"That is true; but Edelmira herself has undeceived me, showing me your answers to her letters."

"My position also obliged me to keep silence," added Rivas, sadly.

"What does your position matter if I love you?" answered Leonor, looking softly in Martin's eyes.

"Oh, Leonor! Repeat those words to me!" said Martin, with frantic joy, as he took possession of the girl's hands.

"Yes, I love you, and I shall hide it from no one," answered Leonor. "This morning I recalled every day since I first saw you, and I know that I have been cruel for pride's sake. If you had died today," she added, turning pale, "I would never have forgiven myself nor been able to console myself. Even before I had received your letter, nothing was able to keep me from thinking that I was the cause of the desperate resolution which you had taken; you did not do well, Martin, to make me run the risk of having to weep for the rest of my life."

"How could I guess my happiness, since you dismissed me from your house?"

"And why did I dismiss you? Was it not because I loved you? Why otherwise could it matter to me that you were in love with this poor girl?"

"My hope—Leonor—never told me so, and how could I have guessed it?"

"Why should you not have guessed it?"

"You forget now," said the young man, smiling, "that you are capable at times of looks that would freeze the blood of the most daring and that many times you did not forbear to give some of those looks to me."

"Chastise me; it is just," replied she, with an adorable smile of submission.

"But this moment repays with interest all that my love has made me suffer," replied Martin, in impassioned accents; and, without thinking of what he was doing, he left his seat and fell on his knees before Leonor—pressing passionately her little hands which she yielded to him.

"We have been very silly, Martin," said the girl, dropping her eyes under the ardent gaze of those which looked on her with ecstasy. "Have we not told each other many times with our eyes that we loved each other? Ah! it is too true! You are always right. It has been my fault. Of all the men who surrounded me, you! you who held the lowliest position, appeared to me the most noble, and I was afraid to confess to myself the preference of my heart. Well! Henceforth I shall repair my fault because I am proud of your love."

"I do not know that I am the most worthy of your love," said Martin, "but I am certain that I love you the most. What power had I to defend myself against your beauty? I felt myself conquered by it without inquiring what hopes I could have. When I sought to combat it I found myself with no strength to fight the passion which had seized me. Since that time nothing could tear you from my heart, neither the thought of self-respect nor the want of hope, nor the disdain with which you sometimes received my glances: thus it was that this morning I risked my life with pleasure, because I thought myself despised by you and knew that death alone could extinguish my love."

The girl drank in each word that fell from his lips and allowed Rivas to kiss her hands passionately. She had prayed so much to Heaven for the man who was now at her feet that she believed she listened to his impassioned language as if it were one of the miracles of his resurrection.

Martin was about to continue when they heard voices and a loud knock on the door.

"Leonor!" shouted Don Damaso, from the other side.

Leonor ran to the door, she looked through the keyhole and saw her father who was accompanied by Ricardo Castanos and some soldiers who remained in the distance.

"You are lost if you don't fly," she said, running towards Martin; "it is an officer and some soldiers."

"Leonor!" shouted Don Damaso again, knocking on the door.

"Fly from this, Martin," said the girl, opening another door. "You know the house; you can go out by my father's study and arrive in the street while they are looking for you in this room."

"Others will follow me there," said Rivas.

The blows were redoubled and the voice of Ricardo Castanos could be heard threatening to burst open the door.

"If you love me, fly, in God's name!" exclaimed Leonor, torn with anxiety.

"If you counsel me to fly I will do so," said Rivas, "but I would prefer to fight for my liberty here if it were not for your reputation."

Leonor pushed him from the room and fell upon a sofa almost senseless.

The voice of her father roused her from her stupor, and going towards the door at which he knocked she opened it softly.

"Señorita," said Ricardo to her, "painful duty obliges me to ask your permission to examine this apartment."

"Examine it, sir," replied Leonor, haughtily. "A conqueror," she added ironically, "does not tarnish his glory while lending himself to what you call a sad duty."

"Girl!" said Don Damaso to her in a low voice; then he added aloud, "It is only right that the defenders of order should pursue the rebels. Look, Señor Officer, you are a witness that I have offered no resistance, we are all right, because I could never hide demagogues who are also Revolutionaries."

Whilst the soldiers were minutely examining every corner of the room Don Damaso followed, abusing the whole Liberal Party, and Leonor sat on the sofa trembling for the fate of Martin.

He, knowing the house, traversed several rooms and arrived in the courtyard by the door of Don Damaso's study.

As this moment Leonor left the room in which the soldiers were following their researches and went out into the courtyard to see if Rivas had left the house.

As soon as Martin found himself in the courtyard he went to the door of the street; but, besides being bolted, he found it in the custody of two policemen, sword in hand. Arriving at the exit Rivas saw that it would be impossible either to proceed or to hide himself, as the two sentinels at the door threw themselves upon him brandishing their batons. The young man, without being disconcerted, put his back to one of the walls of the exit and, drawing his sword, began to parry the wild blows which the police aimed at him. Whilst the two attacked him they shouted at the same time, calling for help. At that moment, and when Rivas had given one of them a blow which made him draw back terrified, Leonor arrived in the courtyard and saw the young man who was attacking the other policeman. Just at this moment, summoned by their shouts, others arrived and encircled the young man, who continued to defend himself with heroic courage, whilst Leonor cried to her father—

"Save him, papa! They will kill him!"

To the shouts of the combatants were now joined the cries of the women, who, with Doña Engracia at their head, had left in the middle of the rosary and arrived in the courtyard at the same time as the soldiers, who had rushed there on hearing the voices of the men whom Martin was getting the better of.

Don Damaso tremblingly approached the group that surrounded Rivas.

"Resistance is useless, Martin," he said; "yield yourself."

"If he doesn't yield I will fire on him," shouted Ricardo Castanos, who not only looked upon the young man as a rebel but also as the cause of his disappointment in love.

Leonor gave a cry on hearing this order, and seeing that two of the soldiers were loading their guns to carry it out, she ran to the entrance terrified.

"Defend yourself no longer, they will assassinate you," she cried to Rivas, who was still fighting with admirable coolness. He obeyed this voice as a command.

The four soldiers seized him and disarmed him.

"I hope," said Don Damaso to Ricardo, "that you will treat this young man with consideration and generosity. I, as a member of the Administration," he added, in an emphatic voice, "will intercede for him with the President."

The order was given to march, and, surrounded by the troop which had taken him prisoner, Rivas left, after having received a look from Leonor, who, paler than a corpse, seemed to wish to send him her very soul in this silent but eloquent adieu.

LX

A fter having brought the soldiers and the officers to Don Damaso's house to arrest Martin, Amador Molina remained in the street, following the dictates of prudence. Joining the crowd that was coming on, and seeing that he ran no risk, he arrived with it at the Fort in which Rivas was to be imprisoned.

During this time the inhabitants of Don Damaso's house were still in a state of consternation caused by the recent scene, and each of them gave his opinion on what had happened, to explain the sudden apparition of Rivas, when they were all so certain that the street door had been firmly bolted the whole morning. The news of Rivas' apprehension circulated in a very short time from this house to the neighbouring ones, from these down the whole street and from that to other streets, and so on, and at the end of an hour Don Damaso's principal salon might have been found full of people of distinction of both sexes who arrived to talk about this notable event.

Don Damaso was in the ante-room surrounded by his friends, and Doña Engracia in the salon surrounded by ladies.

It is worth while to repeat some of the conversation in both these rooms about the events of the day, to depict, on one part, the fruitful invention of imaginary alarms by the ladies, and, on the other hand, the sudden reaction which had taken place in the opinions of the men, who wished to disassociate themselves from the bloody drama of the morning.

"We've had a lucky escape," said Don Damaso to the others, who the day before had called themselves Liberals, as he had done. "What should we have done if the canaille had triumphed?"

"What the Government ought to do now is to shoot on the spot a few dozen of these rebels," observed, in decided accents, a man who had been shut up all the morning in his room praying to all the saints in the calendar to keep him safe.

"But, my dear," at the same time said a lady to Doña Engracia, speaking of Rivas, "this man must be an atrocious person! Is it true that he murdered three policemen here in the courtyard?"

"Ah, my dear!" exclaimed another, "what would I have done if I had had such a man in my house? I think I would have died of fright; but how did he get in here when the door was bolted?"

"By the roof, perhaps," answered another; "these Liberals do not hold anything sacred."

"Or by the sewer, for they stick at nothing."

"To do that he must have got through the grating in the drain!"

During this conversation Doña Engracia contented herself with pressing Diamela in her arms.

In the neighbouring room one of the gentlemen was saying—

"Now is the time when really patriotic men should approach the Government as an example to the demagogues that they are condemned by public opinion."

"That is well thought of," said Don Damaso. "Good citizens should present themselves to the Government. Shall we all go to the Palace?"

"A good idea!" they all replied.

"It is necessary that we ask for energetic measures," said the one who had just spoken about shooting.

They took their hats and went to the Moneda with the airs of conquerors to ask for the death of those who had given them such a dreadful fright that morning.

In the meantime Leonor had returned to her room and was weeping despairingly for the fate of Martin, whilst her memory recalled her recent conversation with the young man, his words of love which resounded in her heart like the echo of celestial music, and the reckless courage with which she had just seen him defending himself against so many united adversaries. If love had before made her heart beat more swiftly, pride also palpitated at these remembrances, and she vowed to endeavour to make her life worthy of such a precious offering. But the idea of new perils surrounding Rivas soon arrived to disturb the ecstasy of her dream; she saw that instead of weeping it was necessary to defend his threatened life, and she went out of her room resolved to try every possible means to set Martin at liberty.

Dominated by this thought she entered Augustin's rooms. Augustin, in order to fortify himself after the weakness he felt from the events of the morning, was drinking repeated glasses of "kirsch."

"Oh! Hermanita! what a terrible day!" he exclaimed on seeing Leonor enter. "I confess to you that I have much compassion for women and cowardly men, because I found I was able to imagine the fear that they must endure."

"What we have got to think about now is how to save Martin," replied Leonor, without paying any attention to her brother's bravado.

"We! and what can we do?" said the dandy, pouring out another cup of liqueur.

"It is necessary that papa should speak with the Ministers, with the President, and with every one who has any influence in the Government."

"Gently, *mi bella* it is a dangerous day to take risks, and as Martin had the unhappy idea of coming and hiding himself here it might be thought that we had taken a part in the Revolution if we speak in his favour."

"Are you afraid to do something for a man to whom you owe such a great obligation? Augustin, I thought you gay, but not ungrateful!" said Leonor, looking disdainfully at her brother.

"No, I'm not ungrateful, dear; but, without doubt, in politics one must be cautious. What the deuce! Let us see what can be done for poor Martin to whom I don't deny we owe gratitude; but you want everything to go by steam."

"The affair is not done by thinking, but by working," replied the girl, in a tone of resolution. "I'll speak to papa, and if he takes the matter as coolly as you do I'll go myself and intercede for Martin with some friends who will not refuse to help me."

"Capital! Hermanita! What a fury you are in! No one would say that it was only on account of a friend—"

"But a lover, that is what you mean to say," interrupted Leonor, impatiently."

"Caramba. She has all the energy that should belong to me as a male and the eldest!" said Augustin, on seeing her exit.

Leonor entered her room, after having ordered a servant to let her know when her father arrived.

An hour afterwards Don Damaso entered the room to which his wife had retired as soon as her visitors had left. Augustin, who had seen him cross the courtyard, entered the same room shortly after him.

"The Palace was full of people," said Don Damaso, taking off his hat. "Nothing but unanimity in the opinion in condemnation of the rebels; the most decided civic valour reigned there, and I think that we would have all marched singing to the fight if it had taken place then."

Hardly had he finished this sentence, in which it would have been very difficult to discover the Liberal who in the morning was preaching the cause of the people, when Leonor entered the room, her head erect, and resolution depicted on her face.

"How did the affair go off, papa?" said she, seating herself beside Don Damaso.

"Perfectly, little girl; the President thanked me for my adherence to the cause of order," replied the caballero, with an air of satisfied importance.

"I was not asking about that," asked Leonor, "what was done about Martin?"

"Ah, Martin! They must have taken him to prison, poor boy!"

"And you have done nothing for him?" asked Leonor, gazing at her father.

"It was not an opportune moment," answered her father; "feeling was running too high, it is better to wait."

"To wait!" exclaimed the girl; "Martin never *waited* to help us!"

"That is true, little girl; I don't deny that Martin would be a most clever young man if he had not been so mad as to become a Liberal."

"It is not for us to judge him," said Leonor; "our duty is to influence every one we can in his favour. It is most important."

"Oh, we'll have influence, don't fear about that; I'm now all right with the Government."

"Yes, but meanwhile time is passing, and Martin may be brought before the judge!" exclaimed the girl, with visible impatience.

"That is inevitable," answered Don Damaso, calmly.

This reply appeared to exasperate Leonor, who rose indignantly.

"Papa, you must go immediately and speak with the Minister of the Interior," she said in a commanding tone.

"That would compromise me, since Martin has been found in my house; we must allow some days to pass," replied Don Damaso.

"Then I will go myself to see the wife of the Minister!" exclaimed Leonor, exasperated with the indifference of her father.

"What a lively interest you have in Martin," said the caballero, in an accusing tone.

"More than interest," replied Leonor, excitedly; "I love him."

These words appeared to produce the same effect on Don Damaso, Augustin, and Doña Engracia as the noise of the battle did in the morning.

Don Damaso got up with a bound, Augustin appeared terrified, and Doña Engracia caught hold of Diamela, who was sleeping beside her, giving her a frightful squeeze.

"Girl, what are you saying?" exclaimed Don Damaso, thunderstruck with what he had just heard.

This exclamation was mingled with a yelp from Diamela, victim of the nervous excitement of her mistress.

"I say that I love Martin," replied Leonor, in a firm voice and with a magnificent look of pride.

"Martin," repeated Don Damaso, helplessly.

Leonor did not deign to reply, instead she turned away with dignity and seated herself.

At this moment Don Damaso well knew the ascendancy that this girl exercised over him, because, whilst wishing to speak severely, he quailed before her serene and determined look, which appeared to defy him.

Don Damaso felt the weakness of his character and lowered his eyes, saying—

"You have no right to make this confession."

"And why not? Martin, although poor, has a noble heart, and high intelligence; these are enough to justify him. Would you prefer that I should hide what I feel? No, you are the natural receivers of my confidence."

Leonor pronounced these words in a manner which admitted of no reply, and the three persons who surrounded her were lacking besides in the strength which it was necessary to possess in order to confront such a determined and haughty character.

Doña Engracia contented herself with pressing Diamela.

Augustin murmured some phrases, half French and half Spanish, under his breath, and Don Damaso began to walk up and down the room to hide his want of will-power.

Leonor continued: "You know, papa, that Martin is a young man of promise, you have said so yourself many times; also he is of a very good family: the only thing that is wanting is that he is not rich, and I am certain that, with his cleverness, which you yourself recognize, he will never be poor. Why should I not love him? He is far superior to the young men who until now have paid me attention, and it is very natural that I should prefer him. Now that he is in grave peril and perhaps from sheer desperation has taken part in the Revolution, we must repay his services by helping him as much as we are able. He saved Augustin from an infamous intrigue which would have made him an object of ridicule to the whole of Society, and besides, he has managed all the business of the house with a skill which you used to praise every day."

"As to that, it's quite true, and I make no mistake in saying that I owe to Martin a great deal of my successful business this year."

Don Damaso said these words with the object of calling a truce, for he certainly found himself unable to impose his authority on Leonor.

ALBERTO BLEST GANA

The girl took advantage of this to continue to persuade her father of the necessity of at once going to help Rivas; and she was so eloquent, that, at the end of a short time, Don Damaso went out to mediate with influential people in favour of Martin. One reflection sustained his weakness.

"I will advise them to banish him," he said to himself, "and once out of the country Leonor will forget him and marry some one else."

Don Damaso, like all weak characters, counted on the help of time to get out of difficulties.

LXI

Martin was brought to the police quarter, and shut up in a small cell at whose door a sentinel was stationed.

Four walls, badly whitewashed, a roof made of bulky poplar boards, a window without shutters, and fastened with a rough iron bar, this is all that offered itself to Martin's eyes in the room that was going to be his prison. There was not a single piece of furniture.

The young man stood on the brick floor, leant his back against the wall and crossed his arms on his chest. In this attitude he hung his head as if the weight of the ideas which were gathering in his brain kept him from holding it upright.

The more recent events of this agitated day first occupied his attention; Leonor's beauty, her impassioned language, her affectionate interest, the awful sadness of her last look, mingled in Rivas' memory, making his heart beat high, and filling the empty cell with rosy and bright images, which, like a luminous fire, irradiate from the spirit of love.

To see the impassioned expression on Martin's face, his eyes gazing into space, you would have said that this young man, shut up in a miserable room, was dreaming of the conquest of an Empire.

But soon his unquiet imagination brought other recollections to his memory and happiness left the prisoner's face, his chest heaved with sighs, and, as if overcome by their weight, he stood up and approached the window. From his lips escaped in profoundest sorrow these words—

"Poor Rafael!"

And tears filled his eyes and the sighs which came from his breast were changed into heavy sobs.

"So noble, and so courageous! Poor Rafael!" he repeated in bitter sorrow.

Thus he wept for a long time, his eyes were scalded with tears; then came to his remembrance the man, the stoic resignation of his courage, the serenity with which he had consecrated his life to a cause which he believed just. "In any case he has been happier than I," he said to himself; "it is better to die fighting than to be shot."

Not a single muscle of his face altered at this idea nor did his colour change; his high spirit calmly faced danger, mocking at the proverb—generally true—that neither the sun nor death can be looked in the face. Rivas possessed that tranquil courage for which neither witnesses nor admirers are necessary. The source of which is a peculiar gift of the nervous organization of the individual.

But at the fall of evening and when he had turned over in his mind not only the scenes of the day, but those of his whole life; when a ray of the sun, after having crossed the chamber diagonally, had almost disappeared, and would soon be blotted out, Martin shuddered, and a bitter thought came to him. He had inevitably arrived at the supposition at which every one is bound to arrive who finds himself borne down by sorrow, and he said—

"Had I not been so proud I should have known sooner that Leonor loved me, and I should not be here, but at her side."

As we have seen—in a few hours—Rivas' imagination had shown him all the phases which the situation in which he found himself could present to him. Yet to have courage without aid! He went and sat down tranquilly in the place he had first chosen, and tired of thinking, sought forgetfulness in sleep.

A few moments afterwards, when Rivas, yielding to the fatigue which had overtaken him, was almost asleep the noise of the door opening suddenly roused him from his doze. A soldier entered, carrying on a large tray some dishes. After him came another carrying a couch, which the first placed in a corner of the room, leaving the tray on the window-sill.

After which he approached Martin with a mysterious air.

"Read this bit of paper and answer at once," he said to him, letting fall a paper folded up very tightly.

And he turned, beginning to arrange the bed whilst Martin, full of surprise, read the following:—

"My father has arranged that we can send you food every day. I send you a bed, in the bolster of which you will find a pencil and paper so that you can reply to this. I have arranged that Augustin, conquering his timidity, should bribe the soldier who brings your food.

"Be of good heart, I am watching over you. I hope to be able to carry out a plan I have made by which I can go and see you. This hope gives me courage, but even if you do not see me, never imagine that it is because you have ceased to reign in the heart of

LEONOR ENCINA

Martin answered—almost breathless with happiness.

"If it is possible for a loving heart to repay the sacrifices that you make for me, you must know that that heart belongs to me. This morning, notwithstanding dangers and the shadow of death surrounding me, your sweet voice, Leonor, opened for me the gates of Paradise; later on, in prison and in solitude, that voice again returned, describing magic images on the sad walls of the cell. Ah! Leonor, my unhappy fate overwhelms me and my mind is disturbed, but in the midst of all this chaos there is one light which shines over me, serene and cloudless, it is a dazzling star. You love me!

"You must have received the news of Rafael's death; he died like a hero; his was a noble heart which the wind of misfortune had withered. My immense happiness in possessing your love is not enough at this moment to dry the tears with which I deplore him. Pardon me, Leonor, this confession. If the happiest of lovers is not able to forget his friend, you may judge by this the place he occupies in my heart."

"Get on, get on," said the soldier, approaching him, "I can't wait any longer."

Martin added swiftly some indications of the place in which he had left his friend's body, praying Leonor to send this news to San Luis' family, and handed his letter to the soldier, giving him the little money that remained to him. Afterwards he tasted his food and saw with indifference the door of his cell once more bolted; with Leonor's letter, which he pressed to his heart, he was able to despise the malice of his enemies, and felt even able to forget them.

The reading of this letter and the dreams which it brought to Martin's mind, helped him to bear his loneliness with patience until the following day; then, through the same medium, he received a second letter from Leonor, in which in tender, simple language she revealed to him the treasures of a love which Martin had never dared to expect.

Two days more of this correspondence and Rivas had begun to think that the days spent in prison were the happiest of his life.

In the meantime the charges brought against him were carried on with the rapidity which then, and to this day characterizes Chilian justice in political affairs. And as Martin, besides being openly convicted of his participation in the riots of the 20th April, had not only confessed to this participation, but also spoken boldly about the Liberal principles which he professed, the prosecution was finished at the end of four days, and the criminal condemned to death.

Leonor received the news of the sentence shortly after having read a letter which her father had just shown her, in which permission was given to Don Damaso and his family to visit Martin at six or seven o'clock in the evening. That hour had already passed, and it was necessary to wait until the following day. The thought of the fatal sentence, and of the long time she would have to wait before seeing him were absolute torture to the girl. During the night she was assailed by all the fears which her family had tried to calm during the day by endeavouring to persuade her that the sentence would not be carried out. Her love at this critical time attained the proportions of an overwhelming passion, and she could not think for one moment of the death of Rivas without thinking at the same time of her own.

After a night of weeping Leonor left her room very early and went to Augustin's apartments. He was sound asleep.

At the voice of his sister the dandy opened his eyes.

"How early you are!" he exclaimed, seeing Leonor standing beside his bed, "and what a pale little sister! Any one would say that you had been awake all night!"

"And that is what I have been," said the girl. "How could I sleep thinking of this terrible sentence?"

"Make your mind easy, the sentence won't be carried out."

"Who can guarantee that?" asked Leonor, her eyes filled with tears.

"Every one says so."

"That is not sufficient, and therefore I have come to pray you to help me."

"*Soi todo a ti, mi bella*—command and I shall obey."

"You must come with me to see Martin."

"That's not so easy as it sounds. How can we do it?"

"By means of a permission which my father has obtained. You will ask him for it saying that you are going to see Martin, and you will come with me."

"Do with me whatever you like."

In effect, when six o'clock struck Leonor and Augustin presented the permission, and were conducted to Martin's cell.

The young man had placed upon the window-sill all Leonor's letters, which he was occupied in reading one by one.

On opening the door Leonor saw him start, and quickly hide the letters. On recognizing the girl, Rivas ran to the door and pressed the little hands which she extended to him.

"Peste!" exclaimed Augustin, looking at his surroundings, "English comfort doesn't reign here! My poor friend," he added, embracing Martin, "this is *degoutant, ma parole d'honneur.*"

"That is the only chair I can give you," he said, placing a straw stool for Leonor: the girl sat down and turned away her head as she dried her tears.

Augustin was also moved to compassion, and said, "Come, little sister, let us have more courage; it is strength of mind that distinguishes us from fools."

Martin could not repress a burst of laughter on hearing this sententious maxim uttered by Augustin in a melancholy voice.

Leonor gazed at her lover full of pride.

"We must take things as they come," said Rivas, not wishing to let himself be afflicted by the sadness of the brother and sister.

"But this sentence!" exclaimed Leonor.

"I expected it from the first day of the trial and it did not upset me," replied Martin, modestly. "But what has made my heart palpitate," he added, in a whisper to Leonor, "has been what I did not expect—your letters!"

Through the tears which wetted the girl's lashes shone a ray of passion from her eyes on hearing these words.

Either intentionally, or accidentally, Augustin came to a halt at the door of the cell before which the sentinel was passing.

Martin took possession of one of Leonor's hands as she continued to gaze upon him.

"The happiness that I feel on finding myself loved," he said to her, "so fills my mind that no place is left in it for the fears that my situation might inspire. Besides," he added light-heartedly, "I don't know that perhaps presently they will tell me I am not to die."

"Nevertheless," replied Leonor, "you must seriously think of escape."

"That seems to me very difficult."

"Not so very; here is a plan that I have thought out; I shall come tomorrow with Augustin at this hour, and I shall wear two dresses: you will take one and go out with Augustin instead of me."

"And you?" asked Rivas, with delight on seeing the enthusiasm that shone in the eyes of his beloved.

"I," she replied, "I shall stay here. What can they do to me when they find it out?"

Martin felt that he would like to go down on his knees to adore as a goddess a girl who, as if it was quite a natural thing, offered to sacrifice her honour to save him.

"Do you think that I would consent to preserve my life at the cost of your honour?" he said to her, passionately kissing the hand which he pressed between his.

"All that I wish is that you should be away from here," replied Leonor, in agitation; "you must not cherish illusions, Martin, the Government is furious against those who have taken part in the revolution. Who will assure us that the council of state will pardon you? What penalty will they substitute for that of death? We know nothing, and all this makes me tremble."

"Caramba!" said Augustin, who just approached them, "Leonor is right, this place has a very sad appearance, you must try to get out of it."

"If you have any courage," said Leonor to her brother, "Martin can come out this moment; remain here in his place, and he can leave with me!"

Augustin turned quite white, and could not hide the trembling which seized the whole of his body at the idea of running such a risk.

"They would recognize him in going out. Who would arrange for my flight?"

"They would be obliged to set you at liberty," replied Leonor.

"Augustin is right," said Rivas, "they would recognize me going out."

"It's as clear as the day," observed the dandy, getting a little calmer, and taking out his watch as if he wanted to see the hour approach when he could get away.

"If Augustin will bring me tomorrow a good file, and a pair of pistols, I will make an attempt," said Martin.

"That's arranged, and there's nothing more to be said," exclaimed Augustin—again looking at his watch—in terror lest his sister might propose some other means of flight which might compromise him.

At this moment a jailor announced that it was time to leave, and Leonor and Augustin said good-bye to Rivas, promising him to do all that they could to help with his escape on the following day.

LXII

B ut this attempt was not carried out because the celerity of the judicial proceedings exceeded all expectations.

When Leonor and Augustin presented themselves asking to see Rivas by virtue of the permission which they showed they received this laconic reply—

"It cannot be done."

"Why?" asked Leonor, apprehensively.

"Because he is condemned," replied the man who had at first answered.

Leonor leant upon Augustin's arm to keep herself from falling, overcome by the terror of these fatal words.

Augustin, trembling with pity, assisted Leonor into the street where the carriage was waiting for them.

The girl threw herself across the seat, breaking into despairing sobs.

"To the house," said Augustin to the coachman.

The carriage began to move.

At the end of a few moments Leonor raised her head. One might have said that through the tears which filled her eyes there shone a slight ray of hope.

"All is not lost!" said the girl, throwing herself into Augustin's arms.

"Of course not, little sister," replied the dandy, without knowing what he was saying; "don't worry yourself, little sister."

"Has any means occurred to you of saving Martin?" asked Leonor, in feverish excitement, deceived by the air of certainty with which her brother had spoken.

"To me! No, nothing whatever occurs to me!" replied the dandy, with the nervousness which he always showed when he feared that Leonor would wish to exact some sacrifice from him.

"But I have had an idea!"

"Let us hear the idea, then."

"Take me to Edelmira Molina's house."

"Why?"

"You will know when you get there."

"It appears to me unsuitable that you—"

Leonor did not allow him to finish his sentence, but lowered one of the windows of the coach and through it said to the coachman, "Stop!"

Then, turning towards her brother, she said to him in an imperative tone—

"Tell him where to go."

Augustin obeyed without a murmur, and the coachman took the road indicated to him.

"We must speak to Edelmira," said Leonor, at the end of a few moments of silence.

"But to go to the house of her mother is not the best, way of doing it," replied Augustin.

"Why?"

"Because they know me there, and since the story that you remember they hate me cordially."

"You are right," said Leonor, pressing her hands to her head, "but it is absolutely indispensable that I should see Edelmira today. Listen!" she added, with feverish impatience, "think of something, invent something; my head is burning, I cannot collect my thoughts."

The afflicted girl hid her face and let her head fall back on the cushion of the carriage, in her breast her sobs were choking, rising and falling in waves of torment.

"I'll invent something," said the dandy, "but don't let us go to Doña Bernarda's house, because we shall lose everything."

"Home," cried Leonor, to the coachman.

Then she turned to her brother. Her eyes shot rays of fire and the contraction of her brows showed the strength of will that she was capable of displaying.

"We shall return to the house," she said, "but I warn you that before two hours you must arrange an interview with Edelmira for me."

"But, little sister, how do you expect me to get her away from her house?"

"I don't know, but I am resolved to speak with her today, and if you are not able to manage it I shall go alone to see her."

"It isn't proper that you should go there *toute seule*," replied the dandy, exasperated.

"I shall go! I shall go!" replied Leonor, excitedly, "nothing will prevent me; don't you see that Martin is condemned? Don't you see that if they shoot him I shall die also?"

Augustin could say nothing in reply to this cry from the heart of his sister, and he was convinced that to prevent her from taking some desperate step he must do everything possible to accomplish her wishes.

The young man remembered at this moment the insatiable greed for money which constantly dominated Amador.

"I have found a way by which you can speak to Edelmira," he said.

"How?" asked the girl, eagerly.

"It is by giving some money to her brother, and he himself will bring her to our house."

At this moment the carriage arrived in the neighbourhood of Don Damaso's house.

"I will give you money," said Leonor, "as soon as we leave the carriage; wait for me in your room."

And in effect, in a very short time Leonor returned with thirty ounces of gold, which she gave him.

"Take it," she said, "I have confidence in you, you do not wish to see me weep all my life, do you?" And in saying this she showered on the dandy affectionate kisses.

"Caramba!" exclaimed Augustin, "you are a Crœsus, little sister! How rich you are!"

"Papa has just given me this money, I explained my plan to him in a few words."

"In the meantime nothing has been explained to me, so that I wander in the dark."

"Wander first, afterwards you will know all."

Augustin left the house, and Leonor fell upon her knees imploring the protection of Heaven for the success of her enterprise. At the end of a few moments of fervent prayer, she went to Augustin's desk, and began to write a letter to Rivas in which she told him her plans, showering upon him the most ardent protestations of that love, which, slowly awakened in her breast, had now become an irresistible passion.

In the meantime August in had arrived at Doña Bernarda's house. Crossing the threshold of the door all the remembrances of the scene of the supposed marriage, in which he had been forced to play the part of victim, returned to him, and made his heart beat with fear; but the conviction that he must at all risks obey Leonor gave him strength to knock at the door of Amador's room.

It was Amador who opened the door, and who replied with an uncertain salute to Augustin's bow, not knowing the object of his visit.

"I desire to speak with you alone," said the dandy.

"We are alone here," replied Amador, showing him in and bolting the door.

"I have come, frankly, to make use of you," said Augustin, without sitting down.

"I am pleased at that; there's nothing like frankness," exclaimed Amador.

"Do you wish to earn fifty pesos?"

"Fifty pesos! What a question, who does not like money? Will you smoke?" said Amador, in the midst of his exclamations, passing a paper cigarette to the dandy.

"No, thank you. The service which I ask of you is very simple."

"Make no excuses, I am at your service."

"My sister wishes to speak with your sister Edelmira at once."

"About what?"

"I don't know, but I suspect that it may be to ask her to intervene with some one in favour of Martin Rivas, who is condemned to death."

"Poor Martin, it was I who had him taken prisoner, and now I'm sorry for it. Look here, I'll bring Edelmira, not on account of the fifty pesos—although I'm very poor—but to do something for Martin."

"Magnificent! As soon as you arrive at the house with Edelmira you will get the money."

"I tell you that although I am as poor as a goat, I'm not doing it for reward."

"I can well believe it, but money is always welcome."

"That's true; and to me it is always wanting."

They parted, Amador promising that in half an hour more he would be in Don Damaso's house with Edelmira.

Very shortly after Augustin had recounted to Leonor the result of his interview Amador and Edelmira arrived at the house.

Leonor brought Edelmira to her room, leaving her brother with Amador.

When the two girls found themselves alone in the apartment, of which Leonor had bolted the door, both looked at each other with curiosity, and both showed surprise after the first glance.

Edelmira found, instead of the haughty expression which she had noted before in the beautiful daughter of Don Damaso, such sorrow in her looks that she felt an irresistible sympathy for her.

Leonor saw that the rosy tints of Edelmira's cheeks had been replaced by the pallor of suffering, that the vivacity of her looks was effaced by the gloom of a melancholy plainly to be seen, and knew, with the penetration of a woman in love, that Edelmira had not ceased to love Rivas.

This idea, which under other circumstances would have annoyed her, on the contrary now appeared to cheer her.

"Do you know the situation in which Martin is placed?" she said, as she made Edelmira sit down beside her.

"I knew that he was in prison," the latter replied, "but now," she added, in a trembling voice, "my brother tells me that he is condemned to death."

The girl who spoke and the girl who listened looked at each other with their eyes full of tears.

Leonor threw herself into Edelmira's arms, exclaiming, "You are my only hope! He must be saved!"

The heart of Edelmira beat painfully on hearing these words which disclosed a confession of the love which Leonor had concealed on their first interview.

Leonor continued excitedly and without stopping to dry the large tears which rolled down her cheeks.

"Until now I have done all that I can and I pictured to myself that Martin would be reprieved, but it appears that they must fear him greatly, since they refuse to pardon him. I am tired out trying to devise means for his escape, and although I am quite ready to sacrifice myself for him, there is nothing to help to make it possible. This morning, desperate on hearing the fatal news that he has been condemned, I thought of you—I know not why. Tell me that I had a happy inspiration! You told me when you were here some time ago that you wished to do Martin a service: the occasion has arrived to show your gratitude, you know that he is so noble and so courageous, and they wish to murder him!"

Edelmira felt herself deeply moved at the sight of the desperation with which Leonor said these words. The wonderful beauty of Leonor, in the midst of such bitter affliction far from arousing the jealousy that the beauty of a rival creates in the heart of a woman, appeared to exercise over Edelmira a species of fascination.

"I, Señorita," she said, "am ready to do anything that you tell me to save Martin."

"But if I can think of nothing, *por Dios!*" exclaimed Leonor, pressing her forehead with her hands, "it seems as if ideas escape me directly they arrive. . . Let me see. . . Why did it occur to me that you could save Martin? Ah! is there not a police officer who wished to marry you?"

"There is."

"He is young, is he not?"

"Yes."

"This young man must love you still, you are beautiful enough for him to continue to love you, although you have slighted him. I am certain that he loves you. Well, then, Martin is a prisoner in his district, and you can get him to help in his escape, offer him anything he may ask; money, advancement, my father does not deny me anything. Do not refuse me this service, I will thank you for it eternally."

"Señorita," said Edelmira, "I will do all I can. If you consent that Amador comes with me to see Ricardo, perhaps we may succeed in saving Martin."

Leonor embraced Edelmira frantically, rewarding her with the tenderest caresses for this reply."

"Let us go and see your brother," she said after this, "because we have no time to lose."

They left the apartment in which they were talking, and entered that of Augustin.

Amador was swallowing the tenth glass of liquor which Augustin had offered him, and was smoking a priceless Havana of enormous size, with the gravity of a magnate, conscious of his importance.

Leonor explained her new plan in a few words, and after begging Amador with insinuating words to accompany Edelmira, she approached Augustin to ask him for the money which she had given him.

The dandy quietly slipped the thirty ounces into the hand of Amador, whose face was illuminated with indescribable joy.

"To save Martin, who has been my friend," he cried, "I will do what you wish me, Señorita."

"You will accompany them to bring me back the answer," said Leonor to Augustin, taking him on one side, "and don't spare expense; if the officer makes any difficulty tell him that papa will provide for his future, I will answer for that."

Then she embraced Edelmira with the tenderness of a sister, and carried her heroism to the point of pressing the hand of Amador, who exhaled an odour of tobacco almost insupportable.

"Send me by Augustin the news of the result," she said to Edelmira, when crossing the courtyard, "you are my only help."

"Don't fear, little sister," said Augustin, "I'm here to arrange everything. May the furies take me if we don't save this poor Martin from prison."

They said farewell at the street door, and Leonor returned to her room. There she threw herself on a sofa, torn with emotion and anxiety.

LXIII

Immense surprise was depicted on Ricardo Castanos' face when he beheld three people entering his room, whom we have seen setting out in search of him from the house of Don Damaso Encina.

Ricardo Castanos belonged, as may have been observed in the course of this story, to that class of lovers who are able to support the disdain of their inamoratas with the resignation which philosophers counsel in the difficulties of life. Although he had seen himself jilted by Edelmira, his love still lived and was as strong as it was in those days when he was about to be united to the girl by indissoluble ties. Thus it was that on seeing her enter the room which he occupied in the building, the beating of his heart was hastened in such a manner that besides the surprise which was shown in his eyes, a rosy tint dyed his cheeks with the waves of blood that the rapid beating of his heart transmitted to his face.

Confused, and without being able to formulate a distinct phrase, he offered a seat to Edelmira and the two young men who accompanied her.

Edelmira broke the silence which succeeded; in a steady voice and with a firm expression of face, she said—

"We have come here to speak to you about a very important affair."

"Señorita, I am at your service," he replied, getting still more furiously red.

"Although these gentlemen," continued Edelmira, turning towards Augustin and Amador, "know my reason for coming, I would prefer to be alone with you, when I could explain myself more fully."

"We have no lawyers here, so to speak," said Amador, smiling, "who would bear witness afterwards if you should say something to your prejudice."

"The señorita is right," replied Augustin, "I am in favour of a *tête-à-tête*, and in the meantime we can go and smoke a cigar."

"Come on, then," said Amador, "let us go and smoke."

The two young men went out and began to walk up and down the corridor outside the door of the officer's room. Ricardo had remained standing and was racking his brains to find some means of opening the conversation.

Edelmira saved him this trouble by saying to him—

"You must be very surprised to see me here."

"Oh no, Señorita; but certainly I didn't expect it," replied Ricardo.

"I know I have not behaved well to you, and I am sorry for it," continued the girl.

"You are very kind, Señorita; I thank you for it."

"Do you love me now?" she asked, looking fixedly at the young man.

"You can imagine that I love you," exclaimed Ricardo, "the proof of it is that I pass your house every day, just to look at it."

"You can give me now a proof which will convince me more than any other."

"Say no more, you will see if I am speaking the truth!"

"I want you to save Martin Rivas."

Ricardo started with surprise.

"Even if I could do so, I would not!" he said in a furious tone.

"Yet if you wish to prove to me that you love me, you have to save Martin."

"That would indeed be a fine thing! In order that he should marry you! No! it would be better to shoot him and thus finish all!"

The officer of police uttered these words in a terrible tone, which convinced Edelmira that the love of this man had never ceased.

"If they shoot him we shall never meet again, you and I," said the girl, rising from her seat.

"Prove to me that you don't love him, then!" exclaimed Ricardo, passionately, "if that should be the case we might be able to discuss the matter."

"I am disposed to do so if you will save him."

"How will you prove it to me?"

"I will marry you, if you like."

These words caused the officer to hesitate for some moments, during which they remained in silence; then he spoke—

"And now, why are you so anxious about him?"

"Can you keep a secret?" asked Edelmira.

"Why not?"

"Then I tell you that I want to save him because I promised Augustin's sister—Augustin is here only to carry her back your answer."

"Then this lady loves Martin?"

"Yes,"

"And you don't love him?"

"No."

"And how can I save him, then?"

"Cannot you undertake his guardianship tomorrow?"

"It is not my duty."

"But you might be able to change with some one whose duty it is?"

"That might be possible."

"If you were the guardian it would be very easy to enable Martin to escape, bribing the sentinel to fly with him."

"That's true; but I will tell you one thing, I have no money."

"Augustin will provide that."

"And who will guarantee that after Martin is free you will keep your word?"

"I will swear if you like before witnesses, in the presence of my mother, who up to the present is always speaking of you to me."

"Listen, Edelmira," said Ricardo, after a few seconds' reflection, "you know that I have loved you, and that I love you still, what better could I desire than to marry you; but the condition that you impose on me is very hard. If I let Martin escape they can dismiss me from my post."

"Ah! If you think more of your career than of me—"

"I don't mean to say that, but if I lose my salary I shall be out in the street, and I love you too much to drag you down to poverty at my side."

"If it's nothing more than that I don't believe you have anything to fear."

"How so?"

"Supposing a rich person, grateful for the service which you have rendered by setting Martin at liberty, would promise to ensure your future—would you then find a difficulty in doing what I ask?"

"I would find no difficulty; but I tell you, I am doing it for you."

Edelmira called Augustin, who at this moment had arrived with Amador at the door of the room.

"Will you kindly repeat to this gentleman all the messages with which the Señorita Leonor charged us when we were setting out," she said to him.

"Capita! that is not so easy, my sister talks like a parrot, and I don't shine on account of my good memory," replied the dandy.

"But perhaps you have not forgotten," replied Edelmira, "what she said in case that Ricardo should lose his employment."

"Ah! that part of it, no. She said that papa would answer for everything, and Leonor may well say so for she leads papa about by the point of his nose."

"You can see that I am not deceiving you," said Edelmira, in a low voice to Ricardo.

This confidential tone, used by one who had formerly always shown herself disdainful, caused the face of the officer to shine with happiness and love.

"I do not say that you are deceiving me in this," he replied, "tell me that you'll keep your word and marry me, and not throw me over afterwards if I become poor?"

"If Martin is free tomorrow evening," replied Edelmira, making silent efforts to overcome her emotion, "I will marry you any day you like."

"He shall be free or I lose my name," said the official, taking one of Edelmira's hands, and sealing with an ardent kiss this species of oath.

The girl made him repeat over and over again that he would not break his word, and Augustin undertook to bring the necessary money to bribe the sentinel who was to aid in the flight.

Edelmira and Amador returned with Augustin to the house of Don Damaso, where Leonor awaited them in a state of anxiety bordering on madness.

When Edelmira told her that Martin would be saved, Leonor uttered a cry of joy, and falling into her arms, overwhelmed her with frantic kisses.

"And how have you managed this?" asked Leonor, without remarking that Edelmira, the prey of the profoundest dejection, had hidden her face in order to hide the tears which bathed it.

"I swore that I would marry him," replied the girl.

And in making this reply she appeared to abandon the courage and the resignation which she had displayed during her interview with Ricardo, for sobs almost choked her last words.

Leonor gazed at Edelmira for a few moments with an indefinable expression; admiration and jealousy (which sleeps in the depths of all true love) occupied her mind together. During this moment, which passed rapidly, she said to herself—

"She loves him as much as I do, and—Poor girl, she has the heart of an angel."

And, as we have said, this moment of involuntary reflection passed rapidly, for Leonor again threw herself into Edelmira's arms.

"God alone," she said, "is able to recompense you for such generosity. If my eternal gratitude is of any value accept it, Edelmira, and permit me to be your friend."

These words uttered with all the warmth of a generous heart, calmed Edelmira's grief, and her serenity returned.

Leonor repeated a thousand times her protestations of gratitude, mingled with caressing words, and tried to make Edelmira forget the social difference between them.

On the morning of the following day Ricardo and Amador presented themselves at Don Damaso's house and arranged with Leonor and Augustin the scheme for Martin's escape, which was fixed to take place on the evening of the same day.

LXIV

M artin in the meantime was bidding a sad adieu to life and to love—that second life of youth.

In these farewells were found—although naturally coupled with sadness—the serene resignation of courage. Besides, love occupied such a large place in his mind that the idea of separating from Leonor for ever saddened him far more than the thought of losing his life in the flower of his youth. In this frame of mind Rivas calmly occupied himself with his last farewells. Not possessing any worldly goods, the anxieties of material interests did not rob him of any of the precious moments that remained to him.

But he possessed an immense treasure of love to which he wished to consecrate his entire mind in these solemn moments.

He wrote a long and affectionate letter to his mother and sister. Every phrase in this letter had for its object to fortify them beforehand for the terrible shock of grief that awaited them.

"In any case," he said to them at the conclusion, "death will not be for me an evil under the present circumstances. Almost insuperable obstacles present themselves to me if I live, to prevent my realizing the happiness which Leonor has given me the right to aspire to, and besides in fighting them I would have to suffer cruel humiliations. I have confidence in God and I am not wanting in courage, your prayers will smooth the road that I must travel in order to appear before the Divine Judge."

When he had closed this letter, it appeared to him that he could now devote himself to thoughts of Leonor. In order to speak about his deep love, he wrote her the story of how it had begun and how it had increased in his heart. Simple and eternal story of love, full of ideal aspirations, and bitter pain already obscured by the memory of the happiness of the last days. The tragic end which awaited him was the only cloud on this picture painted in diaphanous colours by youth and love. Martin dwelt upon it with the predilection of an artist for his favourite work, and was adding a sentence of affection to the thousand which already embellished it when the door of his prison was quietly opened.

It was evening, and Martin saw a man, whose face was partly covered by his cloak so that he did not recognize him at first. The man drew aside his cloak and approached the table at which Martin was writing by the poor light of a candle of grey tallow.

"What is the object of this visit, Señor Don Ricardo?" asked Martin, with a certain haughtiness, on recognizing Ricardo Castanos.

"Read this paper," replied the officer, handing Rivas a letter.

Rivas read the following:—

"All is planned for your escape; Ricardo Castanos will bribe the sentinel who will show you the best way to get out; take advantage of this chance and be prudent, remembering that upon the success of this step, not only your own life depends, but also that of your loving

LEONOR ENCINA

Martin, his eyes shining with hope, looked at Ricardo, and at the same time carefully held the letter.

"Would it not be better to burn it?" said the officer to him.

"Why?" asked Martin, who guarded as treasures Leonor's letters.

"Because, if unfortunately they catch you, this paper would compromise me."

"You are right," said Rivas, burning the letter.

"Good," said Ricardo, "now I am here you have nothing to do but go out, the soldier on guard will conduct you by a safe path."

"One word," said Martin, approaching Ricardo, "you are now doing me a service that I never expected, and much less expected that it should come from you, who have looked upon me as an enemy."

"That is not the case," said the officer, "I pursued you and took you prisoner because we were fighting."

"Nothing more than that?" asked Rivas, "speak to me frankly. You always thought I was your rival?"

"That's true."

"Nevertheless you have deceived yourself. I have never spoken of love to Edelmira, I assure you on my word of honour."

"Is that true?" exclaimed Ricardo, joyfully.

"It is true. If formerly you might have considered that this confession, made by me to you, was humiliating, now that you are trying to help me, believe that I have made it without knowing the cause why you should do so. If you love this girl," added Martin, "I believe that this confession will destroy the prejudice that you may have formed against her; anyway

ALBERTO BLEST GANA

I have no other means of showing my gratitude than by making this confession and begging you to accept my friendship."

"I thank you," replied Ricardo, with effusion, pressing the hand which Rivas offered him.

The officer went out leaving the door open, after telling Rivas to put out the light before following him.

In Martin's flight there were none of the hair-breadth escapes which novelists take advantage of to excite the interest of their readers. The soldier who guarded his prison abandoned his post and conducted Martin by lonely paths until they arrived at a courtyard also solitary, where by means of a staircase they escaped over the roof to get down into a street.

"Adios, patron," said the soldier to Rivas; and he wandered down the street thinking of the onzes of gold that rattled agreeably in his purse after having been given to Ricardo Castanos by the white and shapely hand of Leonor.

Rivas perceived a carriage not far from the place where the soldier left him, and went straight towards it. A man rose to receive him, saying, in a well-known voice—

"You are saved, Martin, let me embrace you!" and Augustin Encina clasped him fraternally.

"My sister is there waiting for you," added the dandy, pointing to the carriage.

"These moments have been full of mortal inquietude for me," she said to Rivas, allowing him to press the hand which she had given him. "Every moment I expected to hear the alarm given."

"Come, we must get in, *et nous mettrent en route*," said Augustin. "This place is too near the prison to be pleasant."

Leonor seated herself in the carriage with Martin beside her. Augustin sat opposite them.

"In a place close by," he said to Martin, "we expect to meet a young man with horses, which will be more useful in taking bridle paths, if the authorities should take a fancy to follow you."

"I shall never be able to repay the services you have done me," said Martin, full of gratitude.

"It was not without selfishness on my part that I wished to save you, I was saving also my own happiness which was threatened with extinction," Leonor murmured in his ear.

"What nonsense to talk of repayment," said Augustin, at the same moment; "it is we who are repaying you what we owe you. You have forgotten that it is you who have saved me from the misfortunes of having that insatiable devourer of pesetos—Amador—for a brother-in-law. Remember the French proverb, *'Un bienfait n'est jamais perdu!'*"

Augustin continued to keep up the conversation during the drive whilst Leonor and Martin whispered to each other in broken words; those words, interrupted by heart-beats which lovers find a thousand times more eloquent than the most brilliant conversation. They arrived at a narrow, lonely street in the suburbs, close to the street of San Pablo, which is on the road to Valparaiso, and the coach stopped at Augustin's order.

The three got out of the carriage and Augustin turned to a man who was on horseback, leading another horse by the reins.

"We must separate here," said Leonor to Rivas. "Write to me whenever you possibly can. Is it necessary for me to swear to you that I will think of you every moment?"

"No, but tell me once more, Leonor, that what has happened to me in these last few days is true, for at times I think that all is a dream. Above all, is this love for which I never dared to hope except in the solitude of my heart, true also?"

"This love, Martin, is as true as all the rest."

"And will always remain. Is it not so?" murmured the young man, passionately pressing Leonor's hands.

"It will be the only love of my life," she said, "and don't think this is a vain oath rising from a passing affection. I have never loved any one except you in the world. Who would have told me when you arrived at our house that I was going to love you?"

"And I," said Rivas, "who looked upon you as a goddess! Ah! Leonor, how small I felt then before the proud haughtiness of the glance with which you received my salute."

"And how could I imagine," exclaimed the girl, in a gay accent, "that beneath the exterior of a poor Provincial was hidden the heart which would take me captive! Martin, you have scolded me for my pride, and in return I love you all the more."

These last words were pronounced in an accent of impassioned melancholy, which formed a strong contrast to the vivacity of the first.

"Are you sorry that you have made me happy?" asked Rivas.

"I am sorry, on the contrary, not to have let you know sooner that I loved you," replied the girl, in the same melancholy tone.

"What does that matter, when those words alone make me forget all the past?" replied Martin.

"But now we must separate, and I resign myself to this parting because I know that your life depends on it."

"And I also accept it with pleasure, because, Leonor, the remembrance of it will help me to fight against evil fortune if such awaits me, because I know also that there will be a superb reward for my perseverance when I can return to your side, and hear from your own lips words such as you have just uttered."

"We must wait for our happiness until then," said the girl, sighing as the idea came to her that in a few moments more she would cease to hear her lover's voice.

"And that day will soon come, will it not?" said Martin, who, having forgotten for a moment the separation which awaited them, was brought back to the reality of the situation by the girl's sigh.

"Soon? Yes, it will arrive soon, because I shall never rest until your pardon is signed. Happily I feel strong enough to overcome all obstacles. Neither the commands of my parents nor the foolish gossip of the world will frighten me. Ah! I have strength and courage enough for everything. Do you know that you have almost worked a miracle, I don't understand it myself, but I know that your will will be stronger than mine, that your desires will be commands for me—the only thing I shall refuse to obey you in will be if you order me to cease to love you."

Rivas fell from the heaven into which he had been wafted by these words, uttered in the sweetest tones of a loving woman, on hearing the voice of Augustin, who approached them, saying—

"Come, Martin, my friend, you must finish your farewells and get on horseback."

Before giving this advice the dandy had smoked half a cigar as he chatted with the rider not far from the carriage, muttering to himself from time to time—

"I must be kind and leave them to make their last farewells in peace. Caspita! the poor boy has suffered so much that I may at least let him have this little recreation."

Under cover of darkness Martin printed an ardent kiss on Leonor's forehead, and left the carriage.

Leonor covered her face with her hands and allowed full course to the tears which during this conversation she had had such difficulty in restraining.

Then Rivas warmly embraced Augustin, and mounted his horse.

"We shall work hard for you," said Augustin to him, "and on your part take care they don't catch you before you get to Valparaiso. The boy who accompanies you has a valise with some clothing, and in it you will find some letters of recommendation to certain merchants in Lima, friends of papa's, and, besides, some money which you will require for the necessities of life, and the purchases which you will be obliged to make in Lima, the rest is provided for in the letters of which I have spoken. Vamos! Now, good-bye; good luck *en route!*"

The two young men shook hands with cordial affection, and Martin started at a gallop, after having given one look of farewell to Leonor, who, motionless in the carriage, was hiding her face, bathed in tears, between her hands.

LXV

Letter from Martin Rivas to His Sister

Santiago, Oct. 15, 1851

"Five months of absence, my dear Mercedes, instead of diminishing, appear to have increased my love for Leonor. I have returned to Santiago to find her more beautiful than ever. The proud maiden who returned with such sovereign disdain the salute of the poor young man who came from the provinces to solicit the patronage of her father, now showers on him the treasure of a love which dazzles him. When she looks at him, her eyes are those of an angel, yet they are the same eyes whose mocking glance were once sufficient to make him tremble. Those rosy lips are the same which, formerly disdainful, now smile on me and murmur words of love. In fact it is really the beautiful and imperious Leonor, now my beloved, who is thus transfigured by the mysterious influences of love.

"From Lima I wrote you all the particulars of the life which I led in Santiago from the day of my arrival. In these letters predominated the egotism of a lover, dwelling on his remembrances, recalling the past on every opportunity in order to forget the sadness of the present. Thanks, therefore, to this egotism you are acquainted with all the personages who have had to do with me, and I want to finish my work by telling you how I found them on my return.

"Augustin, always immaculately dressed and always using as many French phrases as possible, had married Matilde a few days before. Speaking to some one of his happiness he said, 'We are as happy as two angels, we love each other *à la folie.*' The day following my arrival being Sunday I went to the Alemada; Leonor accompanied me taking my arm, so you may easily imagine the pride I felt. We had not gone far when we perceived a couple coming towards us. We soon recognized Ricardo Castanos, who with an air of triumph had offered his arm to Edelmira. We approached them and had a long conversation. Since this encounter, I ask myself if this poor girl is happy, living in a circle mentally inferior to her feelings and sentiments, and I have not been able to give myself a satisfactory reply; for the tranquillity, and tone of vivacity which I remarked in her words were contradicted by the melancholy expression of her eyes. Anyway, I am told that Edelmira has consecrated her life to the happiness of the man to whom her noble heart has united her, and for those who like myself knew the nobility of her nature that is the answer nearest the truth.

"To tell you all that relates to this family I will mention that I learned from Augustin that Edelmira's sister, Adelaida, has married a German clerk in a carriage factory; that Amador now wanders in hiding, pursued by his creditors who want to have him imprisoned, and that Doña Bernarda lives with Edelmira and cultivates more ardently than ever her passion for cards and mistela.

"One of the first visits I paid was to Rafael's aunt. The poor lady related to me—her eyes filled with tears—the steps her brother, Don Pedro, had taken to recover the body of my unfortunate friend. I left her house with a heavy heart after visiting Rafael's rooms—which his aunt kept exactly as we had quitted them on the night of the 19th April. This is the only cloud which shadows my happiness. Rafael's vigorous character, his noble and manly heart will live eternally in my memory; I cannot think, without deep grief, of the loss of such a splendid intellect. Sorrow, which had given his eyes the sad expression which appeared in his face, was not strong enough to overcome the noble instincts of his mind. In the heart of this despairing lover the call of liberty woke a new world of love in which passed away like a shadow the melancholy of the old. You will understand the intensity of affection which I have for Rafael's memory, dear sister, when I tell you that I talk to Leonor as much about him as of our future happiness.

"Knowing Leonor's character so well from my frequent descriptions, you will understand how she has contrived not only that her parents, but all her family, have joyfully consented to our marriage. She wished it, and they have yielded. Don Damaso who with much trouble obtained my pardon, made a point of informing every one, that he—on his marriage—was not in any better position than I am.

"Doña Engracia has shown herself—as usual—submissive to her daughter's will. Augustin treats me like a brother, and all the relations of the family follow his example. After this—what more can I desire. To picture my happiness is impossible. Leonor appears to have reserved for me a new sweetness and docility of which no one would have believed her capable. She says she wishes to efface from my memory the haughtiness with which she treated me at first. Speaking just now to me of Edelmira's sacrifice, she said, 'You who have taught me the meaning of love, have also taught me the meaning of egotism.'

"If I were to continue to describe to you, my dear Mercedes, more pictures of my joy and felicity this letter would never cease, and the post leaves today.

"With all loving messages to our mother, I am your affectionate brother,

MARTIN

Five days afterwards Rivas again wrote to his sister, telling her of his marriage to Leonor. This letter was shorter than the other.

"I should have liked to have gone in person to bring the news to you, but in this matter Leonor has shown her former determination. 'Go,' she says, 'but with me.' We are coming soon, you alone are wanting to complete my happiness."

Don Damaso handed all his business matters over to Martin, in order to give himself more time to attend to the fluctuations of politics, which he hoped would one day procure him a seat in the Senate. He belonged to the numerous family of illustrious shufflers, who, to hide their lack of conviction, use the word Moderation.

THE END

A Note About the Author

Alberto Blest Gana (1830–1920) was a Chilean novelist and diplomat. Born in Santiago, he was raised by William Cunningham Blest, an Irishman, and María de la Luz Gana Darrigrandi, a Chilean aristocrat. After studying at the Military Academy and in France, Blest Gana pursued his political and literary interests. Inspired by the works of French novelist Honoré de Balzac, Blest Gana employed European writing techniques popularized by the Realist movement, authoring ten novels on the impact of history and politics on individual lives. His book *Martín Rivas* (1862), the first Chilean novel, is recognized as a masterpiece of Latin American fiction, but the success of its publication led to an increased demand for his diplomatic work. After a serving as an administrative official in Colchagua province, Blest Ganawas appointed Chilean ambassador to France and Britain and served for many years. He returned to literature upon retirement and continued to publish novels until the end of his life. Blest Gana is celebrated today for his for his mastery of style and intuitive sense of sociopolitical reality.

A Note from the Publisher

Spanning many genres, from non-fiction essays to literature classics to children's books and lyric poetry, Mint Edition books showcase the master works of our time in a modern new package. The text is freshly typeset, is clean and easy to read, and features a new note about the author in each volume. Many books also include exclusive new introductory material. Every book boasts a striking new cover, which makes it as appropriate for collecting as it is for gift giving. Mint Edition books are only printed when a reader orders them, so natural resources are not wasted. We're proud that our books are never manufactured in excess and exist only in the exact quantity they need to be read and enjoyed.

Discover more of your favorite classics with Bookfinity™.

- Track your reading with custom book lists.
- Get great book recommendations for your personalized Reader Type.
- Add reviews for your favorite books.
- AND MUCH MORE!

Visit **bookfinity.com** and take the fun Reader Type quiz to get started.

Enjoy our classic and modern companion pairings!

Printed in the USA
CPSIA information can be obtained
at www.ICGtesting.com
JSHW022205140824
68134JS00018B/863

9 781513 282558